# An Inconvenient Woman

ALSO BY DOMINICK DUNNE

*The Winners*
*The Two Mrs. Grenvilles*
*Fatal Charms*
*People Like Us*

# An Inconvenient Woman

## Dominick Dunne

CROWN PUBLISHERS, INC.
*New York*

Portions of this book have appeared in *Vanity Fair*.

Grateful acknowledgment is made to Warner/Chappell Music, Inc. for
permission to reprint a portion of lyrics from "You Better Go Now"
(Bickley Reichner, Robert Graham), copyright 1936 (renewed 1963) by
Chappell and Co. All rights reserved. Used by permission of Warner/
Chappell Music, Inc.

Published by Crown Publishers, Inc.
201 East 50th Street, New York, New York 10022

CROWN is a trademark of Crown Publishers, Inc.

Manufactured in the United States of America

Library of Congress Cataloging-in-Publication Data

Dunne, Dominick.
An inconvenient woman: a novel/by Dominick Dunne.
p. cm.
I. Title.
PS3554.U492I6 1990                                                    90-1602
813'.54—dc20                                                              CIP

ISBN 0-517-57763-1

*For Griffin and Carey Dunne*
*with love*

LATER HE WAS vilified and disgraced; Archbishop Cooning denounced him from the pulpit of Saint Vibiana's as a corruptor, and the archbishop's words spread throughout the land. But before the disgrace and the vilification Jules Mendelson was, seemingly at least, on top of the world: awesome in appearance, brilliantly married, and revered in the manner that the very rich are revered in America.

Clouds, the Mendelson estate, which looks down on Los Angeles from its lofty mountaintop, remains unlived in but cared for, although the massive iron gates that once fronted a ducal residence in Wiltshire have become dislocated, their hinges pried loose by vandals. The caretaker on duty has backed the gates with plywood boards to keep the curious from staring in; but, even if they could stare in, they would see nothing of the house and gardens, for a few hundred feet up the drive there is a sharp turn to the right. Pauline Mendelson's greenhouse, where she grew her orchids, has fallen into disrepair, but the kennels are kept up still, and a pack of police dogs patrols the grounds at night, as always.

There was a time when people said that the views from Clouds were the prettiest views in the city. Pauline Mendelson, mindful of this, had created one room to take best advantage of the sunrise over the downtown skyline, where she and Jules were meant to have breakfast together, but never did, except once; and another room for watching the sunset over the ocean, where, on most evenings, she and Jules did indeed meet to drink a glass of wine together and discuss the events of the day before dressing for dinner.

Probably no one ever conducted herself so well in a scandal as Pauline Mendelson. Everyone agrees on that. She held her head high and invited neither pity nor scorn. The city, or that part of the city that figured in the lives of these people, was beside itself with excitement. Nothing so thrilling had happened in years, except among the movie people, and no one they knew saw the movie people. Within a year of the events that riveted the city for so many months, Pauline became Lady St. Vincent and moved to England. She not only married quickly but also, being by birth one of the McAdoo sisters, the marrying McAdoos, as the papers often called them, married extremely well, even under the terrible circumstances. People say that all traces of her life as Mrs. Jules Mendelson have been totally obliterated, and in her new life she is not at home to people who knew her in Los Angeles, not even Rose Cliveden, and, God knows, if anyone was a good friend to Pauline Mendelson, it was Rose Cliveden.

There were splendid times at Clouds for over twenty years. You had only to look at the signatures in the guest books when they came up for auction at Boothby's, along with the furniture, the personal effects, and, of course, the extraordinary art collection, to get an idea of Pauline Mendelson's voracious appetite for what she always called "interesting people." As to the pictures, or the auction of the pictures, there is still rage in the art world today. The Metropolitan Museum in New York said it had been promised the collection. The County Museum in Los Angeles said the same, as did the Kimball in Fort Worth. And there were other museums, with lesser claims. But that was typical of Jules Mendelson. He liked being called on by heads of museums—being courted by them, as he put it—and hearing them praise his magnificent collection. He enjoyed walking them through the halls and rooms of his house, spelling out the provenance of each picture, as well as the stage in the life of the artist at the time the picture was painted. He liked letting each one think it was his museum to which the collection would go, in time; and surely he meant to leave it to one, because he often said, even in interviews, that he never wanted the collection to be broken up, and that he was leaving money for the construction of a wing, the Jules Mendelson Wing, to house it. But the fact remained that he did not make such a provision, although he had intended to, just as he had intended to make a provision for Flo March. Or poor Flo, as she came to be known. It was Pauline who decided to break up the collection and auction it off along with the furniture and personal effects, minus van Gogh's *White Roses* and the bronze cast of Degas's fourteen-year-old ballerina, with the original pink ribbon in her hair, which, some people say, are already installed in Kilmartin Abbey in Wiltshire.

Pauline Mendelson was one of those people totally at home in the inner circles of several cities, although she seemed to belong to none. Even after twenty-two years of living in Los Angeles, and becoming a prominent citizen there, Pauline always seemed like a visitor rather than a resident. Her parties at Clouds were famous, and rightly so. She left nothing to chance in the planning of her evenings. It was through one such party that young Philip Quennell was brought into the orbit of the renowned couple. Pauline liked to ask writers and artists to her house to mix with her grand friends. Once Philip had seen her take communion at Andy Warhol's memorial service at Saint Patrick's Cathedral, and he had met her once before that, by accident, during the intermission of a play in New York. Pauline knew the stepmother of the woman he was with, and, after introductions, she and his companion chatted briefly while Philip stood by, simply watching her. She spoke in a fashionable contralto. "Awfully light, isn't it, but I'm being amused, aren't you?" she asked, about the play. They answered yes. "Dreadful about Rocky, isn't it?" she asked, about someone Philip didn't know, but his companion did, whose private plane had recently crashed. "Both his pilots were killed, but he'll be fine, in time," Pauline added. And then the bell rang, and it was time for the second act, and they didn't see her again. Given this minimal exposure to Pauline Mendelson, Philip Quennell was therefore surprised to find an invitation to her party, hand-delivered to his hotel by her chauffeur, on the very day he arrived in Los Angeles for what turned out to be a considerably longer visit than he could ever have anticipated. It was his birthday. He was twenty-nine, turning thirty that night, but of course that milestone, known only to himself, could have nothing whatever to do with the invitation from Mr. and Mrs. Jules Mendelson, as their names read in engraved script on the ecru-colored card.

He was late. The parking valet told him so. So did the maid who opened the door. Inside, on a hall console table where little envelopes with dining-table numbers inside had been alphabetically placed, there was only one left, his. The convivial sound of sixty voices, talking and laughing, could be heard from an interior room. Even late, however, with a butler hurrying him toward the voices— "They're about to sit down," he insisted—it was impossible for Philip to be oblivious to the grandeur of the interior of the Mendelson house. There were six ground-floor doors opening onto the front hallway. A curved staircase of superb proportions seemed to float upward on invisible pinions, its green moiré wall lined with six Monet paintings of water lilies, Philip's first glimpse of the Mendelson art collection; below, at its base, were masses of orchid plants in blue-and-white Chinese cachepots and bowls.

"Beautiful," said Philip, to no one in particular.

"It's Mrs. Mendelson's hobby," said an efficient, secretarial-looking woman.

"What?" asked Philip.

"The orchids. She grows them herself."

"Ah."

"Will you first sign the guest book, please," she said. She handed him a pen, and he wrote his name beneath the names of one of the former Presidents and his First Lady and that of the great film star Faye Converse, now in retirement. His eyes scanned the signatures. Although he knew no one, he recognized many of the illustrious names. It was not the sort of crowd that Philip Quennell was used to dining with.

Just then one of the six doors opened, and the party sounds increased in volume as Jules Mendelson entered the hall. He closed the door behind him again and strode across the marble floor with the purposefulness of a man who had been summoned to take an important telephone call. He was enormous, both in height and in girth, unhandsome and compelling at the same time, the possessor of an appearance that was likely to intimidate the fainthearted. His aura of power enveloped him like a strong scent. But people discovered on meeting him that he could be surprisingly gentle, and, more surprisingly still, a gentleman. When biographers of great men questioned him for his reminiscences of their subjects, Jules invariably replied (if he could not get out of replying) with kindness and benevolence, even about great men he had disliked or done battle with, for he was always aware that his own biography loomed as a certainty at some future time.

Philip stared at him, fascinated, in a way that he would come to see many people stare at Jules Mendelson in time to come. Introduced by the secretary, Mendelson shook Philip's hand in passing, met his eye, and sized him up in an instant as one of Pauline's "interesting people," in whom he had very little interest. Political figures, senatorial and up; ambassadors; business tycoons, like himself; and heads of museums were the kinds of people who interested him. It was once written about Jules Mendelson in a magazine article that he had simplified the spelling of his family name from Mendelssohn to Mendelson because he figured he wasted seven and a half minutes each day correcting or explaining its spelling. His great-grandfather had been a second cousin of the Mendelssohns of Berlin, one of the most important families of the Jewish upper bourgeoisie and minor nobility before the war. Born in Chicago, Jules Mendelson had taken his inheritance and turned it into a vast fortune. All that was part of his public story.

"I'm sorry to be so late, sir," said Philip. "My plane got in from New York this afternoon, but one of my bags, the one with my dinner jacket in it, couldn't be found." Jules didn't care, nor did he want to be involved in such a drab story. He had a mission of his own on his mind.

"Go in, go in, Mr. Quennell," he said, directing him with a wave of his hand to a room on the right. "Pauline is in the drawing room. I must take a call and will join you then."

Last year, when Malcolm McKnight, who is writing the biography of Jules Mendelson, asked Philip Quennell what his impression of him was the first time they met, Philip remembered this moment and hesitated.

"What came into your mind?" Malcolm persisted.

Philip couldn't bring himself to tell McKnight that what came into his mind was how wonderfully cut Jules Mendelson's dinner jacket was, for such an enormous man. What he did say to Malcolm was, "I thought that this was a man that I would never like to cross," which had been his second thought.

For a newcomer without connections, Philip was extremely well seated that night, placed between Camilla Ebury, with whom he was to fall in love, and Rose Cliveden, a past-middle-age social celebrity of the area who would, inadvertently to be sure, cause havoc in the life of her great friend Pauline Mendelson. The reason for Philip Quennell's excellent *placement*, however, had nothing to do with his desirability as a guest. A man named Hector Paradiso had switched their place cards before dinner, for reasons known only to him, and had moved himself to what Rose Cliveden considered a more advantageous position at a table where the former First Lady was seated.

"Live by the place card, die by the place card," said Rose Cliveden to Philip's left. She was slightly tipsy and greatly miffed as she revealed Hector Paradiso's social disloyalty for the third or fourth time. Her neck had just the suspicion of a goiter, which moved up and down as she spoke in a voice deepened by years of heavy smoking. "Imagine Hector moving the place cards. He's gotten entirely too full of himself lately."

"Be careful what you say to Rose," said Camilla Ebury, to his right. "No matter how drunk she gets, she remembers everything. Total recall."

"Who is Rose Cliveden?" asked Philip.

"Old Los Angeles. Old money. Old friend of Pauline's. Married three times. Divorced three times. Once had an affair with Jack Kennedy. In the White House. In the Lincoln Bedroom. Or so she says. She's been known to exaggerate. What else do you want to know?"

"That's pretty good coverage," Philip replied. "You could be in my business."

"Your business is what?" she asked.

"I've only arrived here today, to write a documentary film. Quite honestly, I'm surprised to have been asked here tonight."

"Pauline collects people," replied Camilla Ebury. She was pretty in a quiet way that was not at first apparent to Philip. Her blond hair was parted in the middle and held back by two gold barrettes, a style he associated with the debutantes he used to watch at dances when he was at Princeton. She was, Philip found out in due course, a recent widow, although she was only a year or two older than he.

Like Pauline and all of Pauline's grand friends, Camilla's range of conversation was on a more elevated scale, at least economically, than his. "Don't ever die in a foreign country if you don't speak the language," she said, recounting her husband's sudden death on a street in Barcelona. "It's an absolute nightmare. The embassy was useless. Thank God for Jules Mendelson. He made a few calls and straightened everything out, and I was able to ship poor Orin home."

At that point, noticing that he was listening attentively, she picked up his place card and read his name, although he had already told it to her twice. "Philip Quennell. Why have you come out here to the Golden West?" she asked.

"To escape the heat," he said.

"What heat?"

"Something I wrote offended some very important people, and I thought it best if I left New York for a while."

"Oh, my lord! Are you the one who wrote that book that made everyone so angry in New York?" she asked.

He was. "Yes."

"No *wonder* Pauline invited you," said Camilla, smiling. "That's the sort of thing she adores." When she smiled, dimples mysteriously appeared in both cheeks and her eyes twinkled. Each of them looked at the other with more interest. "Didn't someone hit you? I think I read that."

He had indeed written a book, on a particular leveraged buyout, that had offended several important people in the New York business community. One well-known figure on Wall Street threatened to have his legs broken, and Philip did not think of his threat as simply a figure of speech, nor did his lawyer. The well-known figure was known to have "connections," as they are called. When Casper Stieglitz, a Hollywood producer, contacted him through his agent to see if he would be interested in writing a screenplay for a documentary based on the proliferation of drugs in the motion picture industry, he leapt at the opportunity, although he knew absolutely nothing about either the motion picture industry or the proliferation of drugs in it. He leapt at the opportunity because he thought a four- or five-month paid sojourn in Southern California might be just exactly what he needed in his present circumstances.

"This is a very swell party," said Philip, looking around the room.

Camilla, following his look, nodded. "It's always very swell at Pauline's," she said.

"Is there an occasion for an evening like this? I mean, is there a guest of honor, or is it a birthday or an anniversary, or something like that? Or do you people out here just have sixty for dinner with rare wines and a flown-in orchestra on a nightly basis?"

Camilla laughed. "You're right. It is quite special. I shouldn't act like I take it for granted, but I've been coming to parties here for so many years that I might have lost my sharp eye."

"You mustn't ever lose your sharp eye, Mrs. Ebury," said Philip. "Or ear, for that matter. You might miss something."

Camilla looked at Philip, interested. "Camilla," she said.

"I'm Philip," he answered.

"I know."

"What kind of people are these?" Philip asked, holding his hand out to indicate the guests. "Aside from the former President and the film star, I mean."

"Oh, the core, I suppose. My father used to describe them as the kind of people who can keep things out of the newspapers," said Camilla.

"What kind of things?"

"Oh, things."

"The woods are full of bodies, you mean?"

She laughed. "In a manner of speaking."

Philip looked around the room again. "This is all quite glamorous in a way. At least it is for me."

"I suppose it is when you're traveling like you are, staying a few days or a few weeks; but if you were to stay longer, you would begin to see that each evening is a variation on the same theme, except at the Mendelsons', where it's a little more extravagant, but then the Mendelsons aren't really Angelenos in the sense that the rest of us are who were born and brought up here. There are about two or three hundred of us who dine together in various combinations, and we rarely widen the circle, and you rarely read about us in the newspapers." She smiled almost apologetically and made a helpless gesture.

"Go on. I'm fascinated," said Philip.

"Well, we never mix with the movie crowd, and only sometimes with the people from Pasadena, except for civic evenings or certain charities, like the museums or the Music Center. I'm not saying it's right, but it's the way it is and the way it always has been. If you want to know the truth, I'd love to know a few movie stars."

Philip laughed. Camilla looked at Philip and saw that he gave her his full attention. She moved in closer to him and spoke in a lowered voice. "Now that you mention it, I think there was originally a point for this party. We all thought that an announcement was going to be made tonight that Jules was being sent by the President to Brussels to head up the American delegation at the statehood of Europe. It would have meant staying there for the whole of nineteen ninety-three, at least, and Pauline was looking forward to it enormously. She speaks perfect French, and I think she sometimes gets bored here."

"It's not to be?" asked Philip.

"Oh, yes, it is to be, but not to be announced as yet, apparently."

Philip nodded. "Good soup," he said.

"Marvelous."

A MENDELSON PARTY was, even for the initiated, a heady experience. The food was prepared by their own chef, a famed figure in gastronomic circles, and the wine, from Jules Mendelson's own cellar, was superb. There were orchids, and antiques, and priceless art on every wall in every room. In the library, which the Mendelsons used for a sitting room when they were alone, there were more French paintings, and English furniture, and armchairs and sofas covered in glazed chintz. There was a long table for photographs in silver frames, including several of Pauline and Jules with Presidents and First Ladies at White House dinners, as well as signed photographs from the monarchs of Spain and Great Britain. There was a matching table on the other side of the room for magazines, changed weekly or monthly, and newspapers, changed daily. Tall French windows, elaborately curtained and swagged, opened onto a terrace with umbrellaed tables, and a garden beyond, and a lawn beyond that. People who visited the Mendelsons always said about this room, "How marvelous!" So Philip Quennell, a newcomer to such grandeur, can be excused for gasping and exclaiming aloud when he wandered into this library, looking for a lavatory, and saw van Gogh's *White Roses*, which just happened to be his favorite picture, hanging over the fireplace.

"Good God," he said, walking over to it and staring upward. It was worth, he knew, forty million dollars at least, even in a depressed art market. He wanted to touch the thick vivid paint, and almost did, but resisted. Then he had a sense that he was not alone in the room. He turned, and there was Pauline Mendelson, sitting in a chair by the telephone, or, rather, perched on the edge of a chair by the telephone.

"That's my treasure," she said, about the painting. "It was my wedding present from Jules twenty-two years ago."

She looked, as she always looked in the photographs he had seen of her, resplendent, and was dressed, he was sure, from Paris, from the couture, black velvet cut in a classical fashion, having nothing to do with the trend of that season. She was more elegant than beautiful, although *beautiful* was always the word used to describe her in social columns and fashion magazines. She was tall and slender, and, even without the two strands of grape-sized pearls she was wearing, he would have noticed her astonishing neck. In a flash he remembered the Avedon photograph of her exquisite neck. It was no wonder that she was married to one of the country's most powerful men. It would have been unthinkable to imagine her in a lesser sort of union.

"I saw this picture at the van Gogh exhibit at the Met," he said.

"So you did," she replied.

It couldn't possibly be, he thought, that she had been crying, but there was a trace of moistness in her eyes and something about her face that was in disarray. She rose and walked over to a table over which hung a Chippendale mirror. From a box on the table she took out a compact and lipstick and expertly and quickly rearranged her face. He noticed that she seemed quite comfortable away from her sixty guests and in no hurry to be finished with him to return to them.

"I often wondered who owned it. I remember it said 'On Loan from a Private Collector.' "

"That was its first and last loan-out, believe me. I'll never let it go out of this house again. It was a nightmare. It seemed as though the whole mountain was blocked off when they took it out of the house to fly it east."

"Why?"

"Security. You wouldn't believe all the security, even police helicopters hovering above. They were terrified it was going to be hijacked, because of all the publicity. It's worth, they say, oh, I wouldn't even dream of telling you what they say it's worth, but it's ridiculous, I know, considering that poor Mr. van Gogh was never even able to sell it."

She spoke rapidly, barely stopping for commas and periods, in a low whispery voice, with that kind of accent that no one can really duplicate who hasn't had English nannies and French governesses and been educated at a school like Foxcroft. Philip understood why fashionable people were intrigued by her, quoted her, imitated her.

"Besides," she went on, "I missed it, all the time it was gone, hanging there over the fireplace. I find it such a comforting picture, and this room was forlorn without it. I kept trying other pictures there, but nothing looked right, after the *White Roses*. I'm mad about that color green in the background."

"Oh, yes," he replied, looking back at it.

"Is it true that Reza Bulbenkian threatened to break your legs?" Pauline asked, unexpectedly.

"Yes."

"Do you think he meant it?"

"I'm not sure."

"Hmmm," she said.

"Do you know Reza Bulbenkian?" asked Philip.

"Jules is on his board, and he's on Jules's board, and I sometimes have lunch with Yvonne Bulbenkian when I'm in New York."

"She's a piece of work."

"Isn't she?" Pauline agreed, smiling. "Hector says—have you met my friend Hector Paradiso? Terribly naughty, but very amusing. Hector says that Yvonne has calluses on her hands from social climbing." Pauline laughed. "She called her twins Oakley and Ogden, can you imagine, and speaks to them in French, poor little creatures. New York is so changed now. I've rather lost my taste for it, I'm afraid. It's not at all the way it was when I lived there." She walked over to a cymbidium plant and picked off a dying bud. "How long will you be staying in California?"

"Several months, if all goes well. I'm here to write a film."

"I heard that. For Casper Stieglitz."

"You do know everything."

"I don't know Casper Stieglitz. We don't see many of the movie people."

"Except Faye Converse."

"Faye's different. Faye belongs to the world, not just Hollywood. Faye talks about things, not just what's going on on the set, which is so boring, don't you think? Movie talk drives Jules mad."

"It was nice of you to ask me tonight, Mrs. Mendelson," Philip said.

"You're quite an addition, having been threatened by Reza Bulbenkian; and it's Pauline, not Mrs. Mendelson, and, of course, I'm going to call you Philip. You seem so young to have caused so much trouble. How old are you?"

"I'm twenty-nine until midnight, and then I'm thirty."

"Heavens, we must do something to celebrate."

"Oh, no, please," he said, meaning it. "I would hate that. I'm sure you don't remember, but we met once before."

"Indeed, I do. At the theater, at that silly play. You were with Mary Finch. Her stepmother was one of my bridesmaids, in my first wedding."

"How's Rocky, whose plane crashed and whose two pilots were killed?"

"What a memory you have! Rocky's completely recovered. Getting married again. Even bought a new plane."

"Atta boy, Rocky," said Philip.

"How are you getting on with Camilla?"

"She's very nice."

"Recent widow."

"She told me her husband dropped dead in Barcelona."

"He did. You know who she is, don't you?"

"No."

"Sam Worthington's daughter."

The name meant nothing to Philip. "Is that good?" he asked.

"Natural gas."

"I guess that's good," said Philip, and they both laughed.

Then Jules Mendelson came into the room. His massiveness filled the doorway. "Pauline, people are looking for you," he said.

"Yes, I'm coming, Jules," said Pauline, turning to him.

"I feel lost at these parties unless you're there," he said to her, as if Philip were not there.

"Oh, Jules, don't be silly."

"It's you they come to see, you know. Things slow down when you're not there."

"Isn't he sweet, this husband of mine?" asked Pauline, looking at Philip and indicating Jules with a wave of her hand.

"What are you doing in here?" asked Jules.

There was a pause, and she said, "Kippie called."

Jules looked at his wife. "Kippie? Called from France?"

"No, here. He's back."

"Here? In Los Angeles?"

"Yes."

"Is he coming over?"

"No."

"Where was he calling from?"

"I don't know, Jules. He wouldn't say."

"Everything all right?"

"No," she replied. For an instant they looked at each other. Aware of Philip's presence, Jules persisted in the conversation, but in a lower voice, as if Philip could not hear.

"What did he want?"

"Money, what else?" answered Pauline, matching his lowered tone.

"I won't."

"I know, Jules. I told him that."

"We'll talk about it later, after the party. I'll wait up," he said, looking over at Philip.

"Yes," said Pauline. Philip was struck by the sadness in her voice.

"Your friend Hector changed the place cards," said Jules, in a chiding voice meant to distract his wife from her problem.

"I know he did. It's a long story. I didn't realize Hector and Rose aren't speaking at the moment," said Pauline. Philip noticed that Pauline was making an effort to shake off her sadness over whatever was troubling her and return to her hostess role. "But you know Hector, Jules. By tomorrow everything will have been straightened out between him and Rose, and he'll make a hilarious story out of it."

"My enthusiasm for Hector is more restrained than yours, I'm afraid," replied Jules.

"Not now, Jules. Have you met Philip Quennell?"

"How do you do, Mr. Quennell," he said, offering Philip a hand to shake. He seemed not to remember having met him an hour and a half earlier in his own hallway.

"Did you like the red wine?" Jules asked Pauline.

"Marvelous, Jules."

"From the Bresciani auction. Château Margaux."

"Oh, I know, darling. Everyone commented at my table."

"Did you notice the color? And the body? Jean-Pierre said it has all the characteristics of *une grande année*."

"Superb. Everyone thought so," said Pauline.

"What did you think of the red wine?" Jules asked Philip.

"I'm afraid I'm one of those people who put their fingers over the rim of the glass when the waiter pours," answered Philip.

"Don't drink?"

"No."

"You must try this. It's exceptional. The quintessential 'eighty-five Bordeaux."

"No, thank you. I won't," said Philip.

There was an unmistakable look of disdain on Jules's face, as if to say his young guest was a fool to pass up such an opportunity to sip, for free, one of the great wines of France. "A problem?" asked Jules, in the direct manner he had of asking blunt questions.

"Far less dramatic," answered Philip. "Simply no taste for it."

Pauline, observing, quickly came to Philip's rescue. "As you can see, my husband is a wine enthusiast. Philip has come out to write a film for Casper Stieglitz," she explained.

Jules, disinterested, nodded.

Pauline was not deterred. "It was Philip Quennell's legs that Reza Bulbenkian threatened to break," she said.

Jules turned to him now, his interest captured. Suddenly his stern face broke into a wide grin, and the sternness evaporated. "So you wrote *Takeover*. I thought your name was familiar," he said. "Whoever told you all those things?"

Philip smiled but didn't reply.

"You were pretty damned accurate, I'll say that for you. You must know you're high on Reza's shit list," Jules continued.

"Oh, yes, I know."

"It's all talk, though. Reza Bulbenkian wouldn't hurt a fly. Or, have a fly hurt."

Philip wasn't so sure of that, but he replied, "I'm sure."

"It's inexpensive to have someone killed, but it's very expensive to have someone's arms or legs broken, because they can identify you," said Jules.

"What curious information to have at your fingertips, Jules," said Pauline.

"Reza, you know," continued Jules to Philip, "was the only one who didn't go to jail."

"Yes, I know," replied Philip. "He didn't go to jail because he testified against his former partners."

Jules looked at Philip. "Can't wait to tell Reza that you've been here to dinner," he said, chuckling at the thought.

"Will he be annoyed?"

"If he is, he won't say anything."

There was a moment's silence. Then Pauline said, "If you should move hotels, or take an apartment, Philip, make sure you let Miss Maple know."

"Miss Maple?"

"You met her when you came in, at the guest book. She's Jules's secretary. I'll want her to know where to reach you." Philip understood that he had passed inspection. He was going to be invited back.

"Pauline," said Jules again, giving a toss of his head toward the music to prompt her to return to her party. She put her hand beneath his arm.

"Tell the orchestra not to play too loud, Jules. It kills the conversation. Remember what happened at Rose's party? The music was so loud everyone went home by eleven, and they hadn't even wheeled out the birthday cake yet."

"That was because Rose was loaded and forgot to tell them to wheel it out," said Jules.

"Oh, darling, you shouldn't say that," said Pauline, giggling. "Poor Rose. She'd die if she heard you say that."

"You mustn't let her drive home tonight," said Jules. "She's in no condition to drive anywhere."

"I've already told Blondell to turn down the bed in the guest room," said Pauline.

Jules patted her hand in approval.

"Somebody's kissed you," said Pauline. She took his handkerchief from his breast pocket, touched her tongue to it, and wiped the lipstick off his cheek.

"Rose," he said, grimacing.

Pauline laughed and put the handkerchief back in his pocket. Jules smiled at her, and they returned to their party. Philip watched them. However rarefied their existence, he thought, they were married, a couple, committed, bonded in long wedlock. It was what he wanted for himself.

WHEN PHILIP got back to his table, Camilla Ebury was not there. He looked out at the dance floor and saw her being whirled around by a tall, dark man, too tanned, who was almost too good a dancer, Philip thought, like an instructor in a tango palace. He moved too elegantly, too sleekly, his left shoulder assuming a slightly delicate twist as he steered Camilla through the dancers. Camilla was laughing in a carefree manner, and Philip, to his astonishment, felt a twinge of jealousy, although he scarcely knew Camilla Ebury.

On the other side of him, Rose Cliveden, drunk, was waving her arms as if she were leading the orchestra, and the red wine in her wineglass spilled onto her blue satin dress. Rose, Philip decided, was in her fifties, looked older, because of drink, and must have been very pretty at twenty, thirty, and forty.

As if understanding what he was thinking about her, Rose said, "A dim railway light is still becoming to me."

Philip, embarrassed, laughed.

"Out, out, goddamn spot," said Rose, dipping her napkin into her water glass and then vigorously rubbing her discolored blue satin dress with it.

"What did you spill?" asked Philip.

"Red wine," answered Rose.

"Awfully good red wine to spill," said Philip. "From the Bresciani auction. Château Margaux. The quintessential 'eighty-five Bordeaux. *Une grande année.*"

"A pain in the ass is what it is," said Rose. She had a cigarette hanging from the corner of her mouth. She removed it and stubbed it out in the brown sugar crystals, mistaking the silver bowl for an ashtray.

"Rose, look what you've done!" cried a lady from the other side of the table, but they were all used to Rose in their group and thought the things she did when she had too much to drink exceedingly funny.

Rose, oblivious, went on talking. "This dress cost me an arm and a leg, first time I ever wore it, bought it new for Pauline's party," she said. She unpinned and then repinned at an awkward angle a diamond brooch on her left bosom. She wore big-stoned old-fashioned jewelry, with settings never updated to the current fashion. "Heavens, why would I do that?" she would often say in a voice expressing astonishment at such a suggestion, and then relay that the piece being admired had been Granny's, or Mummy's, or left to her by Aunt Minnie MacComber, or Aunt Mildred Waymouth, and that took care of that.

"Who's Kippie?" asked Philip, suddenly.

"The difficult son. Used to have a kleptomania problem. All the shops in Westwood and Beverly Hills were alerted."

"I didn't know they had a son."

"They don't. Pauline does. Terribly good-looking. By her first marriage, to that fool Johnny Petworth."

"Never heard of John Petworth."

"Johnny, they call him. They keep Kippie stashed away in France somewhere, kicking drugs, I think. He got Madge White's daughter pregnant when they were both only fourteen. Oh, what a to-do there was about that!"

"He's here," said Philip.

"At this party?"

"No. In L.A."

"Kippie's here?" She seemed astonished.

At that moment Pauline walked past Rose and Philip, in the company of Faye Converse and the former First Lady.

"Pauline!" called out Rose.

"Oh, please," said Philip, quickly, not wanting Pauline to think he had been discussing her.

"I want to ask Pauline about Kippie," said Rose. She started to get up to follow Pauline.

"Would you care to dance, Mrs. Cliveden?" he asked, rising also, as if to take her to the dance floor.

"Can't dance, and I'm the best dancer you would have ever danced with," replied Rose.

"Then why can't you?"

"I have a broken toe. So why don't you stay right here and talk to me. Camilla has been monopolizing you for the whole night. That son of a bitch Hector ditched me, did you know that? Changed the place cards."

"Yes, yes, you told me," said Philip, who had heard the account several times and did not want to hear it again.

"He's mad because the orchestra played so loud at the birthday party I gave for him last week, everybody went home before his birthday cake got wheeled out, and no one sang 'Happy Birthday' to him. He loves being the center of attention. That's why he's not speaking," said Rose.

"These are not what I think of as major life problems," said Philip.

Rose, surprised, looked at Philip for a bit. "Hand me that bottle of red wine, will you? If you wait for these waiters to pour it, you could be waiting for an hour. Now, as my problems are unimportant, you tell me, what kind of conversation do you want to have?" Looking about, she saw that Pauline was returning. "Oh, Pauline," she called out.

"Tell me, Mrs. Cliveden, what kind of a fuck was Jack Kennedy?" asked Philip, forestalling her from speaking to Pauline about Kippie.

"Oh, marvelous, simply marvelous," said Rose. She turned to him, giving him her full attention. "He was so good-looking. And so attentive. And so passionate. Until he came, and then he simply couldn't stand to be touched anymore, no affection whatsoever, just when a girl needs it most, when it's all over, the lust, I mean. I put my hand on his back when he was putting on his shoes, and he simply shrank from me. It's that Irish Catholic guilt. They all have it, those Irish people."

Suddenly, she looked at Philip and picked up his place card. "Who are you? Why are you asking me all these questions?"

"Here you are, delivered back to your table," said the dark man, pulling back Camilla Ebury's chair. "I've never cared much for purple flowers, but look how marvelously Pauline has arranged these, mixing them with the pink. It's perfect."

"You're a shit, Hector Paradiso," said Rose haughtily.

Hector elaborately ignored Rose.

"Hector, this is Philip Quennell, whom I've been telling you about. Hector Paradiso."

"Delighted," said Hector. "Oh, look, there's Pauline. I promised her this dance." He was off.

"I thought you were going to dance with me," said Camilla, taking hold of Philip's arm. "You don't mind if I borrow Mr. Quennell, do you, Rose? Come on, let's go." She almost pulled him from his seat and led him onto the dance floor. "I think Rose is going to be sick soon, so let's get out of the way so we don't have to help."

"I take it the Latino twirling you around was the place-card mover Hector Paradiso?" asked Philip, as he allowed himself to be led out to the dance floor.

"Yes, that's Hector. He's one of those men who's never off the dance floor," answered Camilla.

"All the ladies seem smitten with Hector," said Philip.

"Yes, in a way, I suppose," said Camilla. "He and Rose aren't speaking at the moment, but they're best friends at heart."

"I gather. She has a broken toe."

"Rose always has a broken something. She falls a lot."

"What do they all see in Hector?" Philip asked.

"He's really Pauline's pet. Pauline adores him. He makes her laugh and tells her all the gossip. They say Hector's in love with Pauline, but I don't see it like that. Just very close friends," said Camilla.

"Why do I think that under all that Latin charm and cha-cha-cha, he leads a very complicated life."

"I think it's only fair to tell you that Hector Paradiso is my uncle."

"Oh, God. That's the second time in fifteen minutes I've put my foot in it. Want me to take you back to the table?"

"No, but I wouldn't mind if you danced a little closer. There, that's better. I was supposed to go home with Rose, but I wouldn't dream of driving down the mountain with her in the condition she's in."

"Not to worry. She's staying here for the night. Blondell has already turned down the bed in the guest room."

"You certainly know a lot for a stranger in these parts."

"True."

"You're a pretty good dancer too," she said.

"Thanks."

"I asked my uncle Hector to drive me home, but he said he wanted to stay until the bitter end and talk over the party with Pauline," said Camilla.

"Just between us, I think Pauline and Jules are going to want to be alone when the party ends," said Philip. "Kippie is back in town."

"Kippie? He is? How in the world do you know that?"

"I just know."

Camilla nodded, looking at him, but did not miss a beat of her dance step. "Maybe Hector just had a late date and didn't want to tell me. It wouldn't be the first time. God knows where Hector ends up when the parties are over."

"Tell me about Kippie."

"Handsome. Hair too long, or was, the last time I saw him. Always in trouble. He got Madge White's daughter pregnant when they were both only fourteen. Oh, what a to-do about that! Takes drugs. Or did, I don't know about now. He's been in a rehab, somewhere in France," said Camilla.

It was the sort of answer Philip liked. "Succinct," he said.

"What?"

"Your answer."

"Thanks."

"How old?"

"Kippie?"

"Yes."

"I think he was three, or maybe four, when Pauline married Jules."

"So, twenty-five or twenty-six now," he said.

"Why this sudden fascination with Kippie?"

"You know what? I don't know," he said, and they both laughed.

They continued to dance. Behind them Jules and several friends were helping Rose, who was loudly singing the lyrics to "Camelot," to make as graceful an exit as possible. Blondell, Pauline's maid, stood waiting at the entrance of the room for her. Then Philip remembered that it was his birthday.

"What time is it?" he asked.

"Midnight," she answered. "Don't tell me you have jet lag, and it's really three o'clock in the morning your time, and you have to go home. I hate jet-lag stories."

Philip laughed. "I wasn't going to say that. I was going to say something entirely different."

"Like what?" asked Camilla.

"Like how about a club soda at your house?"

"Oh, the wickedness of it."

"Well?"

"I do need a ride home," she said, pulling back her head from his cheek and looking at him.

"I was hoping you'd say that," said Philip.

## Flo's Tape # 1

"I was perfectly content to be his mistress. The guy had a wife. I understood that. I couldn't have done the things his wife did, all those parties, all that swank. He needed that kind of wife for his kind of life. But I could do things his wife couldn't do. I mean, the guy had a dick like a mule's. Not many girls could handle that. I could. I mean, you know, we're all good at something. That's what I'm good at."

# 2

JULES MENDELSON always arose at five o'clock to be shaved by a barber called Willi, who came to his home every morning at five-thirty, when it was still dark. It was a practice that Willi had been performing for Jules for twenty-five years, and for which he was handsomely recompensed with a small and very successful barber shop on Sunset Boulevard that was backed by Jules's money. It was understood that Willi would not speak unless spoken to, as Jules liked to think about the business affairs of the day ahead during that time, except on the mornings when a haircut took place as well as the shave, and then the two men exchanged baseball and football scores, for both were passionately interested in spectator sports.

Jules was in the habit of leaving Clouds for his office by six o'clock, in order to receive telephone calls from his associates in New York when the stock market opened and to talk with his partners in London. Invariably, with a private sign to Pauline, he slipped away from their parties at eleven, without saying good night to anyone, so as not to break up the evening, and Pauline carried on until the last guest left. The last guest was always Hector Paradiso. Hector liked to wander through the rooms with Pauline, helping her blow out candles and making sure the butler and maids had emptied all the ashtrays. Then it was their habit to settle down in the library with a last glass of champagne, beneath the van Gogh picture of the *White Roses*, and discuss every detail of the evening. It was a ritual they both enjoyed and looked forward to as the perfect denouement of the party. So it was a surprise to Hector, who had something urgent to say to Pauline, when Pauline, after she had blown out the candles, told him that she had a killing headache, "simply killing, darling," and was going directly to bed without their usual postparty chat and glass of champagne. She did not tell him that Kippie had returned to town.

Hector Paradiso loved Pauline Mendelson without ever having to play the role of lover, a relationship understood by them both, without its ever having been verbalized by either. Never was Hector happier than on those evenings, which had become increasingly frequent, when Jules was busy working, or away from the city, and he was pressed into service as Pauline's escort at a charity benefit, or a museum or ballet or opera opening. The photographers always went

22

mad over Pauline Mendelson, who had achieved celebrity status in
the social and fashion press, and Hector stood by her side smiling
widely, sometimes even waving, as if the media acknowledgment were
equally for him and his family's place in the history of the city.

Driving down the mountain from Clouds after the Mendelsons'
party, Hector marveled at Pauline, at the utter perfection of her.
Hector was a gossip. It was a thing about him everyone knew, and no
one knew better than Pauline, but one of the people he never gossiped about was Pauline Mendelson. For Hector never to have mentioned to a single soul in the whole world what he knew about Jules
Mendelson and Flo March was a measure of his utter devotion to
Pauline.

Hector led a compartmentalized existence; people who were intimate with him in certain areas of his life knew nothing of the other
areas, and it had always been so with him. Tall, dashing, bald, and
fit, he looked younger than his forty-eight years. He was that rare sort
of man whose looks had improved with the loss of his hair. Dancing,
he always said, kept his waistline as slim, or almost as slim, as it had
been at twenty-five, although tennis, which he played on Rose Cliveden's court every weekend, also helped. He was often described as
being a descendant of one of the Spanish Land Grant families, like
the Sepulvedas and the Figueroas, who had major boulevards named
after them, in recognition of their involvement in the founding of the
city; and he never did not enjoy the moment when a new person
heard his surname, Paradiso, and asked, "As in Paradiso Boulevard,
on the way to the airport?"

The fortune his family once possessed had long since evaporated,
but he lived more than comfortably, for a person who didn't work, on
a trust fund left by his sister, Thelma Worthington, the mother of
Camilla Ebury, who had killed herself a dozen years ago after an
unhappy love affair. His small but perfect house on Humming Bird
Way, between Oriole and Thrush, in the Hollywood Hills, had been
photographed for a house magazine and had been the scene for many
a cocktail party through the years. He often said that his was one of
the few houses where the many diversified groups of the city over-
lapped. They did, but not at the same time.

Anyone who wanted to know anything about Los Angeles society
always called Hector. He knew the answers because he knew everyone, and those he didn't know, he knew about. "We may not all know
each other, but we all know who each other is," he was fond of saying.

23

He was able to interconnect the old families of the city for generations back. Like old Bronwyn Doheny, Caroline Phillips's mother, age ninety-one, whose funeral was to be held the next day at All Saints Episcopal Church in Beverly Hills. "Bronwyn was born a Parkhurst," he said to his friend, Cyril Rathbone, who wrote a social column for *Mulholland,* explaining it all in a nutshell. "She was Judge Parkhurst's second daughter. Her grandfather built that enormous French house on West Adams Boulevard, which is now the Center for the Church of the Heavenly Light. That whole neighborhood has gone black, you know. When I was just a child, I used to go to Caroline's birthday parties in that house before they moved to Hancock Park. Now, Bronwyn's first husband—who was *not,* I repeat not, Caroline's real father, that's another story entirely—was Monroe Whittier, and then when Monroe died, she married Justin Mulholland, who embezzled the money, do you remember that story? Now Justin Mulholland, who died in jail, was the first cousin of Rose Cliveden." When Hector Paradiso wasn't dancing, that was the sort of conversation he could carry on for hours, and did, when he was spending the evening with the kind of people he had grown up with, or, at least, the first part of the evenings, the part that preceded midnight. He was, furthermore, and had been for many years, the man who led the cotillion and taught the debutantes how to curtsy to the ground at the Las Madrinas Ball, where the daughters of the Los Angeles elite made their bow to society.

After midnight, Hector Paradiso's life took on a very different aspect, one that might have shocked some of his Angeleno friends. Even as sophisticated a couple as Pauline and Jules Mendelson could not have guessed the extent of his late-night adventures, looking for strangers to pay to kiss. Although they might have suspected there was another element to Hector's life—he had, after all, never married —it was not a subject ever voiced, even by people like Rose Cliveden, who often fought with Hector, but who fully intended to leave him the life use of one of her trust funds, should she die before him. Earlier, in his youth, there had been women in his life, like Astrid Vartan, the late ice skating star to whom he had once been engaged, and even, briefly, Rose Cliveden herself. Rose, who was never at a loss for words, reported that his equipment, as she called it, was minimal—"a rosebud, darling, no more"—but that he was marvelously adroit with his tongue. After midnight, Hector visited places that his friends in high society had never heard of, much less visited.

One of these, more reputable than some he frequented, was Miss Garbo's.

Miss Garbo's was a late-night cabaret club located on a short street in West Hollywood called Astopovo, between Santa Monica Boulevard and Melrose Avenue. Hector, ever mindful of his own importance, even in an area where it was highly unlikely that he would run into any of the kind of people he knew from the main part of his life, pulled his small Mercedes into the rear of the parking lot himself, rather than give it to a parking boy in front of the club, so that, when he left, he would not have to stand in front of the club, possibly with a companion in questionable dress, and wait for his car to be brought around for him. A stickler for appearances, Hector always thought of things like that. He wished there were a rear door that he could enter, and it occurred to him to speak to Manning Einsdorf, the owner of Miss Garbo's, to put one in so that people like himself, who didn't like to be talked about, could enter and leave the club in complete anonymity, especially when wearing a dinner jacket like he was that night, having come directly down the mountain from the Mendelsons' party.

"Hi, Hector," a loud voice called out from the crowded bar, and he turned to see Joel Zircon, a Hollywood agent who was also a regular in the place, standing at the bar with a friend.

"Hello, Joel," replied Hector, not matching the familiar tone of Joel's voice.

"Say hi to Willard Parker," said Joel, introducing his friend. "Willard's Casper Stieglitz's butler."

"Hello, Hector," said Willard, putting out his hand. Willard already knew who Hector Paradiso was, and was anxious to make his acquaintance so as to be able to claim the social figure as a friend.

Hector nodded but did not take the hand that was offered. He had not come to Miss Garbo's to make conversation, especially with a movie producer's butler.

"What kind of night are they having here?" asked Hector.

"Not bad. Not bad," said Joel.

"Where's Manning Einsdorf tonight?" asked Hector.

"He'll be out in a few minutes. He's got a new singer opening in the next set," said Joel.

"I want to get in and out before the new singer goes on. I've heard enough of Manning Einsdorf's discoveries," said Hector.

"Well, you're looking pretty spiffy," said Manning Einsdorf, coming up to the bar. He was sixty, and his gray hair was combed upward and sprayed into place to cover his bald spot. He wore large rings on each hand. "You always add a touch of class to the place, Hector."

Hector, in his gleaming white shirtfront and black tie, preened a bit as he felt himself to be the center of attention of this admiring group, knowing that he was different from them, more important, better even. He nodded in acknowledgment, and turned to watch the action in the room.

"Been to one of your high society functions?" asked Manning.

Hector nodded yes. It was a game they played out together. He took a cigarette from a gold case in his pocket and lit it with a pack of matches labeled MISS GARBO's that Manning handed to him.

"Whose?" asked Manning. Like the outsider he was, Manning Einsdorf had an enormous curiosity about the social lives of his clientele, and Hector Paradiso, who greatly enjoyed his reputation as a social figure, could not resist impressing the impressionable Manning.

"Pauline Mendelson's," answered Hector, in a lowered voice, always aware of the impact of her society name.

"Oh, la de da," said Manning. "And how was Pauline dressed tonight?"

Pauline Mendelson would have been greatly surprised to know how frequently her name was invoked in the name of style and swank among the customers of bars like Miss Garbo's, as well as the hairdressers, and florists, and picture framers, and lampshade makers in the area of West Hollywood.

"Like Madame X herself. Black velvet. High neck. Low back. Very classical," answered Hector.

"And what jewels tonight? Lemme guess, the emeralds?" asked Manning.

Hector shook his head. "Two strands of her perfect pearls the size of grapes, and a plain diamond bracelet."

"Class, the woman has class," said Manning. "Have a drink on the house, Hector."

"I'll have a scotch and soda, Zane," said Hector to the bartender.

"Coming right up, Hector. How's it going?"

"Okay, Zane. You're looking pretty good for an old man."

Zane, who was forty, laughed. "You want to know the first time I made it with Hector, Manning? Nineteen sixty-eight. Right, Hector? Met him at Numbers up on the Strip."

"He was a hot number in those days," said Hector.

"Speaking of hot numbers, I got a couple of new hot numbers here tonight," said Manning.

"Start pointing them out. It's getting past my bedtime," said Hector. "And nothing Third World."

"Take a look at the far end of the bar, the one nursing the beer, with the leather jacket and the blond hair," said Manning.

Hector glanced down the bar. Sitting on a bar stool was a young man, aware that he was being looked at. He looked back and smiled. He was, in the dim light of the bar, very good-looking.

"Go no further. That'll do just fine," said Hector. "What's his name?" asked Hector.

"Lonny," answered Manning.

"Lonny what?"

"How the fuck do I know Lonny what? Lonny was what he told me," said Manning.

"You ought to get both names."

"For what? These guys aren't trying to get into the *Los Angeles Blue Book*. They have something else on their minds. Guys like that give you two names, nine times out of ten, the second name is a phony, so why waste time learning it?"

"What's Lonny's claim to fame?" asked Hector, staring at the young man.

"You're gonna love this one, Hector. This guy is supposed to have the rest of the missing manuscript of *Candles at Lunch*," said Manning. "Took it off Basil Plant one night when Basil was drunk and belligerent and wouldn't pay up. He thought Basil would come after him the next day and pay him a fortune for it, but Basil was so far gone on pills and booze he didn't even remember the incident, and a short time later he died. And Lonny's got three hundred and ninety-eight pages of a novel he's too stupid to read, but he brags about it a lot."

"That wasn't exactly what I meant when I asked what was his claim to fame," said Hector. "Let me put it this way: when I came here tonight, I didn't have in mind a night of literary pursuits. Let me be more succinct. Is he hung?"

"I have no personal experience in the matter. I've only seen his videos," said Manning.

"Well?"

"Extended, it rises two inches above his belly button. Is that what you want to know?" asked Manning.

"Yes, Manning, that's exactly what I want to know. Introduce me, and get the charges all set now, up front, so there's no misunderstanding later. I had a little trouble with that Puerto Rican number you set me up with last week."

"So I heard."

"I pay seventy-five, no more."

"It's a hundred-dollar market these days, Hector."

"Seventy-five," repeated Hector.

"And the pretty boy at the end of the bar that you've taken a fancy to is a hundred and a half, take it or leave it, no bargaining with him."

"How do you know?"

"He told me. He considers himself a video star."

"That is an outrageous amount of money," said Hector, with indignation in his voice.

"Let me put it in perspective for you, Hector," said Manning. Manning Einsdorf was an astute businessman and used to dealing with the penurious Hector. "A hundred and fifty bucks wouldn't pay for one centerpiece at Pauline Mendelson's party tonight, and you can't fuck a centerpiece."

Hector smiled. "I always said about you, Manning: you're a man with class."

"Do we have a deal?"

Hector turned to the bartender. "Zane, send another beer down to Lonny at the end of the bar. Compliments of Mr. Paradiso, tell him."

"I bet you five bucks he'll say, 'As in Paradiso Boulevard, on the way to the airport?' " said Zane.

"That's the point, Zane," said Hector. "They all say that. It worked with you in 'sixty-eight, and it's still working today."

Zane laughed and took a beer down to the end of the bar. Lonny accepted it, and raised it in a salute to Hector. Hector walked down to the end of the bar, and the two men shook hands.

There was a roll of the drums, and Manning's voice came out on the loudspeaker. "Lady and gentlemen, Miss Garbo's is proud to present the Los Angeles singing debut of Miss Marvene McQueen." The orange curtains parted to reveal a blond singer, in a black evening dress with thin shoulder straps, standing in the curve of a piano. She wore her long hair in the style of a forties movie star, like Veronica Lake, so that one eye and half of her face were obscured by it. As she began to sing "Moanin' Low," in what she hoped was the manner of Libby Holman, she threw back her head to get the hair out of her eyes. The customers turned to look and listen, but their interest in her musical efforts quickly waned, and the business of the bar went on.

"Is this a guy in drag?" asked Hector.

"Hector, please," said Manning. "She's a woman."

"Looks like a guy in drag."

"Well, she's not." Manning was annoyed. "Shhh," he went to some customers who were talking too loudly and not paying attention to his discovery.

"How much are you paying her?" asked Hector.

"Actually, she's paying me. This is her debut."

"Not so hot-looking for a nightclub singer."

"I think it's a very interesting face," replied Manning.

"Her family never heard of braces, I see."

"Braces?"

"She's got buckteeth."

"Well, they're not exactly buck. One of the two front teeth is in front of the other."

"Where I come from, that's buck. You're not going to tell me she makes a living at this?"

"Why?"

"Look around. Nobody's listening to your new discovery. How does she make a living?"

"She's the literary critic for *Mulholland*, but keep that under your lid. She don't want anyone to know."

"That's Hortense Madden?"

"Herself."

"Hey, Manning," said Zane, the bartender. "The singer's pissed off because you're talking during her number."

"Fuck the singer," said Hector.

"No, thanks. She's not my type," said Lonny, the video star, speaking his first words of the evening.

Hector looked at Lonny and laughed. "Let's get out of here," he said.

LONNY, smoking a joint, looked at all the photographs in silver frames that covered the tables in Hector Paradiso's living room. There were pictures of a great many grand people, as well as recognizable faces of film stars of past decades—Tyrone Power, Rosalind Russell, Dolores del Rio, Astrid Vartan—and they never failed to fascinate Hector's nocturnal visitors. Hector, his black tie off, his shirt open at the neck, sat in a chair with a strong drink of whiskey and watched the young man. In his arms was his dog, Astrid, a West Highland terrier. Astrid was used to the strangers her master brought home most nights of the week. Hector noticed for the first time that Lonny wore black jeans, a black Lacoste shirt, and black running shoes.

"A study in black," said Hector.

"What's that mean?"

"It seems as if all the interesting people dressed in black tonight."

Lonny nodded, disinterested. "Who's this?" he asked, picking up a picture.

"She's called Pauline Mendelson," said Hector.

"Movie star?"

"Oh, goodness, no. Just a friend."

"Looks high class."

"She is."

He picked up another picture, of a young bride, and stared at it. "I've never been to a wedding," he said.

"Never been to a wedding? Really?"

"I mean a real wedding like this, where the bride wears a white veil, and has bridesmaids, and walks up the aisle on the arm of her father. Hey, that's you in the picture? Is this your daughter?"

"No, no, my niece. My sister's daughter. Her father was dead, and I took her up the aisle."

"Wow." He took another toke from his joint. "This is good dope you got, Hector."

"Lots more where that comes from. And other treats, as well."

"How long ago was this wedding?"

"Nine years."

"Is it a happy marriage?"

"It isn't a marriage anymore."

"Divorced, huh?"

"No, the husband dropped dead on the street in Barcelona."

"No kidding? That's sad, really sad."

"What's your last name, Lonny?"

"Edge."

"Lonny Edge. Nice name. Is that your real name or hooker name?"

30

"It's my real name, and I don't like being called a hooker, Hector," said Lonny. There was a menacing note in his voice.

Hector recognized the note and looked at him. Beneath the cushion of his chair was the gun he always had at the ready for protection in case any sort of unpleasantness should break out with one of his night visitors.

"This is what I do for a living," said Lonny, explaining himself. "I have no problem with it."

"Oh, of course," said Hector, smiling nervously. "It was just a figure of speech. No offense, old man."

"I also happen to be a very big name in video," continued Lonny.

"Yes, yes, I think I may have seen some of your videos, now that I think of it. *Hard, Harder, Hardest*? Wasn't that you?"

"Yeah, man. That was me," said Lonny, pleased that he was recognized.

"Marvelous film. Why don't you come over here, Lonny," said Hector, getting down to the business of the evening. He placed the little dog on the floor and then lifted one foot, on which he was still wearing his black patent leather dancing pump, and pointed it at the crotch of Lonny Edge's black jeans. Hands on hips, ready for anything, Lonny watched the rich bachelor. Hector drank from his whiskey glass and slowly moved the toe of his black patent leather dancing pump up and down on the fly of Lonny's jeans, smiling at him at the same time.

"Let's see if what you've got in there is as good as Manning Einsdorf says it is, Lonny," said Hector.

THE NEXT MORNING, an hour before dawn, five shots rang out in the living room and library of 9221 Humming Bird Way. Hector Huberto Luis Paradiso y Gonsalvo, the last member of the great Paradiso family that had helped to found the city, turned and stared in disbelief into the mirror over his mantelpiece and saw the blood drain from his tanned face, leaving it a purplish gray color. Beyond in the mirror, his eyes met the eyes of his killer as that person looked back in haste before making for the front door. Astrid, his dog, barked furiously at the departing figure.

Leaning against the wall for support, Hector edged his way to the door of the library, trailing blood as he slowly moved toward the telephone. On his desk was a pile of blue stationery from Smythsons on Bond Street in London, with his name, Hector Paradiso, engraved across the top of each sheet. The stationery had been a favorite gift from Pauline Mendelson. "So personal, so thoughtful, so typical of Pauline," Hector had said at the time to Cyril Rathbone, to whom he sometimes flaunted his close friendship with the grand lady. As he leaned over the top sheet and wrote the name of the person who had fired the five shots that were causing his death, several drops of blood fell on the piece of paper, partially covering his childlike scrawl. The dog, Astrid, hugged his leg, crying.

Hector buzzed the intercom that connected with the room of his houseboy in the pool house across the lawn.

"Sí?" came the sleepy voice of Raymundo.

"Police," Hector whispered into the phone. "Get the police."

"You all right, señor Hector?" asked Raymundo.

"Get the police." His voice was so weak it could scarcely be heard.

Raymundo, alert, hopped out of bed.

From the intercom came the last words of Hector Paradiso. "And get rid of all the porn before my niece gets here."

## Flo's Tape # 2

*"There's something you've got to understand. I never for a moment expected Jules Mendelson to divorce his wife and marry me, and he never gave me any line like that either, in order to keep me hanging in there. If he had any complaints about his wife, he never talked about them to me. The thing is, the Mendelsons had an ideal marriage, like a great partnership, except that he was in love with me, as well as being in love with Mrs. Mendelson. He just loved us in different ways.*

*"Jules was a guy who'd had his own way all his life. And he thought he could have the two of us, and he could have as far as I was concerned, but it just didn't work out that way.*

*"You see, I had no intention of letting happen what happened between us. You've certainly seen enough pictures of Jules; he was never going to win any prizes in the looks department. And I'd never gone out with a guy that age before. There's something about power that's very sexy, you know, and what Jules lacked in the looks department, he more than made up for in the power department. When Jules walked into a room or a restaurant, people turned around. My friend, Glyceria, who was Faye Converse's maid, told me that in her time, women used to think Henry Kissinger was attractive. It's another version of the same thing, you know.*

*"And he was good to me. He wanted to improve me. He once said to me, 'You've got to start reading the newspapers, not just the gossip columns.' And then he started asking me about stuff in the news, like Gorbachev, and Bush, and the deficit, and stuff like that, and he could explain things to me so that I could understand. If you should happen to have any questions about the European currency after 1992, for instance, I'll probably be able to help you out, because he talked about that all the time. And he wanted me to wear nice clothes, and he began to buy me classy gifts, like this ring here with the sapphire and the diamonds, and these yellow diamond earrings. When I was seeing that putz Casper Stieglitz before I met Jules, all that he ever gave me was black satin underwear from Frederick's of Hollywood. And pretty soon, I started to fall in love with Jules."*

# 3

THE NIGHT BEFORE, Philip Quennell and Camilla Ebury had made love for the first time, as well as the second and the third, each time experiencing increased acts of intimacy. Awakening later than Camilla, Philip lay in bed without moving and watched her as she brushed her hair, with a raised arm and long hard strokes, at the same time gazing into her dressing table mirror with an intent stare. The strap of her nightgown had fallen from her shoulder, and her concentration on her hairbrushing was complete.

"When I was a child, my nanny—Temple she was called, short for Templeton—made me brush my hair one hundred times each morning, no matter what. I used to hate it, but it became a habit, and now I find that my day is imperfect if I don't do it the first thing. Of course, I don't think about my hair when I brush it. It is for me a time for thinking," said Camilla.

"How did you know I was awake?" asked Philip.

"I could see you in the mirror," she said.

"Nice back," he said.

"Hmmm?"

"Nice back, I said."

"Thanks."

"It's a good look the way your strap has fallen off your shoulder."

"I'm experiencing shyness, if you can believe it."

He smiled at her.

"Do you always sleep with your pearls on?"

"Always. They belonged to my uncle."

"The place card changer, that uncle?"

She laughed. "Uncle Hector, although I never call him uncle. Hector Paradiso."

"As in Paradiso Boulevard, on the way to the airport?"

"Yes. The Paradisos were a Land Grant family. Hector's great-grandfather, or great-great, I'm not sure, I never get it straight, was one of the founders of the city, way back when. My mother was his older sister."

"Now let me get this straight. On your father's side, according to Pauline Mendelson, you're natural gas, and on your mother's side, you're from a Land Grant family. Right?"

"Right."

"You're what's called well connected, where I come from."

"I cover all the bases, at least in Los Angeles."

"I know it's none of my business, but why did Uncle Hector have a pearl necklace?"

"It belonged to his mother, my grandmother, whom I never knew. When Hector was in the army, he wore it under his uniform. He claimed the pearls brought him luck. After the army, he gave them to my mother, and when Mummy died, they came to me. I almost never take them off, except when I bathe, of course, or go swimming—the chlorine in the pool is terrible for them—or when I wear Mummy's diamond necklace, which isn't often, because it's a bore to get it out of the bank and then back the next morning, because of the insurance."

Philip laughed.

She looked at him, confused. "What did I say that was funny?"

"Rich people stories always strike me funny," he said.

Her hundred strokes finished, she stood up and walked toward the bed and pulled the bedclothes off him. "Time to get up," she said. Looking down at him, she spoke again. "Oh, heavens!"

Philip, embarrassed, smiled bashfully.

"Is that because of me or because it's morning?" she asked.

"Both," replied Philip. He reached up and flicked off the second shoulder strap, and her nightgown slipped down to her waist. "Nice front, too," he said, quietly.

She folded her arms in front of her breasts but did not turn away.

"Don't do that," said Philip. He reached up and took down her protective arms and stared at her breasts. With his first finger he lightly touched the tip of her nipple and then moved his finger in a circular motion. "Perfect," he said. The night before, at the Mendelsons' party, he had thought she was attractive, but not quite beautiful. Now, seeing her, he revised his opinion.

"That's really nice," he said.

"What's really nice?" she asked.

"Your modesty."

"Listen, Philip, I don't want you to think I'm in the habit of picking up men at parties and bringing them home," said Camilla. "I'm not." She wanted to say, "This is the first time since my husband died," but she didn't, although it was true, because she knew it would sound like a protestation.

"That's not what I think at all," said Philip gently. For a moment they stared at each other. Then Philip reached out and took her hand and brought her down to the bed beside him.

"There's something I meant to tell you last night," she said.

"What?"

"I do think that's an awfully odd place down there for you to have a tattoo."

LATER, CAMILLA WENT downstairs to make coffee and brought it back up to the room. She could hear Philip in her bathroom, with the water running. He was standing nude with his back to her, intent on shaving. Although she had spent the night with him, making love in endless variations, and repeated the process in the morning, she felt like an intruder on his privacy as she walked in on him in her bathroom.

"Oh, excuse me," she said.

He smiled. "It's all right."

"I need the Floris bath salts."

"Come in. It's your bathroom. I borrowed a razor."

"What are you using for shaving cream?"

"Just soap. It works all right."

Passing him, opening the cabinet, her body brushed against the front of him. Philip, always responsive to touch, responded. They both noticed. They both smiled.

The telephone rang in the bedroom.

"What? No extension in the bathroom?" joked Philip. "I thought this was the movie capital of the world."

"Not the group I'm in," said Camilla as she walked toward the ringing telephone. "We don't even speak to the people in the movie capital. It's probably Bunty. Did I tell you I had a daughter?"

"No."

"Age eight. She's spending the weekend at her friend Phyllis's family's ranch in Solvang. Otherwise, there'd be no way you would ever have spent the night here. Hello? Oh, good morning, Jules. What a marvelous party that was. I had such a good time. I was going to call Pauline to thank her, but I thought it was too early."

There was a long silence, and then Philip heard Camilla say, "No!" There was another silence, and again she said, "No! I simply can't believe it. How could this happen?"

36

Again there was a silence, and Camilla said, "Where are you calling from, Jules?"

Philip wrapped himself in a towel, walked into the bedroom, and stood by Camilla. He perceived at once from Camilla's face that something serious, possibly calamitous, had occurred.

"From Hector's house." He was able to hear Jules Mendelson's deep voice.

"I'll be right there," said Camilla.

"No, no, Camilla, don't come over," said Jules. He spoke hastily. "There's no point in that. It would only upset you terribly. I can handle everything here. What you should do is go up to Pauline's and stay with her, or I could tell Pauline to come to you, and I'll meet you in an hour or so."

Camilla was dissatisfied with this arrangement, but, as it was Jules Mendelson who was advising her, she capitulated to his wishes.

"Yes, of course, Jules. Have you told Pauline yet?"

"Yes, I called her," said Jules.

After she hung up, Philip asked, "What is it?"

"Hector's dead," answered Camilla.

"How?"

"Shot, apparently."

They looked at each other. He put his hand over her hand. "I'm sorry."

She nodded. "My father, my mother, my husband, now my uncle. What the hell's wrong with me?"

"Get dressed," said Philip. "I'll drive you there."

"Jules said not to come, that it would only upset me. He said for me to go up to Pauline's and that he would meet me there and fill me in."

"Is Jules Mendelson related to your uncle?"

"No."

"Was he his best friend or something?"

"No. Hector was Pauline's friend really. I never thought Jules liked him all that much. Why do you ask?"

"You are Hector's only living relation, aren't you?"

"Yes."

"How come Jules Mendelson knows your uncle is dead before you know it? Why would the police call him?"

Camilla looked at Philip. "I don't know, but it is so like Jules to handle things. Underneath that stern facade, he is an incredibly kind man, who would do anything for his friends. I told you how he helped me when Orin dropped dead in Barcelona."

"Yes, I understand all that," said Philip. "But I still don't understand why the police called him and not you."

"I suppose you're right," she said.

"Don't you think you should go to your uncle's house?"

"Jules said to go up to Pauline's."

"Somehow you don't strike me as the kind of woman who stays away just because someone tells her to stay away."

"I'm not."

"C'mon. I'll take you there."

## Flo's Tape # 3

"Once Jules told me he sometimes felt inadequate around Pauline's family. I couldn't imagine Jules ever feeling inadequate about anything, but he said he did. Pauline's father was a great sportsman, and Jules never participated in sports, except to watch football on television. What almost no one knew was that Jules had a little spindly leg, just about this big around. He was very sensitive about it. When he was a child in Chicago, he had one of the last known cases of polio. So he didn't play golf, or tennis, or any of the things that were important to Pauline's father.

"He also felt that Pauline never really lost her Eastern Seaboard background, even though she had become a fixture of the Los Angeles social scene. He said he thought of her as a permanent visitor. When her sisters came to visit her, as they did several times a year, he told me that he felt like an outsider among them, while they giggled and talked about people they had known whom he had never heard of. He said that sometimes they spoke in French together.

"Once he said that if anything ever happened to him, he was sure that Pauline would be gone from Los Angeles with the year."

# 4

TO HAVE THE NEWS of a misadventure before anyone else, even the media, was not an altogether new experience for Pauline Mendelson. In times past, because of the prominence and influence of her husband, she had known of certain minor misadventures involving her son and only child, Kippie Petworth, before anyone, even the police. Kippie's teenage kleptomania had long since come to a halt, but not without several highly embarrassing situations that had had to be covered for, atoned for, and hushed, all thanks to Jules, who was no more than the boy's stepfather. But, as everyone they knew knew, Kippie's real father, Johnny Petworth, was hopeless in any sort of crisis, except in cards and backgammon.

No amount of familiarity with misadventure, however, could have prepared Pauline for the shock of the early morning telephone call that aroused Jules and sent him flying out of their house at such an ungodly hour.

"But what is it, Jules?" she asked from their bed, seeing the haste with which he hung up the telephone, after an indecipherable conversation, and leapt from the bed and dressed, without either bathing or shaving. She feared, of course, for her son, who had returned unexpectedly the night before, having abandoned his clinic in France months before the time the doctors had prescribed as necessary for his treatment.

Standing at the door of their room, ready to go, Jules said to her, "It's Hector."

"Hector!" said Pauline, nearly collapsing with relief. "Oh, thank God. For a moment I thought it was Kippie again."

"He's dead," said Jules.

"Hector?" whispered Pauline, aghast. "How? What happened?"

"I don't know anything. I'll call you when I get there."

"Was it an automobile accident? What? How?" she asked.

"I don't know, Pauline," he replied again.

"Where are you going?"

"To his house."

"Oh, Jules, should I do anything about Camilla?"

"No."

"Of course, if they called you, they undoubtedly called her."

Jules nodded. "Do you have much on your agenda for today?"

"Whatever it is, I'll clear it."

"Good. Stand by."

Outside, a moment later, she could hear the frenzied barking of the police dogs that patrolled the grounds at night, as they rushed around Jules on his way across the courtyard to the garage. "Hi, boy, hi, boy, down, down," she could hear Jules say to the dogs. However fierce the dogs were to other people, they responded totally to the commands of Jules Mendelson. "Call them off, will you, Smitty. It's me."

"Anything wrong, Mr. Mendelson?" asked Smitty, the night guard, who had been with the Mendelsons for fifteen years.

"Apparently," answered Jules, without elaborating further. "I have to get up to Humming Bird Way. Remind me how to get there. I can't remember."

"Off the Strip, up Doheny, turn right on Oriole, and it turns into Humming Bird," said Smitty.

"I'll know it when I see it. I've been there a hundred times," said Jules.

"I hope everything's okay, Mr. M.," said Smitty.

Alone, Pauline turned on the All News radio station, but there was nothing on it that pertained to her life, or Hector's, as far as she knew: rapes, murders, gangs, drug deals gone awry, and a television star's divorce. Still stunned by the suddenness of the news, and the incompleteness of it, she could not yet cry, although she felt an ache of loneliness for her friend. In days to come, she would say over and over, dozens of times, "He was my first friend here when Jules and I moved to Los Angeles." She could only remember that Hector had wanted to stay on the night before after the other guests had left, as was their habit, and bring a bottle of champagne into the library to talk over the happenings of the party, especially his latest contretemps with Rose Cliveden, but she had said no. My God, she thought, perhaps if he had stayed, whatever has happened might not have happened. And then she remembered that Rose was sleeping down the hall in one of the guest rooms, having been too drunk to drive to Holmby Hills, let alone down the mountain from Clouds.

I'll wake up Rose, thought Pauline.

ON SUNSET BOULEVARD the traffic moved at a snail's pace and then stopped entirely. Philip Quennell and Camilla Ebury, en route from Camilla's house in Bel Air to Hector Paradiso's house in the Hollywood Hills, sat in impatient silence in the car.

"It's driving me mad, this sitting here," said Camilla, tapping her fingers on the dashboard. "The traffic usually moves on Sunset."

"There must be an accident, or something, up ahead," said Philip.

"More likely, some great event at the Beverly Hills Hotel. That's the holdup, I'm sure," said Camilla.

Philip pressed on the horn several times.

"Honking is not going to do any good, you know," she said.

"I know. I can't stand people who blow their horns, but I can feel how anxious you are."

"Perhaps if you turned left when we get to Roxbury, and got over on Lexington, we could go behind the hotel, and then come out again on Sunset," suggested Camilla.

"Did Hector keep great sums of money in his house, do you think?" asked Philip.

"I know he didn't. In the first place, he didn't have very much money."

"What do you mean, he didn't have much money?"

"I mean, people who don't have any money will think he had a lot of money, but people with money will say he didn't have any money."

"Money is a relative thing, is that what you're saying?" asked Philip, amused.

"Something like that. Jules explained that to me. And in the second place, Hector was extremely tight. Anyone who knew him will tell you that."

"Has Hector ever been married?" asked Philip.

"Engaged a few times, once to an actress, Astrid something, before my time, but he never married," said Camilla. She looked out the window.

"Why don't you cry?" asked Philip.

"I don't know you well enough to cry in front of you," she replied.

"Yes, you do."

"I only met you last night."

"We've come a long way in a short time, don't forget."

"I want you to know one thing."

"What's that?"

"I'm not in the habit of bringing men home from parties."

"You already told me that, and it wasn't necessary to say it the first time. I knew that."

She reached over and patted his hand on the steering wheel.

"Thanks for coming with me," she said.

"May I ask you a question?"

"Of course."

"About your marriage?"

"All right."

"Didn't you love your husband?" asked Philip.

"Why do you ask that?" replied Camilla, with surprise in her voice.

"You spoke of him very casually."

"How did I speak of him very casually? And when? I don't remember."

"Last night, at the Mendelsons'."

"What in the world did I say?"

"You said, 'Don't ever die in a country where you don't speak the language. It's a nightmare.' "

"But that's true."

"I'm sure it's true, but it's also a very casual way to talk about a husband who dropped dead on the street in Barcelona."

"Do you think I sound callous?"

"I don't know, but I'm curious."

She looked straight ahead, thinking before answering. "Oh, I suppose we would have gotten a divorce in time if Orin hadn't died. We weren't really happy, but Bunty adored him, and I wasn't desperately unhappy, just not terribly happy. Satisfied?"

"Honest answer."

"Now tell me something."

"Okay."

"Do you always remember everything people say?"

"Yes."

"I better be careful about what I say."

"Look, the line's moving," he answered.

"I'M SORRY, ma'am, there's no one permitted to go in the house," said the policeman posted outside Hector Paradiso's house on Humming Bird Way. Already the driveway had been roped off with orange masking tape strung between trees. There were police cars lined up on both sides of the street, and a news van from one of the local television stations was driving up and down the street looking for a place to park. An ambulance, with its rear door open, was parked in the driveway, and the driver leaned against the fender smoking a cigarette. Across the street, neighbors, still in nightclothes, were huddled together, watching the scene.

"No one admitted here," said a policeman, holding up his hands, as Camilla Ebury and Philip Quennell walked up to the entrance of the house.

"I am Mr. Paradiso's niece," said Camilla.

"I'm sorry, ma'am, I can't let you in. Those are my orders," said the policeman.

"This is Camilla Ebury, officer," said Philip Quennell. "Mrs. Ebury is Hector Paradiso's only living relative."

"I'll go inside and ask, Mrs. Berry, but not at the moment," said the officer. "I'm really sorry for your trouble, but I'm just doing what I was told. The coroner's in there now."

"If you could just tell them inside that I'm here," said Camilla. "It's Ebury, not Berry. E-B-U-R-Y. My mother was Mr. Paradiso's sister. Mr. Jules Mendelson called me with the news."

Always, whenever it was mentioned, in any circumstance, the name of Jules Mendelson seemed to bring about a change in attitude. As the officer headed toward the front door, it opened, and two policemen came out with a young man between them, his hands in handcuffs behind his back. The television van had parked and unloaded, and the cameraman ran forward to get a picture of the trio. The handcuffed person in the middle shouted out, "Hey, man, don't photograph me," and bent his head down and turned it away from the camera. As he looked up from his bent-over position, his eyes locked with Camilla's.

"I didn't do this, Miss Camilla! I swear to God! I was asleep in my room in the pool house. Your uncle buzzed me on the intercom and said there was trouble, and by the time I got dressed he was dead, and whoever did it was gone. I swear to God, Miss Camilla."

"Oh, Raymundo," said Camilla, staring at him.

The policemen moved him on toward the police car. One opened the door, and the other pushed Raymundo into the car.

"Who's Raymundo?" asked Philip.

"He's my uncle's houseboy, has been for a couple of years," said Camilla.

From the front door, the policeman called out, "You can come in now, Mrs. Ebury, and your friend."

Walking toward the door, aware that they were being photographed by the cameraman, Camilla reached into her pocketbook and took out a pair of dark glasses and put them on.

"There was a blond man, looked like an off-duty marine, who ran out of the house," yelled a voice from behind some trees.

"Who's that?" asked Philip.

"The crazy lady next door," said Camilla. "She made Hector's life hell, spying on him all the time, imagining all these insane things."

They walked inside the house. There was a small central hallway. To the left was the dining room. To the right was the living room, and beyond that the library. The house was filled with police and medical people.

"This is the niece, Captain," said the police officer.

Philip took hold of Camilla's arm and walked her forward.

"Captain Mariano, Mrs. Ebury," said the captain, introducing himself.

Camilla nodded. "Mr. Quennell," she said, introducing Philip and looking around at the same time. The living room was in shambles. A shot had been fired into the mirror over the fireplace, and the glass top of the coffee table had also been shattered by a shot. There was blood on the blue upholstery of a sofa, and a trail of blood leading into the library. Camilla gasped when she saw the bare legs of her uncle's bare body in the room beyond.

"Will you be able to identify the body, Mrs. Ebury?" asked Captain Mariano.

She had turned pale. She looked as if she was going to faint. She looked at Philip.

"Didn't Mr. Mendelson identify him?" asked Philip.

"Mr. Mendelson didn't go in that room," answered Mariano.

"May I identify the body, Captain?" asked Philip.

"How well did you know the deceased?"

"Not at all well. Hardly at all, in fact, but we were at the same party last night, and I know what he looks like," said Philip.

"That all right with you, Mrs. Ebury?" asked the captain.

Camilla nodded. Philip walked into the library. Lying facedown on the floor, in a pool of blood, was Hector Paradiso, nude and dead. There appeared to be several shots in his torso, and red marks on the cheek that was visible to Philip, as well as on both his buttocks.

Philip nodded. "That's Hector Paradiso," he said. He thought of Hector last night, dancing so elaborately, his white teeth flashing in his tanned face. Too tanned, he remembered thinking at the time. Now the too-tanned face looked ghostly and white beneath the red welts on it.

"How many times was he shot?" asked Philip.

"There appear to be five shots fired in all," said the captain.

"What are those red welts on his backside?" he asked.

"The victim seems to have been slapped across the face and buttocks by his black patent leather dancing pumps," said the captain.

Philip nodded. From the other room he heard Camilla's voice. "I am stunned, simply stunned, that Raymundo could do such a thing," she said. "My uncle has been responsible for bringing Raymundo's family up here from Mexico and getting them green cards so they could work legally and sending them to schools where they could learn English."

"We're not at all sure that Raymundo is responsible, Mrs. Ebury," said a police officer.

"I saw him myself in handcuffs outside this house being put into a police car," she said.

"I'm not a bit convinced about Raymundo," said the captain. "Do you happen to know where your uncle was last night, Mrs. Ebury?"

"Yes, he was at Jules Mendelson's house," replied Camilla.

"I know that. We've talked to Mr. Mendelson. I meant, after Mr. Mendelson's."

Camilla looked at the police captain and understood what he meant. "No. I would have no way of knowing that."

Philip walked back into the room. "Where is Mr. Mendelson?" he asked.

"He left," said Captain Mariano.

"How long ago?"

"He only stayed a few minutes."

"Perhaps you should call him at home," said Philip to Camilla.

"Yes," she answered.

"I don't think he went home," said the captain. "I heard him telephone Sandy Pond and ask to see him immediately."

Camilla nodded

"Who's Sandy Pond?" asked Philip.

"The publisher of the *Tribunal*," answered Camilla.

"Comin' through," called out a voice from the library.

"Step over here, will you, Mrs. Ebury, Mr. Quennell," said the captain.

Two stretcher-bearers made their way through the living room carrying the last remains of Hector Paradiso zipped into a black rubber body bag. In the silence that followed, the crying of a small animal could be heard.

"What's that?" asked Captain Mariano.

"What?" answered one of the policemen.

"Like crying?"

"Oh, my God," said Camilla. "Astrid."

"Who's Astrid?" asked Philip.

"Hector's dog," said Camilla. She called the dog several times. "Astrid. Astrid."

The sounds of crying became louder as Camilla went into the library. She knelt down on the floor and peered under the sofa. "Astrid, come out, you sweet thing," she said in a gentle voice. She reached under the sofa and pulled the small West Highland terrier out. The dog appeared terrified, and Camilla clutched it in her arms, kissed its head, and petted it. "Rose gave Hector this dog," she said to Philip. "I'm going to bring it back to Rose."

"That little dog knows who killed Hector Paradiso," said Philip.

"Too bad Astrid can't talk," said Captain Mariano.


"I DON'T give a shit if Mr. Einsdorf left strict orders he did not want to be disturbed until noon or not," yelled Joel Zircon into the telephone. "Wake him up!"

Several minutes later Manning Einsdorf, enraged that his sleep had been disturbed, came to the telephone. "This is outrageous, Joel. I need my rest. I didn't close the club last night until four."

"Have you heard about Hector Paradiso, Manning?" asked Joel.

"Oh, my God. AIDS?"

"No, Manning. Shot five times."

"What?"

"That's right."

"Dead?"

"Of course dead."

"Oh, my God. You don't think that Lonny . . . oh, my God. Is it on the news?"

"No, not a word so far."

"How'd you hear?"

"A sometime trick of mine was working on the ambulance. He called me."

"Oh, my God."

"You said 'oh, my God' three times now, Manning. You better get your ass in gear and get over to the place and destroy any records or phone numbers you have of hustlers and johns or you're going to be in deep shit."

"That fucking Lonny," said Manning Einsdorf.

"What was that lousy singer's name with the buckteeth?"

"Marvene McQueen."

"Tell Marvene she didn't see Hector Paradiso in your place last night. And Zane too."

"Don't worry about Zane," said Manning.

## Flo's Tape #4

*"Jules used to say that if you could visualize yourself as something, you could become it. I can't tell you how much that meant to me when he said it. You see, I always thought I would be famous, only I never could visualize what I would be famous at. He knew, he always knew, he told me, that he would become an important person, and he certainly did.*

*"When I visualized myself as famous, it wasn't this kind of fame."*

# 5

LATER THAT DAY, Philip Quennell returned to the Chateau Marmont, an apartment hotel on that part of Sunset Boulevard known as the Strip that was frequented by the movie and art crowd. Casper Stieglitz's secretary, Bettye, had booked him a room, or, as Bettye described it, a junior suite. A junior suite, Philip discovered, was a bedroom and sitting room in one.

"Perfect for your writing," Bettye had told Philip when she called him in New York to confirm his reservation. "All the writers who come out from New York stay there." Philip, who was not a chatter on the telephone, even with a full-time chatter like Bettye, said the arrangement sounded fine, but Bettye sensed a dissatisfaction, where there was none, and added, as a further enhancement of the charms of his future lodging, "It's the place where John Belushi OD'd."

"Oh, right," Philip had added.

"But that was in one of the bungalows. Not the room where you will be."

"Right," said Philip.

The lost luggage had been returned by the airline to the hotel, and Philip showered again and changed the clothes he had worn since the morning before when he boarded the plane in New York, and had then worn to the Mendelsons' party the night before, and on the mission that morning to Humming Bird Way to identify the body of Hector Paradiso, and then back to Clouds at the top of the mountain to deliver Camilla Ebury into the comforting hands of Pauline Mendelson.

That time no butler or maid opened the door to receive them. Pauline herself was standing in the open door waiting for them when Philip drove his rented car into the courtyard. She walked to Camilla's side of the car and opened the door. When Camilla got out, the two women embraced.

"So awful," said Pauline.

"Poor Hector," answered Camilla. "What a good friend you were to Hector, Pauline. He adored you."

"And I him. I'm livid with myself that I didn't let him stay on last night after everyone left. He wanted to talk over the party, and I said no."

"Oh, Pauline, it's not your fault," said Camilla. "Anyway, I heard that Kippie was back, and of course you wanted to be with him."

Pauline smiled distantly in acknowledgment of the mention of her son's name, but did not reply.

Camilla continued. "How is he?"

"Oh, coming along," said Pauline. In the short silence that followed, the sound of a tennis ball being hit with great force against a backboard issued from an unseen court somewhere behind the house. Pauline was wearing a cashmere sweater over her shoulders, and she pulled it together in front of her as if she were chilly, although it was not cold. Instinctively, both Camilla and Philip realized that the player was probably Kippie. Turning, Pauline greeted Philip warmly. If she was surprised to see him in the company of Camilla, wearing the same clothes he had been wearing the night before, she gave no such indication.

"I don't see Jules's car," said Camilla.

"He went out very early this morning, as soon as he got the call, and he's not back yet," said Pauline.

"Who called him?" asked Camilla.

"I don't know. The police, I suppose."

Camilla and Philip looked at each other.

"Is Rose still here?" asked Camilla.

"Heavens, yes. On her second Bloody Mary already and her fortieth cigarette. I'm always afraid she's going to burn down my house," replied Pauline. She was back to being herself again, charming, and in charge.

"How's she taking the news?"

"In absolute despair, calling everyone. Blaming herself for everything. If only they'd been speaking, this never would have happened, that kind of talk."

"Like most lifelong friends, they were always not speaking," said Camilla, and both she and Pauline laughed.

From within the car, the dog started to whine.

"What in the world is that?" asked Pauline.

"Oh, my God, I forgot," said Camilla. "It's Astrid. We brought Astrid. I couldn't leave her in that house. Poor little thing, she was hiding under the sofa in the library. I thought Rose might want her back, as she gave her to Hector in the first place."

"That will be just what she needs," said Pauline. "She's planning the funeral already. High Mass at Good Shepherd in Beverly Hills. She wants Archbishop Cooning to officiate, can you imagine, and she's going to give a big lunch after the funeral at the Los Angeles Country Club. Are you going to mind that she's taken over completely?"

"Hell, no," said Camilla. "Rose is at her best when she's planning a party, and that's exactly what she'll turn this into."

"Now, come in, the two of you," said Pauline.

Philip, who had been watching Camilla and Pauline, said, "The papers are going to have a field day with this story. I'm surprised they're not buzzing your bell down at the gates now."

"Oh, no, I shouldn't think so," said Pauline.

"I mean, it has all the elements, doesn't it? Land Grant family. Prominent social figure. Millionaire, or at least one presumes. Uncle of Camilla Ebury. Close personal friend of Mrs. Jules Mendelson. It all sounds very front page to me."

"Oh, no. I shouldn't think it would be played up," repeated Pauline, shaking her head.

"But why not?" asked Philip.

"That's what Jules said when he called. He was at Sandy Pond's office at the *Tribunal*."

"But, Pauline, they took Raymundo away in handcuffs," said Camilla. "I saw him with my own eyes."

"They've let him go by now. A mix-up, apparently. Anyway, come in. Rose will be having an anxiety attack."

Philip, a newcomer and an outsider in the group, declined. Twenty-four hours earlier he had not known any of these people, and now he felt awkward among them in such personal moments. "I won't come in, Pauline. I'd better get back to the hotel and check on my luggage and call Casper Stieglitz to tell him I've arrived."

Pauline looked at him and smiled. "Happy birthday," she said.

Philip smiled back, touched that she had remembered.

"I didn't know it was your birthday, Philip," said Camilla.

"So much has happened since last night, I'd forgotten it myself," he said.

"How old are you?" she asked.

"Thirty," he answered.

"I'm thirty-two," she said.

"I like older women."

Camilla laughed. "I can't thank you enough for seating me next to this wonderful man last night, Pauline," she said. "I don't know what I'd have done without him."

Camilla and Philip looked at each other.

"I'll call you," he said.

As Philip was driving out of the courtyard, Jules Mendelson came up the driveway in his dark blue Bentley. He stopped the car by the front door and got out. Walking over to where Pauline and Camilla were standing, he put his arms around Camilla and hugged her. To Philip, leaving, he appeared weary.

WHEN PHILIP QUENNELL told Jules Mendelson the night before, after refusing his Château Margaux wine from the Bresciani auction, that he did not have anything so dramatic as a drinking problem— "simply no taste for it"—he was not telling the truth, but it was an untruth with which he had long since come to terms. There had been in his past a problem, one with dire consequences, and as a result part of his life, a part that he never discussed with anyone, was spent in atonement. Twice each year he returned to the small town in Connecticut where he was born. He was the son of the town doctor, long dead, and had gone to good schools on scholarships. Across the causeway that separated Old Saybrook from Winthrop Point, an enclave for wealthy summer residents from Hartford and New Haven, was Sophie Bushnell, who had lived her life in a wheelchair since the accident that crippled her.

At seven o'clock on the morning following Hector Paradiso's death, Philip was seated in a small hall on Robertson Boulevard in West Hollywood, reading the *Los Angeles Tribunal* and drinking coffee from a cardboard container while waiting for the AA meeting to start. He tore through the paper looking for news of the violent event in which he had become involved. It surprised him that it was not mentioned on the first page, or in the first section. It surprised him more that it was not mentioned in the section known as the Metro section, which covered local news. Finally, on the obituary page, he found it in an inconspicuous position, quite easily missable, a small announcement of the death of Hector Paradiso. He folded the paper in half and then refolded it in quarters in order to read the item again to see if it bore some clue.

"Something fishy there," said a girl on a chair next to him, who was reading his newspaper over his shoulder.

"Hmmm?" said Philip.

The girl, who smelled of expensive bath oil and perfume, tapped a beautifully manicured fingernail on the story of Hector Paradiso's death.

"I said there's something fishy about that story," she repeated.

Philip turned to look at her. She was young and very pretty, with dark red hair and vividly blue eyes that met his with a look that hovered between flirtatious and humorous. Although she was fashionably dressed, her manner, her voice, and her way of sitting were at odds with her expensive clothes. She exuded sensuality rather than fashionableness and seemed to Philip a curious but dazzling presence at such an early hour in the drab surroundings of an AA meeting on Robertson Boulevard.

"I was thinking the same thing," he said.

"Want to know how I see it?" she asked.

"Sure."

"He went to Pauline Mendelson's party, right?"

"How do you know that?"

"He always goes to Pauline Mendelson's parties. He was her pet. You know how all those society ladies have their pets?"

Philip smiled. He liked her. "But how do you even know Pauline Mendelson had a party?"

"I read it in Cyril Rathbone's column in *Mulholland*," she answered, shrugging. "I always read the society columns."

"Go on."

"In my scenario, on the way home he stops at Miss Garbo's."

"What's Miss Garbo's?"

"You new in town, or something?"

"I am. Yes."

"It's a bar, with a cabaret. It's a place where well-to-do gentlemen of a certain persuasion go on their way home from fashionable places, like a Pauline Mendelson party, if you get my drift."

Philip, nodding, got her drift. "How do you know so much?" he asked.

"My last job. I used to know guys like that."

"Like Hector Paradiso?"

"Yeah. I even knew Hector."

"What was your last job?"

"We're talking about Hector, not me," she said.

"Of course. What's your name?"

"Flo."

"Flo what?"

"Flo M.," she replied, emphasizing the M.

"Oh, yes, sorry. I'm a little lax in the anonymity department some-times," said Philip.

"You shouldn't be. I abide by the rules. No last names in AA."

"You're right. I'm sorry. I'm Philip Quennell."

"K," she corrected him. "You're Philip K."

"No, not K. Q," he said. "I'm Philip Q."

"Well, I was never much of a speller," said Flo, smiling. "Do you mind if I smoke?" she asked.

"No."

"Some of these people freak out. They've got so many no-smoking meetings now. This is the main reason I come to this one, at this ungodly hour of the morning—because I can smoke."

She opened a bag that hung from her shoulder on a gold chain and took out a gold cigarette case. Philip noticed that her name, Flo, was spelled out in sapphires on the top. "I'd give up smoking, but I love this cigarette case too much to put it in a drawer and never use it again." She lit her cigarette with a matching gold lighter.

"That's not a good enough reason," said Philip.

"For me it is," replied Flo. "I get a charge every time I open this pretty case. When I was still doing drugs, I used to carry joints in it."

Philip laughed. He was about to ask her another question, about Hector Paradiso, when the meeting started. Flo moved to a chair in the row behind him. Neither raised a hand to participate in the meet-ing, but each paid careful attention to the speaker and to the people who raised their hands to share.

At the end of the meeting, during the prayer, Philip looked around at Flo. She was saying the Lord's Prayer with her eyes closed, holding the hands of the person on each side of her, with a cigarette dangling from her lips.

"Will I see you at the Rodeo Drive meeting on Friday night?" he asked, as they were leaving the meeting.

"Oh, no, I never go to the Rodeo Drive meeting. Or the Cedars-

Sinai meeting on Sunday mornings either. Too social for me. This is the meeting I like. You never see anyone you know."

Philip, puzzled, nodded. "You wouldn't want to have dinner one night, would you?"

Flo looked at him and smiled. "No, I'm spoken for," she said.

He nodded, understanding. "I wasn't coming on, if that's what you were thinking," he said.

"Oh, yeah?" said Flo, smiling, with a hand-on-hip gesture.

Philip laughed. "Is that what you thought?"

"The idea had crossed my mind," she answered. "You're not exactly hard to look at, you know."

"Neither are you," he said. "But that wasn't what I had in mind, really. I thought it would be nice to have a cup of coffee and talk."

"Oh, I see. We've moved down the scale from dinner to a cup of coffee, have we? To discuss sobriety, is that it? Hey, good line, Phil Q. I bet it works. Most of the time." She smiled at him and waved good-bye with a left-handed circular gesture and a toss of her red hair. He watched her as she walked away from him up Robertson Boulevard. There was a sway to her walk that he could not help but admire. Whether she meant it to be provocative or not, it was. Philip could imagine that she had been whistled at in her day. She turned into a parking place in front of an outdoor furniture shop that was not as yet open for business. She got into a red convertible Mercedes-Benz. He wondered where her money came from.

THAT DAY Philip Quennell was to have his first meeting with Casper Stieglitz, for whom he was to write a documentary on the proliferation of drugs in the film industry. Casper Stieglitz had an office at Colossus Pictures in the San Fernando Valley. Once a studio unto itself in Hollywood, Colossus now occupied part of the lot that used to be called the Warner Bros. Studios. Philip, unused to the freeways, and armed with a map provided by the Chateau Marmont, left an hour before his appointment for fear that he might get lost on the drive from West Hollywood to the San Fernando Valley. Much to his surprise, he found the studio with no difficulty at all, and was thirty-five minutes early for his appointment. Not wanting to inconvenience Casper Stieglitz, he decided to find a diner or coffee shop and have another cup of coffee rather than arrive too early. He pulled into the parking lot of a House of Pancakes. On the sidewalk in front of the restaurant, there were bins for the Hollywood trade papers, the *Reporter* and *Daily Variety*, as well as several city newspapers that Philip, being new to the city, had never heard of. Thus far, he had only seen or heard of the *Times* and the *Tribunal*. He put a quarter in one of the bins and took out a paper called the *Valley Sentinel*.

Sitting at the counter drinking a cup of coffee, he found an article on the third page of the first section that read, "Death of Millionaire Socialite." The facts in the piece were minimal. Hector Paradiso, descendant of a Spanish Land Grant family, had been found dead "under mysterious circumstances" in his Humming Bird Way house. Several shots had been fired. Cyril Rathbone, the social columnist for *Mulholland*, who described himself as Hector's closest friend, was quoted as saying about him, "He was like a Spanish don." Rose Cliveden, who was called a Los Angeles socialite, said by telephone from her home in Holmby Hills, "He was my lifelong friend. The world has lost a courtly gentleman." A Mexican houseboy, Raymundo Perez, who had been questioned by the police and released, was quoted as saying, "Mr. Paradiso was helping me get my green card. He was a very generous man."

"More coffee?" asked the waitress behind the counter.

Philip looked at his watch. It was getting close to the time of his appointment with Casper Stieglitz. "No, thank you," he said. He ripped the page out of the paper and put it in his pocket, grabbed the check, left a tip, and dropped the money on the counter of the cashier's desk.

Driving up to the gates of Colossus Pictures, he felt awed by the prospect of entering a Hollywood studio for the first time. At the guard's booth, he said, "I have an appointment with Casper Stieglitz. My name is Philip Quennell."

The guard was wearing dark glasses and did not reply. He picked up the telephone, consulted a list, and dialed an extension.

"I have a Mr. Quennell here to see Mr. Stieglitz," he said.

"Could I pull into that space over there?" asked Philip, pointing to an empty parking space.

"You do, and you'll be talking in a soprano voice," said the guard. "That's Marty Lesky's space."

"Oh, sorry," said Philip. Even Philip knew that Marty Lesky was the head of Colossus Pictures.

Philip could hear a person rattling on at the other end of the guard's telephone call to Casper Stieglitz's office. Bettye the chatterbox, probably, he thought. The guard hung up the telephone. "Bettye says to tell you Mr. Stieglitz had an unexpected appointment off the lot this morning and would like you to meet him instead at his house late this afternoon, for drinks."

"But I don't know where Mr. Stieglitz lives," said Philip.

"Bettye says call her when you get back to your hotel," said the guard.

## Flo's Tape #5

"I was going to live in Brussels when Jules went over there to head the American delegation during the year of the statehood of Europe. I'm sure you know all about that. There's going to be only one currency, like we have here in this country, no more French francs and Italian lire and German marks, and all that stuff. I can't remember what they're going to call the new money, but it's all going to be the same from one European country to the next.

"Jules had this apartment already picked out for me on the Avenue Hamoir, I think it was called. It was supposed to be a good address in a good neighborhood in Brussels. Of course, Jules and Mrs. Mendelson had taken a very swell house on the Avenue Prince d'Orange. I hope you notice my French accent on the Prince d'Orange. He sent me to French lessons at Berlitz.

"I mean, the guy really did a lot for me. I'll say that for him."

# 6

ROSE CLIVEDEN said it for everyone when she said, "Everyone adored Hector," to a reporter from the *Valley Sentinel* who quizzed her as she was going into Hector Paradiso's funeral. Rose, however, was never able to settle for anything so simple as a three-word answer to anything and added, quite unnecessarily under the circumstances, "He didn't have an enemy in the world."

"Except one," said the reporter.

Rose glared at him through her dark glasses, with what she meant to be a withering look.

The reporter, knowing he had gotten to her, pressed further. "It only takes one."

"Excuse me," said Rose grandly, and proceeded past the reporter up the steps of the Good Shepherd Church in Beverly Hills, trying to catch up with Pauline and Jules Mendelson, who had walked past the reporter without replying. Still using a cane, because of her broken toe, she stopped inside the vestibule to gaze about.

"Did you ever see such a crowd?" Rose said to Madge White at the holy water font, dipping in her white glove and making the sign of the cross in a single sweeping gesture. "There's Loretta Young. Doesn't she look marvelous? And Ricardo and Georgiana Montalban. Look, Cesar Romero. All the Catholic stars are here. They all loved Hector. Jane Wyman couldn't come. She's shooting her series, and you know Janie. Work, work, work. But she sent beautiful flowers. Yellow lilies, from Petra. Oh, there's Faye Converse." She waved hello to Faye Converse and one or two others, all the time maintaining a properly solemn face. "Poor Hector," she repeated over and over.

The church was filled beyond capacity. Those unable to obtain seats, or standing room, or space in the choir loft, remained outside on the church steps or on the lawn. Monsignor McMahon later said, at Rose Cliveden's lunch at the Los Angeles Country Club, that only at midnight Mass on Christmas Eve had the crowds been comparable. It was not that Hector Paradiso had been that great a man in life, or even that beloved. It was the bizarre circumstance of his death that created all the momentary excitement, far more than the death of a more important person would have caused, and people came who had only a passing acquaintance with Hector, or even none at all, and only wanted to stare at the grand or celebrated friends of the dead man.

All the ushers were old friends, but Rose decided to wait for Freddie Galavant, who looked so distinguished, she thought, in a gray suit that matched his hair, to take her up the aisle to her place. Freddie had been given an ambassadorship to a Latin American country during the previous administration, a reward for campaign funds raised, and his presence as an usher, together with Winthrop Soames, Sandy Pond, Sims Lord, and Ralph White, indicated the importance of Hector Paradiso in the community, although none of the men had been known to be particularly close to him. "Their wives were," Rose had said, when the plans were being drawn up. Jules Mendelson, stating that he was not a Catholic, had refused to give the eulogy. Jules said that Freddie Galavant, who still liked to be called Ambassador Galavant, would be far better in that capacity than he, although Freddie was not a Catholic either.

The person most put out by the choice of Ambassador Galavant as eulogist was Cyril Rathbone, the society columnist for *Mulholland*. Cyril Rathbone thought of himself as Hector Paradiso's closest friend and the natural choice to speak at the service. Cyril was known to be entranced with the sound of his own mellifluous English voice, and he imagined himself, from the moment he first heard of Hector's death, speaking beautiful thoughts from the altar of the Church of the Good Shepherd in the presence of the group he most admired in the city, particularly Pauline Mendelson, who had thus far resisted his charms. But his offer was declined by the funeral planners, Jules Mendelson in particular, when Sims Lord, Jules's lawyer, came up with the information that a morals charge was pending against Cyril. "A beating of some sadomasochistic variety," said Sims.

"That's all we need," said Jules, when he heard this news. "Freddie, you do it."

"But I hardly knew Hector," said Freddie Galavant.

"We'll fill you in," said Jules, ending the discussion and solving the problem. He was used to not having his decisions questioned, even by ambassadors.

Rose was seated, finally, in the row behind Camilla Ebury, next to Pauline and Jules. Although Philip Quennell had ridden to the church in a limousine with Camilla, he chose not to sit in the front row with her, feeling that he was too new a friend to take such a prominent position. Camilla understood, and Pauline, who observed the moment of Philip's removing himself to a seat farther back, admired the good taste of the young man. She leaned forward in her pew and whispered into Camilla's ear, "Be sure to bring Philip back to the house afterwards." Camilla smiled and patted Pauline's hand.

Rose whispered to Pauline, "Aren't the flowers lovely?" Pauline, praying, nodded her approval without involving herself in conversation, knowing that Rose enjoyed whispered conversations. Rose could not stand funeral wreaths and had instructed Petra von Kant, the florist her group all used—"She knows us all, she knows what we like" —to decorate the church with birch trees and great baskets of yellow and pink tulips and hyacinths, knowing that all the real friends of Hector would order their flowers through Petra. The others, the wreaths of gladiolus and carnations, with starched ribbons and gold lettering, the sort of flowers and arrangements that Rose and her friends abhorred, had been placed on the side altars, so as not to cause disharmony in the color scheme that Rose had worked out with Petra. Only the enormous spray of white phalaenopsis, which had come from Pauline Mendelson's greenhouse at Clouds, broke with Petra's scheme; but, as everyone knew, Pauline knew more about orchids than anyone in the city, and Pauline had been the friend that Hector liked best. Her spray had been placed on top of Hector's mahogany coffin.

As far as Rose Cliveden was concerned, the single disappointing note of the otherwise perfect funeral was the absence of Archbishop Cooning, who had declined her persistent requests to officiate at the Requiem Mass, even though she had contributed handsomely to the redecoration of the archbishop's residence in Hancock Park. The archbishop, renowned for the fiery sermons on the decline of morality in the nation he delivered each Sunday from the pulpit of Saint Vibiana's, was not unaware of the secret life of Hector Paradiso, having heard his confession on more than one occasion, and he suspected that the circumstances of his death were other than were being reported. Mercifully, a conference at the Vatican called him from the city, and he was able to adhere to his standards without seriously offending Rose Cliveden.

□   □   □

PAULINE was the person most devastated by Hector's death. She had fostered the story—without ever stating it—that Hector, had he been able to love women, would have loved her. When Hector kissed her, as he sometimes did, in moments of affection, after parties, his kiss and even his embrace were not the kiss and embrace of a lover. Pauline understood that even with encouragement from her, which, of course, was not forthcoming, the kiss and embrace would lead to nothing more. It was an arrangement they both enjoyed. And Hector had loved Pauline, in his way, so sincerely that even Jules, who had grown more sophisticated during the years of his marriage, had no objection to the "love match," and even found himself amused at times by Hector, who was funny and knew all the gossip about everyone, after an initial period of disliking him. "I have trouble with people who don't do anything," Jules said. On several occasions Hector had been their sailing companion when they chartered yachts and cruised the Dalmatian coast, or the Turkish coast, or the Greek isles. Pauline could not bear to think that Hector had died in sordid circumstances, and so had reluctantly accepted the suicide theory that Jules proposed when finally they were alone, after Camilla and Rose had departed.

"It's better this way," Jules had said.

"Why?" asked Pauline.

"It is a shabby and distasteful death," said Jules.

"How so? Tell me."

Jules blushed. "His sexual inclinations were, perhaps, pederastic," he said.

"How arch, Jules," said Pauline.

"You knew, then?"

"Of course I knew."

"And didn't care?"

"Oh, Jules, really. He was my friend."

"This sort of death, if the circumstances get out, will reflect badly on Hector, on his family, and on everyone concerned."

"His only family is Camilla, and she is only a niece, and his death is certainly not going to reflect badly on her."

"Well, his family that founded the city. It will reflect badly on the name Paradiso."

"And the 'everyone concerned' you speak about? Does that mean us, Jules?"

"The fact that he was here in our house until a few hours before it happened, and the fact that you are known to be his great friend will certainly involve us, yes. It is the sort of publicity that will be bad at this moment, with the appointment to the economic conference in Brussels coming up for nomination. There is bound to be fallout, and it is best that this be the solution."

"That he committed suicide?"

"Yes."

"But who would believe such a story, Jules? People are not such fools."

"That is a theory that I do not agree with at all."

"But *I* don't believe that story, Jules," said Pauline quietly.

"Believe it," he said.

"Are you ordering me to believe something I don't believe?"

"Yes." There was a harshness in his voice that she had never heard when he spoke to her. "Hector was ill, we will say, and Dr. James will confirm it. He was to have an operation, we will say. A bypass. I thought about saying he had AIDS, but this heart thing is better. More respectable. He was terrified of the operation, we will say, and terrified that he would be an invalid afterwards, and a burden to his friends. He had perhaps a few too many drinks, and he did this tragic thing."

"Jules, please. Dr. James was Hector's friend. He wasn't actually his doctor. Mickie Cox was his doctor."

"Only you know that, Pauline, and you've just forgotten it," said Jules. He leaned over and kissed her cheek.

"But, surely, Dr. James will deny such a story, about an operation and a heart problem."

"No, he won't," said Jules, quite emphatically, and Pauline understood that he meant that Dr. James would do as he said.

The suicide story began to be spread at the church, both before and after the Mass. "No, no, no," said Sims Lord, when he was asked if Hector's death had been a murder. "No, no, no," said Freddie Galavant to the same question. Both Sandy Pond and Ralph White replied in a similar manner, as did several other public figures of the city. Then the word *suicide* was mouthed. It was a disappointment to many that they were being deprived of the excitement of a murder, which some continued to believe was the case, although they would shortly cease to express that belief.

□   □   □

PHILIP QUENNELL, sitting toward the back of the church, was surprised to see the girl who had introduced herself as Flo M. at the AA meeting walk up the aisle and take a seat two rows in front of him. Her expensive bag was suspended from her shoulder on a gold chain, and she lifted it as she genuflected in the Catholic manner. Once seated, she knelt, made the sign of the cross, and bowed her head in prayer. Unlike most of the people present, she did not look around to see who was there, but a man with long hair swept upward to cover his bald spot, sitting directly in front of Philip, nudged his two companions and indicated the young woman. They smiled at one another in recognition. The men, unknown to Philip and to most of the mourners present, were Manning Einsdorf, the owner of Miss Garbo's, Joel Zircon, the agent, and Willard, Casper Stieglitz's butler, all of whom had talked with Hector shortly before his death.

During the Mass Pauline turned to Jules, who seemed deep in thought.

"What are you thinking about?" she whispered.

"I have a meeting with Myles Crocker from the State Department tomorrow," he whispered back. "About Brussels."

"You're thinking of that now?"

"Yes."

"Do you never pray?"

"No."

During the eulogy, the former ambassador spoke about Hector as a great friend to many people. "He cherished his friends," said Freddie Galavant, looking at Pauline and Camilla and Rose as he spoke. "He was a man of such great taste and sensitivity that he chose to spare those friends from certain aspects of his life, which can only account for this great tragedy. Good night, sweet prince. May flights of angels sing thee to thy rest."

Several sobs could be heard in the church, as well as a single chortle from Cyril Rathbone, who whispered to those around him that he would have done better. Ahead of him, Philip noticed that Flo M. was crying. He saw her open her bag to get a handkerchief and realized from her searching in the bag that she had forgotten to bring one. When she wiped her tears away with her fingers, Philip took his own handkerchief from his pocket. He leaned forward through Manning Einsdorf and Joel Zircon, tapped Flo's arm, and handed it to her. Flo nodded her head in thanks, but she did not turn to look at the person who gave her the handkerchief. She knew it was Phil Q. She had seen him out of the corner of her eye when she passed his pew looking for a seat.

During communion, the Catholics went to the altar, edging their way past the coffin to the rail where the monsignor, officiating at the Requiem Mass in the place of Archbishop Cooning, waited with lifted chalice. Among the communicants was Flo March.

Outside, after the Mass, on the steps of the church, Rose Cliveden raised her dark glasses and surveyed the crowd while the casket was being placed into the hearse by the pallbearers. "I was in floods the whole Mass," she said to Pauline, who was standing next to her. Her powdered cheeks were smeared with the tears she had shed during the eulogy, and she made no attempt to wipe them away. "Such a lot of strange people at this funeral," she continued, but Pauline was not in a chatting mood as she watched the proceedings. The unwelcome wreaths that Rose had so hated were being placed in a follow-up hearse, to be placed eventually on the gravesite at Holy Cross Cemetery, where the Paradiso family had a mausoleum.

Rose was undeterred by Pauline's lack of response. "I thought I knew all of Hector's friends. Who do you suppose these people are? Look at that amazing man with his gray hair swept up over his bald spot." She was staring at Manning Einsdorf, who was standing with Joel Zircon and his friend Willard, watching the people emerge from the church. "Did you ever see so much hair spray? He looks like Ann Miller. I can tell you for a fact that our Hector would never know anyone like him, or his friends there. I think these people are just sightseers looking for celebrities, don't you? Faye Converse, that's who they're looking for."

Out of the corner of her eye, she saw Jules talking with an unfamiliar young woman in the crowd.

The young woman spoke nervously when Jules Mendelson approached her. "Do you know what they call this church? Our Lady of the Cadillacs. The only poor people in this parish are the rich people's maids."

"What in the world are you doing here?" Jules asked. "I almost fell out of the pew when I saw you at the communion railing." He talked to her without looking at her, as if he were looking for someone else.

"I knew Mr. Paradiso," the young woman answered, defensively. "What do you think, I go to funerals of people I don't know?"

"Hector? You knew Hector?"

"Yes."

"Wherever from?"

"When I was a waitress at the Viceroy Coffee Shop, I used to serve him his coffee and croissant every morning," Flo said. "He was a cheap tipper, all the girls said so, but he told me good stories. I could tell you a couple of Hector Paradiso stories that would make your hair curl, about the kind of people he used to see after he left all the society parties. I don't buy this suicide story at all. I'll tell you what I think happened."

"I don't want to hear," Jules said brusquely, as if he were afraid she might start to tell him then and there. He signaled his chauffeur with a wave and indicated for him to bring the car around to the side street rather than wait behind the other limousines on Santa Monica Boulevard.

"Well, excuse me," she said, grandly.

"I have to go. There's my car."

"You're ashamed to be seen talking to me, aren't you, Jules?"

"No," he said quickly.

"Yes, I can see it. I can feel it."

"I'll be up later," said Jules quickly, and then he moved on.

Looking away, her eyes met the eyes of Philip Quennell, who was watching her. She nodded to him faintly and mouthed the words "Thanks for the handkerchief." He nodded back and smiled, but she did not go toward him, nor did he move toward her to speak.

"Look, Pauline, Jules is waving at you to go to the Bedford Drive side of the church," said Rose. "Are you going to the cemetery?"

"No, we're not," said Pauline.

"But you're coming to my lunch at the Club, aren't you?"

"Actually, we're not, Rose. You do understand, don't you?"

"Yes, of course, darling, but you're very foolish to feel like that about the Los Angeles Country Club."

"Call me later."

"Isn't it wonderful, Pauline, the way the Catholic church has relaxed its ban on burying suicides?"

## Flo's Tape #6

"I never knew how terrible it was to be poor until I had money. All that I ever wanted to do about my childhood was forget it, never to even think about it. It was terrible. My mother burned to death in a fire in a welfare hotel. I never knew who my father was. She used to say he walked out on us when I was one year old, but the older I got I came to believe that she didn't actually know which one he was. It was like that."

# 7

WHEN, TWENTY-TWO YEARS EARLIER, it was suggested a week
before their marriage, during a meeting at the law firm that represented Jules Mendelson's interests, that Pauline McAdoo sign a prenuptial agreement that would limit the amount of her settlement in
the case of a divorce, Pauline read through the agreement without
comment. When Marcus Stromm, Jules Mendelson's lawyer of many
years, handed her a pen from a penholder on his desk to sign the
prenuptial agreement, Pauline tossed the folder back at him with such
force that the pen fell out of Marcus's hand and spattered black ink
over the monogram on his custom-made white shirt. Then Pauline
rose without looking at Jules, who had been seated at her side silently
observing the scene, and left the office. No amount of protestations
on Jules's part at the bank of elevators could dissuade Pauline from
entering the first car that arrived, without answering him or looking
in his direction as the doors closed behind her. For Pauline, from a
distinguished New York and Northeast Harbor family, the affront of
being asked to sign such an agreement, as if she were a groupie
marrying a rock star, only confirmed the deep reservations that her
sisters had expressed from the beginning when she had told them she
was considering marrying Jules Mendelson as soon as her divorce
from Johnny Petworth was final. Her marriage to Johnny Petworth,
which read well in the social columns, had been a disappointment
almost from the beginning, and she could not envision a life with a
man who had no more ambition than to be the very best in squash,
backgammon, and bridge at the smartest clubs in the smartest resorts.

"No, no, Pauline," her sisters had said to her, both separately and
together, "I don't care how much money Mr. Mendelson has. He
won't do. He won't do at all."

Her father, whom she revered, and who doted on her in return,
said only this as a point of dissuasion to his daughter's proposed marriage: "Jules is very nice, Pauline, and certainly very rich, but he's not
eligible for any of the clubs." She knew what that meant. It was a
phrase she had heard all her life to distinguish people like themselves,
the McAdoos, from the others. For their kind of life, clubs were very
important. An early McAdoo had founded a dynasty that produced

fortunes in shipping, trade, iron, railroads, land, and textiles, but those fortunes had evaporated over the century, and the present McAdoo fortune was minimal by the current financial standards, although there was no lessening of McAdoo social standards.

"That would not bother me, Poppy," said Pauline.

"It will, in time," her father had answered.

Such familial disapproval had only increased her determination to go ahead with the marriage to Jules. What she felt most was that he would be an ideal stepfather to Kippie, who was then only three years old, and, as described by everyone, adorable, but badly in need of male supervision.

That night, following the incident with Marcus Stromm, Pauline left Los Angeles for New York. In her life there was still another man, whom she loved more than she loved Jules Mendelson, although his prospects were less, and it was to his side that she flew. Jules, fascinated by her independence and intimidated by her pedigree, followed, and placed on her finger a diamond ring larger by far than the diamond he would have placed on her finger a week earlier.

"My word," said Pauline, astonished by its size, wondering if it was perhaps too big, like the one owned by the actress Faye Converse. She knew that her sisters would scoff at it, but she also knew that they would say, finally, "Oh, Pauline, you're so tall you can get away with it."

"It's the de Lamballe," Jules said, as proud as he was the day before, when he had purchased van Gogh's *White Roses*, which was to be his wedding present to her.

"My word," said Pauline again, for she had heard of the de Lamballe diamond. He sketched its provenance: a French princess, a daughter of a German munitions maker, an American heiress, twenty years of oblivion before it resurfaced at an auction in Geneva. "It's too lovely," she said.

The following week Pauline and Jules were married in Paris, with only Sims Lord, who had replaced Marcus Stromm as Jules's lawyer, present. Although Jules could never stand to be away from the business of finance for more than a few days at a time, they went for their honeymoon to the Mamounia Hotel in Marrakech. One evening, sitting on the balcony of their suite at sunset, he said to her, "There's something I must tell you."

"What is that?"

"I got into a jam once when I was young. Please don't ask me about it. It happened. I can't undo it."

"Then why did you bring it up if you won't tell me?" asked Pauline.

"Please bear with me, Pauline."

"Do you have a police record?"

"No. One of the advantages of having rich parents," said Jules.

He looked so pained at that moment that Pauline did not pursue the subject. She felt that he would tell her in time.

"Oh, yes, I know all about that," she said, to cheer him up. "I had an uncle Harry. Harry Curtis. My mother's sister's husband. He was found dead in a seedy hotel on the West Side, and not a single one of the New York papers reported that he was in women's clothing. Poppy handled the whole thing."

"Harry Curtis? In women's clothes? I've heard a lot of things about Harry Curtis, but I never heard that," said Jules.

"Poor Aunt Maud. She's never been the same."

"Well, I wasn't in women's clothes," said Jules. "You can be sure of that."

Pauline laughed. The subject, whatever the subject was, was never mentioned again.

Jules would have lived anywhere Pauline wished. It was her idea to settle in Los Angeles and buy the old von Stern mansion on the top of a mountain and rebuild it into the famous estate that would become known as Clouds. The asking price was five million dollars, a sum considered outrageous and exorbitant at the time, but Jules Mendelson never quibbled over money when he wanted something, and he knew that his new wife wanted that particular property. He and Pauline arrived at the house for a final look, and then he handed a check for the full amount to the dumbfounded Helmut von Stern.

"I have been thinking, Mr. Mendelson," said von Stern, staring greedily at the check in his hand.

"Thinking what, Mr. von Stern?" asked Jules.

"Second thoughts."

"On selling your house, you mean?"

"On the price, actually. More like five point five million, I was thinking."

"I see," said Jules. He reached out, removed the check from von Stern's hand, and tore it in half. "Are you ready, darling?" he said to Pauline. "Good-bye, Mr. von Stern."

Jules took Pauline's arm, and they headed for the front door and the dilapidated courtyard.

Von Stern, aghast, saw the mistake he had made. The house had been on the market for three years and was in a deplorable state of repair. As the Mendelsons got into their car, von Stern called after them. "Come back, we must talk." There was an element of panic in his voice as he envisioned five million dollars driving out of his courtyard.

Jules, with Pauline behind him, followed von Stern back into the front hall of the house. "I have had second thoughts myself," he said.

"About what?"

"The price. My top price is now four point five. Take it or leave it," said Jules.

Pauline, fascinated, watched her new husband in a business transaction. That afternoon the Mendelsons purchased von Stern's estate and renamed it Clouds.

The clubs, which mattered so much to people like them in Southampton and Palm Beach and Northeast Harbor and Newport, did not matter so much in Los Angeles, and the problem of Jules's ineligibility to join them was less pressing. Both Rose Cliveden and Sims Lord had made an effort on Jules's behalf, but Freddie Galavant, who later became a friend, said to the admissions committee, "Look at it this way. If he weren't so rich, would you still want him to be a member?" No one answered, and the matter was never brought up again.

In the years since their marriage, Jules and Pauline had become a renowned couple in the world of wealth and power, and all earlier misgivings on the part of Pauline's family had long been forgotten. Pauline's sisters even took pride in their fascinating brother-in-law and entertained the Mendelsons in grand style several times each year. Jules had been a prominent background figure at all of the economic conferences under two Presidents, and, on at least two occasions, in Paris and in Toronto, had been photographed in the Presidential motorcade, in deep conversation with the Chief of State himself.

"Ask Jules," people would say, when matters of finance were under discussion. When Jules spoke, Pauline gave him her full attention, not only at parties when people asked him questions about the economy or the elections, but also at home, alone, with no one watching. Her ability to listen so intently to the man she loved was considered one of her most attractive traits. Only she, and not a single soul else, knew that she was sometimes able to plan the seating of a dinner party in her head at the same time. Their marriage was considered perfect. And it was, in its own way.

JULES HAD NOT wished to go to Rose Cliveden's lunch at the Los Angeles Country Club after Hector's funeral. Although there would be denials if such a claim were made in print, the club, a bastion of the old wealth of the city, had never taken more than a token member from the film industry or from certain religious and racial groups. In the case of the Mendelsons, it was felt that they were "perhaps too well known," an excuse delivered by Rose to Pauline that amused both Jules and Pauline. But it was not that he was ineligible to join the club that kept Jules from wishing to enter its white colonnaded portal after the funeral. He would have been quite welcome as a luncheon guest of Rose Cliveden. He knew, however, that there would be gossiping in every corner of the rooms, all to do with the prevalent excitement over the mysterious death of Hector Paradiso, and he did not wish to be questioned about the circumstances of the death, which, he knew for a fact, was about to be officially declared a suicide. He was abetted in his decision not to go by Pauline, who was truly grieving for her friend Hector and was afraid that the lunch, meant to be solemn, would take on a party atmosphere, as did all the events in Rose Cliveden's life.

Philip Quennell, accompanying Camilla, was pleased to be asked to lunch quietly with the Mendelsons at Clouds rather than attend Rose's lunch at the club, where there would be a lot of people he did not know and endless speculation about the demise of their beloved Hector, about which he knew a great deal more than they. He was pleased to be given a tour of the art in the house by Jules himself, while they were waiting for lunch to be served. It interested Philip to watch Jules gaze on each of his pictures as if he were looking at it for the first time. For every one he had a story about its provenance, or the state of mind of the painter at the time, or the subject matter, or even the price. They stopped beneath a Bonnard of Misia Sert sitting on a sofa in a drawing room. "That's only one of several pictures Bonnard painted of the old girl," he said. "Baron Thyssen has one in Lugano, and one of the Annenberg sisters has one in Palm Beach, but mine is the best by far. Look at her expression. I paid eight hundred thousand dollars for that picture only three, maybe four years ago, bought it at Boothby's at the Elias Renthal auction when he went to the slammer, and just last week I was offered fourteen million for it. Pauline hates it when I talk money in relation to the art, but you can't help not talking about it, when the prices are continuing to skyrocket the way they are. Of course, I wouldn't dream of selling it, or any of the other pictures for that matter, except to upgrade the collection, because I want to keep the collection together."

Philip nodded.

"This conversation is, of course, off the record," Jules continued.

"Of course," answered Philip.

"You are here as a guest of my wife, and with Camilla, who is an old family friend," Jules said, as if reminding Philip of the obligations of being a guest in such a grand household.

"Of course," repeated Philip, knowing that Jules was thinking of the book that he had written about Reza Bulbenkian.

"What kind of money do you earn?" asked Jules.

"Not enough to become seriously involved with a girl like Camilla Ebury, if that's what your train of thought is," replied Philip.

Jules chuckled at having been read through. He liked Philip's answer. Since Pauline had pointed out to him that Philip had written the book that so enraged Reza Bulbenkian, Jules had, surprisingly, taken a liking to him, even though Reza was a friend, or, at least, a business friend.

They passed through the open doors of the library out onto an awninged terrace. A Rodin sculpture of a naked woman stood at the top of the stone steps leading down to the lawn. Beyond, on the lawn and beneath the trees, was Jules Mendelson's sculpture garden.

"Good God," said Philip, looking out at the sight.

Jules, pleased by Philip's reaction, chuckled again. "It's amazing how many people don't notice this, you know, just think it's statues in a garden. Over there is my latest, the Miró. One of the few he ever made. Exquisite, isn't it? I'm not sure I have it placed correctly yet. I have them moved around several times until I finally decide. The Rodin here was my first piece of sculpture. Years ago it belonged to my grandfather, and then it went out of the family, and when I saw it in an auction catalog, I bought it back and started the sculpture garden with it. Then came the Henry Moores. If you're interested, walk over behind the orange tree and look at the rear of the Maillol. It's my favorite."

Philip walked behind the round and sensuous lady, amused that Jules had asked him to view the rear of her. From nearby came the sound of dogs barking and jumping against a fence.

"That's a fierce sound," said Philip.

"The watchdogs. Nothing to worry about. They're in the kennels. They're only let out at night to patrol the grounds," said Jules.

"They sound as if they would tear you apart," said Philip.

"They would, if you were the wrong person," said Jules, very matter-of-factly.

Behind them, Pauline came out onto the terrace. She had removed the hat she wore in church. "Jules, I want to borrow Philip, and Camilla wants to talk to you about Hector's will before lunch," she said. "She's in the library."

"That means Pauline wants to show you her garden," said Jules, smiling. As he went back up the steps to the terrace, he affectionately put his arm around Pauline's waist. "Did you like Freddie's eulogy?" he asked.

"Most of it," replied Pauline. "I could have done without flights of angels singing Hector to his rest. I didn't believe that for a minute."

Both Jules and Philip laughed.

"Scratch my back, will you, darling. I have an itch," said Jules, pointing over his shoulder to a spot on his upper back.

Pauline moved over to him and rubbed the area where he had pointed. "Here?" she asked.

"No, higher. A little to the left. That's it. Harder."

"Who was that girl you were talking to at the funeral, Jules?" Pauline asked, as she continued to rub.

"What girl?" asked Jules.

Philip, who was watching them in their marital moment, almost answered, "Flo. Flo M." But he didn't. He understood when to listen.

"When you were looking for the chauffeur," Pauline continued.

"I don't know, which one? I talked to a lot of people at the funeral," answered Jules.

"Quite pretty. Red hair. Rather vivacious, I thought," said Pauline. "I wondered who she was." She said "vivacious" in a way that only a very acute ear might have taken as a synonym for "common."

"Oh, yes, her. Some friend of Hector's, she said she was," said

Jules. There was a vagueness about his answer, as if the person was not of sufficient consequence to spend time discussing.

"That was a very good-looking Chanel suit she was wearing. I almost ordered it myself," said Pauline. She was totally unaware that the girl she was talking about was her husband's mistress.

Neither Jules nor Philip responded, nor did they look at each other. Jules did not know that Philip knew Flo, but Philip, ever watchful, had the beginning of the idea that Jules might be somehow connected with the expensive red Mercedes that he had seen Flo drive.

"I don't remember her name," said Jules, shrugging, and went inside to Camilla.

"I'm rather touched by Jules's concern for Hector," said Pauline to Philip.

"How so?" asked Philip.

"In the beginning, Jules couldn't abide Hector. Jules never likes men who, as he puts it, talk about dresses, and parties, and who sat next to whom at dinner the night before, all that sort of thing, and he is absolutely intolerant of any man who doesn't work, so poor Hector had everything going against him, as far as Jules was concerned. But Hector was an awfully good friend to me when I first moved out here. Women like me need a Hector in our lives, to tell us we're still pretty, or look good that night, the sort of things our husbands are often too busy to remember to say."

Philip turned to look at Pauline. Her lovely face was momentarily sad. Seeing him look at her, she smiled and continued talking. "In time Jules, although he wouldn't admit it, grew rather fond of Hector. The fact is, Jules really adores hearing all the gossip about everybody; he just pretends he doesn't. Last summer, in Greece, Hector was really a godsend on the boat. He was so funny the whole time, kept us in stitches."

As she talked, Philip and Pauline walked across the lawn to the orangerie, which had trellised walls and espaliered trees. Through the orangerie was a cutting garden, in full bloom.

"This is very beautiful, Pauline," said Philip.

"What's a house without a garden? I always say. I brag about very few things, but I do brag about my garden and greenhouse. Look at my perennial border here. Roses, peonies, delphiniums, poppies, asters. Heavenly, isn't it?"

Philip nodded.

"Come see the greenhouse, and then we'll go back to lunch," said Pauline. "The cook says if we're not seated by one on the dot, the soufflé will fall. She is always full of dire predictions."

They walked inside. There were orchids everywhere. An older man in jeans and a sweater came up and nodded a greeting to Pauline.

"Hi, Mrs. Mendelson," he said.

"This is Jarvis. My treasure. People say about me that I am the most expert of orchid growers, but it's not true at all. It's Jarvis who does it all, and I get all the credit. This is Philip Quennell, Jarvis."

The two men shook hands.

"That's not true for a minute, Mrs. Mendelson," said Jarvis, smiling at Pauline. He turned to Philip. "Mrs. Mendelson knows more about orchids than anyone."

"Jarvis and I are perfecting a yellow phalaenopsis that we hope will startle the orchid world," said Pauline.

Philip nodded, but he was interested in people, not orchids.

"You see, Jarvis," said Pauline, laughing. "Mr. Quennell has no interest whatever in our botanical experiments."

Walking up the lawn to the house, Pauline turned to Philip and saw him smiling.

"Why are you smiling?" she asked.

"I suppose that less than one percent of the country lives the way you and Jules live, Pauline, and I'm just glad I got to look at it," said Philip.

"Do you think that's true?" she asked. "Less than one percent?"

"Certainly, I do."

"I never thought of that."

"IT'S JUST US," Pauline said when they entered the garden room for lunch, as if Philip might have been expecting a lunch party. It was a semicircular room, entirely enclosed in glass. "You come here by me. Camilla there. And Jules there."

They sat around a glass table on Regency bamboo chairs, looking out on the lawn. For a time Camilla and Pauline talked about the service: the eulogy, the music, the flowers, and the crowds of people. Dudley, the butler, passed the wine. Philip put his hand over his glass. Blondell, the maid, passed the poached salmon and cheese soufflé.

"It amazes me that the papers have not played up this case more," said Philip. No one replied, and he continued. "It has all the elements for front-page stuff." Again there was no reply. "Who do you think killed Hector, Mr. Mendelson?" asked Philip.

There was silence at the table.

"No one killed Hector," answered Jules, quietly. "Hector killed himself."

"Oh, but I don't believe that," said Philip, in a dismissive voice.

Jules was a man unused to having his statements challenged, let alone doubted. "The facts are incontrovertible," he said. There was a tightening of his neck muscles, and his voice was purposely measured. "There can be no reasonable doubt. I have checked this out with Detective McDaniels, who solved the shooting of poor Madge White's father two years ago in the garage of her house in Bel Air. You remember that, Pauline?"

Pauline, silent, nodded.

"Incontrovertible." Jules repeated the word. "It was the word Detective McDaniels himself used." He put stress on the word *detective*, as if that proved his point. "Suicide, he said. And the coroner agreed, a Japanese, I've forgotten his name. I was there. I heard."

"But certainly you don't believe that, do you, Mr. Mendelson?" asked Philip.

Jules looked at him without answering. It was a look that Philip remembered long afterward.

"I mean," continued Philip, persevering, "we've all seen enough movies to know that a single shot in the mouth or the temple would do the trick far more effectively than five shots in the torso, not to mention the fact that it is virtually impossible for a person to shoot himself five times in the torso."

There was silence again. Then Jules, red in the face now, threw his napkin on the table and slid back his bamboo chair on the marble floor with such force that the action produced a screeching sound. He stood up without speaking and headed toward the hall that separated the garden room from the house. Passing through, his massive body hit against the Degas sculpture of a fourteen-year-old ballerina, her feet in the fifth position, her hands held gracefully behind her back, with the original pink satin ribbon in her hair. It toppled from the marble pedestal on which it had stood in the Mendelsons' garden room for fourteen years.

"Jules, the Degas!" screamed Pauline, rising.

Turning, amazingly agile for such an enormous man, Jules reached and grabbed the head of the ballerina at almost the same instant that it hit the marble floor.

"Oh, marvelous, Jules," said Pauline. "Is she all right?"

He turned the piece of sculpture over in his arms as if it were a child he had pulled from a wreck or a fire and stared at it. When they were alone together, Jules and Pauline called the young dancer Clotilde. When he spoke, he spoke very quietly. "You were right, you know, Pauline, you always wanted me to have a Lucite case made for her, and I thought it spoiled her to be encased."

"Is she broken, Jules?" asked Pauline.

"Cracked," he said.

"Oh, Jules, how disappointing," she said, with a concern that was less for her devalued treasure than for her husband's concern for that treasure.

"Well, we can love her more, I suppose," he said. He spoke gently, in a father's voice.

"I'm very much afraid this is all my fault," said Philip. "I had no idea I was making you angry, sir."

Jules looked at Philip and left the room without replying, carrying the sculpture with him.

Philip looked to Camilla for confirmation of his position. She had been with him on Humming Bird Way. She had seen her uncle's body, the blood on the walls, the shots in the mirror and on the ceiling.

Camilla, silent until now, lowered her eyes. "Certainly if there were something awry, Philip, the coroner and the detective would not have both arrived at the conclusion they did," she said.

"I don't understand you people," said Philip, differentiating himself from the others. His voice had become perturbed. "A man has been murdered, and a cover-up is taking place, and you are all buying it, or participating in it."

"You must understand, Philip," said Camilla. "Jules believes it is for the best."

"But the best for whom?" persisted Philip.

"You must not misunderstand my husband, Philip," said Pauline. "There is no ulterior motive to what he has said. He is simply trying to protect the reputation of a great family. You heard him yourself say that the coroner said it was suicide."

Philip nodded his head. "There's something wrong," he said simply. He pushed back his chair. It was clear he was going to leave, but he had more to say. "Let me for a moment accept the theory that Hector's death was a suicide, which, of course, I do not believe. I was there. I saw the body. I saw the number of shots. Five. The suicide of a prominent man from a distinguished family who shot himself five times is a story in itself, and yet no such story is being written. It smacks to me of cover-up."

"I really don't understand why it should concern you so," said Pauline, quietly, as she moved a spoon back and forth over her linen place mat. She was torn in the conversation, knowing Philip was right, but unwilling to counter the position of her husband.

"I'll tell you why," replied Philip. "I do not believe that powerful people have the right to decide what the public should and should not know."

"Sometimes it's necessary," said Pauline.

"I don't think so."

"If it comes out, it could cause a great deal of grief."

"If it doesn't come out, that means I will be party to the same concealment tactics as you, and I can't do that."

Philip rose, aware that he was a guest who had overstepped a guest's boundaries, but still unwilling to make anything less than a dignified exit. "Of course, I will leave, and I am very sorry for the trouble I have caused you, Pauline, but I have to say before I leave that the reason it is so hard for me to say that it is all right for all of you to foster this bogus story is that a killer is being allowed to walk free. Remember that. I find that unconscionable. Good-bye."

He nodded to both Pauline and Camilla and walked out of the room. In the hallway by the garden room, he was momentarily confused as to whether to turn left or right to find the front hallway and door of the enormous house. The butler, Dudley, walked into the hall and anticipated his question. "This way, sir," he said, walking to the left toward the library, and then to the right toward the drawing room, and then to the left again to the hallway. There, on one of the console tables, Philip noticed that the Degas ballerina had been placed in a lying-down position facing upward. She looked forlorn, as if she were aware that she would no longer be desired by museums. Passing her, Philip did not stop to examine the crack.

The butler opened the door, and Philip nodded to him as he walked out. Dudley, who always assumed the attitudes of his employer, did not return the nod. Philip's car was standing where he had left it earlier, but he noticed that Jules's dark blue Bentley was missing. Turning on the ignition, he backed the car around, wondering why he had taken such a stand in a house of strangers. As he headed for the entrance of the courtyard that led to the driveway, he heard his name called.

It was Camilla, running toward him. "I'll go with you," she called.


PHILIP lay in Camilla's bed, naked, with his hands clasped behind his head, staring at the ceiling.

Camilla, next to him, ran her hand over his chest lightly and then leaned over and kissed his nipple. "I've had such an incredible desire to do that," she said.

"Be my guest," he said. He watched her for a few moments as she kissed his chest, and then began to rub his hands over her head. When she looked up at him, he smiled at her and brought her up to him to kiss her on her lips.

Later, after their lovemaking, they lay in each other's arms. "You would have walked out of Pauline's house today and left me there, wouldn't you?" said Camilla.

"Yes. I meant what I said, you know," answered Philip.

"Oh, I know you did. You've made yourself an enemy. You must know that."

"Jules. I know."

"A severe enemy."

"I know. Imagine having antagonized Reza Bulbenkian and Jules Mendelson in the same year."

"Something could happen to you."

"It won't."

Later, when Philip was leaving, Camilla walked with him to his car.

"Beautiful night," said Philip.

She kissed him good night. "Pauline likes you, I know, and Jules worships her," said Camilla, as if she had been thinking about the problem.

"Yes, I think he does," agreed Philip, "but I think Pauline would prefer love to worship any day."

"What in the world does that mean?"

"Think about it."

## Flo's Tape #7

"I mean, Jules was a rich and famous man, and I was very flattered that he was devoting so much of his time to me. It was much more than a rich guy getting into my pants, believe me. I wouldn't have stayed with him so long if that's all it was. He taught me. He wanted me to better myself. Once he said to me, 'Don't say stoodent, say student.' At first, I thought he was putting me down, but then I found out he wanted me to do things right.

"Have you ever seen an older guy and a young girl in a restaurant together? And they're making forced conversation because they have absolutely nothing to say to each other once they aren't in the feathers? Well, Jules never wanted that to happen with us. That's why he was always teaching me things. And let me tell you something, I wanted to learn."

# 8

PHILIP QUENNELL was still unused to the streets of Beverly Hills, and he had difficulty finding the small cul-de-sac called Palm Circle where Casper Stieglitz, the film producer, lived. "Sunset to Hillcrest, right on Hillcrest to Mountain, left off Mountain to Palm Circle, the last drive on the left by the cul-de-sac," said Bettye, Casper's secretary, over the telephone to Philip, who wrote down the instructions on a Chateau Marmont scratch pad. Then Bettye added, as if it would simplify things for Philip, "It's the old Totie Fields house."

When he buzzed the intercom at the gate, a red light went on on the closed-circuit television. "Philip Quennell to see Mr. Stieglitz," he said, looking up into the camera.

"Proceed along the driveway past the tennis court to the front of the house and enter by the front door," said a voice, English in inflection, but not English.

The wooden gates, less grand by far than the gates at the Mendelsons' estate, opened slowly and laboriously, as if they needed a caretaker's attention. As Philip drove by the tennis court, he heard screams of laughter and saw two extremely pretty girls, one blond, one brunet, in extremely short shorts and angora sweaters, playing what appeared to be an extremely amateurish game of tennis.

"That shot was *not* in, Ina Rae, and you know it wasn't, you big cheater," said the blond girl.

"Fuck you, Darlene," said Ina Rae.

Ina Rae's language was greeted with more screams of laughter.

At the front of the house was a courtyard, with cobblestones, smaller by far than the Mendelsons' courtyard. He pulled his car around a center island with a birdbath and a great many geranium plants to the front of the house. Looking up, he could see that the house had once been Spanish, but the arches had been squared off, and a mansard roof replaced what had once been a red tile roof, giving the Spanish house a French look. The front door opened, and a butler, rather informally clad in dark trousers and a white shirt with the sleeves rolled up, stood in the doorway. He wiped his hands on a long green apron.

"Excuse my appearance, Mr. Quennell," he said, in an extremely friendly manner, "but I've been doing the silver. Messy job."

Philip nodded.

"If you'll follow me," said the butler. "My name is Willard, sir. Mr. Stieglitz is in the pool pavilion."

They crossed through a hall to the living room, which looked to Philip as if it had been decorated by a studio set dresser. Large paintings with white backgrounds and various colored dots lined the walls. Philip glanced at them.

"Mr. Stieglitz is quite the collector," said Willard.

"Yes," replied Philip.

They went out a pair of French doors to a terrace. He followed the butler around a swimming pool at the edge of the terrace to the pool pavilion, where the butler pulled back a long sliding glass door.

"Mr. Quennell is here, Mr. Stieglitz," he called in. He then stepped back so that Philip could enter first. Inside, the large room was in total darkness, except for the light let in by the open door and a small lamp at the far end of the room. Heavy curtains were drawn tight on all the windows. For a minute, the darkness blinded Philip after the bright sunlight outside, and he stood in the room, unsure which way to look.

"Could I get you a drink?" the butler asked.

"No, thank you," said Philip. "It's very dark in here. I can't see a thing."

"This is Mr. Stieglitz's projection room as well," he said. "He's been watching a rough cut. He keeps the blackout curtains drawn."

"I see."

A toilet flushed. "Mr. Stieglitz will be out directly," said the butler, with an English affectation. "Would you like coffee?"

"No, thank you."

"Perrier, Diet Coke, anything like that?"

"No, nothing, thank you."

"Sit down."

Philip sat in a deep chair. On a massive coffee table in front of him were bowls of gumdrops, small candy bars, chocolate pretzels, and a variety of nuts. There were also dozens of scripts in cardboard covers of varying colors.

The toilet flushed again. The door opened. Into the projection room walked Casper Stieglitz. He was dressed entirely in loose black velour, both shirt and trousers. On his head was a wide-brimmed plantation-type hat with a black ribbon around it, pulled down on his forehead to just over his eyebrows. His face was very tanned, as if he spent a great deal of time under a sunlamp rather than in the sun. He wore black-rimmed, thick-lensed dark glasses, through which it was impossible to see his eyes.

"Willard, tell those twats at the tennis court to keep their voices down. They're turning my place into a fucking slum with that filthy language," said Casper Stieglitz. He sneezed. "Don't they realize they're in Beverly Hills? Not wherever it is they come from." He spoke in a catarrhal voice, as if his nose were stuffed.

"Hello, Mr. Quennell. I'm Casper Stieglitz."

Stieglitz gave Philip his left hand to shake, at the same time sneezing again and speaking the word "Bursitis," in reference to his right hand, in a hoarse voice. Philip wondered why he wore a hat in the house.

"You seem to have a terrible cold," said Philip. He noticed that his nose was dripping.

"I do, yes, I do," said Casper. He reached into the pocket of his black velour trousers and pulled out a handkerchief and blew his nose, although the blowing seemed more noisy than nostril cleansing. "I liked your book on that Wall Street guy," he said.

"Thank you," said Philip.

"You get any flak from Reza Bulbenkian?"

"A bit, yes."

"He wanted to break your legs, right?" asked Casper.

"There was such a threat, yes," answered Philip.

Casper laughed. "I like the way you wrote it, kind of tough, a good style. I thought you'd be an older guy than you are. How old are you?"

"Thirty."

"Thirty, huh? Thought you'd be older. Now, uh, the picture I got in mind is quite a different proposition. We have this problem out here in the industry, you know, with drugs."

"Yes, that's what my agent told me you wanted to do this picture about."

"This is not a picture for the theaters, though. You understand that."

"Oh?" said Philip, surprised. "That's what I assumed."

"No."

"Television then?"

85

"No, not television."

"I'm confused."

Casper Stieglitz laughed again. Philip noticed that his bright gleaming teeth—too even, too large, too perfect—resembled Chiclets. In the minutes that followed, as his eyes became used to the dim room, it occurred to him that Casper's tight unlined skin was the result of a face-lift, a feeling that was confirmed when he saw the red scars of recent surgery behind his ears. Casper leaned over and put his hand into a bowl of nuts and started eating them as he talked, tossing them in his mouth one or two at a time. "You see, I was falsely arrested on a drug charge a few months ago. There was a shipment of drugs from Colombia that, uh, inadvertently got into the hands of an employee of mine who brought the package to this house under the impression that he was delivering film of some dailies of a picture I have shooting in Central America." For a moment he seemed to lose his train of thought. "It's a long story."

Philip stared at Stieglitz. "I am at a loss to understand what my position is in all this," he said.

"That is what I am coming to," replied Casper, remembering where he was in his story. He sniffed and blew his nose again. "The judge in the case, realizing the terrible mistake that had been made, asked me to make a film on the proliferation of drugs in the film industry that could be shown to groups, like, uh, Cocaine Anonymous, and different places like that, rehabs, et cetera, where they are fighting this terrible battle against drugs."

"In return for which, no charges are to be brought against you, is that it?" asked Philip.

"It's ridiculous, the whole thing," said Casper. "I'm a total innocent bystander in this thing, and, uh, what we thought, my lawyers and I, that rather than have the terrible publicity that such a thing would entail, it would be easier to just go ahead and make the fucking film, and have a clean slate. Like a, you know, a form of community service. At a very high level, you understand. Do you know about community service?"

"Yes, I know all about community service," said Philip quietly. "I really don't know if I am interested in doing that, Mr. Stieglitz."

"Casper. Call me Casper, Phil. Listen, uh, would you like some nuts?"

"No."

"Cashews. No? You like candy?"

"No, thanks."

"Did the fagola offer you a drink?"

"Who?"

"Willard, the butler. Did he offer you a drink?"

"He did, thank you. I don't want anything."

"Beer?"

"No. We must talk about this," said Philip. "This is not what I thought it was going to be. My agent told me this was to be a feature motion picture."

"Look, you get paid the same kind of bucks as if you were writing a feature, for a first-time feature writer, that is, which you are. I mean, you never wrote a picture before, and it's more money than you got for your leveraged buyout book. What we have here is like a documentary, interviewing this law enforcer, and that drug dealer, and so on, and arrangements can be made to get you in on a drug bust, and include that in the picture. It will be a terrific start for you in the industry."

Philip nodded.

"They'll show it to the various groups, you know, that deal with the drug problem, and you'll have a showcase for yourself to show the other studios what you've done. Will you excuse me for a second. I'll be right back. I've gotta take a leak." As he rose, he sneezed again and the partially chewed cashew nuts in his mouth flew all over Philip's face. "Oh, sorry, man, here," he said, reaching into his pocket and bringing out his soiled handkerchief. Philip declined the handkerchief with a shake of his head. "I gotta take a leak," Casper said again and disappeared into the bathroom. The sound of the door locking behind him could be heard.

Philip looked at his sneezed-upon face in the mirror behind the liquor bottles of the bar. Semimasticated nut particles stuck to his eyebrows and nose. He turned on the water tap to wash his face but noticed there was no bar towel. He went to the sliding glass door through which he had entered the projection room and walked out into the bright sunlight. Retracing his steps around the swimming pool onto the terrace, he reentered the house through the same French door by which he had left it twenty minutes earlier. The butler was nowhere in sight. He opened a door, looking for a bathroom, and found it was another mirrored bar. He opened another door and found a hallway that led to what turned out to be Casper Stieglitz's bedroom, its massive bed covered with a spread of the prevailing color scheme of orange and brown. Through it were his bathroom and dressing room.

Inside the bathroom, Philip turned on the gold-plated hot water fixture and washed his face thoroughly with a bar of sandalwood soap from a gold-plated soap dish in the shape of a shell. He then dried his face on a brown face towel, elaborately monogrammed with the intertwined initials *C.S.* in white satin, from a set of brown monogrammed towels on a heated towel stand. Still feeling soiled, he repeated the process.

When he finished, Philip looked at some of the dozens and dozens of framed photographs on the bathroom walls and the walls of the dressing room beyond. In almost every picture Casper Stieglitz, in younger times, was with a different beautiful girl, at awards ceremonies, or industry dinners, or premieres of films. In all the pictures he was laughing, happy, glamorous; they bespoke a life of fame and success. There were photographs showing him having a script conference by the side of his swimming pool and toasting a blond starlet with a glass of wine while lying on an inflated rubber raft in the middle of his swimming pool.

His clothes were arranged in cabinets, dozens of silk shirts hung on hangers, next to dozens of sport coats, next to dozens of suits, next to a variety of styles of tuxedos, in midnight blue, and maroon, and black. An open cabinet showed sweaters, all cable stitch, all cashmere, in the entire spectrum of colors, folded painstakingly one on top of the other. On the counter level there were bottles of aftershave lotions, gold-backed brushes, and a fitted leather case for dozens of pairs of cuff links, as well as an immense silver tray on which dozens of pairs of sunglasses were neatly arranged.

There was a knock on the bathroom door. "You in there, Phil?" asked Casper.

"Yes, I am," replied Philip. "I'm washing my face."

"The guest bathroom is off the front hall," called in Casper. There was an unmistakable tone in his voice that Philip was trespassing. "I'm not keen on people using my bathroom."

"I had no way of knowing that," called out Philip. At that moment his eye caught sight of some strange objects on the top of the clothes cabinets. At first they appeared to be hat stands, of the variety used in millinery shops, but then he saw that they were wig stands. He counted them. There were thirty-one, and on each was a full toupee, going from freshly cut hair to long hair in need of a haircut.

"I'll be out in a minute," said Philip.

Beyond the dressing room, he could hear the girlish laughter of Ina Rae and Darlene in an adjoining bedroom.

"Where's the dildos?" asked Ina Rae.

"I thought you brought them," answered Darlene.

"No, stupid, you were supposed to bring them. Casper's gonna be furious."

"How come you need a dildo, anyway?"

"The guy's got a dick like a Tampax," said Ina Rae.

Darlene shrieked with laughter.

Philip walked out of the bathroom. Casper was standing there. On his face was an anxious expression, and Philip understood that he was concerned that he might have seen his toupees.

"Interesting house you have, Mr. Stieglitz," said Philip.

"I did a total gut job when I bought the house. Got rid of all the Spanish shit and gave it this French look. Thelma Todd built the house," he said. "She was murdered. Remember that?"

"No," said Philip.

"Way before your time. Way before my time too, as a matter of fact. I was gonna make a picture about the case once. Faye Converse was gonna play Thelma, but it never got off the ground. Couldn't get all the elements together."

There was a silence.

"About this drug picture," said Casper.

"I think I'm not the right choice for this, Mr. Stieglitz," said Philip.

"Fifty thousand down. Fifty thousand when you turn in the first draft. Another fifty when we go into production. Not bad bucks for a young guy like you. You only got fifty for the whole fucking book you wrote on that chiseler Reza Bulbenkian."

Philip laughed. "I'm at the Chateau. Let me talk to my agent, and I'll call you."

"Call me when? I gotta let the guy from the community service know, or I'll be in violation."

"This evening. Tomorrow morning at the latest."

"Some guys would get down on their knees and kiss my hand at an offer like this."

"I'm sure," said Philip. "But I'm also sure that's not the kind of guy you want for a project like this."

He walked back through the living room and hall and opened the front door. Outside the sun was blinding. He covered his eyes with his hand. He would have to buy dark glasses, he decided, although he had an antipathy toward dark glasses. When he got into his car, he heard his name called. Turning, he saw Casper Stieglitz's butler standing at the front door. Philip rolled down the window, and the butler walked up to the car.

"Yes?" asked Philip. He couldn't remember the butler's name.

"Of course, it doesn't matter a bit," said the butler.

"What doesn't?"

"About the house."

"What about it?"

"It wasn't built by Thelma Todd at all. He always gets it wrong." He shook his head in exasperation. "Thelma lived, and died, bless her soul, on the Pacific Coast Highway in Santa Monica."

Philip stared at him.

"Mr. Stieglitz isn't really interested in the history of Hollywood. This house was built by Gloria Swanson, when she was married to the Marquis de la Falaise. After they were divorced, Mr. Hearst tried to buy it for Marion Davies, but Miss Swanson didn't want Marion Davies to have it for some reason, and she sold it instead to Constance Bennett. It was Miss Bennett who put on the mansard roof. To the best of my knowledge, Thelma Todd was never even in the house."

"I thought Totie Fields owned it," said Philip.

"Oh, later. That was much later," said Willard, dismissing Totie Fields's contribution to the house.

Philip felt that this was not the reason the butler had called him back.

"As I said, it doesn't matter a bit," said the butler.

"Interesting, though. I'm sorry, but I can't remember your name."

"Willard."

"Oh, right, Willard. Do you have to clean all those wigs when you're not cleaning the silver?"

Willard gasped. "You saw Mr. Stieglitz's toupees? He'll die, absolutely die. He thinks nobody knows he wears a rug."

"I won't tell."

"I saw you at Hector Paradiso's funeral."

"You do get around, Willard."

"Terrible thing."

"Was Hector a friend of yours?"

" 'Acquaintance' would be a better word."

"Suicide, they say it was," said Philip.

"You don't believe that, do you, Mr. Quennell?"

"That's what they say, even in the autopsy report," said Philip.

Willard looked back toward the house. "I better get back. Mr. Stieglitz will wonder what's happened to me."

"I think Ina Rae and Darlene are taking pretty good care of Mr. Stieglitz by now, although they forgot the dildos," said Philip.

"Aren't they the two cheapest?" asked Willard, shaking his head in disapproval.

Philip turned on the ignition. "I'll remember that about Gloria Swanson and Constance Bennett," he said.

Suddenly, Willard started to talk very rapidly. "Did you ever hear of a bar called Miss Garbo's?" he asked.

"No," replied Philip, although it was the same bar that Flo had mentioned to him at the AA meeting.

"On Astopovo, between Santa Monica and Melrose?"

Philip shook his head.

"Not exactly on your beat, I wouldn't imagine."

"What kind of a bar?"

"The kind of bar that after midnight caters to gentlemen of a certain age, looking for, uh, companionship, for, uh, a price."

"I see. Why are you telling me this?"

"Hector Paradiso was there on his way home from Pauline Mendelson's party."

"I thought Hector Paradiso was a great ladies' man," said Philip.

"Hector Paradiso was as gay as pink ink, Mr. Quennell," said Willard.

"How do you know he was at Miss Garbo's that night?" asked Philip.

"I was there myself that night," said Willard. "I saw him. I even talked to him. Joel Zircon, the Hollywood agent who works for Mona Berg, introduced me to him."

"How can you be sure it was the same night?"

"He was in a dinner jacket. He'd been to Pauline Mendelson's party. He said Pauline was wearing black velvet and pearls and looked like Madame X, in the Sargent picture."

"Hector said that?"

"Yes."

"To you?"

"To Manning Einsdorf."

"Who's Manning Einsdorf?"

"Owns the place. He was at the funeral too. Gray hair combed in an upsweep?"

"Willard!" came a voice from the house.

Willard, jumping to attention, turned and started back toward the house. Then he turned back to Philip and spoke very quickly. "Hector left with a blond about two in the morning. I saw him."

"A blonde? Like Darlene?"

"A boy blond, called Lonny."

WITH THE EXCEPTION of some personal bequests, written by hand on blue stationery from Smythsons in London, Hector Paradiso had died intestate. "Typical," said Jules Mendelson, shaking his head in exasperation, when this information was passed on to him. Hector, everyone knew, was never one for business. In his personal bequests, which were neither notarized nor witnessed, he left his Paradiso family silver service to Camilla Ebury, his Flora Danica china to Pauline Mendelson, his dog, named Astrid, after the skating star he had once been engaged to, to Rose Cliveden, and a thousand dollars to Raymundo, his houseboy. "If that's not a fruit's will, I never saw one," said Jules to Sims Lord, the attorney who handled all of Jules's business affairs, as he tossed the blue notepaper on Sims's desk. It was Pauline who had suggested to Jules that it might be a nice gesture if Sims Lord would step in and handle the disposition of Hector's estate, such as it was, and expedite matters so that everything could be brought to a conclusion as soon as possible.

In the days that followed, Sims Lord had a telephone call from a woman named Mercedes Sandoval, who pronounced her first name Mer*the*des, in the Castilian manner. She had done part-time secretarial work for Hector for years, such as writing out his party invitations, paying his bills, and balancing his checkbook. Mercedes told Sims Lord that a check had come in written by Hector on the night of his death and cashed the next day. The check was made out to someone Mercedes had never heard of before called Lonny Edge.

"Should I send it over to the police?" asked Mercedes.

"Send it over to me," said Sims Lord. "I'll see that it gets to the police."

"Oh, thank you, Mr. Lord. I don't know what we would have done without you."

## Flo's Tape #8

"I don't know if I actually thought of it at the time, but the more I think of it now, of everything that happened, Jules started to grow old right in front of my eyes. There were an awful lot of things that were coming down on him, all at the same time. But I didn't know that. I was bugging him too, about buying me a house, but I realize now he had other things on his mind. When Jules was young, he was in a big jam in Chicago in 1953, I think it was. I don't want to besmirch his memory, although I guess it's pretty besmirched anyway, because of the way he died, but it's an important part of the story. There was a girl he took to a hotel. It was the Roosevelt Hotel, I remember that. She wasn't a hooker or anything like that, but she was a kind of low-class girl he picked up in a bar. Like me, I suppose. What you have to understand about Jules is that he was a very sexually oriented man, even though he wasn't a sexy-looking man. The girl got frightened of him. He had a dick like a mule's. Have I told you that? I think I did. Anyway, the girl ran out on the balcony of the hotel, and he grabbed her by the arm to bring her back in and, somehow, her arm got broken, and somehow she went over the balcony. Everything was hushed up. Jules's family paid through the nose. The girl's family was taken care of. There was never any record of it. But Arnie Zwillman knew. And Arnie Zwillman blackmailed him."

# 9

WHEN CAMILLA EBURY asked Pauline Mendelson a few days later if Kippie would be available as a fourth for a few sets of mixed doubles —"I told Philip that Kippie has the best backhand ever," Camilla said—Pauline informed Camilla that Kippie had returned to France, to the drug rehab in Lyons that had been so highly recommended by the headmaster at Le Rosay, the school in Switzerland that had expelled Kippie twice, even after Jules Mendelson had offered to build a new library for it in Gstaad. Pauline seemed to be her old self again, less tense when Kippie's name was mentioned, and Camilla ventured to ask a few questions about him, between backgammon games.

"I thought perhaps he'd finished there, in Lyons," she said.

"Oh, no. He has to stay another three months, at least. It's part of the program," said Pauline.

"Why was he home then?" asked Camilla.

"To see the dentist. He dislodged a front tooth somehow. An altercation, I would think, but he was very noncommittal. You know what he's like. And he simply refused to go to one of those French dentists, especially in Lyons, and I don't blame him a bit. Dr. Shea saw him for a few appointments, implanted a new tooth, you could never tell. And then he went back."

"How was he?"

"Oh, you know Kippie. Utterly enchanting. Blondell spoils him rotten. The cook loves him, made him mashed potatoes and chicken hash, and all the kinds of things he could eat with a missing tooth. The butler couldn't do enough for him. Jules and he are forever at odds with each other. That's a given. And I try to be the peacemaker in the middle." For an instant she was silent, and then she added, "But he seems to be behaving. He even seemed quite anxious to get back to France, which came as a complete surprise."

"What will he do when he gets out of the rehab?" asked Camilla.

"He's thinking of opening a restaurant, can you imagine? At least, that's this week's scheme."

They went back to their backgammon.

□    □    □

A WEEK BEFORE, on the night of the Mendelsons' party, Kippie Petworth had telephoned his mother to tell her he was back in Los Angeles. The news came as a complete surprise to her. Pauline was listening to the former President, who was seated on her right, tell a long anecdote about a verbal altercation between his wife and the wife of the Soviet leader, which Pauline had heard several times before, when her butler, Dudley, came to fetch her. With both elbows on the table, she gracefully cupped her chin with one hand and gave her distinguished guest her full attention, as if she were hearing the tale for the first time, and smiled and laughed at the appropriate moments. She held her hand up to caution the butler not to interrupt until the former President had arrived at his punch line.

"It's really too funny," she said at the end of the story, laughing heartily with the other guests. The President's story caused the convivial laughter accorded to a distinguished man, although the same story, if told by a lesser individual, would have gone unremarked upon or unlaughed at. She then turned to Dudley to hear his message, expecting him to tell her of a crisis in the kitchen, or a problem with the band that had arrived to play for dancing.

"It's Kippie," said Dudley, whispering in her ear.

"Kippie?" she asked, turning to Dudley. There was astonishment in her voice, although even the person sitting on the other side of her, Sims Lord, her husband's lawyer, was not aware from her voice that a possible family crisis was at hand.

"On the telephone," whispered Dudley. "I told him you were having a party, but he insisted on speaking to you."

"Is he calling from France?"

"I don't think so. I think he's here," answered Dudley.

"Would you excuse me, Mr. President," said Pauline, placing her damask napkin on the table and rising. "There seems to be a slight soufflé problem in the kitchen."

"Woman's work is never done," said the President, and everyone laughed appreciatively at his joke.

"I'll send Rose Cliveden over here to keep my seat warm," said Pauline. With that, she was off. "I'll go into the library, Dudley. Will you stand outside the door and make sure no one comes in?" Several guests waylaid her on her way through the atrium to the library, and she returned each greeting or salute charmingly but never stopped moving. "What a marvelous dress that is," she said to Madge White,

whose daughter her son had impregnated when they were both fourteen years old. "Thank you, Sandy. I'm glad you're having a good
time," she said to Sandy Pond, whose family owned the *Los Angeles
Tribunal*. "Faye, if there's a line for the powder room, use my bathroom upstairs. Blondell will let you in," she said to Faye Converse.

"Pauline, I must talk to you," said Hector Paradiso, grabbing her
arm.

"Naughty you, moving the place cards, Hector," she said to him,
still walking toward the library. "Why in the world did you do that?
Jules will be furious."

"I felt wasted where you seated me," said Hector.

"I won't be angry if you promise to dance with Rose. I think you
hurt her feelings."

"But Pauline, there's something I must tell you."

"Not now, Hector." She walked into the library and closed the door
behind her, shooing him off when he tried to follow her into the
room. As always, she looked up at the van Gogh painting of the *White
Roses* over the mantelpiece, and it brought her a momentary sense of
calm. She picked up the telephone. "Hello? Hello? Kippie, it's
Mother."

KIPPIE had been calling from the house of Arnie Zwillman, although
he did not tell his mother that. Even if he had, his mother might not
have known who Arnie Zwillman was, although Jules Mendelson,
Kippie's stepfather, certainly would have. Arnie Zwillman, in the eyes
of people like the Mendelsons and their friends, was undesirable,
which might have been part of his attraction for Kippie Petworth.
Arnie had once owned a hotel in Las Vegas called the Vegas Seraglio,
and the insurance money from the conflagration that razed the Vegas
Seraglio was the basis of Arnie's original fortune. If someone wanted
to incite Arnie's ire, which could be formidable, he had only to describe Arnie as the man who burned down the Vegas Seraglio for the
insurance money. A lot of people had done that, and a lot of those
same people were sorry that they had. On most other occasions,
though, Arnie could be, as many of his friends claimed, "as nice a
guy as you'd ever wanna meet."

Arnie always said, when a guest admired his house, that it was the
old Charles Boyer mansion, although anyone who had ever seen the
house when Charles Boyer lived in it would have been hard pressed

to recognize any of the architectural elements, for sliding glass doors had replaced whole walls, and floor-to-ceiling mirrors had covered the French boiserie, and a steam room and spa were now where the old library had been. Turquoise, pink, and orange, the favorite colors of Gladyce Zwillman, who had been Arnie's fourth wife, dominated what Gladyce always called her decor. Now Gladyce was gone, and Adrienne Basquette had moved in and hoped she could retain Arnie's attention and affection until the legalities of Gladyce's severance could be worked out and she could become the fifth Mrs. Arnie Zwillman.

Adrienne heard the chimes and went to the door and turned on the outside lights. The door was bullet-proof glass, fifteen feet high, with a wrought iron design in front of the glass for privacy and safety. Through it, Adrienne could see a handsome young man with blond hair, and blood coming from his mouth. He's adorable, she thought to herself. Women always thought Kippie Petworth was adorable.

"Where's Gladyce?" he asked, when she opened the door.

"Where have *you* been?" asked Adrienne, in a tone of voice that let him know that Gladyce had been out of the picture for some time.

"France," he answered.

"Ooh, la la," said Adrienne. "Your mouth looks yucky."

"Feels yucky too," said Kippie. "Arnie in?"

"Who shall I say is calling?"

"Kippie," said Kippie.

"He's expecting you?"

"Ask him and find out." He smiled a smile he knew was beguiling, without opening his mouth. One of his front teeth was missing.

Adrienne closed the front door and left him standing there for a few minutes. He looked to see if anyone was watching and then spat a mouthful of blood into a terra cotta container holding a bonsai tree by the side of the front door. When Adrienne returned, she opened the door wide and indicated that he was to come in.

"Arnie will be out in a minute," she said. "He's taking a sauna. Can I get you anything?"

"A box of Kleenex," said Kippie.

"What happened?" she asked, pointing to her own mouth as a way of inquiring what was wrong with his.

"Could you get me some Kleenex and then we can chat?" asked Kippie, impatiently.

"You act like a spoiled brat," she said.

"I am a spoiled brat," he answered.

She went into a powder room off the hall and returned with a turquoise container holding pink Kleenex. "Don't drip on Arnie's carpet, for God's sake," said Adrienne. "Arnie will freak out."

Then Arnie Zwillman came into the room. He was deeply tanned, wore a terry cloth robe, and was slicking back his full head of wet silver hair with a comb. A diamond ring glistened on his pinkie finger. Kippie had once described him as handsome, in a Las Vegas sort of way. For an instant he stared at Kippie, taking him in.

"I couldn't imagine who was coming to call at ten o'clock at night," said Adrienne, breaking the silence.

"Get lost," Arnie said in a growl that sounded like "gedloss," with a toss of his head and a wave of his thumb, indicating for her to remove herself. Adrienne retreated to another room without a word. "Come on in the sauna," he said to Kippie. "We can talk there, and for chrissake, don't drip none of the blood on my white carpets." Moving ahead of Kippie, he straightened two Lucite picture frames and removed a speck of dust from a brass-and-glass end table on the way to the steam room.

"What kind of trouble are you in?" asked Arnie, when Kippie had undressed and followed him into the sauna.

"Who said I was in trouble?"

"Don't bullshit me, junior."

"What's it to you?"

"I can help you out of it, that's what it is to me."

"How?"

"You got Judge Quartz for your preliminary hearing, right?"

"Yes. How'd you know?"

"It's my business to know these things. I knew ten minutes after they busted you. Friend of mine came in on the same flight from Paris. They were looking for what he was carrying, and instead they found what you were carrying."

"I couldn't understand why they hit on me like that," said Kippie. "It was nothing, what I was carrying, a couple of joints, and they acted like I had a shipment from Colombia. You ought to see what they did to my luggage."

"Assholes picked the wrong guy, that's all," said Zwillman.

"My family's going to kill me."

"You lose a tooth?"

"Yes."

"How?"

"The cop hit me."

"Cops don't usually hit preppy boys like you. Did you pull your rich kid act on the cop?"

"Something like that."

"Called him a mick or a spic?"

Kippie nodded. "A mick."

They looked at each other and laughed. "I can read you like a book, Kippie."

"There were these two big cops the customs agent called. One held me under my armpit here, and the other held me under my other armpit, and they lifted me up so that my feet didn't touch the floor and carried me though the Pan Am waiting room. Not one of the great looks, you know. This is after they made me take my clothes off and shoved their finger up my ass looking for drugs. I was pissed off."

Over the intercom in the steam room came the sound of a woman's voice. "Ready for your massage, Mr. Zwillman," she said.

Arnie turned to the box and pushed a button. "Okay, Wanda. I'll be in in a minute. Get the table set up." He turned back to Kippie. "Wanna massage?"

"No thanks," said Kippie, who didn't want to be in the steam room either.

"This Wanda's good," said Arnie. "She'll bring you off if you get a hard-on."

Kippie shrugged. "Okay," he said.

"I take it you haven't contacted Jules and Pauline with your little adventure?" He said the names "Jules" and "Pauline" with an exaggerated pronunciation, in an outsider's allusion to their grandeur.

Kippie shook his head.

"You better call them from here," said Arnie. "Just don't tell them what happened. Don't tell no one, except your lawyer. I'll get you a lawyer. Gonna cost you ten grand up front."

"Are you going to lend me the ten grand?" asked Kippie.

"I bailed you out, sonny boy. There's a limit to my generosity."

"Where am I going to get ten grand?"

"Your rich mommy."

"She won't. I know it. She said so the last time."

"Be adorable, Kippie, like you know how to be, and she'll come

99

through. Then when you go before Judge Quartz on Monday morning, the case will be dismissed. Count on it."

"What do you want for all this, Arnie? I can't think you're doing all this for me because you think I'm such a swell kid."

"Smart boy."

"What do you want?"

"An intro."

"Who the hell could I introduce you to?"

"Your father."

"My father? My father lives on Long Island, is now married to the former Sheila Beauchamp, and plays bridge all day every day in Southampton, or Palm Beach, or the Racquet Club in New York, or at Piping Rock, wherever he happens to be. What possible reason would you have to want to meet Johnny Petworth?"

"Don't get snotty with me, you spoiled brat. I'm talking about Jules Mendelson."

"He's not my father. He's my stepfather."

"All right, your stepfather. I want to meet your stepfather."

Kippie hesitated. He knew from past experience that he could not promise his stepfather. "My stepfather does not think highly of me," he said quietly.

"You want to get your case fixed without your family knowing about it, don't you?"

"Arnie, please, man. My stepfather will never come to your house. I know it."

"I know that, junior. What I want you to do is arrange for both your parents to have dinner and see a film at Casper Stieglitz's house. I'll be there too, but that's the part you don't tell them."

"Who's Casper Stieglitz?"

"The film producer."

"But my mother and stepfather don't mix with people like that. I'm not saying it's right. I'm just saying they don't."

"Arrange it, asshole. You don't want your name in the papers, do you, for getting busted on Pan Am flight number three from Paris? I don't think Jules and Pauline are going to care much for that, with the economic conference coming up in Brussels and all."

Kippie, abashed, only stared at Arnie Zwillman.

"What's Piping Rock?" asked Arnie.

"A club," answered Kippie.

"Where?"

"Long Island."

"What kind of club?"

"The kind that wouldn't let you in."

"As a member, you mean?"

"Not even as a guest of a member. Not even for lunch."

"How come?"

"You're not their type."

Arnie nodded. "Now, you better call your mama and tell her you're in dire need of ten thousand dollars. I'll take my massage first."

AS A FAMILY, Jules and Pauline and Kippie had met only once during the days that followed. Although Hector Paradiso lay dead in an open casket at the Pierce Brothers Mortuary, life went on as usual in the city, despite the endless speculations as to the cause of his death. The Freddie Galavants decided not to cancel their dinner dance in honor of the visiting Brazilian ambassador. Polly Maxwell saw no reason not to go ahead with the fashion show luncheon at the Bel Air Hotel for the Los Angeles Orphanage Guild, even though Pauline Mendelson, Camilla Ebury, and Rose Cliveden had telephoned in their regrets. And Ralph White, despite Madge's protestations, refused to back out of a long-planned weekend of trout fishing on the Metolious River in Oregon, but did promise to be back for the funeral at the Church of the Good Shepherd.

It was a particularly busy time for Jules as well. The economic conference was coming up in Brussels, with all its attendant preparations. A group from the National Gallery in Washington had been promised lunch at Clouds and a tour of the collection, with him as their tour guide, and they could not be put off. And there were the arrangements for Hector's funeral going on concurrently, in which Jules seemed to have an inordinate interest. It surprised Pauline that he seemed so insistent on lining up former ambassadors and other prominent figures in the city to act as pallbearers, when none of them were known to have been more than acquaintances of Hector's.

Kippie was mostly silent during those days, saving his conversation for Blondell and Dudley, to whom he was not a disappointment, or hitting a tennis ball against the backboard on the tennis court for hours at a time, or going for several appointments to Dr. Shea to have a new front tooth implanted, or to Dr. Wright to have the forefinger of his right hand attended to, where Astrid, Hector Paradiso's dog, had bitten off the tip. When Kippie was alone with his mother and stepfather, he strummed on a guitar, which drove Jules mad, but Jules said nothing. There had been a time, before he wanted to become a restaurateur, when he wanted to become a guitarist.

Casper Stieglitz's secretary, Bettye, had telephoned Jules's secretary, Miss Maple, that day and invited Mr. and Mrs. Mendelson to a Sunday night dinner and screening of a film to be held at a date sufficiently in the future to ensure an acceptance.

"Tell him no," said Jules, when Miss Maple telephoned him at home to repeat the invitation. "We don't even know Casper Stieglitz."

Kippie looked up from his guitar playing and struck a chord sufficiently grating so that Jules looked up in annoyance from the telephone conversation.

"No, Jules, don't tell him no," said Kippie.

There was an authoritative tone in Kippie's voice that made Jules react to his stepson. He covered the mouthpiece of the telephone with his hand. "What are you talking about?" he asked.

"I'm telling you, accept that invitation."

"What do you know about this invitation?"

"Tell Miss Maple to say yes, Jules," said Kippie.

Jules and Kippie stared at each other. "Hold off on it, Miss Maple," said Jules, and hung up. "Your mother will never go to Casper Stieglitz's house."

"She will if you tell her she has to."

"There's a beat missing here for me," said Jules. "Do you know this Casper Stieglitz?"

"No."

"How do you know about this?"

"I just know."

"What's your connection?"

"Someone's going to be there who wants to meet you."

"Who?"

"I can't say."

"You better damn well say."

"Arnie Zwillman."

"Arnie Zwillman?" said Jules, in a shocked voice.

"Do you know him?" asked Kippie.

"Of course I don't know him. Do you?"

"Yes."

"How did you ever know such a person?"

"You sound like my mother," said Kippie. "She says things like 'How do you know such-a-person?' "

Jules ignored the remark. "This man is a gangster," he said. "He burned down the Vegas Seraglio for the insurance money."

"He's never been busted," said Kippie.

"And he cheats at cards. He has an electric surveillance system in the ceiling of his card room, and a man hides above the ceiling and sends him mild shocks telling him what's in the other players' hands."

"You know a lot about Arnie for not knowing him."

"Tell me, Kippie. What's your connection with him?"

At that moment Pauline came into the room, dressed in black. She had come from the calling hours at the funeral home where Hector Paradiso's body was on view.

"What was it like?" asked Jules.

"A nightmare," said Pauline. "Poor Hector. He would have hated it. Such sobbing. The Latins do cry so audibly. The rosary went on until I thought I'd die. And the flowers! You've never seen such awful flowers. Pink gladiolus. Orange lilies. Everything I hate. Tomorrow, the funeral will be better. Rose Cliveden and Camilla are handling everything, and Petra von Kant's doing the flowers herself." She turned to Kippie. "How are you, darling? How's the tooth? Let me see. Oh, look. He's doing such a good job, our Dr. Shea. How's the finger? Does it hurt terribly? I'm so glad that little dog is out of our house. Get me a glass of wine, will you, darling. Your mother's a wreck."

Kippie poured his mother a glass of wine. When he brought it over to her, she was lying back on a chaise, her feet up. "Thank you, darling. Isn't this nice, just the family, at my favorite time of day. It's been so long since we've been together like this."

She looked at her husband and son and smiled. Neither returned her enthusiasm, but both nodded. For a moment there was a silence.

"Casper Stieglitz has asked us to go there for dinner," said Jules.

"Casper Stieglitz? Whatever for?" asked Pauline, with a chuckle at the absurdity of such a notion.

"And a film," added Jules.

"Oh, heavens, all those people we don't know," said Pauline. As far as Pauline was concerned, there was no more to be said on the subject.

Jules turned to Kippie and shrugged, as if to point out that he had tried, and failed.

Kippie, looking at Jules, began to strum on his guitar again. "This is my latest composition," he said. "Kind of a catchy lyric." He began to sing in a low muffled voice.

> *"Flo is the name of my stepfather's mistress,*
> *She lives on a lane called Azelia.*
> *Each afternoon, at a quarter to four—"*

Jules, rarely stunned by the events of life, looked at Kippie, stunned.

"Whatever that is, it's lovely, darling, but I can't stand guitar music at the moment. I have such a terrible headache."

"Sorry, Mom," said Kippie, putting down his guitar. "Arnie Zwillman will be there too."

"And who, pray tell, is Arnie Zwillman?" asked Pauline. Pauline had a way of saying a name like "Arnie Zwillman" that left no doubt what her feeling was about such a person, without voicing a single derogatory word against him.

"You'll like him, Mom. Arnie Zwillman's from an old mob family. Old mob money. Listed in the Mafia Register. None of your new people stuff. You'll love him."

Pauline laughed. "Do you think my son is making fun of me, Jules?" she asked.

Jules did not reply.

"How do you know such a person?" she asked Kippie.

Kippie laughed. He dearly loved his mother. He was proud of her beauty. At all the schools he ever attended, the other boys and the teachers vied with each other for him to introduce them to her, and she was never not charming to them in return. He was always thoughtful to her on her birthdays and at Christmas. But he was also bewildered by her life in society, and he could not bear Jules Mendelson. He never confided in her, although he knew that his secrets would be safe in her keeping.

"I wish my son would spend more time in the company of the sort of people he was brought up with, instead of the marginal types he's constantly with," she said. "I simply don't understand how you get to know these people, Kippie."

"Look, Pauline," said Jules suddenly, rising from his chair at the same time. "I think we'd better go to Casper Stieglitz's. Just this one time."

"I never thought I'd hear that from you, Jules. I thought you couldn't stand all those movie people," said Pauline. " 'All they ever do is talk about movies.' Isn't that what you always say about them?"

"I think we'd better go," Jules repeated softly, looking at Pauline with a married look that indicated she should go along with his wishes.

"Suit yourself, Jules," said Pauline. "You go, but I have no intention of going. I don't know that man, and I don't know why I have to go there for dinner."

Jules looked at Kippie again and made a loose gesture that indicated he would talk Pauline into going when the time came.


ARNIE ZWILLMAN had been having his daily massage from Wanda when Kippie Petworth came to call. Kippie sat reading a magazine in another room until Wanda was finished.

"Wanna massage?" asked Arnie, when he came out of his workout room, tying the belt of his terry cloth robe.

"No, thanks," said Kippie.

"She'll bring you off if you get a hard-on," said Arnie.

"No, thanks," said Kippie.

"See you tomorrow, Wanda," said Arnie. He walked over to the bar and poured himself a glass of grapefruit juice. "This stuff's good for you."

Kippie nodded.

"What'd your stepfather say?" asked Arnie Zwillman.

"He'll go," answered Kippie.

"Good boy, Kippie. What about your mother?"

"My mother's iffy."

"Iffy, huh?"

" 'All those people we don't know' were her exact words," said Kippie.

"Very hoity-toity."

"That's my mom."

"You tell your mom—"

Kippie held up his hand in protest. "I can't tell my mother where to go. Only my stepfather can do that. He'll get her there."

Arnie Zwillman nodded. "What happened to your finger?"

"Dog bit me."

"You lost your finger?"

"Part of it."

"Yech. I hate blood," said Arnie. "What'd your old man say about me?"

"He's not my old man. I told you that."

"All right. What did your *step*father, Jules Mendelson, say about me?"

"He said you burned down the Vegas Seraglio for the insurance money," said Kippie.

Arnie Zwillman turned red and shook his head. "That fat dickhead."

"Hey, you're talking about my stepfather."

"What else did he say about me?"

"He said you cheated at cards."

"Big fucking deal. I don't know anybody who don't cheat at cards. That's part of the game to me. It's a case of cheating the cheaters."

"He said you had an electrical surveillance system in the ceiling of your card room."

"How the fuck did he know that?"

"Listen, Arnie, you're not hearing any criticism from me. I'm just the message carrier."

"Your arraignment's tomorrow. Judge Quartz will dismiss the case. Will your parents be going to the courtroom with you?"

"My parents don't even know. Besides, they'll be at a funeral."

"COME IN HERE a moment, Kippie," Jules had said the next morning. He was standing in the door of the library, darkly dressed for Hector's funeral, holding a coffee cup in his hand, as Kippie made his way to the sunrise room for breakfast. "There's something we must discuss before your mother comes down."

Jules returned to his chair beneath van Gogh's *White Roses* and moved some newspapers aside. Kippie entered the room and closed the door behind him, but he did not sit down.

"I have called the rehab in Lyons," said Jules. "I talked to Father LaFlamme. They'll take you back. I think it's where you should be."

Kippie nodded.

"Miss Maple has booked your flight."

Kippie nodded again. "Much obliged," he said.

"Just get one thing straight. I did this for your mother. I didn't do it for you," said Jules.

"Much obliged, anyway," said Kippie.

## Flo's Tape # 9

*"They had me down on the books as a consultant, although God only knows what I was a consultant for. I'll say this for Jules Mendelson, he was a very generous man. Each month my check came addressed to F. Houlihan. Houlihan's my real name, although I haven't used it for years. March is only a made-up name, in case I became an actress or a model, none of which ever worked out, incidentally. Sometimes, if Jules ever had to write me about anything, he always started out the letter, 'Dear Red.' That was supposed to fool the secretary into thinking F. Houlihan was a guy instead of a girlfriend, and Miss Maple went along with the act. Only you couldn't fool Miss Maple. She always knew who I was. One day she called me up on the telephone and told me, in a very nice way, that she thought I was spending too much money. Of course, Jules never knew she called me. If only she'd said to me, 'Put some of that money in the bank and save it for a rainy day.' But even if she had, knowing me, I probably wouldn't have listened. You see, the big mistake I made was that I thought the merry-go-round was never going to stop."*

# 10

HAD FLO MARCH known how unserious the conflagration was going to be, she would have reacted with less alarm than she did when someone, a woman, running, had screamed the word *"Fire!"* in an altogether hysterical voice in the corridor outside her suite in the Meurice Hotel in Paris at two o'clock in the morning. Later, she told the person most affected by her action that her mother had died in a fire in a welfare hotel in downtown Los Angeles. Had she reacted with less alarm, Flo's picture would not have appeared on the front page of *Figaro* and two other Paris newspapers, as well as the *International Herald Tribune*, with her lovely red hair in total disarray, wrapped in a blanket over her silver fox coat, and carrying a small Louis Vuitton case—its newness evident even in the photograph—that could only have contained jewels. Even that might have passed unnoticed, for Flo March was relatively unknown, as most mistresses are, but her benefactor and lover, dressed but tieless, was in the background of the same picture, another fleer from a four-alarm fire that turned out to be no more than a burned mattress caused by the dropped cigarette of an inebriated television star in an adjoining suite. And Flo March's benefactor and lover was extremely well known. He was so well known that it was known he was staying at the Ritz Hotel in the Place Vendôme several blocks from the Meurice and could only have been having a midnight rendezvous at that hotel, as Cyril Rathbone, the gossip columnist for the Los Angeles magazine called *Mulholland*, who happened to be in Paris at the same time, noted on the clippings that he sent back to his old friend Hector Paradiso in Los Angeles.

"Poor Pauline!" Cyril wrote in his spidery handwriting, on the border of the newspaper. Cyril Rathbone had never liked Pauline Mendelson, because she refused to allow him to cover her parties for his column, and no amount of persuasion, even on the part of her great friend Hector Paradiso, could make her change her mind. "Darling," Pauline had said to Hector at the time, "don't persist. We cannot have newspeople like Mr. Rathbone in our home. Jules hates that sort of social publicity. And besides, Mr. Rathbone seems to write a great deal about us *without* coming to our house." So, in Cyril Rathbone's code of behavior, the very grand Mrs. Mendelson was fair game.

On several occasions, as recently as at the Mendelsons' party on the night he died, Hector had tried to impart this information to Pauline, in order to save her from embarrassment should the photograph become public. Each time he approached his unpleasant task with reluctance, and each time he felt an inner gratitude that he had not been able to carry out his mission, because he knew how deeply hurt she would have been.

No man was more content with his marriage than Jules Mendelson. From the moment he first saw Pauline McAdoo Petworth twenty-three years earlier, at Laurance Van Degan's birthday dance at the Everglades Club in Palm Beach, he had known that it was she for whom he had been waiting. She was dancing that night with Johnny Petworth, whom she was also divorcing, and she epitomized everything to Jules that was proper and swell. Jules was not thought to be a great catch in those days. He was at the time ungainly and vaguely untidy, a large rumpled-looking sort of man who gave no thought to his appearance. And, moreover, word of his immense wealth and financial genius had not penetrated the world in which Pauline, as young as she was, was already a fixture.

Palm Beach people found him dull and difficult to seat. "Darling, do you mind terribly that I've put you next to Jules Mendelson?" hostesses said to their best friends. It was in that way that Pauline was seated next to Jules on the following night at the home of Rose Cliveden and immediately saw the possibilities of him. Once Mr. Forbes began publishing his annual list of the four hundred richest people in America, and Jules Mendelson was listed so near to the top, the very people who had found him dull in the beginning became the first to find him fascinating. "Lucky me, Jules, sitting next to you," the same ladies now said, but by then Pauline had been Mrs. Jules Mendelson for many years. No one who knew him then ever suspected that he would allow himself to be done over, as Pauline had done him over, in much the same way she had done over the old von Stern mansion in Beverly Hills that Jules had bought and Pauline had turned into a showplace. She totally redid his appearance. She instructed Willi, his barber, to raise the part in his hair and shorten the length of his sideburns. She picked out his ties and cuff links and studs. She took him to the tailor in London who had made her father's suits for years, as well as to her father's shirtmaker and shoemaker, and made his decisions for him until he understood the look of her kind of people. Everyone remarked on his greatly improved appearance, as well as his ability to carry on a conversation at a dinner party.

"DO YOU HAVE a mistress, Jules?" Pauline had asked him once, more than a year before Cyril Rathbone had seen the picture of Flo March, with Jules in the background, in the Paris press. She waited until Dudley had set up the drinks tray and left the room before asking her surprising question, a question that surprised even her when she asked it. Although she was not an overly passionate woman, Pauline was feeling worshiped but untouched, and a certain feminine instinct brought forth the question more than any knowledge of such a fact. The conversation took place in the sunset room, where the Mendelsons met each twilight to have a glass of wine together and talk over the business of the day before they dressed for dinner.

"What does that mean?" asked Jules, astonished, turning away from the red and orange sunset to give her his full attention.

"Just asking," said Pauline, holding up her hands in a defensive gesture.

"But what does such a question mean?" Jules asked again.

"You keep repeating yourself, Jules. 'What does that mean? What does such a question mean?' Surely you can think up a better answer than that, you, a man used to handling hundreds of millions of dollars." For Pauline, usually so serene, she had become slightly shrill.

"Why are you being like this, Pauline?" he asked, with the attitude of a man who had nothing to hide.

"More questions. You answer me with questions. That might work in your business life, Jules—intimidation, putting people on the defensive—but it doesn't work with me. I'm probably one of the few people you've ever met who isn't afraid of you."

Jules smiled. "I know that, Pauline," he said. "I've always known that, from the time I saw you throw the prenuptial agreement at Marcus Stromm and splash black ink all over his shirt. That's one of the many things I love about you."

"You have a peculiar way of showing your love," she said.

"I can only answer you with a question again. What does that mean?"

"I am considered to be a beautiful woman. At least people tell me that I am beautiful, and magazines and newspapers write me up as a beautiful woman. I say this with no braggadocio. It is something I have been told about myself since I was a child. It is something I work on. It is the reason I swim forty laps in the pool every day, rain or shine. It is the reason I spend part of each day with Pooky for my hair and Blanchette for my nails. It is the reason I go to Paris twice a year for my clothes."

"I know all that," said Jules.

"Oh, yes, I know you do. I also know that you like to have me by your side when you enter those endless dinners you have to attend. I know you like and even need the way I am able to entertain and attract interesting people to your parties when you want to impress men you have business dealings with."

"Yes, that's true."

"It's not enough for me anymore, Jules. I might as well be married to Hector for all the love you show me."

"I do love you."

"You do understand that I am talking about love in the lovemaking sense of the word *love*. I am more than a mannequin. I am more than a hostess."

Of course, he understood. He worshiped his wife. He could not imagine life without her. His marriage was a contract as binding as any business contract he had ever signed. Forestalling further suspicion, he became attentive again to the obligations of his marriage, at least for a while, but a complication had set in, a sexual complication, that he had never imagined could happen to him.

HER NAME had been Houlihan, Fleurette Houlihan, and she could not bear the sound of it. "You don't think I look Irish enough, without having a name like Fleurette Houlihan?" she often asked, shaking her red hair at the same time. When she thought she might become an actress, and worked as a waitress at the Viceroy Coffee Shop on Sunset Strip, she renamed herself Rhonda March, after Rhonda Fleming, a red-haired film star her mother had admired. The Viceroy was said to serve the best coffee in West Hollywood, and that was where she had met Jules Mendelson, who was a coffee drinker, ten cups a day. He had walked into the Viceroy Coffee Shop on a day when the coffee machine in his office was not working. She was wearing a name plate with RHONDA on it.

Jules Mendelson was not the type of man who spoke to waitresses in coffee shops, but that day, for a reason he did not understand, he had said to the red-haired girl wearing the name tag with RHONDA on it, "I suppose they call you Red."

"No, they don't," she answered quite emphatically. She was a pretty girl who was used to dealing with lascivious older men. "I don't like being called Red, as a matter of fact."

"What do they call you?" he asked.

There was in his tone a genuine interest in her answer, and she felt she had mistaken him for lascivious. "Do you mean what is my name?"

"Yes."

"Rhonda," she said, tapping a red fingernail against her name plate.

When he looked up from his *London Financial Times* and watched her wipe off the table with a turquoise-colored sponge, he said to her, "You don't look like a Rhonda."

"I was thinking of changing it to Rondelle," she said.

"Oh, no," he said, "not Rondelle."

"You want coffee?" she asked. "We got the best coffee in West Hollywood here."

"Yes."

When she put the cup down in front of him, he asked, "What was your name before you changed it?"

"You don't want to hear," she said.

"Yes, I do," he said.

"Fleurette Houlihan," she said, almost whispering. "It makes me cringe. Imagine that up on the screen."

He laughed.

"I kind of like the Fleurette part," said Jules.

"You don't!"

"Kind of."

"You're nuts." She liked talking about herself, though.

"How about Flossie?"

"Sounds cheaper than Fleurette."

"Flo?"

"Hmmm." She gave it some thought.

"I once knew a Flo," said Jules. He hadn't meant to get so deeply mired in such a conversation. "She was a very pretty girl too."

So she became Flo.

FLO MARCH was then twenty-four years old, perhaps not the smartest girl in town but one of the nicest and, certainly, one of the prettiest, if red hair, blue eyes, and creamy-colored skin were an appealing combination for her beholder. She sometimes dated minor agents she poured coffee for in the morning, but they never took her to screenings or to dinners in restaurants, which were the sorts of things she yearned to do. They took her to dinner in other coffee shops and were after one thing and one thing only, and she usually gave it to them, because it was easier to say yes than to say no and have to deal with all that hassle. Hector Paradiso, who lived in the Hollywood Hills above the Viceroy, had breakfast there every morning, and often told Flo stories of where he had been the night before: at Faye Converse's party, or Rose Cliveden's, or, best of all, Pauline Mendelson's. Flo loved hearing about parties, especially Pauline Mendelson's parties. She read every word about Pauline Mendelson in the society columns and in the fashion magazines that Hector sometimes brought by for her after he had finished with them. Flo, no fool, knew all about the other part of Hector's life too, the part no one ever talked about. All the hustlers from the Strip came into the Viceroy too, and they told her about their adventures with the rich guys who stopped their Mercedes-Benzes and Rolls-Royces, made their deals, and took them to their houses.

Jules had returned to the Viceroy Coffee Shop every day since the first day, always carrying a financial newspaper, and sat at the same table, though the management frowned on a single person tying up a booth for four customers and only ordering coffee. But there was something about Jules—although the manager, whose name was Curly, had no idea who Jules was—that kept him from asking Jules to sit at the counter instead of the booth, especially after Rhonda, who now wanted to be called Flo, told the manager that the big man always left a ten-dollar tip, even though he only had coffee.

"I don't want you to think for a single instant that this is what I intend to do for the rest of my life," said Flo, a few days later, pouring Jules a second cup of coffee with one hand and wiping off the Formica top of the table with her turquoise-colored sponge with the other. *"This,"* continued Flo, referring to her job as a waitress in a coffee shop, "is only a means to an end."

"And the end, of course, is stardom," said Jules, watching her over the top of the *Wall Street Journal.*

"I'd settle for less than stardom," said Flo, quite seriously.

"What would you settle for?"

"I'd like to be the second lead in a TV series, best friend of the star, where the whole show wouldn't rest on my shoulders, and when it gets canceled after thirteen weeks, I wouldn't be blamed and would just go on to another series, again as a secondary lead. Or even just a running part would do."

Jules laughed.

Flo blushed. "What are you laughin' at? I'm serious," she said, defensively.

"It is a laugh of enchantment, not derision," he said.

"A laugh of enchantment, not derision," she repeated slowly, as if she were memorizing it so that she could repeat it in conversation. "Hey, that's really nice," she said.

"Are you doing anything about it?" asked Jules.

"What do you mean?"

"Studying, getting an agent, going on calls, or whatever it is actresses do to get ahead. You're not waiting to be discovered at the coffee counter, are you?"

"You have to have pictures," said Flo. "Or they don't want to see you."

"Then get pictures," said Jules, simply.

" 'Get pictures,' he says." She rolled her eyes, as if Jules Mendelson had said something stupid. "Do you have any idea what pictures cost?"

"You seem to be defeated without even starting," he said. "Let me tell you something. If you can visualize what you want to be, you'll make it, believe me."

She looked at him earnestly. It was not the sort of flirtatious conversation she was used to with her customers. "The thing is, I have this great desire to become famous, but I don't know whether I'm good enough at anything to become famous."

□   □   □

"YOU LOOK very well today," Jules had said another day, noting the fresh pink uniform that she was wearing.

"My mother used to say that Maureen O'Hara was the first redhead in movies who had the courage to wear pink on the screen," said Flo.

Jules, bewildered, nodded. He didn't understand most of what Flo said, but he had grown to like listening to her talk. She had opinions on everything. His secretary, Miss Maple, whom he had had for years, couldn't understand why Jules left his office every morning around ten o'clock to go and have coffee at the Viceroy Coffee Shop, when Beth, her assistant, made perfectly good coffee right there in the office; but Jules said he liked to get the fresh air and to be able to read the *Wall Street Journal* and the *London Financial Times* in peace. Miss Maple didn't ask any more questions.

Flo looked out the window of the coffee shop. There, parked by the curb on Sunset Boulevard, was a dark blue Bentley.

"That your car out there?" she asked.

Jules looked out the window at the car, as if it were not his, and then looked back at her.

"Why would you think that was my car?" he asked.

Flo shrugged. "You kinda match each other," she said. Jules did not reply.

"And nobody else in this joint looks like they could afford a car like that. Do you have that on a lease, or do you own it?"

Jules, embarrassed, muttered, "It's mine." He wanted to terminate the subject.

"Sure, I'll go for a ride with you," she said, and then roared with laughter, blushing at the same time. "Hey, I'm only kidding. All my life I wanted to go for a ride in a Rolls-Royce."

"It's not a Rolls," said Jules.

"What is it?"

"A Bentley."

"A Bentley. What's a Bentley? Never heard of a Bentley." There was great disappointment in her voice.

"Well, it's like a Rolls, made by the same company," said Jules, as if defending his car. He knew it was an absurd conversation, unworthy of him.

"Like a cheaper model sort of thing?" Flo asked.

"Yes, I suppose it is, but not by much," he said. Looking at the next booth, he wondered if the people were listening, or if they knew who he was. He wanted to leave the orange Naugahyde booth where he was sitting. He visualized himself rising, leaving a large bill on the table to cover cost and tip, and walking out, but he did not. Instead, he pushed his coffee cup toward her to indicate that he wished another cup of coffee.

LIKE A MOTH drawn to a flame, Jules began to visit the Viceroy Coffee Shop more frequently. Outside the window of the booth where he always sat could be seen a tall building. The golden letters on the side of the building proclaimed it as the Jules Mendelson Building, which was where his office was, although so far no one in the Viceroy had connected him with that name, or that building.

One morning Flo kept him waiting while she joked with a young man at the counter, whom Jules recognized from previous visits. He saw that the young man was handsome, dressed in black jeans that were far too tight, and it surprised him how much anger and jealousy he felt. When, finally, Flo approached his table, he was cool and distant with her.

"Cat got your tongue?" she asked. She frequently used expressions that he could not bear.

"Who's that guy you're talking to at the counter?" he asked after she had brought him his coffee.

"What guy?"

"With the blond hair."

"Oh, him. That's Lonny." She made a thumbs-down gesture.

"You looked quite friendly with him."

"Oh, please!"

"What's he always hanging around for?"

"Drinking coffee, like you. Hey, you're not jealous of Lonny, are you?"

"Jealous. Of course not. Why should I be jealous? I just wanted to know who he is."

"Let me fill you in on Lonny. Lonny is *not*, repeat *not*, interested in pretty young girls, like me, believe me. Lonny is interested in rich old guys like you, who drive the kind of car you drive."

Jules reddened. He did not like to be described as an old guy. He was then fifty-three years old, and he did not think of himself as old. He had started to lose weight. He had started to eat only proper things

—grilled sole and leaf spinach—and declined bread and dessert. Even Willi, his barber who shaved him every morning at five-thirty, had remarked only that morning that he was looking fit and years younger.

Flo realized she had insulted him. "I didn't mean *old*," she said. "I meant *older*. Lonny was a friend of that famous writer who died. What was his name? I'm sure you've heard of him." She tapped her finger on her upper lip as she tried to remember the name. "Basil Plant, I think it was. Anyway, Lonny's supposed to have stolen the manuscript of his unfinished novel, or something like that. Somebody told me the story, but I hear so many stories here at the Viceroy that I can't keep them all straight."

Jules shook his head. He was disinterested in the young man's story.

"Curly thinks you've got a crush on me," said Flo, changing the subject.

"Who's Curly?"

"The manager. Over there, talking to Lonny. He says you'll only sit at my table when you come here and that you leave the biggest tips of anyone who comes into the place."

Jules did not answer. He lifted the *London Financial Times* higher, as if he had discovered something in the news that it was urgent for him to read, in order to hide the reddening of his face. The thing he most feared was to be talked about, although he was sure that Curly, or any of the people at the Viceroy, did not know he was Jules Mendelson. He wondered if he himself knew Jules Mendelson. The Jules Mendelson he knew would never be sitting each day for over an hour in an orange Naugahyde booth in a coffee shop on Sunset Boulevard in order to stare at a red-haired waitress called Flo March. That day he asked Flo March to go for a drive in his Bentley.

HER DRESS had been cheap and a bit showy. Jules felt that it did not suit her. He thought that the skirt was too short, even though she had beautiful legs. He was used to seeing her in her pink waitress uniform, which had a simple style to it, and he was at first disappointed in her appearance away from her job.

"You know what I like about you, Jules?" she asked.

"What?"

"You were awkward and clumsy about asking me out, like you weren't used to picking up girls like me. I was touched by that."

"I thought it was the car that got to you."

"That too," she said, and they both laughed. He noticed that she seemed to enjoy her own humor. If she said something funny, she laughed heartily along with her listener at her sometimes boisterous stories.

"You don't laugh enough, Jules. Did anyone ever tell you that?"

"I guess that's so."

"You want to know what else I like about you?"

"Sure."

"You didn't come on to me the minute we were alone in your car."

"That doesn't mean I didn't want to."

"I understand that, but still, you didn't come on. You acted like a gentleman, which is something I'm not used to with the kind of guys who ask me out.

"I don't even know your last name," Flo said to him, getting out of the Bentley in the parking lot behind the Viceroy, where her car was parked.

"What difference does it make?"

"No, c'mon, tell me."

"Mendelson," he said quietly.

She looked at him. Her mouth fell open. "Like in the Jules Mendelson Family Patient Wing at Cedars-Sinai Hospital?"

Jules nodded.

"That's you?"

Jules nodded.

"That's where my mother died. In the burn unit. She was burned in a hotel fire."

"I'm sorry."

Her high spirits had vanished. She had become quiet.

"G'night," she said. She stepped out of the car and slammed the door behind her. She started walking toward her own car and then turned back to look at him. He was sitting in the driver's seat, looking out at her. She opened the door of his car again and put her head inside.

"Does that mean you're married to Pauline Mendelson?" she asked.

He nodded his head in an almost imperceptible manner. He had heard that florists and hairdressers and people in shops called his wife by her first name, but it was the first time he had ever heard it himself.

"No wonder you didn't want anyone to know your name," said Flo. "You better get home. Your wife's probably having a party and is wondering where you are." She slammed the door again and got into her own car.

THE NEXT DAY Flo had been distant. After Jules was seated in his regular booth, she asked Belle to take her tables—her station, she called it—saying she was going to take her break early. Then she sat at the counter and joked with Joel Zircon, the Hollywood agent, and Manning Einsdorf, who owned Miss Garbo's, in a boisterous manner. Jules, furious, read his *Wall Street Journal*.

Out the window behind him, Flo noticed for the first time the gold lettering on the tall building that read THE JULES MENDELSON BUILD-ING. He stayed for only two cups of coffee, rose, and left Belle the same ten-dollar tip that he always left Flo. She did not get up from the counter when he left.

The next day he brought a gift with him, a small blue box from Tiffany tied with a white ribbon.

"For you," he said, sliding it toward her on the Formica table.

"Really?" There was a childlike look of joy on her face.

"Open it."

"Now?"

"Sure."

She untied the white ribbon carefully, as if she were going to save it. She smiled at him. Then she slowly opened the small blue box. Inside was tissue paper, which she tore aside. Beneath was a layer of white cotton. Under the cotton was Jules's gift. She picked it up. Disappointment registered on her face.

"Do me a favor, will ya, Mr. Big Bucks? Take your little silver trinket from the economy counter at Tiffany's, and shove it. My ex-boyfriend, Mikey, from the Mobil gas station over there, would have given me something better than a silver key chain with a heart charm hanging off it. What was it, a leftover from your office Christmas gifts? Save it for your receptionist's birthday. Hey, Belle, will you take my station? I'm gonna take my break."

Jules sat there, grim-faced. It was a cheap gift for the intention he had for it, and she had called him on it. She had also called it right; it had been a leftover from the office Christmas gifts, an accompani-ment to the bonus that each of the girls on his staff received.

That night, as he was dressing for dinner, he telephoned her at her apartment to apologize. It was the first time he had ever called her, as well as the first time he had ever called another woman from his house. Her line was busy. He showered and then telephoned her again, and her line was still busy. He put his studs and cuff links in his dinner shirt and dialed again, but her line was still busy. He tied his black tie. The line was still busy. He put on his black patent leather shoes. Still busy. He put on his dinner jacket. Busy.

"Jules," called Pauline. "We're going to be late."

"Coming," he called back. One last time, he thought. He dialed again. Her telephone rang.

"Hello?"

"Your line was busy," he said. There was a tone of annoyance in his voice.

"Yes, it was," she said coolly.

"Who were you talking to?" He knew it was the wrong question to ask, even as he was asking it.

"None of your fucking business."

"What's the matter?"

"You're speaking to me in an annoyed voice, as if I have no right to talk on the telephone."

"I'm sorry. I'll tell you what. Call the telephone company tomorrow and have another line put in. I'll take care of it."

"You're some big gift giver, Bucks," she said.

There was a knock on the door of his dressing room, and then the door opened and Pauline walked in. "Jules! Please! We're going to be late! It's a surprise party for Madge, and Rose will be livid if we spoil it."

"I'll be right there, Pauline. I'm just finishing this call with Sims."

"My God, is that Pauline?" asked Flo, enchanted. "I can't believe it. Pauline Mendelson. 'Jules! Please! We're going to be late! It's a surprise party for Madge, and Rose will be *livid* if we spoil it.' " Flo spoke in an exact imitation of Pauline's upper-class voice.

"Jesus," said Jules, panicked. For him, familial domesticity of the highest order, such as he shared with Pauline, and love of the most sexual nature, such as he yearned for but had not yet shared with Flo March, were not incompatible, but it was unthinkable for him that the two could ever intermingle. "Look, I have to go."

"Bye," she said. Her indifference exasperated him.

"You still mad?" asked Jules.

"No."

"Who were you talking to before?" he asked.

"One of my lovers from Watts," she said, and hung up.

The next day Jules contacted a furrier in the San Fernando Valley that was not likely to be frequented by any of the people Pauline knew. He sent Flo a silver fox coat.

"Now we're talking," said Flo, after she tore open the box and pulled it out.

EVEN WOMEN who were jealous of Pauline Mendelson, for the silver platter that her life had been handed to her on, had to concede that she would be marvelous as the wife of the head of the American delegation in Brussels during the year of the statehood of Europe. Although Jules had not as yet been confirmed, the President had assured him that his confirmation was a foregone conclusion and preparations could be made. First the possibility of that high office, which Jules craved, and then the certainty of it, kept things on keel for him during the private torment of his obsession with Flo March.

On her twice-a-year trips to Paris to buy her clothes, Pauline had made several side excursions to Brussels and had secured for them a large house set in a verdant park on the Avenue Prince d'Orange, where it was expected she would entertain magnificently during the year of their stay. Mr. Jensen, the French decorator, had flown over from Paris with Pauline, and they had chosen the colors in which the rooms would be redone and had decided in what locations the paintings she intended to bring from Clouds, like van Gogh's *White Roses* and the six Monets and the Degas and the Bonnard of Misia Sert, would be placed. Pauline, who was meticulous in all things, had over the years perfected her Foxcroft schoolgirl French so expertly that even her French friends, who were numerous, praised her on the faultlessness of her tenses and the elegance of her pronunciation. Jules, on the other hand, had no aptitude for languages other than his own. He spoke the kind of French that the French smile at, but no one ever smiled at Jules Mendelson in a condescending way, for he was too awesome in manner, posture, and wealth.

WHEN PAULINE had gone to China with her sister and brother-in-law, Louise and Lawford Ordano from Philadelphia, Jules took Flo to

Paris, where he had business. They sat in different sections of the Concorde and never once spoke during the flight, because Jules knew several people on board. In Paris they stayed at different hotels. The Mendelsons always stayed at the Ritz on the Place Vendôme, and that is where Jules stayed. Flo stayed nearby at the Meurice. Jules lived in fear that one of Pauline's friends would see him with the young and beautiful redhead.

In the limousine leaving the Charles DeGaulle Airport for the city, Flo stared out the window of the car, overwhelmed to be in Paris. "Is that the Eiffel Tower?" she asked.

"No, that's the airport tower," Jules replied.

"Oh. It looks like the Eiffel Tower," she said.

"No, it doesn't," replied Jules. "It looks like the airport tower."

"To me, it does," insisted Flo.

He gave her a credit card to shop with and told her to go to any of the couturiers, except the one that Pauline went to, but he would not accompany her to the fashion showings, and she had no idea what clothes to order. A sympathetic vendeuse, sensing her confusion, advised her to try Chanel. "You can't go wrong at Chanel," she said. On the first day she went to Chanel, Flo ordered four outfits. On the second day, she ordered six more. When a fitter asked her questions about length and color, she turned to the vendeuse and said, "Just do whatever you think is right. I'm putting myself in your hands."

In two days she had spent nearly fifty thousand dollars. An accountant, who did not recognize her face or name, noticed the amount of her order and telephoned to check out her credit. He was told that there was a sufficient amount to cover whatever Miss March charged. He was told she had unlimited credit.

Each night they dined at her suite in the Meurice. It was there that Jules finally made love to Flo for the first time. He discovered that his sexual appetite was limitless. His requests for specific acts were not plebeian, and Flo denied him nothing. In the beautiful young woman who was once named Fleurette Houlihan, Jules Mendelson had found his perfect sexual partner.

If she was unhappy with the limited scope of her Parisian adventure, she did not let on. At that time in her life, just to have been in Paris at all was enough, even hidden from view. For her to be able to say, "When I was in Paris," when she was in conversation with her friends from the Viceroy Coffee Shop, or her hairdresser, Pooky, or even a stranger, thrilled her. Only the four-alarm fire that turned out to be no more than a burning mattress in the next suite brought the trip to a halt before its natural expiration.

For all his passion for Flo, Jules never once entertained the idea of a divorce from Pauline. Each was necessary to him, and it did not occur to him that he could not have both. He shut Flo out of every part of his life except his sex life and allowed her to have no life of her own that did not revolve around him. For this he paid her a great deal of money. If in the totally improbable event that the two women in Jules's life had ever met and compared notes, each would have found that the other woman had that part of Jules that she most wanted. The beautiful and elegant Pauline would have liked a more romantic relationship with her husband, instead of being kept on a pedestal by him, and the sexy and erotic Flo would have liked to receive guests and sit at the head of dinner tables full of famous and rich people.

JULES WOKE at three in the morning and could not go to sleep again. Pictures and thoughts of Flo March filled his mind. He yearned to be with her. He ached with desire for her. Turning, tossing, wanting to cry out her name, he pulled the bedclothes over him in such an abrupt fashion that he pulled them off Pauline, lying next to him.

"Jules, for heaven's sake, what is the matter with you?" asked Pauline, awakened now, and cold. She pulled the covers back.

"I'm sorry," he said. There was such a forlorn tone in his voice that it was impossible for Pauline to feel annoyance with him for ruining her sleep.

"Jules, is there something you want to discuss? Is it the conference? Has something gone wrong?"

"No, no. I'm sorry, Pauline. Go back to sleep. I'm all right. It's just—"

"Just what?"

"Nothing, really. Nothing." He began to snore lightly to show that he had fallen asleep again, which he had not. He had not meant to fall in love with Flo March. He had meant only to set her up and visit her when he felt like it, to give her gifts, to have her at his beck and call. It had never occurred to him that he might want to change his whole life and make her the dominant figure in it.

## Flo's Tape #10

*"Jules once told me about this guy who had made him so mad he knocked over the statue of the Degas ballerina, which was one of the real treasures of his collection, but I never realized the guy he was talking about was Philip Quennell. If I had known that Jules had such a problem with him, I never would have gone to Philip's room at the Chateau Marmont on the night I decided to leave Jules, after he pretended he didn't know me when he ran into Madge White at that steak house in the Valley. I found out later that Philip had questioned Hector Paradiso's death right from the first day. After all, he was one of the few people who had actually seen the body and been in the house. He refused to accept Jules's suicide story, and then he called the publisher of the* Tribunal *to see why the paper hadn't covered the story, and that really pissed Jules off.*

*"Jules could be the nicest guy in the world, but he could be a bastard too. I actually never saw that side of him, but I know for a fact that it was Jules who got Philip Quennell fired off the picture he was writing for Casper Stieglitz."*

# 11

"HOLLYWOOD IS VERY unforgiving of failure," said Casper Stieglitz, whose last four pictures had failed. He had taken to tutoring Philip Quennell in the thought process of the film industry. "It will forgive you, even overlook your forgeries, your embezzlements, and, occasionally, your murders, but it will not forgive you your failure."

Casper looked through his black-framed, dark-lensed glasses, which he never removed, and observed the restaurant quizzically. He shook his head and expressed disappointment with the noonday crowd. "I'm the biggest name here today," he said glumly. For a moment he wondered if Michel, the maître d', had put him into the wrong room, and he considered making a fuss and demanding a table in the rear room, where he had seen Marty Lesky, the head of Colossus Pictures, seated when he went to the men's room. Le Dôme, he had pointed out to Philip Quennell when he called to arrange the lunch date to discuss the progress of their project, catered to people in the film business and the music business, and it was a good place to be seen to get talk going about a new project.

Casper opened his large napkin with a flourish and placed it in his lap. Philip noticed that his toupee was in its mid-month phase, fifteen days from its last "haircut" and sixteen days away from its next, and he wore it that day in a ponytail, tied back with a rubber band. Ponytails tied back with rubber bands were the smart look of middle-aged producers and executives in the industry that season, and Casper, Philip noted, was always in the forefront of filmland fashion. His black velour Armani jacket was open over his T-shirt, on which was a reproduction of a section of Picasso's *Guernica*. Philip had to admit that the toupee was nearly undetectable. He wondered if Willard, the butler, who appeared to be fastidious, assisted in its placement on Casper's head each day and helped with the taping and gluing, or whatever had to be done.

Casper, still worried about his table, remained in a highly nervous state, constantly sneezing and blowing his nose. "I gotta take a leak," he said, and jumped up from the table. As he rose, he spotted Mona Berg. "Oh, look, Mona's here," he said to no one in particular, but his voice calmed considerably when he saw that someone as important as Mona Berg was in the same room that he was.

"Hi, Mona," he called over to her table.

"Hi, Casper," Mona Berg called back, making a gesture that indicated they should talk by telephone later in the day.

"Say hi to Philip Quennell," Casper said, as a way of introduction. "Mona Berg here is the top agent in this town."

Philip and Mona Berg called out hellos.

"And, Mona, Phil here wrote that hot hot hot book on Reza Bulbenkian, called *Takeover*. Did you read it?"

"I never have time to read anything but scripts, Casper. You know that," said Mona Berg. "But I'll make time to read your book, Phil. I promise. What did you think of my idea of Elliott Carver for the role of Bligh?" she asked.

Casper shook his head in an elaborate negative shake. "Elliott Carver has had six flops in a row. Elliott Carver is ready for a sitcom, on cable, not the lead in a Casper Stieglitz picture," he said.

"You're making a big mistake, Casper," insisted Mona, who was known to be relentless in the selling of her clients. "Marty Lesky ran the rough cut of *Career Girl* at his house last night, and said Elliott's fabulous. Even Sylvia Lesky thought he was great, and you know how hard to please Sylvia is."

"Excuse me a second. I gotta take a leak," said Casper.

"One of these days he's going to drop dead with all that stuff he's putting up his nose," said Mona.

Philip, who agreed, did not answer.

"I hear you're writing the drug documentary."

"Yes."

"Thankless task."

"I'm finding that out."

"If you don't go with actual cops, and do actors playing cops, which always works better, call me. I'd like you to meet Elliott Carver."

"Sure thing, but that will be up to Casper."

"Here's my lunch date, the putz. You almost kept me waiting, Joel," she said, looking at her watch. There was admonition in her voice.

"Sorry, Mona," said Joel, sitting down in the booth.

"I hate to be kept waiting, Joel."

"I said I was sorry, Mona. I got held up in traffic."

"What was your name?" she called over to Philip.

"Quennell. Philip Quennell."

"Joel Zircon, Philip Quennell."

"Didn't I see you at Hector Paradiso's funeral?" asked Joel. "You're the guy who gave his handkerchief to Flo March, right?"

"YOU GOTTA do something about the way you dress, Phil," said Casper Stieglitz, when he returned to the table. Philip had started to notice that each time Casper returned from one of his numerous trips to the bathroom, he had a new train of thought, about which he was momentarily passionate.

"What's wrong with the way I dress?" asked Philip.

"It's not the right look for out here," said Casper. "Blue blazer, gray flannels, Brooks shirt. Gimme a break. That look went out years ago. And you gotta lose the polka dot ties. You look like a history teacher, not a screenwriter. All you need is a fucking pipe to complete the picture. Especially for this kind of documentary we're doing. The narcs won't talk to you dressed like that."

"I thought you said you loved what I'd written so far."

"I do. I do."

"So the narcs *are* talking to me, blue blazer, gray flannels, Brooks shirt, polka dot tie, and all."

"I mean, the look is wrong for out here, that's all I'm saying."

"Look, Casper. I don't like the way *you* dress. Black velour was never very high on my list, but it's none of my business how you dress, so I don't mention it, just like it's none of your business how I dress. So you dress your way. I'll dress my way. Okay?"

"Okay, okay. Don't get hot under the collar. I'm just trying to explain California to you, that's all," said Casper.

"I'm just here in California temporarily," replied Philip.

Casper snapped his fingers. "Listen, you just gave me an idea. All of a sudden I like the way you dress. Including the polka dot ties. I got a favor to ask you."

"About the picture?"

"No, about coming to dinner a week from Sunday night."

"Oh, thanks, I can't. I'm going to be at my girlfriend's ranch outside of Solvang," said Philip.

"So? Come back early."

"Why?"

"I'm having some swells to dinner, and it occurred to me you'd fit in perfectly. I never know what to talk to people like that about."

"Who are you having?"

"Arnie Zwillman."

"Who's Arnie Zwillman?"

"He's the man who burned down the Vegas Seraglio for the insurance money."

"That's your idea of a swell?"

"No, he's no swell. The other people are swells."

"Who are the other people?"

"Jules and Pauline Mendelson."

"Jules and Pauline Mendelson are coming to your house for dinner?" asked Philip, not making any attempt to hide the astonishment in his voice.

"Do you know them?"

"Please tell me you're not planning on having Ina Rae and Darlene at the same dinner."

Casper laughed. "Did I tell you about the T-shirt Ina Rae was wearing last night?"

"No."

"It said 'Warning, I Scream When I Come.' Laugh, I thought I'd bust a gut. That girl is a riot."

"That should strike Pauline Mendelson as really funny," said Philip.

"I don't think Ina Rae's right for this group," said Casper, thinking over what Philip had said. "I could have her in for the movie later, but skip the dinner part. I'll need another girl to fill out the table. What about that girl you're seeing. What's her name?"

"Camilla Ebury."

"Actress, model, dancer, what?"

"None of the above."

"Bring her."

"Sunday nights she spends with her daughter. They have dinner together at the Los Angeles Country Club. A family ritual."

"Tell her I'm running a picture."

"She wouldn't care."

Casper snapped his fingers again. "Hortense Madden. That's who I'll get. She'll class it up."

"Who's Hortense Madden?"

"The literary critic for *Mulholland*."

"For heaven's sake."

"You know her?"

"No, I don't know her. She panned my book on Reza Bulbenkian."

"That's Hortense for you. She pans everything that's popular."

"What is the point of this evening, Casper?" asked Philip.

"Arnie Zwillman wants to meet Jules Mendelson, that's all I know, and he asked me to set it up."

Philip thought for a moment. "Okay, I'll come," he said.


"THAT WAS SWEET of you to take Bunty to the movies this afternoon," said Camilla.

"She's a great kid," said Philip.

"She adores you. She told me she thinks you're handsome," said Camilla.

"I don't suppose I could talk you into coming with me to Casper Stieglitz's house for dinner a week from Sunday," said Philip.

"Not unless I can bring Bunty," said Camilla.

"I somehow don't think Bunty is right for an evening at Casper's."

"That's what I figured," said Camilla. They both laughed. "Although I'd love to see his wig collection. Or Ina Rae. I don't know which fascinates me more."

"The Mendelsons are going."

"The Mendelsons are going to Casper Stieglitz's?" asked Camilla. "I don't believe that for a minute."

"That's what Casper said at lunch today."

"Must be some business something or other," said Camilla, shaking her head. "I'll make you a bet."

"What?"

"They'll back out at the last minute. I know Pauline."


AFTER PARIS, where they had become lovers, Jules Mendelson, in the throes of his passion, decided to lease a house for Flo to ensure their privacy. She stopped working at the Viceroy Coffee Shop, moved out of her apartment in the Silverlake district, and lived temporarily in the Sunset Marquis Hotel in West Hollywood. Jules's first intention was to take an apartment in a high-rise condominium on Sunset Boulevard, but when looking there, using an assumed name, he ran into Marty Lesky, the head of Colossus Pictures, in the eleva-

tor. The two well-known men nodded and chatted in a friendly manner. He later found out from the superintendent that Marty Lesky
had an apartment in the building. Judging from Marty's nervous attitude in the elevator, and Jules's certain knowledge that Marty and
Sylvia Lesky maintained one of the largest estates in Bel Air, he suspected that Marty kept a young lady there who was not his wife. Jules
did not return.

"I saw a very nice house in Bel Air today," said Flo. It thrilled her
to be looking at houses in what she referred to as the ritziest parts of
town. House hunting was a new adventure that she enjoyed enormously. Jules leased her a bright red Mercedes, and she had taken to
driving around for hours, discovering the expensive areas of Beverly
Hills and Holmby Hills and Bel Air that she had never seen before, in
the company of a real estate agent called Elaine, who used to be an
actress and knew the history of every house. "That's where Lana
Turner's daughter killed Johnny Stompanato," she said about one
house. "Judy Garland took an overdose in that house," she said about
another. Or, "Jack and Anjelica used to live there." Flo knew she
meant Jack Nicholson and Anjelica Huston, and the information excited her.

"Where?" asked Jules.

"Up Stone Canyon, past the Bel Air Hotel. Elaine says it used to
belong to one of Amos Swank's ex-wives."

"Bel Air? Oh, no, no," said Jules, shaking his head at the idea. "Not
Bel Air."

Flo had come to know that whenever Jules said "Oh, no, no" to
one of her requests, and shook his head at the same time, it meant
that she had inadvertently encroached on his main life, the life that
he shared with Pauline. For Jules, a house in Bel Air, where so many
of the Mendelsons' friends lived, posed a danger in that he ran the
risk of passing people he knew on the narrow roads of the exclusive
enclave. Being ever protective of that part of his life, he could imagine
one of Pauline's friends, specifically Rose Cliveden, saying to Pauline,
"I saw Jules in Bel Air this afternoon." "This afternoon? I can't imagine what Jules could have been doing in Bel Air this afternoon," he
imagined Pauline answering. "Up Stone Canyon, past the hotel,"
Rose, the informer, would continue. "For heaven's sake," Pauline
would answer.

"I think it would be better if you looked off one of the main can-

yons, like Benedict or Coldwater," Jules said to Flo. Benedict and
Coldwater canyons were areas where it was less likely that he would
encounter the kind of people with whom he and his wife dined most
evenings.

"That's a nice area," said Flo, agreeing. She reeled off the names
of several television stars who had homes in the canyons.

Finally Flo found a perfect house, hidden from view by overgrown
shrubbery, on a small street off Coldwater Canyon called Azelia Way.
Elaine said that it was owned by Trent Muldoon, a television star
whose series had been canceled and who had overextended himself
in the four years of his semistardom. "Spend, spend, spend, and now
he's broke, broke, broke," said Elaine. "Let it be a cautionary tale."

"This was Trent Muldoon's house, really?" asked Flo, delighted.

"His wife's taking him to the cleaners in the divorce, and he needs
to get out from under," said Elaine.

Flo was ecstatic that she finally had a house of her own, with a
swimming pool, as well as a Beverly Hills address and a 90210 zip code
and a 274 prefix to her telephone number. She could hardly contain
herself. When she confessed to Jules that she found Trent Muldoon's
mounted cattle skulls and western furniture depressing, he allowed
her to put most of Trent's furniture, which came with the lease, into
storage and redecorate the house herself.

For a time she was never happier, but she was very lonely. Sometimes she felt herself to be no more than a receptacle for the fulfill-
ment of his desires, and she drank a little wine in the afternoons, and
very often she smoked marijuana cigarettes.

"Hello?"

"I'm on my way over."

"Now?"

"Be nude when you open the door."

As requested, she was nude when she opened the door.

"Drink?" she asked.

"No." He stared at her body hungrily and ripped off his tie and
shirt. "Let's go in the bedroom."

There was an absence of endearments in his lovemaking. There
was no fondling, and very little kissing. He wanted only to satisfy his
imperious urge to be within her lovely body, and to stay within her as
long as possible. His lust for her seemed insatiable. At that time he in
no way feared that she would become an important person in his life.
He thought of her as merely an outlet for his increasingly demanding

sexual urges. For Jules, Flo was bracketed in that area of his life only.
He was an art collector and an aficionado of splendid living, and her
taste was too unrefined for him to experience feelings of love. There
were things about her that drove him mad. She pronounced sandwich
"samich," as if it rhymed with "damage." She moved her lips when
she read. She drank soft drinks out of the can. She was uninformed
on important matters.

He had never intended to play Pygmalion to her Galatea, but he
discovered that when he did correct her, if something she did or said
irritated him sufficiently, she was never offended. She even welcomed
his corrections, and she never made the same mistake again. At first
it amused him that she was so quick to act upon his corrections and
suggestions. Then he began to do it in earnest. Her voice improved.
Her carriage improved. Her walk improved. Within himself, he was
aware that the beautiful young woman was wasted living such a hidden life, but he did not want to change that. A simple call to Marty
Lesky at Colossus Pictures would have made it possible for Flo to get
a small part in one of the many television series at the studio, or a
reading for a film, or any of the things she might have done. And
Marty Lesky would have complied. It was the sort of favor that rich
men with mistresses did for each other, but he could not bring himself
to make the call that might have satisfied Flo's yearnings to be somebody. He liked her there for him.

After their lovemaking, when he was spent and satisfied, he began
talking to her in a way that he talked to very few people in his life:
about his business, about the eventual disposition of his art collection, about an apartment in Brussels on the Avenue Hamoir that he
had his eye on for her, when he would have to move there for a year
during the statehood of Europe. The prospect of living in Brussels for
a year thrilled her. Then, invariably, he would look at his watch and
say, "I have to get out of here," and rush from her bed and dress and
leave to get home in time to have his afternoon glass of wine with
Pauline before they dressed for dinner and went out to whatever party
they were attending that evening. Often, on the way home from her
house, he would call her on the car telephone.

"What are you doing?"

"You mean since you came in me the third time eleven minutes
ago?" she replied one day, exasperated. She knew he didn't like her to
be vulgar, except when they were making love, and she used it in
retaliation when she felt that he was overcrowding her. Hearing his

disapproving silence, she relented. "I'm lying here on my brand-new sets of Porthault sheets that you bought me in Paris, exhausted from your lovemaking, Jules, drinking a glass of wine from the Bresciani auction that you brought over to my house. That's what I'm doing." She didn't tell him that she was also smoking a joint. She knew he wouldn't have approved of that. He told her once he had no patience with people who took drugs.

In time Flo became stultified by the persistency of Jules's demanding love in their relationship. He wanted her to be there always for him, in case he should drop in on her unexpectedly, or telephone her, which he sometimes did as often as ten times a day, or more. A busy telephone line could send him into a tantrum. He imagined that there were other men in her life, even though he knew there weren't. She drank more wine. She smoked more marijuana. Several times she threatened to pull away from him, but such threats did not unnerve Jules. There was no doubt in his mind that he was the most exciting thing that had ever happened in Flo March's life. He knew that Flo knew that too. He understood totally the power of money. How gorgeous it was. How easy it was to get used to. How terrifying it was to imagine life without it once one had become used to it.

Except in the evenings, when he drove Pauline to parties, Jules stopped driving his blue Bentley, because he felt that someone might recognize it when he drove each afternoon to Flo's house on Azelia Way. He leased himself an expensive but nondescript Cadillac with darkened windows that he could see out of but passers-by could not see into. One night when Pauline was in New York for a party, he drove Flo back to her old apartment in the obscure neighborhood— at least obscure to Jules Mendelson—known as the Silverlake district, where she had resided before the recent good fortune that had changed the economic circumstances of her life. She went to pick up some mail that her former landlady told her was there. When they stopped at a red light on Melrose Avenue, Flo looked out the window of Jules's car at a bag lady on the street, making her preparations for the night. Terror seized her.

"She reminds me of my mother," said Flo.

"Who?" asked Jules.

"Her." Flo pointed at the bag lady. "I bet that lady was pretty at one time, like my mother was."

Jules nodded.

"My mother died in a fire in a welfare hotel."

"You told me that in Paris," said Jules.

"You're going to take care of me, aren't you, Jules? I can't die poor like my mother. I just can't."

"I *am* taking care of you."

"No, I mean after."

"After what?"

"Nothing."

He knew what she meant, but he could not bear to think of what she meant. They drove on in silence.

EACH MORNING without fail Philip Quennell went to the AA meeting at the log cabin on Robertson Boulevard. He sat reading the newspaper before the meeting started and rarely mixed in conversation with the other members of the fellowship.

A bright red fingernail tapped on the sports page of the *Los Angeles Tribunal* that he was reading one morning. "Think McEnroe will ever make a comeback?" asked Flo.

"Hi, Flo," he said.

"Hi, Phil," she answered. She opened her bag and took out the handkerchief he had handed to her at Hector Paradiso's funeral. It had been laundered and ironed. "Thanks for the loan," she said.

"That was some funeral," he said, taking it.

"Did you see Loretta Young?" she asked. "I hope I look that good when I'm her age."

Philip smiled.

"Who would have thought we would both be attending the same fashionable funeral so soon after meeting?" asked Flo. "I suppose you were at Rose Cliveden's lunch party at the Los Angeles Country Club afterwards."

"No, I wasn't."

"I read about it in Cyril Rathbone's column in *Mulholland*," said Flo. "Poor Rose."

"Why poor Rose?"

"You didn't hear? She fell down and broke her leg at her lunch party. She tripped over Hector's dog, Astrid."

"Did you read that in Cyril Rathbone's column too?"

"That's where I get all my information," said Flo.

After the meeting, when they were leaving, Philip said to Flo, "What was the name of that club you mentioned to me where Hector Paradiso went on the night he committed suicide?"

"I didn't hear you say Hector committed suicide, did I?"

"It seems to be the popular theory."

"I'm surprised you fell for that line, a smart guy like you. Miss Garbo's is the name of the club. Some of the guys who go there just call it Garbo's."

"Where is it?" asked Philip.

"On a street called Astopovo, between Santa Monica Boulevard and Melrose. Somehow I wouldn't have thought it was your kind of hangout."

"You wouldn't want to go there with me, would you? To Miss Garbo's? I'd like to find out who Hector left with that night."

"I'd like to, Phil, but I can't."

"Why not?"

"I told you I was spoken for."

"Listen, I'm not coming on to you, I swear. I meant as pals only. I didn't want to go there alone."

"But I've got a jealous fella. He calls me twenty times a day to keep tabs on me."

"A rejection, huh?"

"Sorry, Phil."

"Actually, it's Philip, not Phil. I really don't like to be called Phil."

"Oh, sorry. Philip. Sounds classier."

"You're sure you won't come?"

"Pretty girls like me they definitely do not want at Miss Garbo's after midnight. But I'll certainly want to hear what you find out. Ask for Manning Einsdorf. He's the one who makes the arrangements."

"So I hear."

"And Phil?"

Philip turned to look at her.

She snapped her fingers. "I mean Philip. A cute guy like you, you better put a padlock on your fly," said Flo.


THAT DAY Philip Quennell placed a call to Sandy Pond, the publisher of the *Los Angeles Tribunal*.

"Will Mr. Pond know what this is in reference to?" asked Sandy Pond's secretary after Philip had identified himself.

"Tell him I am the author of the book called *Takeover*, about Reza Bulbenkian," replied Philip.

"Would you care to tell me what it is you're calling Mr. Pond about?" asked the secretary.

"I wouldn't, no," replied Philip.

"It is customary for me to ask. Mr. Pond is extremely busy."

"I understand."

"Then you won't tell me?"

"No. You have only to ask him and to identify me. Then it's up to Mr. Pond to decide whether he will speak to me, isn't it?"

There was an icy silence. "Just a moment," she said.

In an instant Sandy Pond picked up the telephone. "I certainly enjoyed your book, Mr. Quennell," he said. "Is it true that Reza Bulbenkian threatened to break your legs? That's what we heard."

Philip laughed. "There was something like that, yes."

"I understand from my wife that you're seeing our great friend Camilla Ebury," said Sandy Pond.

"Yes." Philip did not elaborate.

"How can I help you?" asked Sandy Pond.

"I am very curious that your paper hasn't covered the murder of Hector Paradiso," said Philip.

There was a pause. "Murder? What murder?" replied Sandy Pond.

"Death, then," said Philip.

Sandy Pond did not speak.

"You did know Hector Paradiso, did you not?"

"I did, yes. I was a pallbearer at his funeral. A charming man. A great friend of my wife's. She always said he was the best dancer in Los Angeles. It's all so sad, so terribly sad."

"He was shot five times, Mr. Pond," said Philip. "I was there at the house a few hours afterwards, with Camilla Ebury. I identified his body for the police."

"But it was a suicide, Mr. Quennell. I have seen the autopsy report."

"Don't you find it odd that someone could shoot himself five times?" asked Philip.

"Apparently he was deeply depressed. The autopsy report goes on to say that he was a poor shot. I will be happy to have my secretary send a copy of it on to you," said Sandy Pond. His tone of voice indicated that he wished to terminate the conversation.

"But don't you think even that is a story worth covering, Mr. Pond?"

"Would you explain yourself?"

"A prominent man in the city, who moves in the highest social circles, dines and dances at the home of the Jules Mendelsons, and then commits suicide by shooting himself five times in the torso. Where I come from, that's a story. Add to that that he was a member of a Land Grant family and has a boulevard named after him, and that's a front-page story."

"Is that all, Mr. Quennell?"

"I believe that, for some reason I do not understand, there is a cover-up going on, and that your newspaper is a party to that cover-up."

"Ludicrous, and libelous," said Sandy Pond. All trace of pleasantness had vanished from his voice.

Philip, fearing that Sandy Pond would hang up on him, began to speak very quickly. "Isn't it a fact that Jules Mendelson went to see you on the morning that Hector Paradiso was murdered? I beg your pardon, on the morning that Hector Paradiso committed suicide."

"Good-bye, Mr. Quennell."

THAT EVENING at a dinner party at the home of Ralph and Madge White in Hancock Park, Sandy Pond motioned to Jules Mendelson to follow him onto the lanai after dinner, when the other guests were having coffee in the living room.

"Have you ever heard of someone called Philip Quennell?" he asked. "He wrote that book on your friend Bulbenkian."

"Yes, I have. He's seeing Camilla. Why?" asked Jules.

"I had a most upsetting call from him this afternoon."

THAT SAME NIGHT, in a different part of the city, Miss Garbo's was mobbed. Miss Garbo's was mobbed every night. Marvene McQueen, the chanteuse, was in the middle of her set.

"*You are not my first love. I've known other men,*" she sang.

She stared straight up into the spotlight. Her lips puckered over her

protruding teeth. Tears filled her eye-shadowed eyes as she moaned
out her signature number. One of the shoulder straps of her black
evening dress dropped down on her arm. She allowed her hair to fall
over one eye, like a forties film star. It was a wasted performance. No
one in the crowded bar paid the slightest bit of attention to her.

"Zane," called out Manning Einsdorf to the bartender. Manning
sat on a high stool where he could survey the entire room. "Don't
serve any more drinks to Mr. Coughlin and guest at table twenty-six.
They've had enough. And tell the parking boy to call a cab and not
let him drive home either. I'm not going to have the West Hollywood
police closing down my place because of a couple of drunks."

"Calm down, calm down, Manning," said Zane. "It's all taken care
of."

"Miss Einsdorf is very jumpy lately," said Joel Zircon, who was
standing at the bar listening to the exchange.

"Miss Einsdorf has been very jumpy ever since you-know-who left
here with you-know-who and ended up with five bullets in him. She
bites my head off ten times a night," said Zane.

Philip Quennell walked into the club. For several minutes he was
unnoticed in the packed and noisy room. Making his way through
the crowd, he found himself a space at the bar by standing sideways.
Joel Zircon, who had been introduced to Philip at Le Dôme by Mona
Berg, looked down the bar at him in surprise and then stared at him
through the blue mirrored wall behind the liquor bottles. Philip, waiting to be served, concentrated on Marvene McQueen's set.

"*You better go now, because I like you much too much, you better
go now,*" she sang.

"Beer?" asked Zane, when he found time to approach Philip.

"Soda water," answered Philip.

"Lemon? Lime?" asked Zane.

"Lemon."

Zane filled the glass from a rubber tube attached to a spigot and
placed it in front of Philip.

"Who's the singer?" asked Philip.

"Marvene McSomebody," replied Zane.

"Drag queen?"

"No, real girl."

"Buckteeth."

"You can say that again."

"I'm looking for someone called Manning Einsdorf," said Philip. He leaned forward on the bar toward Zane so that he would not have to raise his voice.

Zane looked at Philip. "He's the fella sitting on the high stool at the end of the bar. He's pretty busy tonight. Is he expecting you?"

"No."

"Who shall I tell him wants to see him?"

"I'll tell him myself," said Philip. He pulled out from his position at the bar and walked down to where Manning Einsdorf was surveying the activity in his club.

"Zane!" hissed Joel Zircon. When Zane turned around, Joel signaled for him to come over to where he was standing at the bar. "What did that guy want?"

"Asked for Manning. Who is he? Doesn't look like our crowd, if you know what I mean," said Zane. "But you never know these days."

"No, no. Definitely not our crowd. He's writing a documentary for Casper Stieglitz so Casper won't have to go to jail for being caught with ten pounds of cocaine," said Joel. "Mona Berg told me all about it. What the fuck do you suppose he's doing here?"

"Who?" asked Manning Einsdorf, leaning down from his high stool and putting his hand to his ear.

Philip repeated the name. "Lonny."

"I never heard of such a person," said Manning.

"Blond, handsome, apparently."

"That could be any of a couple of hundred guys who come in here nightly."

"The name means nothing to you?"

"That's right."

"I see," said Philip. "Did you know Hector Paradiso?"

"I didn't, no," replied Manning Einsdorf. He turned away and called out to the bartender. "Zane, they need drinks at table twenty-two. And send Marvene a glass of champagne. Tell her she was terrific tonight. Tell her not to forget 'Moanin' Low' in the next set."

Philip, dismissed, remained. "You say you didn't know Hector Paradiso?" he asked.

"I already told you I didn't."

"But you went to his funeral."

"Who said I went to his funeral?"

"No one said."

"So, where did you get such an idea?"

"I sat in the row behind you. You were with Joel Zircon, the agent who works with Mona Berg, and Willard, Casper Stieglitz's butler."

Manning Einsdorf began to feel uncomfortable.

"Well, of course, I knew Hector slightly," said Manning. "I mean, everyone knew Hector Paradiso, God rest his soul, but he wasn't a close friend."

"I understand he was here in your club on the night he was murdered."

"He wasn't murdered."

"I beg your pardon. I understand he was here in your club on the night he committed suicide."

"No. I don't recall that he was."

"Think."

"Look around you. The place is packed like this every night. I can't remember everyone who comes in here. Miss Garbo's wasn't Hector's sort of place, you know. Hector was a high society sort of person."

Philip persisted. "He came here that night in a dinner jacket straight from a party at Pauline Mendelson's. People tell me he even described to you what Pauline was wearing that night."

"I don't remember any of that," said Manning.

"And you don't remember his leaving with a young blond man called Lonny?"

"How many times have I got to tell you that I never heard of anyone called Lonny, and I didn't see Hector in here that night?"

"Thanks."

"Stick around. My new singer's going to go on again."

"I heard enough of your singer."

In the parking lot, Philip Quennell handed the parking boy his ticket. "Beige Le Sabre," he said.

A back door of the club opened. Zane stuck his head out and, seeing Philip, whistled between his fingers. When Philip turned around to respond to the whistle, Zane signaled with his head for him to come over.

"I'm on a piss break. I gotta talk quick," he said.

"Your boss does not exactly dwell in the palace of truth," said Philip.

"No, no. Truth was never Manning's long suit," replied Zane.

"What's up?" asked Philip.

Zane looked behind him into the club before he spoke. "You're looking for Lonny?"

"Yes, I'm looking for Lonny, and I don't even know Lonny's last name."

"Edge. His name is Lonny Edge. Lives on Cahuenga Boulevard—7204¼ Cahuenga—near Ivar. I don't know the phone number, and he's unlisted, but he left here with Hector about two-thirty that night."

"What's your name?" asked Philip.

"Zane."

"Thanks, Zane. How come you're telling me this? Your boss could fire you."

"Hector Paradiso was a good guy to me, and I don't buy this suicide story. There was no way he was on his way to committing suicide the last night he was in here. No way. Someone's covering up his murder."

Philip nodded. "That's exactly what's happening. What's this Lonny Edge like?"

"You'll see for yourself. He's what's known in the trade as a famous fornicator. Men, women, you name it. He doesn't care if the price is right. Rich guys fly him to New York or Hawaii for the weekend. Like that. He does scenes, in groups, if you know what I mean. And he's a minor porn star in video. Listen, I gotta get back. Miss Einsdorf will have a shit fit. She's very jumpy lately."

"Thanks, Zane."

"You never talked to me, right?"

"Never saw you before, Zane."

As Philip got into his car, he noticed Marvene McQueen leaving the club by the same door that Zane had used. She was wearing dark glasses, as if she were a film star. She walked across the parking lot to an old Honda and got in.

## Flo's Tape #11

*"The trouble is, you can't talk to a Chanel suit. Except for Glyceria, who was Faye Converse's maid, and Pooky, who did my hair, and, I suppose, Nellie Potts, who was the decorator, I never had anybody to talk to. Sometimes I'd call up Curly, who was the manager of the Viceroy Coffee Shop, and we'd laugh a little like old times. Actually, I bought my grass from Curly, if the truth be known.*

*"One day I realized, between the grass and the white wine from the Bresciani auction that Jules insisted on my having on hand for him always, I was stoned almost every afternoon. When I was stoned, I didn't mind so much having no one to talk to. But my skin began looking not so hot, and, without bragging or anything, I happen to have beautiful skin. Everybody tells me that. So I just stopped both the wine and the grass. It was tough, though. Pooky, the hairdresser, who used to do a lot of coke, told me about AA. I mentioned it to Jules. He freaked out. He hated things like that. 'You can't be seen in there,' he said. Pooky told me about the early morning meeting in the log cabin on Robertson Boulevard at seven A.M. From my waitress days, I was used to getting up at that time anyway. That's where I met Philip Quennell."*

# 12

SOMEHOW—NO ONE actually saw it happen, as it happened in the ladies' room—Rose Cliveden fell down and broke her leg at the Los Angeles Country Club during the luncheon she gave following Hector Paradiso's funeral. Madge White swore Rose tripped over Astrid, Hector's little dog, named after the ice skating star he had once been engaged to decades before. He had left Astrid to Rose in his will, although she did not know the dog had been left to her at the time it tripped her, if, indeed, it did trip her. With Rose, when she had her many mishaps, nothing was ever quite crystal clear.

Rose, who loved dogs, would not have a word said against Astrid as the cause of her fractured leg. Not only was the creature her final remembrance from Hector, but, as Rose announced to one and all, she gave great sums each year to the animal shelter. Rose blamed her fall on Clint, the bartender at the Club, whom she claimed made the Bloody Marys entirely too strong, especially for a funeral lunch. She told Madge White she intended doing something about it, like making a complaint to the house committee about Clint. Rose had had it in for Clint ever since it had been repeated to her that he had called her Old Rosie, during a previous mishap, when she dislocated her shoulder, and he had carried her to the ambulance.

When Madge White repeated the story to Pauline Mendelson, Pauline asked, "Why in the world would Rose have had the dog at her lunch at the Los Angeles Country Club in the first place?"

"Wearing a black mourning bow, if you please," said Madge. Pauline laughed. Like all Rose Cliveden's friends, Pauline was both amused and exasperated by Rose's behavior.

"That Astrid is a mean little dog," said Pauline. "You wouldn't believe the way she attacked Kippie after Camilla brought her up here to give to Rose right after Hector died. None of us could believe it. She made a beeline for him when he came up from the tennis court and bit off the tip of his forefinger, right up to here. There was blood everywhere."

Then Pauline remembered that Madge White would have no sympathy for Kippie, no matter how much of his forefinger Astrid had bitten off. Although Madge was one of her best friends, she never mentioned Kippie to her, ever since, years earlier, when they were both fourteen, Kippie had gotten Madge's daughter, little Madgie, pregnant.

"Anyway," said Madge, changing the subject, "Rose gave the dog away already."

"No!"

"She gave it to Faye Converse. Faye always takes in stray dogs."

Pauline returned the conversation to Rose—poor Rose, as they had all started to call her—whose drinking had begun to worry all her friends. "She's getting worse and worse," said Pauline.

Of course, Rose was in deep mourning for her lifelong friend, but her friends knew that if Hector hadn't died, there would have been another reason for her to give as an excuse for her self-indulgence with spirits. Even before Hector died, Rose had said to Pauline, "Oh, what difference does it make if I smoke too much, or drink too much? I'm a sixty-year-old woman, and no gentleman wants to fuck me anymore."

"Oh, Rose," Pauline had said at the time, not knowing how to deal with the statement. Rose, who liked men, constantly bragged that she had once been to bed with President Kennedy, in the White House, in the Lincoln Bedroom, but some of her friends didn't believe her. She had been married three times and divorced three times. With Rose's husbands, one day they just weren't there anymore. There was never a scandal, and never a blow-up, at least publicly. "Where's Bakie?" "Where's Ozzie?" "Where's Fiske?" people had asked about her first, second, and third husbands, after she turned up at several parties alone, and she always answered, quite calmly, "Out of town." And then people would hear, not long after, that a quiet and quick divorce had taken place, usually in a Caribbean country. The things that made divorces long and drawn-out affairs, custody and alimony, never figured in Rose's divorces, because in each case the money was hers to begin with, and her only child, a daughter from her first marriage, whom some people say had had a lobotomy, was in what Rose always referred to as "a home."

She had taken to talking endlessly on the telephone, recounting every detail of every lunch and dinner party she attended, and it was impossible to get rid of her, no matter how hard her listener tried to hang up.

"There I was seated between two divine men. Of course, they were pansies, but at my age, what does it matter? *Such* good conversation! I mean, I'm certainly no intellectual, although I do like to read a good book and see a good play, and these two were divine, absolutely divine, so full of fun and mischief. Oh, how we laughed and laughed."

"I must go, Rose," said Pauline, on the other end of the line, but Rose seemed not to hear.

"Madge White was there," Rose continued. "Poor Madge, in that same dark blue polka dot dress. Don't you hate that dress? I think I can't look at it again. Do you think she'd be hurt if I sent her over some of my old clothes? She could have them let out. She's putting on weight, have you noticed?"

"Rose, darling, I must go, really. Jules has come home," said Pauline, but Rose seemed not to hear. Pauline blew a kiss to Jules, pointed to the telephone, mouthed the word "Rose," and rolled her eyes. Jules smiled. He walked to the bar table that had been set up by Dudley and poured two glasses of wine. It was their time of day to be together.

"Poor as church mice, the Whites," said Rose. "But Madge never lets on, that's what I like about her. Works like a slave in her real estate office and completely supports that husband of hers, who could never make a nickel. He's a big load of snow, Ralph White, if you ask me. The only deduction I could take on my income tax last year was on one of his stock tips. And that little Madgie's such a tramp, you know. Lives with who knows what. A Korean, or something."

"Rose, I'm going to hang up now," said Pauline. Jules placed Pauline's glass on the table beside her. "Jules is here. Yes, I will. I'll tell him. And he sends his love to you. Good-bye, Rose. Good-*bye*, Rose." She hung up. "Oh, God!" she said. "Spare me." She took Jules's hand and kissed it. The unmistakable aroma of another woman's most secret scent was on his fingers. Stunned, she looked up at her husband, as if he had slapped her.

Jules, unaware, asked, "How's old Rosie?"

"Oh, fine, drunk, same as ever," answered Pauline. "Let's not talk about Rose. I've had enough of Rose. She broke her leg at her lunch after Hector's funeral. Aren't you glad we didn't go?" She rose unsteadily from her chair, fearing that she was going to be sick, or faint.

"Look at the colors of the sunset, Pauline," said Jules.

"Fuck the sunset," said Pauline. Her wineglass dropped from her hand and smashed on the terrazzo floor of their sunset room. Jules, who had never heard Pauline use the word she had just used in the twenty-two years he had been married to her, stared at his wife, uncomprehending, as she ran out of the room.

WHEN PHILIP QUENNELL told Camilla Ebury that he had been to a club called Miss Garbo's and learned the name of a young man with whom Hector Paradiso left the club on the night of his death, she became silent and aloof. They were sitting in the library of her house in Bel Air. She moved away from him on the sofa. Then she picked up the remote control and flicked off the television set that had been on in the background.

"How would you even know of a place called Miss Garbo's?" she asked, finally. "I've lived here all my life and never heard of it."

"Casper Stieglitz's butler told me," said Philip. "He was there the same night and saw Hector."

"Wouldn't you know it would be somebody's butler who would have a story like that," said Camilla.

"But it's true," said Philip.

"What kind of a place is Miss Garbo's?" she asked.

"Where rich older men meet young men for hire."

"I just do not believe such a story," said Camilla, shaking her head emphatically.

"You didn't exactly think your uncle Hector was girl crazy, did you?"

"That's not funny, Philip."

"What is it you're afraid of, Camilla? That they're not going to let your daughter come out at the Las Madrinas debutante ball in ten years because her great-uncle died in a gay murder?"

"What's that tacky expression I've heard you use? Smartass, is that it? Well, don't be a smartass with me, Philip," said Camilla.

"I'm not being a smartass, Camilla, and I'm sorry if that's the way I'm coming off, but let's be practical."

"All right, let's be practical. Why do you care so damn much?" she asked. "My uncle's death has nothing whatever to do with you. You didn't even know him."

"Why do you care so damn little?" replied Philip.

Philip could see that his question had made her angry. Her face turned red, and her voice, when she spoke again, had a harsh tone that he had never heard before. "I don't care so little," she said, measuring each word. "We have been through this and through this. My uncle committed suicide."

"No, he didn't."

Camilla looked at Philip for a long time before she spoke. "I understand you called Sandy Pond at the *Tribunal*. Sandy told Jules you'd called him. They seemed to think you were acting in my behalf, so they sent me over the autopsy report. I am satisfied. There is nothing mysterious to me about my uncle's death. Now I wish you would stop minding my business and mind your own damn business."

"One thing I've noticed about your group, when the chips are down you people all stick together."

Camilla, stung, rose from the sofa where she had been seated. "I think you should get out of my house," she said.

"Ah, the classic retort of the rich girl," replied Philip. "Agree with me or get out. Well, I am getting out, Mrs. Ebury."

Camilla was unused to people who were not awed by her wealth. From the beginning, Philip had been indifferent to her money, and it had been refreshing for her. She did not want him to leave, but she could not bring herself to say it. Orin, her late husband, who was the father of her child, always did everything she wanted him to do, like a bought-and-paid-for-husband should do, but Philip was different. She knew he would leave her if she did not stop him, because he was in no way dependent on her. But she remained silent and walked out of the library and started up the stairs to her bedroom above.

Philip followed her to the hall and looked up at her as she ascended the stairs. "Jules Mendelson is trying to tell us that black is white, and because he is so rich and apparently so powerful, most people—but not me—seem to be believing him, at least publicly. I just happen to be a nonbeliever in a social system where someone has the power to pick up a telephone and call a newspaper and say, 'Don't print this story,' and then call the police and say, 'Don't solve this murder.' I realize that the people in your set don't have a problem with that, but I do."

Camilla turned where she stood on a step near the top of the stairs, torn between the standards of her group and the strong feelings she had developed for the man who was walking out on her. "I am at heart a nonbeliever in those things too," she said.

"Good. Then act on them. So long, Camilla. You know my phone number."

"Don't you have things to pack?" she asked, wanting to detain him.

"One of the nice things about disposable razors is that there's nothing to pack when you break up with your girlfriend," he said. He walked out the front door and closed it behind him.

7204¼ CAHUENGA BOULEVARD, the home of Lonny Edge, was not an easy place to find. Bettye, Casper Stieglitz's secretary, thinking the address on Cahuenga had something to do with the documentary Philip was writing for Casper on the proliferation of drugs in the film industry, typed out the instructions on how to find the place on one of Casper's memo pads. Philip drove up Highland Avenue near the Hollywood Bowl and turned right on a small street called Odin. He went under an overpass that led onto Cahuenga Boulevard, a main thoroughfare that had once been bulldozed through a mountain. In the background, from the Hollywood Bowl, could be heard a philharmonic orchestra rehearsing the theme from *Star Wars*, for a concert under the stars that was scheduled to take place that evening. On each side of Cahuenga Boulevard, bungalow dwellings and low-income housing, three- and four-story beige and pink apartment buildings built in the fifties, hugged the mountainsides above. The address numbers at street level for the dwellings above had been vandalized or backed into by vehicles. Occasionally, there was a number intact, in decals stuck on a board with an arrow pointing upward.

When Philip saw a board with a number in the high six thousands, he found a space, parked his car, and sought out Lonny Edge's address on foot. The sidewalk was cracked and littered with refuse— beer bottles, used syringes, used condoms—that homeless people had simply dropped when they searched the trash bins for refundable soda pop cans.

At 7200 Cahuenga Boulevard, there was a wooden stairway in rickety condition, wide enough for only one person to walk at a time. Fifty-five steps above, Philip came onto a courtyard around which were several dozen tiny bungalows of a regional style built in Hollywood in the thirties. Purple bougainvillea bloomed in great profusion, weedlike and untended, covering the roofs of most of the bungalows. In the center of the courtyard was a fountain, its sides cracked and broken, that appeared not to have been used for years. On the ledge lay a half-eaten grapefruit with a plastic spoon and a cardboard container of coffee that appeared to have been abandoned in haste, as if the late breakfaster had been called away to the telephone and forgotten to return.

The door of 7204¼ was open, but the screen door in front of it was closed. The music from the philharmonic rehearsal at the Hollywood Bowl faintly filled the air. A Strauss waltz now, it stopped in the middle of a passage and then started again, repeating the same passage. Philip found the doorbell, but it had been painted over and didn't work. "Hello," he called out, knocking on the frame of the screen door at the same time.

"Hey, you're early, Cyril," came the reply from inside.

Philip, confused, knocked again.

"Door's open," called out the voice again. "I'll take a quick shower. You're early, man. I wasn't expecting you until four, for chrissake."

Philip could hear the sound of the shower starting. He opened the screen door and walked into the small living room of the bungalow. It was sloppy but not dirty. Clothes were scattered on the floor. A black jockstrap hung on a wall light fixture. The furniture was the furniture of a furnished apartment of the period of the bungalow, serviceable but run-down. An open beer bottle had been placed on top of what appeared to be a manuscript in haphazard disarray on a painted wooden table.

"Make yourself comfortable, Cyril," called out the voice from the bathroom over the shower sounds. "The gin's in the kitchen and the ice is in the trays."

Philip, uncomfortable despite being told to make himself comfortable, sat on a kitchen chair that had been pulled up to the painted table. He had arrived without calling first, because Lonny Edge's telephone number was not listed, and he realized that Lonny was expecting a visitor. The telephone rang. It was picked up on the first ring by an answering machine.

"*I can't come to the phone now. Leave your name and number, even if you think I already have it, and the time that you called, and I will get back to you as soon as possible. Wait for the beep.*"

"*Hi, Lonny. It's Ina Rae. How they hangin', babe? Listen, I got us a gig, a four-way at my sugar daddy's on Sunday night, late. Big bucks. You, me, and Darlene. Remember Darlene? You met her at my place? Blond hair. Loves to rim. Bring your own condoms. Joke,*"

Lonny. *Gimme a call, doll. Love ya. And you know the fucking number. Bye."*

Philip watched the answering machine as Ina Rae left her message.
How many Ina Raes could there be? he wondered. She had to be the
same Ina Rae who had forgotten her dildos at Casper Stieglitz's and
worn the T-shirt that said "Warning, I Scream When I Come."

The open bottle emitted the strong aroma of beer, and Philip
picked it up and moved it away from the area of his scent. From
habit, he turned over the top page of the manuscript, wondering if
Lonny Edge, the pornographic video star, might be penning his memoirs. The page was wet from the bottle of beer sitting on it. "Chapter
Four" was typed at the top. He started casually to read. To his astonishment, the prose style was instantly familiar to him. He felt he knew
who the author was, and it was certainly not Lonny Edge. Prior to
the accident that had caused him to drop out of Princeton before his
graduation, he had been writing his senior thesis on the work of the
novelist Basil Plant, who had died in Los Angeles a few years earlier
from an overdose of pills while drunk.

Basil Plant always claimed that *Candles at Lunch*, his long-antici-
pated novel, was finished, although his detractors, of whom there
were many, said that his much-publicized writer's block was a
permanent condition, brought on by drink and drugs, and that his
writing career was over. Three chapters of *Candles at Lunch* were
published in *Monsieur* magazine, causing a scandal that resulted in
Basil's being ostracized by the very people he wrote about. The rest
of the book was never forthcoming, although Basil always assured his
publisher that the book was finished and would be turned in when he
had completed the final refinements. When he died, the manuscript
could never be found, and the first three chapters were ultimately
published as a famous unfinished novel. Philip read:

"I'm looking for a Mr. Burns, a Mr. D. F. Burns? Am I speaking with that
gentleman?"

"You could be and then again you could not be," answered Burnsie.

"That's you, Mr. Burns, I just know. I absolutely know."

"You're from the South, ma'am?" asked Burnsie.

"You are too, I just know."

"With whom am I speaking?" asked Burnsie.

"My friend Kate McDaniels tells me you are a scream, an absolute
scream, and that we should meet."

"Mrs. McDaniels and I are not on good terms, ma'am. In fact, Mrs.

McDaniels fired me from her employ sometime back and has left me in rather embarrassing straits, which is the reason you have tracked me down at such a down-at-the-heel residence as the Yucca Flats Arms in the wrong part of Hollywood. Now, who did you not tell me you are?"

"I'm your fairy godmother."

"Hmmmm," said Burnsie.

"What I have here in my hand for you, Mr. Burns, is an invitation from Kate McDaniels to meet her tonight at the Bel Air Hotel and take her to a party in the Upstairs Room at the Bistro in Beverly Hills."

So fascinated was Philip Quennell by what he was reading that he did not hear the shower in the bathroom turn off. He realized that Basil Plant's manuscript could never be found because it was sitting in the bungalow of a hustler and pornography star on Cahuenga Boulevard in Los Angeles, who had also gone home from Miss Garbo's with Hector Paradiso on the night he was murdered. He did not hear the sounds of Lonny Edge singing "Singin' in the Rain" as he dried himself off either. So he was totally unprepared when Lonny danced into the room, completely naked, and sang "Da-daaaa," in the manner of Gene Kelly.

The two young men looked at each other in astonishment.

"Holy fucking shit," said Lonny.

"Apparently I am not whom you were expecting," said Philip, at the same time.

"You can say that again," answered Lonny. "I thought you were Cyril Rathbone." He grabbed his wet towel from the hook on the bathroom door and wrapped it around his waist.

"I'm Philip Quennell," said Philip. He held out his hand. "I got your address from Zane, the bartender at Miss Garbo's. I would have called first, but he didn't give me your telephone number, and it's not listed."

Lonny looked at Philip appreciatively with wanton, slightly blood-shot eyes, and smiled. "Welcome. Any friend of Zane's, et cetera, et cetera. I mean, I wish I'd known in advance. I've got another trick at four, so we'll have to be quick, or we can set it for tomorrow. The thing is, Cyril's a regular, every Thursday at four, and a fussy one, very precise, gets kind of bitchy if I'm late, so I can't put him off, because it's like, you know, regular income."

Philip was at a loss for words. "Listen, why don't you get dressed so we can talk until your friend comes."

"I'm not cold," said Lonny. He retied the towel around his middle and walked over to the table where Philip had been reading to put the pages back in order.

For a moment, Philip's interest was divided between the manuscript and the reason he had come in the first place. "I suppose you think it's odd that I've come here," he said, trying to get into his subject.

"My God, how come you're paying for it, a good-looking guy like you?" asked Lonny, as he took Philip in. "Oh, I got it. I bet I have this one figured out right. You're married, right? And your wife's having a baby, right? And you're horny, right? Well, you've come to the right house, Cyril Rathbone or no Cyril Rathbone."

Philip spoke quietly. "No. I'm not here for what you think I'm here for, Lonny."

Lonny, suddenly suspicious, walked back to the bathroom and took a terry cloth robe off a hook on the bathroom door. He put it on. On the pocket of the robe was written in green THE BEVERLY HILLS HOTEL.

"What gives?" he asked. "What do you mean? How come you walked into my house like this? This is my private property."

"I wanted to ask you a couple of questions."

"You a cop?"

"No."

"A reporter?"

"No."

"What then?"

Philip did not reply. The questions were not unreasonable. What was he? he wondered. Not a cop. Or a reporter. He didn't know how to explain himself. Lonny Edge was not what he'd expected the killer of Hector Paradiso to be.

"I have curiosity about the death of Hector Paradiso," he said finally.

Lonny, frightened, swallowed. "What the fuck would I know about the death of Hector Paradiso?"

"You were with him when he left Miss Garbo's on the night he died," said Philip.

"Who says?"

"Several people. Zane among them."

"And what are you exactly to Hector Paradiso? Family? Lawyer? What?" asked Lonny.

Again Philip did not immediately answer. He was nothing to Hector Paradiso. He had seen him only twice in his life. Once at Pauline Mendelson's party, dancing the night away, without a care in the world, and a few hours later, lying dead in the library of his house with five bullets in him. He could not even answer, "I am the lover of Hector Paradiso's niece," because he was no longer the lover of Hector Paradiso's niece, and Hector Paradiso's niece seemed as willing as everyone else to believe the theory put forth by Jules Mendelson that he had died a suicide, despite all evidence to the contrary.

"I believe he was murdered," Philip said.

"And you think I did it?"

"I didn't say that."

"Then why are you here?"

"I don't know why I'm here," said Philip, quietly. "I just wanted to see what you looked like, and you're not at all what I thought you'd look like."

For a moment the two men stood in silence and appraised each other.

"What's your name again?" asked Lonny.

"Quennell. Philip Quennell."

"Look, I hit him a bit, because he wanted me to hit him a bit. I slapped him around with the soles of his black patent leather dancing pumps, because that's what he liked me to do to him, and that's how he got his rocks off. And I strapped him with a belt, but that's as far as it went. You know those rich guys? They've got everything in the world, but they hate themselves. And they like someone from the lower orders, like me, to tell them they're shit, and less. Do you know guys like that?"

Philip, who didn't know guys like that, nodded as if he did. "There was no fight, about money or anything?"

Lonny nodded his head. "Yeah, we had words about money. He paid me by check. I don't take checks. This is a strictly cash business, even with my regulars, like Cyril."

"So how did he pay you?"

Lonny shrugged. "By check. He said that was the arrangement he made with Manning Einsdorf. I didn't know he was dead until I got a call from Manning the next day. I swear to God."

"Did you fight over the gun?" asked Philip.

"There was no gun, I swear to God."

"The police didn't question you then?"

"No."

"Did someone called Jules Mendelson question you?"

Lonny stared at Philip. There were footsteps outside the screen door. "Hello-oo," came a voice from outside.

"Jesuschrist, it's Cyril," said Lonny.

"Hello-oo," said Cyril Rathbone again, knocking on the screen door at the same time.

"Come on in, Cyril," said Lonny.

"I brought you some cupcakes," said Cyril, walking into the room with a bakery box in his hand. He spoke in a frothy English voice. Cyril Rathbone was forty, dressed in a double-breasted seersucker suit, with a white shirt and pink tie. On his head was a stiff straw hat worn at a rakish angle.

"This is Cyril. Meet my friend, uh, Phil Quin," said Lonny, nervously making introductions.

Philip nodded to Cyril Rathbone, who turned away. He appeared troubled by an unwelcome stain he discovered on his pink tie.

"Damn," he said.

"What's the matter, Cyril?" asked Lonny.

He pointed to his tie. "Mayonnaise," he said. "Do you have any club soda?"

"I was just leaving," said Philip.

He walked to the door.

"The gin's in the kitchen, Cyril," said Lonny. "Ice is in the tray. Make yourself a drink."

Lonny followed Philip to the door, and the two men walked outside.

"This is my four o'clock appointment," said Lonny.

"I gather."

"Cyril doesn't know I was with Hector on the night he died. They were great friends. He wouldn't have liked it that I tricked with Hector. I don't want him to know."

"I'm not going to tell him," said Philip. "Was the houseboy there that night? Anyone like that?"

"Only that fucking little dog, Astrid," said Lonny.

"You didn't answer me about Jules Mendelson before," said Philip. Lonny paused. "Jules who?"

A voice called out from another bungalow. "Hey, Lonny, you left your grapefruit and your coffee container on the fountain this morning, and the super's pissed off."

"All right, all right, I'll pick it up," Lonny called back.

"He says you're turning the place into a pigsty."

"Jesuschrist," said Lonny irritably. He walked over to the fountain and picked up the remnants of his breakfast. "I gotta go."

Philip nodded and started to walk off. Then he stopped and looked back. "How well did you know Basil Plant?"

"Basil Plant?" asked Lonny, surprised.

"Yes. How well did you know him?"

"I knew Basil pretty well," said Lonny.

"Where did you get that manuscript on your table?"

"That's a long story," said Lonny.

"I'd like to hear," said Philip.

"Stole it from him one night when he was drunk and belligerent. Why?"

"He didn't ever ask you about it later?"

"He didn't remember I took it. And then he died."

"And you never showed it to Cyril Rathbone?" asked Philip.

"Cyril comes here for one thing and one thing only. We don't talk much."

"That manuscript's worth a lot of money, if it's what I think it is," said Philip.

"Really?" He seemed interested.

"I'm at the Chateau Marmont, if you ever want to talk about it."

"Sure. Sorry you're straight. I wouldn't have charged you."

Philip laughed. "Oh," he said, snapping his fingers, as if remembering something.

"What?"

"Ina Rae called when you were in the shower. She wants you for a four-way on Sunday night, late."

Philip walked across the patio to the wooden stairway that led to the sidewalk below and started down.

"I'll tell you one thing," called out Lonny, from the top of the stairs to the retreating figure.

"What's that?" answered Philip.

"I wasn't the only gentleman caller on Hector Paradiso that night," said Lonny.

Philip stared up at him and then started to reclimb the stairs, but

Lonny held up his hand. "Not now, fella. I got a customer waiting. My rent's due."

WHEN PHILIP OPENED the door of his room at the Chateau Marmont, he was surprised to see the door to the balcony that looked down on Sunset Boulevard open. For a moment he thought he had been robbed, or was even in the process of being robbed. Slowly, without getting in the view of the balcony door, he edged his way along the wall toward it and, reaching it, slammed it shut and bolted it. Instantly a woman's face appeared on the other side. It was Camilla Ebury. They stared at each other through the glass for a moment. Then Philip unbolted the door and opened it. Camilla walked into the room.

"I thought it was about time I saw where you lived," she said. She looked at him shyly, as if she were unsure of how he would receive her.

He smiled at her. "Am I glad to see you," he said. "I thought you were a burglar."

"No. Just a lady looking for a guy she missed." She was embarrassed by her straightforwardness.

"I am deeply touched. I hated leaving your house like that."

"I couldn't bear it that you walked out on me," she said. "I didn't realize how incredibly fond of you I was. Oh, I mean I did realize it. I've realized it ever since we met, and I didn't want you to leave me." Camilla seemed close to tears.

Philip walked over to her and took her in his arms. "I'm glad you're here," he said. He held her very tight for several moments and then looked at her, touching her face before he kissed her. It was less a kiss of sexual desire than a kiss of the first stirrings of love.

"I have to tell you something, so there're no misunderstandings between us," said Philip. He stepped back from her and looked at her. "I went to see Lonny Edge."

"Who's Lonny Edge?"

"The guy from Miss Garbo's I heard went home with Hector."

She nodded. "I assumed that's where you went. Was he awful?"

"Not awful at all. A bit dim, perhaps. But not awful."

"Well, tell me. I came after you, didn't I? I want to hear. I want to know. Everything."

"He acts in porn videos and is apparently quite a star in that field."

"Good God. He didn't show you his videos, did he?"

"No."

"Did he leave Miss Garbo's with my uncle?"

"Yes."

"Well, what happened?"

"Something odd."

"What?"

"I don't think he's the one who killed your uncle."

## Flo's Tape #12

"As you know, I always had aspirations to be an actress, but I'd never done much about it, except get my pictures taken for my portfolio. So, after I got my house on Azelia Way in order, I had nothing but time on my hands, and I thought now or never. I didn't know where to start even, and I certainly wasn't going to mention it to Jules because he would have come up with some reason for me not to. Oddly enough, Glyceria, of all people, had an important show business contact, and it wasn't Faye Converse. Her sister was the maid for a casting director at Colossus Pictures, and she arranged for me to meet the casting director, and the casting director sent me up for a reading for a leading part in a miniseries, in the event that they went with an unknown. The part was a wrong-side-of-the-tracks girl who marries into high society and then shoots her husband. The twist is that his mother, who hates her, stands behind her, but you don't need to know the damn plot.

"Well, I got all dolled up. Pooky did my hair, and Blanchette did my nails, and I walked into that office like I owned the world. I talked in my new fancy voice, like I'd once heard Pauline Mendelson talk, and Madge White, and Camilla Ebury. I was great in the meeting, being introduced to the producers and the director, chatting with them and making them laugh. They said incredible things about me, like I could be the new Maureen O'Hara, or Rhonda Fleming, or Arlene Dahl, because of the red hair. Everything was going great. And then they asked me to read. I panicked. I just clammed up. I couldn't do it. I stumbled over the lines, and even mispronounced some of the words. I know I turned beet red, and that kind of red and red hair don't match. I asked if I could start over again, and they said sure, but I knew by the way they said sure that I'd already lost the part.

"I never told Jules about it. The casting director that Glyceria's sister worked for said he'd call me the next time something came up, but I never heard from him again. Anyway, they gave the part to Ann-Margret. I guess they had to go with a name."

# 13

"WHO IS THIS WOMAN?" asked the interior decorator Nellie Potts about her latest client. Nellie was having lunch at the Ivy on Robertson Boulevard with the fashionable florist, Petra von Kant, whose shop was nearby.

"I have my suspicions," answered Petra, tapping her glass and indicating to the waiter that she would like another Bloody Mary.

"She's spending forty thousand dollars for new curtains in a rented house, not to mention knocking down a wall to have her dressing room and closets made bigger," said Nellie.

"All those Chanel suits," said Petra, who had started to arrange the flowers of the lady under discussion.

"But imagine spending all that money when she only has a three-year lease on that house."

"That's not your worry."

"She doesn't have the look of inherited money."

"Heavens, no."

"And yet she doesn't seem to work."

"Or do much of anything," said Petra. "She never stops talking. She wants to hear what parties I'm doing the flowers for and what flowers my clients have ordered, and even how much everything costs."

"She wants to know all about my clients too. She won't make a decision about anything until I tell her that someone very social she's read about in Cyril Rathbone's column has exactly the same sofa, or exactly the same fabric, and then she wants it. I kind of like her though."

"I do too."

"She must be kept by someone very very rich," said Nellie.

"For sure," replied Petra.

"Does she pay her bills?"

"On the dot. Doesn't even wait until the first of the month."

WITHOUT THE BLOND WIG, blue eye shadow, and blue contact lenses she wore in her secret nightclub life as Marvene McQueen,

160

Hortense Madden, the much-feared literary critic of *Mulholland* magazine, reverted to her real life, heaping her contempt on commercial success. Her hair was pulled back in a spinster bun, and she wore glasses so thick they magnified her eyes. Her mouth was set in a puckered expression to conceal her protruding teeth, an expression that she did not relax even when chewing her omnipresent chlorophyll gum, which turned her tongue green.

There was that day a further deepening of the perpetual look of discontent on her face. Unhappiness oozed from her every pore. Not even the devastating review she had just completed of the latest work of a popular novelist—which would most certainly wound the author, as it was intended to do, so personal had she made it—could erase her troubled look, as her devastating reviews often did, or bring momentary surcease to her inner torments.

In her hand was a letter of rejection, made more painful by the fact that it was a form letter, from a disc jockey on an FM station, along with the tape of sad songs of lost love that she had so painstakingly recorded at her own expense. The disc jockey, who was named Derrick Lafferty, worshiped at the shrine of what he called "the long-gone enchantresses of the supper-club circuit," like Libby Holman, Mabel Mercer, Spivvy, and Bricktop, but he had found her tape unfit to be played on his program, even though she sang the same songs as the ladies he venerated. The rejection of her artistry was more painful than she could have imagined.

In the next office, through the paper-thin walls, she could hear Cyril Rathbone, the gossip columnist for *Mulholland,* laughing and chatting on the telephone, accepting invitations, getting tips for his column, and arranging lunch dates at fashionable restaurants. Hortense Madden loathed Cyril Rathbone, whom she considered a philistine.

Just as she was about to pick up her telephone and order a sandwich to be sent in for another lunch alone at her desk, her telephone rang. She allowed her bad mood to permeate her "Hello," which sounded like the bark of an angry dog.

"Hortense?" asked the voice on the other end.

"Who is it?" she replied, with no lessening of hostility.

"Casper Stieglitz."

"Oh, hello, Casper."

"What the hell's the matter with you?"

"Nothing is the matter with me."

"You scared the shit out of me."

Hortense hated that expression. "I'm working, that's all."

"Who are you crucifying today?"

She ignored his question. "Is there a purpose to this call, Casper?"

"I'm calling to invite you to dinner on Sunday night. A little party at my place."

Like everyone else in town, Hortense knew that Casper Stieglitz was on the skids and no longer held in high regard, and she was about to decline.

"Jules and Pauline Mendelson are coming, and a few others," said Casper, not waiting for her reply. There was no mistaking the note of elation in Casper's voice as he dropped the Mendelson names.

Hortense was stunned. She could not believe that she was being asked to a party where the Jules Mendelsons would be. In the next office she could hear the cackling laugh of Cyril Rathbone, as he received some bit of gossip about someone. She knew how Cyril longed to get to know Pauline Mendelson, and she knew that Pauline Mendelson resisted him and never invited him to cover her parties. The prospect of letting Cyril know of her invitation was so delicious to her that, for the first time since the mail had arrived with her letter of rejection from Derrick Lafferty, she felt lighthearted.

"Let me check my book, Casper," she said. She didn't have to check her book, because she had no plans whatsoever, except for her singing engagement at Miss Garbo's, but she allowed a sufficient time to go by before she said, "When is it?"

"Sunday," said Casper.

"I'll have to juggle, but I can," said Hortense.

"Eight o'clock. We'll be running a film after dinner."

"Marvelous, Casper."

FLO MARCH lay on a brand-new lounge chair by her pool, part of a set of brand-new poolside furniture that Nellie Potts, her interior decorator, had told her was the same outdoor furniture that Pearl Silver had at her pool. Flo had taken the bra of her bathing suit off. She lay so that her back and shoulders would get the late afternoon rays, when the power of the sun had lessened a bit. On the table by her side was a timer set to ring after twenty minutes, which her trainer

and aerobics teacher told her was the limit. There was also a white
telephone on a long extension cord in case Jules called, which she
knew he certainly would, as well as an ice bucket, several cans of Diet
Coke, suntan lotion, a copy of the latest issue of *Mulholland* open to
Cyril Rathbone's column, her gold cigarette case with FLO written on
it in sapphires, her matching gold lighter, and her latest purchase, a
pair of binoculars. Flo, who was more lonely than she would ever
admit, had taken to watching her neighbors farther up the hills on
Azelia Way.

She was somewhere between being asleep and awake when the
sound of a small dog crying startled her. Opening her eyes, she removed her large dark glasses and saw staring up at her a white West
Highland terrier.

"Why, he*llo*," Flo said to the dog. "What in the world are you doing
here? Who do you belong to?" She clapped her hands, and the dog
hopped up on the lounge chair with her. "What a sweet little doggie
you are. Are you lost?" She sat up and put back on the bra of her
bathing suit. "Are you thirsty? Do you want some water?" she asked.
She got up and went over to the side of the house, where her new
Mexican gardener had neatly rolled up a garden hose. She ran some
water into the red clay saucer of one of the potted geranium plants
that the gardener had placed around her terrace. "Here's some
water," she called out to the dog. When the dog came over to where
she was, Flo sat down on a chair and watched it while it drank.
Finished, the dog jumped up on Flo's lap again, and she held it to
her, as if it were a baby she was burping. "Oh, you sweet little thing,"
she said. She sat there with the dog, feeling content.

"Par'me, ma'am," came a voice through the tall hedges separating
Flo's house from her neighbor's house. For a moment, Flo did not
answer, never having been called ma'am before, although she listened.

"Ma'am?" The voice repeated the word.

"Are you calling me?" called out Flo, although she could not see
anyone through the thick hedge.

"Have you seen our little dog?"

"Why, yes, she's here," said Flo.

"You mind if I come 'round by the front way and pick her up,
ma'am? Miss Converse is going to be upset with me if she runs away
again. Supposed to be my job to mind her, but I can't run this house

for Miss Converse and keep my eye on that little Astrid at the same time."

"No, no, come around," said Flo. She rose from her chair and walked back to where she had been lying on the lounge chair and put on her terry cloth robe from Porthault, which matched her Porthault pool towels.

"There you are, you naughty little dog," said the maid from next door when she came around to the garden from the front of the house. "I'm sorry she's been botherin' you, ma'am."

"Oh, no, don't scold her. She hasn't been bothering me at all. She's a wonderful little dog, so friendly, aren't you, my darling? What did you say her name was?"

"Astrid," said the maid.

"What a strange name for a dog," said Flo.

"Named after some ice skating star, who died, something like that. I got enough on my mind without having to remember a dog's history. Anyway, Miss Converse, who's my boss, got her from Mrs. Rose Cliveden, the socialite, after Mrs. Cliveden broke her leg falling over Astrid at the funeral lunch, right after she inherited her from Hector Paradiso, who shot himself five times, although they say it was a suicide. Or something like that. I can't keep it all straight with those people." The maid shook her head in an exasperated fashion.

Flo looked at her, fascinated.

"Do you mean this was Hector Paradiso's dog?" she asked.

"Be careful of her, because she bit off some young man's finger too," said the maid. "I forgot his name."

"But she's the sweetest little dog I ever saw. I can't believe she'd ever bite anyone," said Flo. She held the dog in her arms. "What's your name?" she asked.

"Glyceria, ma'am. I'm sorry we're botherin' you like this."

"Oh, no, you're not bothering me," said Flo quickly. Flo had not spoken to anyone, except Jules, since Nellie Potts had been there two days earlier to supervise the hanging of the new forty-thousand-dollar curtains. "Could I get you a drink?" she asked Glyceria, not wanting her to leave.

"A drink? Oh, no, ma'am," said Glyceria.

"I didn't actually mean a *drink* drink. I meant, you know, a Diet Coke, or an ice tea, or something like that."

"Well, maybe an ice tea would be nice, only I won't be able to hear

Miss Converse's telephone if it rings, and she won't like that," said Glyceria.

"Which Miss Converse is that?" asked Flo, cautiously.

"Why, Miss *Faye* Converse, of course," said Glyceria.

"Faye Converse?" cried out Flo. She could hardly contain herself. "The movie star? Faye Converse lives right next door to me beyond that hedge?"

"You didn't know that? You didn't notice the tour bus going by every day?"

"No. No, I didn't. I can't get over it. Faye Converse is my next-door neighbor. I can hardly believe it."

She rushed into the house, singing happily, to open a can of iced tea for Faye Converse's maid. "You can leave little Astrid here any time," she called out. "I'll take care of her if you're busy. All my life I wanted to have a dog."

JULES MENDELSON had seen Astrid for the first time when he went to Hector Paradiso's house after receiving the early morning telephone call telling him that Hector was dead. He did not share that information with Flo, nor did he share Flo's enthusiasm for Astrid, and the little dog, in turn, developed an instant antipathy to Jules. Although Astrid did not bite Jules, as she had bitten Kippie, she barked at him in such an angry fashion when he came to see Flo that Jules became enraged, in a way that Flo had never seen him before.

"I come up here to relax. What I do not need is that angry little shit barking at me like that," said Jules, staring at the dog and breathing heavily.

"She's Faye Converse's dog, Jules. She's just here visiting," said Flo, as if identifying its illustrious owner would lessen the anger of both her lover and the dog. Flo loved being able to use Faye Converse's name in her conversation, now that she had discovered that Faye was her next-door neighbor. It didn't matter to her that the great star wouldn't know who she was in return. "Come up here, you naughty dog, and stop all that barking," Flo said to Astrid, patting a place beside her on her newly upholstered sofa, which Nellie Potts told her was the same gray satin that Rose Cliveden used in her drawing room.

"Get her out of here," said Jules fiercely, pointing to little Astrid. "I don't want that dog around."

After that, as soon as Flo heard Jules's car in the driveway each afternoon, she sent Astrid back through the hole in the hedges, fearing that Jules would forbid her to see Astrid altogether. The little dog had become an important part of Flo's life. Each morning, after she came back from her AA meeting, she whistled what she called her Astrid whistle, and Astrid made her way through the hole in the hedges that separated her property from Faye Converse's property and came to call. The dog could not get enough loving, and Flo never tired of holding her, petting her, and talking to her. She purchased a dog's dish and bought all sorts of treats for her. She loved to break cookies in half and toss them in the air for Astrid to catch.

Often Glyceria came around by the front way to have a glass of iced tea or a cup of coffee, depending on the weather, and a little conversation. Flo, hungry for news of her celebrated neighbor, listened, rapt, to the tidbits of information that Glyceria told her about Faye Converse. Sometimes at night, when she was alone, Flo trained her binoculars on Faye Converse's house and watched the great star, when she was in the city, as she held forth with a constant stream of guests. Flo March longed to mix in the world of famous and fashionable people, but she came to understand that there was nowhere she fit in, except as Jules Mendelson's secret mistress.

## Flo's Tape #13

"*I also took up tennis. I didn't grow up in the kind of background where you play golf and tennis. But there was something about tennis that I always thought was kind of classy. And I liked the outfits, the short shorts and the hats with a visor. So I took lessons at the Beverly Hills Hotel three mornings a week. And guess what? I was pretty good. The pro at the hotel told me he never had a pupil who picked up the game as fast as I did.*

"*When Faye Converse went on location to make her comeback picture, Glyceria said she didn't think there would be any problem in my using Faye's court, as it was just sitting there. It would have been like having my own tennis court. The only problem was, I didn't have anybody to play with.*"

# 14

IT WOULD HAVE BEEN incomprehensible for Hector Paradiso ever to imagine that he had not been remembered, as he was in his time such a vivid figure, always present, always talked about, and both liked and disliked in more or less equal proportions. But it was a fact that he soon faded from memory after his expiration, leaving nothing behind to remind people of him: no heirs, as he had never married; no business, as he had never seriously worked; and no family except his niece.

Rose Cliveden, in bed, ill, never stopped talking on the telephone; it was impossible to get her off. Only the sounds of ice cubes against her wineglass competed with her monologues. "The other day someone said to me, 'Do you remember Hector Paradiso?' Good heavens! Imagine if darling Hector had ever heard anyone ask, 'Do you remember Hector Paradiso?' Are you listening, Camilla?"

"Yes, I'm listening, Rose," answered Camilla.

"Then say something."

"I'll repeat what I said five minutes ago, Rose. I have to hang up now."

Philip kissed Camilla good-bye.

"I wish I could go with you," said Camilla.

"Not a good idea," said Philip.

"I'd just like to see what a porn star looks like," said Camilla.

"My, my, how you've changed, Mrs. Ebury," said Philip.

When Lonny Edge agreed to meet Philip Quennell at the Viceroy Coffee Shop on Sunset Strip, he made only one request: he did not want to talk about Hector Paradiso, and Philip agreed. "It's that manuscript you have. Basil Plant's manuscript," said Philip. "Why don't you bring it along?"

"I'm not lettin' that manuscript outta my sight, man," said Lonny. Ever since Philip Quennell had given him the idea that it might be worth a lot of money, he had begun to look on the tattered pile of pages as a sort of nest egg. Famous fornicators in the age of AIDS were in less demand than before, and Lonny, approaching thirty, had begun to think of his future. He had removed the manuscript from the table in his front room, boxed it, and hidden it behind a stack of Lacoste shirts in the back of his closet.

Curly, who had managed the Viceroy when Flo worked there, nodded at Lonny when he entered. "Long time no see," he said.

Lonny nodded in return. "I'm lookin' for a Mr. Quennell," he said, scanning the premises with a practiced eye.

"He's waiting for you in booth number thirteen," said Curly.

"Flo's old booth," said Lonny.

"Right. I miss the redhead. She got rich, I hear."

When Lonny was seated at Philip's table, they both ordered coffee from the waitress. "Would you like some breakfast?" asked Philip.

Lonny, born poor, was not one to pass up an offer for anything free, even if he'd already eaten, which he had. "Sure," he answered. "Gimme some pancakes and eggs sunny-side up and bacon, crisp. That's all."

"You didn't bring it?"

"What?"

"The Basil Plant manuscript."

"I told you I wasn't letting it out of my sight."

"But I can't tell you if it's worth anything unless I read it," said Philip.

"I thought you read it in my house when I was taking a shower that day."

"I glanced at it for a minute and a half. I *think* it's what I think it is, a famous missing manuscript, but I have to be sure before I go out on a limb. Did you notice, are there any notations on any of the pages?"

"What's notations?"

"Notes? Insertions? Things like that. Like anything handwritten in the margins?"

Lonny shrugged. "I don't know. I never actually read the goddamn thing. What kind of money do you think it's worth if it does turn out to be what you think it is?"

"I can't tell you that. They published three chapters of it, and they could never find the rest after Basil died."

"Basil was a bad drunk. Turned mean. Rest of the time, he was the nicest guy in the world. Like approximately, what do you think it's worth?"

"I don't know. I could find out. It could be a lot, but I have to make sure it's not a hoax before I get involved."

As Philip started to explain to Lonny the complexities of identifying the missing manuscript, he looked up and saw Jules Mendelson walk into the Viceroy Coffee Shop, carrying a copy of the *Wall Street Journal*. Lonny, seated with his back to the entrance, did not see him. Philip watched Curly speak to Jules in a familiar but respectful manner and lead him to a table in the window. When he sat down, Jules spread the *Journal* out in front of him on the Formica-topped table and began to read. He did not look up to acknowledge the waitress who set a cup of coffee on the table in front of him.

"Excuse me," said Philip to Lonny when the waitress arrived with Lonny's breakfast. "I'll be right back."

"It's over there, with the orange door, by the cash register," said Lonny, pointing to the men's room.

Philip nodded and went to the men's room. When he came out a minute later, he walked over to Jules Mendelson's table.

"Mr. Mendelson," he said.

Jules looked up from his paper but did not acknowledge Philip.

"It's Philip Quennell," said Philip.

"Yes," he said, looking back at his paper in a dismissive manner. He had taken a dislike to Philip Quennell since the day the statue of the Degas ballerina had been knocked over and cracked, and he blamed Philip for the accident although it was his own anger that had caused it.

As if reading his mind, Philip said, "I'm sorry about the accident with the Degas ballerina. I wrote Mrs. Mendelson a note of apology."

"She told me," said Jules, not raising his eyes.

"This is not the sort of place I would expect to be seeing you having breakfast," said Philip.

"I'm not having breakfast. I'm having a cup of coffee," said Jules. "I come in here at this time to read my paper." He tapped the newspaper on the table in a gesture meant to dissuade Philip from staying.

"Quite a clientele this place gets," said Philip. "See that guy over there, scarfing down the hotcakes? Jeans, T-shirt, windbreaker?"

"What about him?"

"Hustler. Porn star."

Jules nodded, indicated disinterest, and looked back at his paper. "I didn't realize that was your inclination," he said, chuckling.

Philip smiled and started to move on. "You know what they say about him, don't you?"

"Of course I don't know what they say about him. I never laid eyes on the man."

"They say he's the guy who killed Hector Paradiso."

Jules smiled wearily. "Oh, that old chestnut. Hector Paradiso was a suicide, Mr. Quennell."

"No, he wasn't, Mr. Mendelson."

"You have only to check the police report."

"Hector went to a bar called Miss Garbo's after he left your party that night. It's the kind of bar where rich johns make arrangements of a financial nature to meet young companions. There are several witnesses who will tell you that Hector left Miss Garbo's in the company of that young companion. I've checked the police report. None of those facts are in it. Do you still want to tell me that Hector Paradiso went straight home from your party that night to shoot himself five times?"

"Playing sleuth may be the most important thing that ever happened in your life, Quennell, but it's a matter of absolutely no importance to me," said Jules. He slowly turned the page he was reading and continued to read the story about the release from prison after five years of the Wall Street financier Elias Renthal.

"This thing doesn't have one goddamn thing to do with my life," said Philip. "Why the hell should it matter to me whether or not they catch the killer? If I hadn't been at your house that night and gone home with Camilla Ebury and been with her when you called to say that Hector was dead and then gone with her to Hector's house to identify the body, I probably wouldn't give it another thought, because it doesn't involve me. What *I'm* interested in is why it is being covered up. Chances are it was what the supermarket tabloids refer to as a gay murder. He picked up a trick at Miss Garbo's. He took home the trick. He got into a fight with the trick, probably over money—they say he was tight—and he got killed. Not a particularly uplifting scenario, but it is not a particularly original one either. There was that big decorator in New York it happened to last year. Bertie Lightfoot? Do you remember? I'm sure Pauline knew him. And in San Francisco. The gallery owner. What was his name? Ludovic Cato, wasn't it? Same story. Stabbed to death by a mysterious stranger, all trussed up. But why the cover-up here in Los Angeles? Do you think the people in your privileged group really didn't know Hector was gay? I don't think so. Your kind of group might not have talked about it, but they knew it. Who are you all trying to protect? He had no family who might be embarrassed by such a revelation.

Only a niece, with whom I am involved, and she would now like to have it solved."

"Hey, Quennell," said Jules, looking up from his newspaper finally. His voice had turned harsh. He was not used to people who did not treat him with deference.

"Yes?"

"Read my lips, asshole. You don't know what the fuck you're talking about."

"Ah, the great art collector and philanthropist has spoken," said Philip.

The two stared at each other, and Philip moved on.

SOMETIMES, after they finished making love, Jules—still nude, still in bed—would pick up the telephone and call his office to check with Miss Maple for his messages. Twice he spoke to the President, in the White House, while lying in Flo's bed, with the telephone sitting on his chest. Once Flo heard him say, "Best to Barbara," in a matter-of-fact way, as if, as she told it later to Glyceria, it was no big deal. On this day he signaled Flo with a drinking gesture to bring him something cool to drink, without interrupting his train of thought. Flo was fascinated by the way Jules was able to conduct business involving great sums of money over the telephone. Sell this. Buy that. She felt important just hearing such large sums discussed over her telephone in her house. She grew to know that Sims Lord was Jules's lawyer and closest associate, that Reza Bulbenkian was his contact in New York, and that Miss Maple, whom Jules sometimes called Syrup, was his secretary and had been his secretary for over twenty years. It was Miss Maple, whom Flo had never met, who paid all her bills and mailed her her allowance.

Flo handed Jules a can of iced tea. "I hate canned iced tea," said Jules. "In fact, I hate drinks out of cans, period."

"Oh." Flo always felt hurt if Jules criticized the way she did things.

"Look," said Jules, taking her hand. "What's the name of that decorator you're using?"

"Nellie Potts?" asked Flo.

"Right, Nellie Potts. Tell her to call Steuben in New York. Tell her to order some decent glasses for you. Twelve of each. Water goblets, highball, old-fashioned, the red wine, the white wine, the champagne. Drinks taste better out of good glasses."

AN INCONVENIENT WOMAN

"Wow," said Flo, impressed. "Should I get them monogrammed? You know, like FM? I read somewhere that Dom Belcanto has his glasses monogrammed."

"No, no, monograms are tacky," said Jules. "And they take too long. Just order the glasses. Have them sent out by Federal Express. They'll be here in a couple of days. And then you can serve me my drinks in some decent glasses."

"I'll call Nellie later," said Flo. She was delighted when she had projects to fill up her time.

"Speaking of Nellie Potts," said Jules, reaching out behind him in the bed and grabbing a handful of Flo's new curtains. "Have you any idea how much these curtains cost?"

"Yes, I do, Jules," answered Flo.

"That's a great deal of money, Flo, for some curtains. Did you inquire first about the cost?"

"Yes, I did, Jules."

"And you didn't question such an exorbitant amount?" he asked.

Flo raised her eyebrows. "You can afford it, Jules," she said.

"That's not the point."

"Then what is the point?"

"This is a rented house. To spend forty thousand dollars for curtains in a rented house doesn't make sense. You can't take them with you when you leave, and that has-been TV star you rent this place from reaps the benefits."

"You don't have to point out to me this is a rented house, Jules. And, by the way, the renovations of my closets are going to cost you that much again," said Flo.

"I don't believe this."

"Aren't I worth it, Jules? Any time you're dissatisfied with my services, I shall be happy to make other arrangements," said Flo, grandly.

"Now, let's not get into that kind of conversation, Flo. I'm tired. I have a lot of important things on my mind."

Flo got up from the bed where she had been lying next to Jules. She picked up her terry cloth robe and put it on. "I want you to buy this house for me, Jules," she said. "Trent Muldoon's business manager said he's ready to sell."

"This is not the time to be talking about buying houses," he said. "I just told you I'm tired and that I have things on my mind."

"You keep putting it off, Jules. No time is ever the right time for

173

you. I want something in my own name. I live in a rented house. I
drive a leased car. What's going to happen to me if something happens to you? I've gotten used to living like this."

"You are going to be taken care of. Sims Lord will be making the
arrangements," said Jules.

"You know, Jules, I sit here all day waiting for you to come over. I
have no friends, except the maid next door who works for Faye Converse. I have no job. You're afraid to be seen with me in public, so I
almost never go out. I have thirty Chanel suits, and some forty-thousand-dollar curtains, and I'm about to have a couple of hundred
Steuben glasses without a monogram on them, but it's not really a
fulfilling kind of life. So, I repeat, I want something in my own
name."

"All right, all right, I'll buy you the house," he said.

"Thank you, Jules, and I want the pink slip for the car too, in my
own name."

"I better get dressed," he said, getting out of bed and reaching
around for his clothes.

"Hey, Jules, you have to lose some of that lard around your middle," said Flo. "Pauline's taking you to too many banquets. When you
bend over to tie your shoelaces, your face gets all red and you get
short of breath."

Jules was both annoyed and touched. He did not like to be reminded of his girth. He had recently been infuriated by a magazine
article that described him as a man of ample proportions. But it struck
him how different his relationship with Flo was from his relationship
with Pauline. With Pauline, he dressed and undressed in his dressing
room, as she dressed and undressed in her dressing room, and they
did not present themselves to each other until they were ready to face
the world or ready to go to bed.

Flo came over to him and put her arms around his neck. "Listen,
it doesn't bother me. The way I look at it, there's more of you to
love."

When Jules finished dressing, he walked into Flo's living room. She
was seated on her newly upholstered sofa, reading Cyril Rathbone's
gossip column in *Mulholland*. He was absurdly touched that she
moved her lips when she read.

"Oh, la," said Flo, holding out her little finger in what she assumed
to be a gesture of grandeur.

"What?" asked Jules.

" 'Pauline Mendelson is opening her orchid greenhouse for the Los Angeles garden club tour,' " she read. " 'Mrs. Mendelson, the elegant wife of Jules Mendelson, the zillionaire, has developed a rare yellow phalaenopsis orchid.' Is that how you pronounce that?"

Jules turned away. He could not deal with any overlapping of the segments of his life.

"You know, Flo, you mustn't move your lips when you read," he said.

"Did I do that?" she asked, slapping her hand over her mouth. "When I was in junior high at Blessed Sacrament, Sister Andretta, my home room teacher, used to say to me, 'Fleurette, you're moving your lips,' and all the kids in the class would laugh. I thought I got over that."

"Tomorrow I'm going to bring you over some books I think you ought to read instead of all those gossip columns."

"Not long ones, for God's sake. My lips will be exhausted."


PAULINE MENDELSON had not confronted Jules about the other woman's scent on his fingers after she had kissed his hand and smelled it. Instead, she began to observe him more carefully. There were no telltale signs, nothing so obvious as lipstick traces on handkerchiefs or collars. For the first time since they moved into Clouds twenty-two years before, their habit of meeting in the sunset room each twilight for a glass of wine before they dressed for dinner had been disrupted when Pauline failed to appear for several days following her outburst. When they drove together to and from parties, she had a sense that his mind was elsewhere, although, once having arrived at the house where they were dining, they both automatically fell into their roles of devoted husband and wife, with never a hint, to even the closest observer, of a masquerade being performed. Several times Pauline awoke at night and saw Jules lying beside her in their bed staring up at the ceiling, but she did not speak. She knew the time was at hand to go to see her father in Maine, but she made no mention of her plans.

She had grown used to her role as the wife of one of the country's most eminent figures, and she was not unmindful that there was a dearth of replacements for a man of her husband's importance, even for one of the marrying McAdoo sisters. Caution was the road she chose to follow. Jules, concerned, was aware from the attitude and the coolness of his wife that something was wrong. He even guessed that she may have heard of his involvement, although he had made every effort to keep the affair from being discussed. The very thought of dissolving such a marriage as he had with Pauline was unthinkable to Jules, even though he was in the grips of a grand passion with Flo March.

Under suspicion, facing the loss of a marriage he treasured, he still continued his afternoon visits to Azelia Way, as his ardor for Flo did not diminish for a second. His erotic longings intensified each day; he could not wait for the sight of her alert breasts and ample bush, which were more beautiful to him than her beautiful face. "Be nude," he would say to her on the car telephone so that not a moment of their time together would be wasted. He wanted more and more of her, and she always obliged. "Don't use those scents and unguents down there," he said one afternoon. "Your natural smells drive me mad." He begged her to talk dirty to him during their lovemaking, and she obliged. "Lower," he whispered in her ear once. She understood he did not mean the position of her hands on his testicles, but that he wanted her language to be even baser, and again she obliged. Afterward he said to her, "Where in the hell did you learn how to talk like that?"

She lay back in bed smoking a cigarette, looking up into space, and answered in a surprisingly harsh tone. "Don't go moral on me once you've come, Jules. It's what you begged for."

He looked at her. He knew she was right. The next day he brought her a jewel, a sapphire ring surrounded by diamonds. She was ecstatic. "Like Princess Di's," she said. "Only bigger. I used to think if I ever had a ring, a really good ring, I would love a sapphire. Did I ever tell you that, Jules? I didn't, did I? How did you know?"

"It's the color of your eyes," said Jules.

She was touched. "You are surprising, Jules. Sometimes you're so gruff and unsentimental. I didn't think you ever noticed the color of anything about me, other than my pubic hair."

Jules roared with laughter. He knew she was inferior to him, both in position and intellect, but he loved her. He loved her madly.

"I love you, Jules," she said simply.

"Really?" he asked.

She thought of what she had just said. She perhaps venerated him more than she loved him, but certainly love was present. "Really," she replied.

When he left that day, she walked him to his car. "I'm mad about this ring, Jules. I won't ever take it off. But you won't forget about the house, will you? I want to own this house."

A FEW DAYS later the two women in Jules Mendelson's life met by accident in the parking lot of Pooky's salon. Pauline Mendelson rarely went to Pooky's to have her hair done. She was one of a few very special clients for whom Pooky happily adjusted his busy schedule, going up to Clouds to do her hair in her elaborately outfitted dressing room. But on the day before Casper Stieglitz's party, which Pauline never wanted to attend, Pooky was not able to accommodate her in their usual manner on such short notice, and she drove into Beverly Hills to have her hair done at his salon. As she was parking in the lot behind the shop, a red convertible Mercedes backed into the front of her car. It was Flo March, leaving the shop after her appointment.

"I'm so sorry," said Flo, hopping out of her car and running over to Pauline's. "That was my fault. But I'm insured. Don't worry. And it's not bad. Just a dent."

Looking in the window, she realized the person whose car she had hit was Pauline Mendelson. "Oh, my God, Mrs. Mendelson," she said. "Are you all right?"

"Yes, I'm fine. I hardly felt it," said Pauline. She got out of her car and went around to look at the dent. "Don't worry about it. It was an accident." The girl looked familiar to Pauline. "Do we know each other? Have we ever met?" she asked.

"No, no, we haven't," said Flo. She had become shy and spoke very quickly. "I just know who you are. I recognized you from seeing your picture in the papers and magazines all the time. You're sure you're all right?"

"I'm fine."

"Thank you, Mrs. Mendelson." She felt only fascination for the wife of her lover.

Pauline smiled. "I love your suit," she said.

"Oh, my gosh, coming from you," said Flo, thrilled with the compliment.

Then, looking at the Chanel suit, Pauline remembered. "I know where I saw you. At Hector Paradiso's funeral. Weren't you a friend of Hector's?"

Flo began to get nervous. "Yes, I knew Hector. I have to run. Thank you for being so nice, Mrs. Mendelson."

"Tell me your name. I'll tell Jules I saw you," said Pauline.

"Good-bye, Mrs. Mendelson." She ran back to her car and jumped in. She put her key in the ignition and the car leapt forward. She was bewildered. It had never occurred to Flo March that Pauline Mendelson would be nice.

Although Pauline was in no way the sort of wife who could be bought off with a trinket, no matter how expensive the trinket, Jules made arrangements for a gift for his wife that he felt might thaw the situation between them. He had heard from Pauline's great friend, Prince Friedrich of Hesse-Darmstadt, the head of the jewelry department at Boothby's auction house in London, that a certain pair of yellow diamond earrings were coming up for auction that week, and Jules had instructed the prince to bid on them for him.

On the Sunday of Casper Steiglitz's dinner, Willi, Jules's barber, who usually arrived before sunrise to shave him, came later in the afternoon to cut his hair. Only the day before had Pauline been reluctantly induced to accompany Jules to Casper's party. "It would mean a great deal to me, Pauline," he had said. She read into his voice a need that she did not often hear. She knew that was the moment to confront him about the other woman he was seeing, but she refrained, not wanting to approach that development of their lives in such a sideways fashion. "All right, Jules," she said, simply.

"Wait till I show you what I've bought Pauline," said Jules to the barber, in a rare moment of intimacy with the man who had been shaving him daily in his house for over twenty years. He reached into the top drawer of his dressing table and took out a small velvet box. Opening it, he held out a pair of yellow canary diamond earrings, surrounded by smaller diamonds.

"Look," he said proudly. "She has been looking for earrings to match her canary diamond necklace and bracelet, and I knew these were coming up at an auction at Boothby's in London last week and had my man there bid for me."

Willi, the barber, knew nothing of canary diamonds, but he saw they were large and knew they were expensive and made the appropriate exclamations of admiration. Just then, Pauline walked into Jules's dressing room, wearing a negligee and carrying two dresses on velvet-covered hangers.

"Which of these would be more appropriate for your friends, Mr. Stieglitz and Mr. Zwillman?" she asked, holding them up for his inspection. Jules, who knew better than anyone that his wife's taste in clothes was second to no one's, was not unaware of the slight sarcasm in her tone, but he ignored it. "Hello, Willi," she said to the barber.

"Hi, Miz Mendelson," said Willi. He continued his work of cutting and trimming, but he was aware at the same time that there was a change in the dynamics of the relationship of the couple he had come to know so well. Jules Mendelson was Willi's benefactor as well as client, having advanced him the money to buy the small shop on Sunset Boulevard where he cut the hair of the leading figures in the film industry.

"I would choose that one," said Jules, pointing to one of the two. "You know, Sunday night, not too dressy, don't you think?"

"I've never been to a gangster's party on Sunday night," said Pauline. "So I wouldn't know."

"Mr. Stieglitz is a film producer," he said.

"But Mr. Zwillman is a gangster, or so says Rose Cliveden," replied Pauline. "Rose suggested a corsage."

"I have a present for you," said Jules quickly, wanting to change the subject. "Here." He handed her the velvet box.

Pauline opened the box and looked at the canary diamond earrings. "Very pretty," she said, without the sort of enthusiasm that such an extravagant gift could be expected to engender. It appeared to Jules that she was about to say something else, and he waited, looking at her in the mirror while Willi continued to cut his hair. "I saw them in the Boothby catalog Friedrich sent me. They used to belong to a Mrs. Scorpios. What time are we due at Mr. Stieglitz's?"

Jules and the barber glanced at each other in the mirror. Jules, embarrassed, shrugged.

PAULINE MENDELSON was acknowledged to be one of the most gracious hostesses in society and one of the best conversationalists anywhere, but her skills in those areas applied only when she was with the sort of people she had always known, or with the creative people she mixed in with her own friends at her parties, or with the business, banking, museum, and government officials with whom Jules was involved in his myriad activities. The group of people she expected to encounter that Sunday evening at the home of Casper Stieglitz was not her kind of group at all, and she was prepared to make no effort whatsoever.

When the Mendelsons walked into Casper Stieglitz's living room, they found a larger party than they had been led to expect. At the request of Arnie Zwillman, who exercised a control over Casper Stieglitz, Casper had enlarged his group so that it would be less conspicuous later in the evening when Arnie suggested a private conversation with Jules during the screening of the film. Pearl Silver, the widow of a prominent producer and a hostess of renown in the film colony, had been added only the day before. Ordinarily Pearl Silver would not have gone to Casper Stieglitz's house, but she agreed to come when she heard that Marty and Sylvia Lesky had also accepted. Marty Lesky, the head of Colossus Pictures, was considered by many to be the most powerful man in the film industry, and Sylvia Lesky, whose father had been the head of the studio that her husband was now the head of, was a woman who had been brought up in the film industry and was referred to as Hollywood royalty by such chroniclers as Cyril Rathbone. Marty Lesky was deeply opposed to drugs, and for that reason would not have gone to Casper Stieglitz's home ever, but he was told at a card game at the Hillcrest Country Club the afternoon before that the Jules Mendelsons were going to be there.

"You've got to be kidding," he said. "Jules Mendelson is going to Casper Stieglitz's house? And Pauline too? Will someone explain that one to me, please?"

Certainly Marty Lesky had no social ambitions, but, like many in the film industry, he had developed a great interest in collecting art and had recently been made a member of the board of directors of the Los Angeles County Art Museum. He explained to Sylvia, who didn't want to go to Casper Stieglitz's any more than Pauline Mendelson or Pearl Silver wanted to go, that he thought it would be advantageous to get to know Jules Mendelson better, in the hopes of getting his renowned art collection left to the Los Angeles County Museum, instead of to one of the other art museums that were vying for Jules's treasures.

Dom Belcanto, the famed ballad singer, who was said to have Mafia connections, and his fourth wife, Pepper, were also in the group. Dom was known to play cards every Friday night in Palm Springs with Arnie Zwillman, and it was Zwillman who had asked Dom and Pepper to come. The new additions to what had once been a small dinner were completed with Amos Swank, the late-night talk show host, who almost never went to parties and almost never spoke when he did go to parties, although he kept most of America in stitches five nights a week on his late-night talk show "After Midnight." Amos had just married his fourth wife, and it was she who had talked him into attending a party he would never have accepted otherwise.

Although they were not her friends, Pauline had served on committees with both Pearl Silver and Sylvia Lesky, and greeted them warmly, as they, in turn, greeted her. They all understood, without anyone's saying it, that they were there under duress. Pauline stood by herself, aloof, clasping her gold-and-diamond minaudiere in her hands, and pretended to be looking at Casper Stieglitz's paintings, all of which she hated. Then, in the disparate group, she saw Philip Quennell, whom she had not seen since he had so enraged Jules at lunch at Clouds following Hector Paradiso's funeral and, inadvertently, caused the toppling-over and cracking of their Degas sculpture of the fourteen-year-old ballerina with the original pink ribbon in her hair.

"Admiring the art?" asked Philip, when he made his way toward her.

Jules, standing nearby, acknowledged Philip with a brief nod but did not offer his hand.

"I hate this sort of thing, don't you, big white canvases with a blue dot in the center?" answered Pauline.

"It's not exactly van Gogh's *White Roses*," answered Philip.

Pauline smiled. "We've missed you," she said.

"I don't think Jules has missed me," said Philip.

"Well, I've missed you then."

"You seem different," said Philip.

"How?"

Philip thought for a moment and then said, "Sadder. Is that the right word?"

She smiled at him fondly. "You know, Philip, if I weren't a believer in conjugal vows, and if Camilla Ebury weren't one of my best friends, I'd make such a play for you, even if I am fifteen years older, or maybe it's sixteen, than you are."

Philip, pleased, blushed. "I can't remember when I've felt so flattered."

"This is certainly an unlikely place to have a reunion," said Pauline, indicating the room and the other guests.

"Yes, it is. I couldn't believe it when I heard you were coming."

"Neither could I," she said.

"How's the Degas ballerina?" asked Philip.

"Gone to Paris for repairs. Jules took her over on our plane. There's a marvelous man at the Louvre that Pierre Rosenberg told us about." She clutched her minaudiere to her and looked around the room. "Tell me, Philip. Is Mr. Stieglitz married?"

"He recently became single with a lot of drama, apparently," said Philip. "But they still go to award shows together. My informant is the butler, Willard."

Pauline laughed. "Tell me, who are all these other people? I know Pearl Silver slightly, and Sylvia Lesky and I were co-chairpersons of the Cedars-Sinai benefit, but the others. Who are they? Do you know them?"

"No, but I know who some of them are," said Philip. "I don't know Amos Swank, but he's the talk show host."

"Oh, of course," said Pauline.

"And I don't know Dom Belcanto."

"Oh, I know who Dom Belcanto is. He sang at one of my charities. But who are the others?" asked Pauline. "Who is the prim maiden with the buckteeth?"

"Hortense Madden, the book critic of *Mulholland*."

"And the lady talking movie business a mile a minute with Marty Lesky?"

"Mona Berg, a famous actors' agent, and the man with her is Joel Zircon, another agent."

Whereas the evening was no more than a disagreeable chore for the Mendelsons and the Leskys, it was a great step forward in the social life of Joel Zircon. He had been pressed into service at the last minute as the escort of Mona Berg, who did not wish to arrive alone. Joel had never heard of the Jules Mendelsons, but he was thrilled to be in the same room with the Marty Leskys and the Dom Belcantos and the Amos Swanks, and seemed not to mind that they did not include him in their conversations when he went to stand by them. When he spotted Willard, Casper Stieglitz's butler, with whom he often drank and cruised at Miss Garbo's, he pretended, for propriety's sake, that he had never seen him before.

"And which one is Arnie Zwillman?" asked Pauline. "He is one of those people one hears about, but I haven't a clue what he looks like."

"Deeply tanned, talking to Dom and Pepper Belcanto," answered Philip.

Pauline turned to stare at him. Arnie Zwillman never allowed himself to be photographed. When the *Los Angeles Tribunal* had done a special report on the Mafia infiltration of Las Vegas several years back, they were unable to illustrate their section on Arnie Zwillman with a picture, other than a flash photograph taken at a nightclub in London fifteen years earlier, when he was having a romance with a singer then performing at Talk of the Town.

"Who the hell is Arnie Zwillman anyway?" asked Pauline. "Can you explain him to me?"

"He's the man who burned down the Vegas Seraglio for the insurance money."

"That's all anyone ever says about him. It still doesn't explain him."

"His brother was shot to death in his swimming pool in Las Vegas. His previous wife was hospitalized at Cedars several times after having been beaten up by him, and no charges were ever brought against him. He has been connected with a number of gangland murders, and he has managed to elude the nets of the last six attorneys general. Does that explain him better?" asked Philip.

But Pauline had stopped listening. Entering the room was someone she did not wish to encounter. "Oh, heavens, a host of favorites," she said.

"Who do you see?" asked Philip.

"Mr. Cyril Rathbone," answered Pauline.

"The gossip columnist?" asked Philip. He looked over to where Pauline was looking and immediately recognized the man he had met in Lonny Edge's bungalow on the day he had gone to ask Lonny about Hector Paradiso's death.

"Yes. He drives me mad. He has a fixation on me. Never stops writing about me. I beg of you, don't leave me," said Pauline.

Unused to entertaining, Casper Stieglitz was not the kind of host who took each new arrival around the room to meet the other guests, but then, Cyril Rathbone was not the kind of guest who waited to be introduced. Seeing the famous Pauline Mendelson across the room, he abandoned Pepper Belcanto in midsentence and darted in her direction like a prancing fawn, his hand extended, crying out in his florid English voice, as if they were the greatest of friends, "Pauline! How marvelous!"

"Hellohowareyou?" replied Pauline, the four words becoming one. Pauline was sure that Cyril Rathbone intended to kiss her on both cheeks. While it was impossible not to take the hand that he offered her without creating a minor incident, she had no intention of allowing a man she disliked to do anything so intimate as kiss her. Seeing his face move toward hers, she stepped back away from him. "I have a cold," she said, shaking her head at the same time to forestall such an act.

Rathbone, rebuffed, became very red in the face. Cyril hated Pauline for her aristocratic high-handedness toward him, but he was, at the same time, grovelingly impressed with being in proximity to such grandeur as she represented to him. Had she so much as smiled in his direction, even once, or invited him to one of her famous parties, his hatred would have evaporated into nothingness, and he would have become her most adoring acolyte. But that was not to be.

"Do you know Philip Quennell? Cyril Rathbone," said Pauline.

Cyril looked at Philip, curious to know who the young man was who had been engaged in such deep conversation with Pauline when he entered the room. For an instant Philip looked familiar to him.

"What was your name?" he asked Philip.

"Quennell. Philip Quennell." He remembered that Lonny had not been able to remember his name that day and had called him Phil Quin when he introduced him to Cyril.

"Have we met?"

"I certainly would have remembered if we had," said Philip. If Philip had been standing next to anyone but Pauline, Cyril Rathbone would have instantly remembered the circumstances under which they did meet.

Cyril turned back to Pauline. "Even though you're here, and the Leskys, and Pearl, this is a B-group party," he said, as if he himself, along with the Mendelsons and Leskys and Pearl Silver, stood head and shoulders above the other guests. If he had expected that this comment would endear him to a lady who always resisted him, he was mistaken, as she neither laughed nor agreed with his statement.

"How is your yellow phalaenopsis coming along?" he asked, trying again. He was referring to the rare orchid she was developing in her greenhouse, which he had written in his column she was going to show to the Los Angeles Garden Club.

"Very well," she replied.

"I was thinking just today about our mutual friend Hector," he said, as a last resort for a conversational opening.

She nodded.

"Hardly a day goes by that something doesn't happen that I want to share with Hector," said Cyril. It was Cyril Rathbone who had sent Hector Paradiso the clipping from the Paris newspaper showing Flo March fleeing from a fire in the Meurice Hotel, with Jules Mendelson in the background. "We talked every day."

Pauline was unwilling to be drawn into a conversation about her great friend Hector with Cyril Rathbone. She looked downward. She had never understood why Hector found Cyril so entertaining, and she knew that any statement she made would be printed in his column, and not necessarily correctly. She observed during her downward look that Cyril Rathbone was wearing the tie of an English public school he had not attended and had little feet with highly polished shoes from Lobb on St. James's Street.

At that moment dinner was announced, and Pauline immediately seized the moment to distance herself from the man she found so disagreeable.

"Good heavens," she said, shuddering and wondering again what she and Jules were doing at such a house.

"You weren't very polite to Mr. Rathbone," said Philip.

"Cyril Rathbone is uninsultable," replied Pauline. "I hope you're seated next to me at dinner, Philip."

"If I'm not, I'll pull a Hector Paradiso and change the place cards," said Philip.

IN ANOTHER part of the room, Jules stood in a group with Marty Lesky and Dom Belcanto and their host. He pretended to admire the art on Casper Stieglitz's walls, which had been picked out for Casper by the studio art director who decorated his house for him. Actually, Jules, like his wife, hated the art on Casper Stieglitz's walls, but, as a great art collector, he was always courteous about other people's art, even if he found it inferior. His reputation on matters pertaining to art was so respected that his word was considered authoritarian, and Casper was delighted with Jules Mendelson's false admiration. He wished he could remember the name of the artist who stuck the broken dishes and coffee cups in the canvas when Dom Belcanto asked him, but he couldn't. He excused himself, whispering to Jules man-to-man that he had to take a leak and then check on the dinner. Casper was anxious that the dinner start on time so that the film afterward could start on time, as he was expecting Ina Rae and Darlene and a porn star called Lonny, whom Ina Rae insisted on bringing, for a four-way scene after the film, and he wanted all his fancy guests out of his house before they arrived. Arnie Zwillman seized the opportunity of Casper's disappearance to introduce himself and his about-to-be-wife, Adrienne Basquette, to Jules. Then dinner was announced.

BETTYE, Casper's secretary, had done the place cards. Neither Jules nor Pauline mentioned to the person sitting next to them that their last name had been spelled incorrectly on the place cards, with two *d*'s instead of one in Mendelson, but the error seemed in keeping with the inappropriateness of the evening. Pauline minded that her difficult situation with her husband prevented her from catching his eye and smiling over the misspelling of their names, the sort of husband-wife togetherness that had marked the twenty-two years of their marriage. Or catching his eye and smiling across the table over the black napkins and black dishes. Jules knew how much Pauline hated black napkins and black dishes, but they could not exchange looks over that either, or over the several times the hired waiters from a catering service served the guests from the wrong side, or over the wine, an indifferent Italian Soave in long tapered bottles that had the price tag of $8.00 stamped on them, which Pauline knew would drive Jules mad. Jules was aware that there was a point to the evening and that the point had to do with Arnie Zwillman, and he waited for the other man to make the first move.

Almost everyone at the table deferred to Jules Mendelson in the forced conversation, even Marty Lesky, who was accustomed to dominating the conversation at the tables where he dined. Jules possessed a kind of power in his presence that made the ordinary conversation that people in the industry were used to talking about at dinner—

films and grosses and casting and who was up and who was down in
the studio hierarchy—seem trite, and he was asked questions about
the presidency, about the economy, and, finally, about a senatorial
confirmation hearing then going on in Washington for a presidential
nominee for a vacancy on the Supreme Court, about whom embarrassing personal revelations concerning women and liquor had come
to light.

"I have no firsthand knowledge, but apparently there are things in
John's past," said Jules cautiously, not wanting to get into such a
conversation with these people whom he did not know and who
would certainly quote him the following day, especially the gossip
columnist Cyril Rathbone. In fact, Jules knew a great deal about the
confirmation hearing. He was not unmindful that certain aspects of
the nominee's behavior mirrored his own and could be used against
him when the time came for his own senatorial confirmation, should
the news of his affair with Flo March leak out. A chill passed through
him. He looked across the table at his beautiful and elegant wife and
realized, not for the first time, what a necessary treasure she was to
him. Jules, who never gulped wine, took a gulp of Casper Stieglitz's
cheap wine and grimaced.

"But all public people have discreditable secrets," said Pearl Silver,
who was known to be able to keep any conversation going. "Don't
you think so, Jules? Even Roosevelt, in his wheelchair. He had that
whatshername, Lucy *quelquechose*, who was supposed to be such a
good friend of Eleanor's. I mean, they all have secrets."

"I suppose everyone has something in his past he doesn't want to
come out," said Sylvia Lesky.

"Not me," said Casper Stieglitz, although almost everyone in the
room knew that he had been secretly arrested for the possession of
drugs while on a foreign location for a picture and that Marty Lesky,
the head of his studio, had had to appeal to a Washington figure to
keep him from being sent to jail in that country.

"You are an exception then, Casper," said Pearl Silver, catching
Sylvia Lesky's eye while she said it.

There was a silence. Then Philip Quennell spoke up, although it
was the custom that conversation at such parties was carried on by
the important figures at the table, while the others listened. "I always
figure if you've got something hidden in your past, it's going to come
out at some time or other," he said. He looked across the table at

Jules, but Jules turned to reply to a question asked him by Pepper Belcanto.

"You do?" asked Pauline. She too looked across the table at Jules.

Philip, having caught the attention of the table, continued. "But, believe me, Mrs. Mendelson, some way is always found for people in high places, and people close to people in high places, to beat the rap. As night follows day, this is the truth. It is part of the fabric of power."

There was an awkward silence in the room, and Philip could feel the dark look that was coming in his direction from Jules Mendelson.

"Who's this guy?" asked Arnie Zwillman, leaning over Adrienne Basquette to speak to Casper Stieglitz.

"He wrote a book," replied Casper, explaining Philip.

"Big fucking deal," said Arnie.

Then Casper excused himself and left the table. Philip could see that Casper's frequent trips to the bathroom were beginning to have their effect. He ate almost nothing, and he blew his nose frequently, feigning a cold. Joel Zircon, who had not spoken a word during the meal, followed Casper out of the room, hoping to be invited to participate in what he called a few lines.

Conversations of this type did not usually take place at Casper's house. There had been a time when he had been a popular figure in the social life of the film community, but it had been several years since he had produced a film that in any way approximated the films of his dazzling early successes, and movie people, aware of his questionable habits, had stopped asking him to their parties and had long since declined going to his. The kind of talk he had grown to prefer in the year since his divorce was the kind of talk he had with Ina Rae and the sort of people she brought to his house.

Throughout the meal Hortense Madden sat in angry silence. Her evening had been spoiled by the unexpected arrival of Cyril Rathbone, whom everyone seemed to know, while none of the guests knew who she was when she was introduced to them. Any dreams she had nurtured of being taken up by Pauline Mendelson, as one of the interesting people she invited to her parties, were squashed when Cyril monopolized Pauline before dinner and she did not get to meet her. Philip Quennell was seated next to Hortense, but he gave his full attention to Pauline Mendelson on his other side during most of the meal. On the several occasions she attempted to open a conversation with Arnie Zwillman, her table companion on her other side, he replied only with a yes or a no and then returned his attention to Adrienne Basquette on his other side. Arnie Zwillman never had time for girls who weren't pretty. After Casper left the table, the conversation became less general, and Philip turned to her.

"You're the literary critic for *Mulholland*, Casper tells me," he said.

"I am," she replied importantly. It was her first recognition of the evening.

"I was bruised by the review you wrote of my book," he said.

"Which book was that?" she asked, although she knew which book it was.

"*Takeover*, it was called," answered Philip. "About Reza Bulbenkian, the Wall Street financier."

"Oh, that, yes," she said dismissively. "Not my sort of book at all."

"I gathered as much," said Philip. Then he added, "But it was popular."

"As if that matters." She laughed a laugh that was nearly a snort. "That's all you people care about, isn't it?"

"And you don't care about recognition?"

"Of course not."

"Or applause?"

"No." She shook her head. There was something about her that was familiar to Philip.

She picked up his place card and looked at his name, as if she could not remember it. She squinted her eyes and pursed her lips over her protruding teeth as she read his name. "Do you make your living as a writer, Mr. Quennell?"

"I do, yes," he said.

"Hmmm," she replied. She nodded her head.

Philip watched her. "I know that you don't make your living as a nightclub singer," he said.

She looked at him in a startled way. "What in the world do you mean by that?"

"As Pearl Silver just observed to Jules Mendelson, all public people have discreditable secrets," said Philip.

"I don't have a clue what you're talking about," said Hortense.

Philip began to sing quietly in Hortense's direction, so quietly that even Pauline Mendelson, on the other side of him, could not hear.

"*You are not my first love, I've known other charms, but I've just been rehearsing, in those other arms,*" he sang.

Hortense looked at him, terrified of exposure.

"Marvene McQueen? The chanteuse? Of Miss Garbo's? Speaking of bad reviews, has your cohort Cyril Rathbone down the table reviewed your act yet? I'd be very interested in seeing that review," said Philip. He started to sing again, a little louder: *"You better go now, because I like you much too much, you better go now."*

"What do you want?" she asked.

"I have a manuscript I want you to read."

"By you?"

"No, not by me."

"By whom?"

"That's what I'm not going to tell you. I want you to read it and tell me who you think wrote it."

"What is this, a game?"


THE MARTY LESKYS left immediately after dinner, explaining that they had run the same film the night before at their house. Pearl Silver, pleading a headache, left with the Leskys. Dom Belcanto, his duty to Arnie Zwillman accomplished, also left, saying he and Pepper were driving back to Palm Springs that night. And Amos Swank and his new wife made a tiptoe-out-of-the-room departure, without giving any excuse at all, or even saying good-bye.

Fifteen minutes into the film in the darkened projection room, Arnie Zwillman tapped Jules on his knee and then rose and walked toward the door and left the room.

"If you're not crazy about this film, we can switch to another one," said Casper in the darkness.

"Oh, no, I'm enjoying it immensely," said Adrienne Basquette. "I love the costumes."

"Picture won't make a nickel," said Casper.

Several minutes after Arnie's withdrawal, Jules whispered into Pauline's ear. "I'll be back shortly. I have to make a call to Sims Lord."

He rose from his seat. For an instant he blocked the light ray from the projector in the booth, and his massive shadow nearly obliterated the screen.

"Down in front," came the voice of Hortense Madden, who was no longer impressed with the impressive Mendelsons, as neither had seemed to recognize her name and each had resisted conversation with her during coffee.

As Jules left the room by the same door that Arnie Zwillman had used, Pauline watched him. The evening had been an evening she had never understood since the idea had been introduced to her. She felt that the early departure of Arnie Zwillman from the darkened room had somehow triggered Jules's own departure. She could not understand the connection the two men could have together and hoped it did not have anything to do with Kippie.

"Isn't she divine?" whispered Cyril Rathbone, leaning forward from the seat behind Pauline's. Cyril Rathbone was not a man who gave up easily.

"Who?" asked Pauline.

Cyril named the actress on the screen, who was very beautiful. Pauline nodded agreement without turning. Although she never interfered in Jules's business, she had an urge to follow him.

"See this actor?" said Casper, talking about an actor in close-up on the screen. "He's had seven flops in a row. Nothing for him after this but a sitcom. He was sleeping with the director."

WHEN JULES REENTERED Casper's house, he stood for a moment in the living room, not sure which way to go. The predinner drinks had been cleared away. From the kitchen he could hear the sounds of the caterers cleaning up the dinner dishes and running a vacuum cleaner in the dining room.

"Mr. Zwillman said to tell you he's in the den," said a voice behind him. Jules turned. The butler, Willard, was standing there.

"The den is where?" asked Jules.

"Through that hall. First door to the left," said Willard.

"Thank you," said Jules.

Jules felt uncomfortable with the situation he was in, but he proceeded to the den and opened the door. Arnie Zwillman was seated with a drink in his hand. The two men looked at each other.

"Shut the door behind you," said Zwillman.

Jules closed the door.

"Drink?" asked Zwillman.

"No, thank you," said Jules.

"Sure, have a drink. Clears the air."

"I never drink after dinner," said Jules.

"Except tonight," said Zwillman. He made up a scotch and soda from a drink table and handed it to Jules.

"Your wife always so quiet, or she didn't think the crowd was up to her usual standards?" asked Arnie.

"My wife is not feeling well tonight," said Jules.

"Does she know your grandfather was the bookkeeper for Al Capone and did time for income tax evasion?" asked Arnie.

"No, she doesn't," answered Jules, unperturbed. "But what happened fifty-five years ago is not of much concern to any of us today."

"Don't pull your upper-class bullshit on me, Julie," said Arnie.

"It's Jules, never Julie," said Jules.

"Oh, I beg your pardon. *Jules*," said Arnie, with mock solemnity.

"Look, Zwillman, what is this? I don't need this aggravation from a two-bit arsonist and card cheat," said Jules. He made no attempt to conceal the derision in his voice.

Arnie Zwillman stared at Jules. When he spoke, he spoke quietly. "Does your society-lady wife know about the girl with the broken arm who went off the balcony of the Roosevelt Hotel in Chicago in nineteen fifty-three?" he asked.

Jules blanched.

Arnie Zwillman smiled. "Nor does your friend the President, who's going to appoint you to the economic conference in Brussels, I suppose."

Jules felt a tightness in his chest. His heart was pounding. He put his hand to it.

"That was an accident," he said in a voice barely above a whisper.

"Siddown," said Arnie. He spoke as if he were talking to hired help.

Jules, breathing heavily, lowered his large body into an Eames chair and stared at Arnie Zwillman.

"Over here," said Arnie, tapping the cushion next to where he was seated on a corduroy-upholstered sofa. "I got a polyp on my vocal cord, and I don't like to have to raise my voice."

Jules got up from the Eames chair and walked over to the sofa where Arnie Zwillman was seated and sat down slowly.

"You're carrying around a lot of lard there, fella," said Arnie. "How old are you, Jules?"

"Let's get down to what you wanted to see me about, Zwillman," said Jules.

"How old? Fifty-seven? Fifty-eight? Something like that? You gotta take better care of yourself. Look at me. I'm the same age you are. Look at this stomach. Flat as an ironing board. You know why? I eat vegetables. I eat fruit. I walk five miles a day, every day. I take a massage every day. I take steam and a sauna every day. It sweats the fucking pounds right off you. You gotta lose a little of that lard. Bad for your heart. What's your lady friend think about it? Does it bother her?"

"If Mrs. Mendelson has any complaints, she has not voiced them."

"I wasn't talking about Mrs. Mendelson, Jules."

Jules was silent for a moment. Then he asked, "What are we here for?"

"I'm a friend of your son, Kippie," said Arnie.

"*Step*son, not son," said Jules.

"Oh, right, *step*son. He kept saying the very same thing about you, *step*father, not father. A very naughty boy, your stepson, but charming, I'll say that for him, very charming. Ambition is not high on his priorities, but then with a rich stepdaddy like you, I suppose he has great expectations."

"No, no, he doesn't," said Jules, shaking his head emphatically.

"Perhaps not directly from you, but certainly indirectly through his mother, assuming that you cool first, which is not unlikely," said Arnie.

The idea of death was abhorrent to Jules Mendelson. As successful as he was, he still had plans for himself that would further expand his wealth and power. And there was the crowning achievement of his life so near at hand, his role as the head of the American economic delegation in Brussels during the year of the statehood of Europe.

"It was nice of Kippie to set up this meeting for me," said Arnie. "You're not an easy man to get on the telephone."

"I don't know how my stepson knows you," said Jules.

"Oh, Kippie gets in a little trouble from time to time, as I'm sure you know, and when he can't go to his famous stepdaddy or his society mama, he comes to see me for a little help," said Arnie. "One of these days he'll come to a bad end; you know that about him, don't you?"

Jules listened. It was not the first time he had heard such a prediction for his stepson. Headmasters at several very expensive schools had voiced more or less the same forecast for Kippie Petworth after expelling him.

"I think the preliminaries are over, Zwillman. What does my stepson have to do with this? Why am I sitting here talking to you in the house of this cocaine-sniffing man Stieglitz, whom I have never met before?" asked Jules.

"Not a goddamn thing. I'm not here to talk about Kippie. I'm here to talk about the laundry business, you being, or about to be, so involved in international banking in Brussels. How'd you like to go into the laundry business with me, Jules?"

"PRETTY GIRL, isn't she?" said Pauline, in the darkened screening room, about the actress on the screen. She addressed her remark to Philip Quennell, but it was overheard by Casper Stieglitz, who, now very high, was returning from another trip to the bathroom.

"She's a big dyke," said Casper. He sat down in the row behind Pauline, in a chair next to the controls, where he could speak to the projectionist.

"Oh, no, I can't believe such a story," said Pauline, shaking her head.

"True," said Casper. "She's cleaned out half the muffs in California."

Pauline, shocked, sat in silence for several minutes. She ceased to look at the screen. She wondered where Jules was, and it occurred to her that he had gone home and left her there, as he was by nature too restless to enjoy looking at films or plays. She looked over at Philip. He smiled at her in the dark, realizing her discomfort with the unfortunate remark that Casper had just made. Pauline did not want to involve Philip, as she knew that he was working on a film for Casper Stieglitz. Finally, summoning her courage, she rose from her seat in the darkness. As Jules had before her, she blocked the light ray from the projection booth just behind her and cast a shadow on the screen.

"You looking for the toilet, Pauline?" asked Casper.

"Where is my husband?" replied Pauline.

"Talking to Arnie Zwillman in the house," said Casper.

"How do I get there?"

From the obscurity of the darkened room, Willard, the butler, appeared. "I'll take you back to the house, Mrs. Mendelson," he said.

"Don't you like the picture, Pauline?" asked Casper. He pressed the intercom and spoke in a loud voice to the projectionist. "What other pictures you got in there, Bernie?"

"*I* happen to be enjoying the picture, Casper," said Hortense Madden.

Pauline did not answer. Beside her, Philip Quennell rose. "Are you okay, Pauline?" he asked her.

"Fine, Philip, just sit down. I'm fine. I have to find Jules, that's all," whispered Pauline.

The butler reached out his hand to her, and she took it. He led her through the dark room to the sliding glass door, which he pulled back. "There's a step there," he said to her in a low voice.

Outside Pauline breathed in the fresh night air.

"Sorry, Mrs. Mendelson, for what Mr. Stieglitz said," said the butler.

"I have never in my life heard such an expression—" said Pauline, and then stopped.

"He gets a little hyper when he uses," said Willard.

Pauline looked at the butler, not sure if he meant what she thought he meant, but decided not to question him. She had been brought up with servants and understood what her father had always called the boundaries of communication. "Look at these roses," she said instead. "They need to be clipped. They need to be watered more. This garden is a disgrace."

"He's let the place go since his wife moved out," said Willard.

"He's let himself go too, I'd say," said Pauline.

"We'll go around this way by the pool," he said. "Careful here, some of the outdoor lights have gone out. One of Mr. Stieglitz's guests tripped last week."

"Heavens, I hope I don't trip," said Pauline, holding on to Willard's arm.

"I know your house, Mrs. Mendelson," said Willard.

"You do?"

"They used to call it the von Stern house before you bought it."

"Yes, they did call it that, years ago," said Pauline. "We bought it from Mr. von Stern."

"What most people don't know is that von Stern built it for Carole Lupescu, the silent film star. It's where she committed suicide."

"I didn't know that."

"Turned on the gas."

"Good heavens."

"In the garage, not the house, in a Dusenberg."

"Oh, I see."

"I'm a house freak, a movie star house freak. I know the history of every movie star's house in this town."

"Our house bears very little resemblance to the way it was when Mr. von Stern had it, I'm afraid."

"I know. I heard you did a total gut job on the house and doubled the square footage," he said.

"You know so much."

As they approached the terrace of the house, Willard said, very quickly, "Hector Paradiso was a friend of mine." If Hector Paradiso had been alive, Willard would not have called him a friend, merely an acquaintance; but dead, it was safe to secure the friendship without fear of detection. "I saw you at Hector's funeral at Good Shepherd."

"Such a sad thing it was," said Pauline. They were now on the terrace, and Pauline remembered the way. "Oh, yes, it's through here, isn't it, that we came out? I remember it now."

"Mrs. Mendelson, Hector didn't commit suicide. You know that, don't you?"

Pauline looked at Willard. "No, I don't know that. Suicide was the official finding in the autopsy report," she said, wondering why she felt obliged to explain that to Casper Stieglitz's butler, whom she probably would never see again. At the same time, she knew this man had been kind to her and realized he was sincere in what he was saying.

"Please listen," he said, with an urgency in his voice. "An undesirable called Lonny Edge was the guy who killed Hector. Believe me, Mrs. Mendelson. I only tell you this because I know what good friends you were with Hector."

Pauline did not know what to say. She had never understood Hector's death or her husband's insistence that it was a suicide. Her confusion was interrupted by loud laughter in the night air. Both she and Willard turned around to see where it was coming from. Three people, two young women and a man, all walking in an unsteady fashion, were coming around the side of the house to the pool area.

"And for God's sake, don't run your hands through his hair, because he wears a rug which he thinks we don't notice," said one of the young girls, and the three collapsed with laughter.

Willard recognized the voices but called out, "Who is that?"

"Hi, Willard. It's only us, Ina Rae and Darlene and Lonny," Ina Rae called back.

"Dear God," said Willard, looking at Pauline. "You're early, Ina Rae. Mr. Stieglitz is still running a film. Perhaps you should wait in his room until his guests leave. Go around by the kitchen entrance."

"Got any drinks, Willard?"

"Ask in the kitchen," he said. Then he turned back to Pauline, who had been staring at the young trio. "Next shift," he said simply, in explanation.

"Did she say that young man's name was Lonny?" asked Pauline.

"Yes."

"Is that the same Lonny you were speaking of just now?"

Willard nodded. He opened the door.

"This is a very active household," said Pauline. They stepped into the house. "Where do you suppose my husband is?"

"In the den with Mr. Zwillman."

"Will you show me the way?"

"Through there."

Pauline looked at Willard as if she wanted to remember his face and then opened the door of Casper Stieglitz's den without knocking. Inside, seated side by side in earnest conversation, were Jules and Arnie Zwillman. Both men held drinks in their hands, and the room was cloudy with blue cigar smoke. The men broke apart from their conversation, in surprise at the interruption.

Pauline wondered at the intensity of their involvement. It was the way she had seen Jules look when he talked with his friends from the financial world.

"Jules, I want to go home," said Pauline. She did not move from the door.

Jules looked at his watch. "Is the movie over?" he asked.

"For me it is."

"Is something the matter, Pauline?"

"I have a perfectly frightful headache, and I must leave immediately, with or without you."

"Did you meet Mr. Zwill—?"

"Yes, I did. Are you coming, Jules?" She turned and walked out of the room.


"HEY WILLARD," called out Ina Rae from Casper's bedroom, where she and Darlene and Lonny were smoking joints and drinking margaritas until the film was over and Casper's grand friends left and the orgy could start. "Come in here a minute, will ya?"

Willard was in the kitchen paying off the caterers and complaining bitterly to them that one of Mr. Stieglitz's black dinner plates had been broken.

"What is it, Ina Rae?" he asked, after he had completed what he was doing with the caterer. He wanted to make it perfectly clear that he did not drop everything and run when a person of the caliber of Ina Rae called him.

"My friend Lonny here has something he wants you to do," she said.

Willard looked at Lonny. He had taken off his jacket and jeans and was sitting on Casper's bed in a black jockstrap and T-shirt, with a joint hanging out of his mouth.

"You look familiar, Willard," said Lonny.

"I was at Miss Garbo's on the night you walked out of there with Hector Paradiso," answered Willard.

"The whole fucking world must have been at Miss Garbo's that night," said Lonny. "Poor Hector. Who woulda thought he'd have pumped all that lead into himself?"

For a moment the two men stared at each other. "You wanted something?"

"Yeah. Is Mr. Phil Quennell in the projection room watching the movie?"

"Yes, he is," said Willard, surprised.

"When he comes out, give him this, will you?" He picked up a large manila envelope. On it was written in a very simple handwriting, *Mr. P. Quinel. Personel.* Under it was written *Zerox copy.*

"You writing your memoirs, Lonny?" asked Willard. "You better learn how to spell first."

"Just give it to him, asshole, and don't give me any attitude. All right?" said Lonny. He reached over and put his hand on Darlene's knee and brought it all the way up the inside of her thigh, at the same time looking at Willard.

"Listen, you cheap hustler. Don't use any of Mr. Stieglitz's Porthault towels for cum rags. Got it?"

"I know the rules, Willard," said Ina Rae. "I know where he keeps the cheap towels. When's this movie going to be over, for God's sake? We may start without him. This boy's gettin' hot here."

□   □   □

JULES'S BENTLEY was parked in the courtyard of Casper Stieglitz's house. He opened the door for Pauline to get in and then went around to the driver's side and got in himself. Both strapped on their seat belts without speaking. As he backed the car up, he crashed into the side of a small Honda.

"Good God," said Jules.

He opened the door of his car and looked out. "I should go in and tell the butler I hit that car," said Jules.

"No, you shouldn't, Jules," said Pauline.

"It might be Zwillman's."

"Zwillman wouldn't have a little car like that, believe me. At least you didn't hit the gold Rolls over there. That's probably Zwillman's. You can call tomorrow. It's just a dent."

"About a nine-hundred-dollar dent," said Jules.

"It's not as if you can't afford to pay for it. Let's go. I want to get away from this house," said Pauline. "I've never had a worse time anywhere."

He drove the car out of the driveway onto the cul-de-sac and made his way toward Mountain Drive, where he went through a stop sign.

"Are you drunk?" asked Pauline.

"I am a bit, yes," answered Jules.

"You're driving dangerously."

"Would you like to drive?"

"Yes, I would."

Jules pulled the Bentley over to the side of Mountain Drive and put the gearshift into neutral. He unstrapped his seat belt, opened the door of the car, and walked very slowly around to the other side. Pauline unstrapped her seat belt and slid across the leather seat to the driver's side. Then they both strapped their seat belts again. Pauline put the gearshift into drive and pulled out onto Mountain Drive, heading toward Sunset Boulevard.

"Mr. Zwillman," Jules said when the car stopped at the stoplight on Sunset Boulevard.

"What about him?"

"I never drink after dinner, ever, as you know, but he made me three drinks," said Jules.

"You didn't have to drink them."

"I know, but I did."

"Was Mr. Zwillman not the reason we went to that dreadful party in that dreadful house?" asked Pauline.

"Yes."

"At some time in the future, if someone asks you, the police or the grand jury, for instance, 'How did you get to know Arnie Zwillman?' you can now say, 'I was introduced to him at a party at the home of Casper Stieglitz, the film producer. My wife and I dined there. We saw a film there. Mr. Zwillman was also a guest, along with Marty and Sylvia Lesky, the head of Colossus Pictures, et cetera et cetera.' Is that it?"

"You're very perceptive, Pauline. Zwillman knew we wouldn't go to his house, and nobody else but a cocaine sniffer like Casper Stieglitz, who is himself no longer invited anywhere, would have him to theirs. He's a leper these days."

"And yet you bring me there, to the house of a cocaine-sniffing leper, while you meet up with a gangster," said Pauline. "It will all read wonderfully in Cyril Rathbone's column. I wonder if he'll include Ina Rae and Darlene and Lonny."

"Who?" asked Jules.

"The late shift was arriving as I was leaving."

"Jesus," said Jules.

"What did Mr. Zwillman want? Some nonpublic information for his stock portfolio?" asked Pauline.

"It had to do with the statehood of Europe in 1992," said Jules.

Pauline laughed. "What possible interest could Mr. Arnie Zwillman, who burned down the Vegas Seraglio for the insurance money, have in the statehood of Europe?"

"It is less the statehood of Europe than the role I am going to be playing in it, representing the United States," said Jules slowly.

"Don't make me pry this out of you, Jules, step by step. Keep talking until I get your point," said Pauline. She turned the Bentley off Sunset Boulevard onto Benedict Canyon and drove to Angelo Drive, where she turned left and proceeded up the winding hillside with the hairpin curves, which strangers in the city found too frightening to drive at night. It was a rare occurrence for Pauline to drive Jules, and he, although slightly drunk, was impressed with her ability.

"Mr. Zwillman is apparently involved in drug trafficking, and has at his disposal immense sums of money, immense beyond description, that he assumed I could facilitate his operation with by putting into circulation through the European Common Market," said Jules. He hiccuped.

"Why would he think you would be amenable to such a thing?"

"He threatened me."

"With what?"

Jules looked out the window of the Bentley and did not answer.

Pauline looked over at him. "What did you tell him?" she asked.

"To go fuck himself."

"It didn't appear to me when I walked into the room that you had just told Mr. Zwillman to go fuck himself," said Pauline. "That was not the impression I had at all."

Jules didn't reply.

"Are you going to report this to the police, or the FBI, or the CIA, or the President, or someone?" asked Pauline.

They looked at each other.

"No," said Jules quietly.

"Years ago, when we were first married, you told me that something had happened in your past, when you were young."

"I don't want to talk about that," said Jules quickly.

"You don't trust me, Jules, after twenty-two years of marriage?" asked Pauline.

"I trust you implicitly, Pauline, but I don't want to talk about that."

"Then just tell me one thing. Does Arnie Zwillman know about whatever it was that happened that you don't want to talk to me about?"

Jules stared out the window again.

"How do you know he wasn't wired?" asked Pauline.

"I don't," replied Jules. "I never thought of that."

They drove in silence for several minutes, as Pauline maneuvered a curve in the road. "Has it occurred to you that our lives, our so-called perfect lives, are unraveling, Jules?" she asked.

"Yes."

"Is it a matter of any concern to you?"

"Of course it is, Pauline. I don't want this to happen," said Jules. "What can we do?"

"I'm not the one who's having the affair," said Pauline. At the same moment she turned the Bentley sharply to the right, pulling up to the closed gates of Clouds. She pushed the button that lowered the window on the driver's side and reached out and pressed a seven-digit code on the calculator buttons of a computerized lock in the red brick wall adjoining the gates. Slowly, the impressive gates opened.

Jules, watching her, said, "You're an amazingly efficient woman, Pauline." Farther up the hill toward the house, the frenzied sound of the watchdogs' barking could be heard.

She looked at him. "I know," she said. The car started up the hill, and the gates swung closed behind them. As they pulled into the cobblestone courtyard, the police dogs, barking ferociously, surrounded the car.

Jules opened the car door. "Okay, boys, okay, now down, down, down. Smitty? Are you there, Smitty?"

"Over here, Mr. Mendelson," said the guard.

"Call the dogs off, will you?" said Jules.

"You boys calm down now, just calm down. I'll open the door for you, Mrs. Mendelson," said Smitty. "Hope you folks had a nice evening."

"Thank you, Smitty. We did indeed," said Pauline. Pauline's father had taught his three daughters that no matter what state their lives were in, it was important always to keep up appearances in front of the servants.

"You'll put the car away, Smitty?" said Jules.

"Sure thing."

Inside, in the hallway of their house, with the curved staircase and the six Monet paintings, Pauline started up the stairs with her hand on the railing.

Jules, following her into the house, reached out and covered her hand with his. "Perhaps we could have breakfast together in the morning," he said. The invitation was an unusual one, as Jules was always gone from their home for several hours by the time Pauline rang to have her breakfast tray brought up by Blondell. They had never once used Pauline's sunrise room for breakfast, as had been the plan when the sunrise and sunset rooms had been added on to the house.

"I had planned to sleep late," Pauline replied, withdrawing her hand from beneath Jules's hand on the banister. She continued up the stairs. The third of the six Monet paintings on the stairway wall appeared crooked to her, and she stopped to straighten it.

"Whenever you are available in the morning," replied Jules, watching her from below, "I will be here."

She turned halfway up the stairs and looked back at him. They both knew the time had come for them to talk. Then she said, quite arbitrarily, in the first of several arbitrary decisions she would make in the next year to assert her authority in her house, "I don't want to lend these Monets to the Carnegie Museum in Pittsburgh for their exhibit after all."

"But they've been promised," said Jules. "I'm sure their catalog has been printed by now."

"I don't care," she said. "I don't want to lend them. I want them here when the garden club comes."

"All right," said Jules, lifting his eyebrows. Her decision upset him, because he took his obligations in the art world very seriously, but he knew, being a dealmaker of renown, when to concede a point. While looking up at her, he made a mental note to think up an acceptable excuse before contacting the curator of the Carnegie Museum in the morning.

Looking back at him, Pauline thought, for the first time, that her husband had started to look old.


THE FEW GUESTS who had actually sat through the movie at Casper Stieglitz's house were leaving. Casper, glad to be rid of them, had not come to the parking area to see them off but, instead, had made straight for the bedroom where Ina Rae and Darlene and Lonny were waiting for him.

Philip Quennell opened the door of his rented car and was surprised to see a large manila envelope on the driver's seat. He picked it up, saw that his name was misspelled on the front, and knew immediately what it was and who it was from.

"Hey! Somebody put a dent in my car," screamed out Hortense Madden, as she went to open the door of her Honda. "I bet it was that ass-kissing Cyril Rathbone. As soon as Pauline Mendelson left the projection room, he lost all interest in the evening and took off in a snit. He's just the type who would back his car into yours and drive off into the night without leaving a note. I'm going to get that little prick tomorrow and make him pay through the nose."

Philip slammed the door of his car and went over to Hortense's, with the envelope in his hands. "Nasty dent," he said. "Will the door open?"

"Let me see," said Hortense. She tried her door and it opened.

"Could be worse," said Philip.

"That fucking Cyril Rathbone," said Hortense, seething with rage. " 'Pauline! How marvelous!' " she said, in an exact imitation of Cyril's florid voice.

"I don't blame you for being in a bad mood, and this is probably the wrong moment, but this is the manuscript I was talking to you about at dinner," he said.

"What do you want me to do with it?" she asked.

"Just read it," he said. "And tell me who you think wrote it. I'm at the Chateau Marmont."

## Flo's Tape #14

"A lot of people think I went to Pooky, the hairdresser, just because he was the hairdresser to Pauline Mendelson, but that is not the case. That's not the kind of thing I would ever do. I knew Pooky from my days at the Viceroy Coffee Shop. He was a regular, every morning. Juice, whole wheat toast, tea. Never varied. One day he said to me, 'Rhonda'—I was still called Rhonda then, before I became Flo— 'you've got really beautiful hair, but you're wearing it in the wrong style. Come on in, and I'll do it for you.' I almost died. I mean, there were articles about Pooky in the paper, about all the famous ladies whose hair he did, like Faye Converse, Sylvia Lesky, and Pauline Mendelson. I said to him, 'Are you kidding? I could no more afford you.' He said, 'On me.'

"So, of course, I went. I've been wearing my hair this way ever since, and that was before I ever met Jules Mendelson. After I started seeing Jules, when I started wearing all the great clothes, and driving the Mercedes, and living in Beverly Hills, I began to pay the same price all the society ladies and the movie stars paid. I know he must have wondered where all the money was coming from, but he never asked any questions. I knew he was happy for me, though, that things had started to go my way.

"He always did Pauline Mendelson's hair at her house. I only saw that house once, and I never went upstairs, but I understand she had a whole, like, beauty shop of her own right off her dressing room, because she didn't like going into Pooky's shop. But one day when I was having my hair done, she walked in. I almost died. She was going back east to visit her father, unexpectedly I guess, and needed to get her hair done quickly. Wouldn't you know, I was sitting there reading about her in Cyril Rathbone's column at the time?

"That was the first time I ever thought Pooky might have suspected about me and Jules, because he quickly pulled the curtain behind me, as if he didn't want her to see me, and went outside the curtain to speak to her. When he came back in to finish me up, he never said a word."

# 15

"DUDLEY, please throw out the peonies on the upstairs hall table. There're petals everywhere," called Pauline the next morning from the top of the stairs.

"Yes, Mrs. Mendelson," replied Dudley, running up the stairs.

Dudley treasured his employment with the illustrious Mendelson family, and wished things to continue as they had always been. It was no secret among the help in the grander houses of the city that Dudley was recompensed for his services at a salary that far exceeded any of theirs, a knowledge that elevated him to a sort of celebrity status in domestic circles. On the numerous occasions throughout the years of the Mendelson parties, he knew that the guests attending were the greatest and grandest in the land, and it pleased him to be called by name by many of them, especially several of the former Presidents of the country who were regular visitors in the house. It was a measure of the high esteem with which Jules Mendelson held him that only he, and no one else, was allowed to dust van Gogh's painting of the *White Roses*, which was the most favored possession in the art-filled house.

When Pauline came down to meet Jules for breakfast, she was dressed for traveling in a tweed suit. Her mink coat, which she wore only in the East, had been placed on a gilded chair in the front hall. The size of her two bags, which had already been carried downstairs by Dudley, indicated that she planned only a brief trip. In her hand was a list of things to be attended to in her absence by her staff.

"And Dudley, I forgot to tell Blondell that the Kleenex in Mr. Mendelson's bathroom should be white, not pink ever. Make sure she changes it."

"Yes, Mrs. Mendelson," replied Dudley.

Jules, hearing Pauline descend the stairs, came out from the library, where he had been on the telephone with his various offices while waiting for her. In his hand he was carrying a coffee cup. "Where are you off to?" he asked, surprised, when he saw her bags and traveling clothes. He had expected to see her in one of her filmy negligees, which she favored for mornings in her house.

"I'm going back east for a few days to see my father," answered Pauline.

"Is he ill?"

"No more than he has been, but I haven't seen him for months, and I thought this would be a perfect time."

He had heard of no such plan the night before. "When did you decide this?"

"During the night."

He turned to go back to the library. "I'll make arrangements for you to take the plane," he said.

"No, no, don't bother. I've already made arrangements with Miss Maple," said Pauline. "The plane's going to fly me to Bangor and will turn around and fly right back so it can take you to Fort Worth for your meeting at the museum tonight."

"You're very efficient, Pauline," he said.

"You told me that last night, Jules."

"Have you had breakfast?"

"No, of course not. I thought we had a date for breakfast."

Her matter-of-factness bothered Jules. He was used to her in a different way, warm and compliant, and he was unsure of himself with her when her manner was so chilly. She preceded him down the hallway into their sunrise room, which they had never used together before for breakfast, as their morning hours had turned out to be so different. Pauline appraised the table and nodded. Her written instructions for Blondell the night before had been carried out exactly. The table was set with a Porthault cloth and napkins. Freshly cut roses from the garden were arranged in a low vase in the center of the table. Her favorite Minton breakfast china in the morning glory pattern was set at the two places. The morning papers from New York and Los Angeles were placed one on top of another on a side table. Even with a life in the beginning of turmoil, no detail in the running of her house was unworthy of her attention.

Jules watched her. "This looks very pretty," he said.

"It does, doesn't it?" she replied.

Dudley, whose instincts were keen, was aware of the unusualness of the breakfast. With proper solemnity, he entered the room with two silver pots on a tray and poured tea for Pauline and then coffee for Jules.

"Thank you, Dudley," said Pauline. "I will have only melon and one slice of toast. Tell Gertie to use the whole-grain bread. I'm sure you know what Mr. Mendelson will have."

"Yes, ma'am," said Dudley.

"Leave the coffee right here, Dudley," said Jules, rapping his knuckles on the table by his coffee cup. "I like to pour myself."

"Do you still drink six cups of coffee with breakfast?" asked Pauline.

"Something like that."

"Can't be good for your heart."

"My heart. All that I'm hearing these days is about my heart," said Jules.

"From whom else?" asked Pauline.

"Last night, from Arnie Zwillman."

"Oh," she said, in disgust, and waved her hands at the mention of Arnie Zwillman's name, as if a bad odor had suddenly permeated the room.

Dudley came into the room with Jules's scrambled eggs and bacon in a covered silver dish. Pauline lifted her delicate Minton cup with both hands and, elbows on the table, watched as Jules helped himself from the dish that Dudley held.

When Dudley retreated from the room again, she said, "I'm giving you back these yellow diamond earrings, Jules." She shook the diamonds in her hand as if they were dice and then shot them in his direction across the tablecloth.

Jules, surprised, took them. "You didn't like them?"

"Oh, yes, they're very beautiful, but I would never wear them."

"I thought you liked them last night."

"I didn't say I didn't like them. I said I wouldn't wear them."

"Why?"

"Because there is guilt attached to them. You bought them for me because you had been found out, as a sort of atonement. Rose always says the more unfaithful the husband, the greater the jewel collection," said Pauline.

"That sounds like something Rose would say," answered Jules. He put the earrings in his pocket. "I'll keep them. I'll put them in the safe. Maybe later."

"What do you mean? For Christmas? For my birthday? No, Jules. I don't want them. Send them back to Boothby's."

"All right," he said, quietly.

On the wall by her chair was a small painting of grapes and pears by Fantin-Latour. She stood up and straightened it by a fraction of an inch. "I've always loved this picture," she said.

"Do you remember when we bought it?" he asked.

"Of course." It seemed for a moment that she would recall the incident, but she chose not to. "Do you think we were ever happy, Jules, or was this all one big twenty-two-year show of a marriage?"

"Oh, Pauline, don't talk like that, please."

Dudley came in again, carrying the silver dish with the scrambled eggs and bacon, but Pauline waved him away, even though Jules would have taken more if they had been offered to him.

"Imagine dividing all this up," she said.

"All what?" he asked.

She made a gesture that indicated the whole of the contents of their house. "Everything," she said, looking at him.

A deeply troubled expression took over his face. At that instant his possessions and his position meant more to him than his obsession, and he was willing to abandon the latter.

"Don't even kid about something like that," he said.

"Oh, I'm not kidding, Jules. Not for an instant am I kidding." Pauline had no fear of meeting her husband's eye. She met it.

"No, of course you're not," he said.

"When you asked me to marry you all those years ago, my father advised me not to marry you, and now I'm going back to my father because I need to talk to someone I can trust to see whether I should stay married to you, or to end it."

"Listen to me, Pauline. I will do *anything* to keep from losing you."

"What about this woman with the red hair?"

"What woman with the red hair?"

"If you're not going to be honest with me, even now, there is no point whatever in continuing this conversation. Months ago I was sent a clipping, anonymously of course, from a Paris paper about a fire in the Meurice Hotel, with a photograph of you in the background, behind a young woman carrying a jewel case. I knew you were staying at the Ritz at the time. I chose to ignore it. I chose to forget it even. But subsequent signs have made it impossible to ignore and forget."

"Like what?"

"I smelled her on your fingers, Jules," said Pauline.

Jules's face turned scarlet. His expression was as clear as a signed confession. "All right, it's true, but it was nothing. It was meaningless. It will be over, I swear to you. I've never heard of anything so absurd in my whole life, that a marriage like ours must end because of an infidelity," he said.

"This hardly qualifies as an infidelity, Jules."

"It was an aberration, no more, I swear to you. I'm fifty-seven years old. Perhaps it was panic. I simply was carried away with an over-whelming feeling."

"Do you think I don't occasionally have feelings like that for other people, Jules?" asked Pauline.

Jules looked at her, as if the idea had never occurred to him.

"I do," she said. "Young Philip Quennell, for instance. I think he is very attractive. I even told him that last night at that terrible party."

At the mention of Philip Quennell's name, Jules winced. He could not bear Philip Quennell.

"I could visualize having an affair with him if I were the kind of woman who had affairs. But I *didn't* have an affair with him, Jules."

Jules was aghast at the thought of his wife even thinking of having an affair. "Because of Camilla?" he asked.

"That, yes. But also, Jules, because of you, because of our mar-riage, which is something I have taken very seriously."

"So have I."

"No. You want an ornamental wife, that's all, and that's not good enough for me."

There was a silence between them.

"Philip Quennell, by the way, has made no such offer to me, nor has he shown the slightest interest of that sort in me."

"I have taken a dislike to your friend Quennell," said Jules.

"He doesn't believe that Hector committed suicide," replied Pau-line. "Neither did the butler at Mr. Stieglitz's last night."

Jules shook his head in impatience. "Who cares what people like that think?"

"I don't believe it either," she said.

"Believe it," he said.

"Are you ordering me to believe something I don't believe?"

"Yes." There was a harshness in his voice.

Puzzled, she looked at him.

There was a knock on the door, and Dudley entered with an atti-tude of anxiety, interrupting what he knew to be an important private meeting between the two people he had served for many years. "I'm sorry to interrupt," he said.

"That's all right," said Pauline.

"The car is here. The bags are in," he said.

"Yes, I'll be right there. Put these newspapers in the car, will you, Dudley?"

When Dudley left, Jules said, "I'll drive out to the airport with you."

"Oh, don't be silly, Jules." She took a final sip of her tea.

"You don't have to hurry, you know. Have another cup of tea. The nice thing about having your own plane is that it's not going to leave without you," said Jules.

Pauline shook her head. His remark was one she had heard often before. When she got to the door of the room, she turned back. "This room is really quite pretty, don't you think? Isn't it too bad we never used it?" She walked out.

Jules rose and followed Pauline out of the room, down the corridor to the hallway, and out the front door to the courtyard.

"Have you put Mrs. Mendelson's bags in the back?" he asked, even though he had just heard from Dudley that the bags were in the car already.

The chauffeur stood holding the door. As she was about to get in, Pauline turned to the butler and said, "Dudley, there's a crack in the windowpane of the lavatory off the library. Ask Joe to replace the pane, will you?" She stepped into the car. "Oh, and one more thing, Dudley. Will you check and see if one of the Flora Danica salad plates is missing? I counted only twenty-three yesterday."

Jules stepped up and nodded to the chauffeur that he would close the door. "Give my best to your father," he said.

"I will," replied Pauline.

"How long will you be gone?"

"I don't know exactly, Jules. Not long."

"When you're ready to return, let me know, and I'll arrange for the plane to fly to Bangor and pick you up," he said. He did not want her to leave.

Pauline pulled on her gloves. "Good-bye, Jules," she said.

"I'll miss you," he said.

Pauline nodded. "All right, Jim, let's go," she said to the chauffeur.

Jules stepped back and closed the rear door. As the car started to move forward, he raised his hand to wave to her. After the car pulled out of the courtyard and started down the driveway, Jules remained standing there, not moving.

In the upstairs hall, standing back from the window, Blondell watched the departure. She did not understand why she felt sadness. From the main hallway downstairs, Dudley also watched with a sense of foreboding.

It surprised Jules that he felt bereft. He had never acknowledged to himself that Pauline was necessary to him as a component part of his existence. Throughout his adult life and great worldly success, Jules had been much sought after to sit on the boards of directors of businesses and hospitals and museums. He had been asked to serve as pallbearer or eulogist at the funerals of a President of the United States, six senators, two governors, and numerous chief executive officers of banks and businesses. As the husband of Pauline Mendelson, he was considered a prize and a catch at social functions. And, yet, he knew deep inside him that he did not have a single intimate friend to whom he could turn in time of trouble. Except Pauline.

"DO YOU ever go to the doctor's, Jules?" asked Flo.

"For what?"

"Checkups? Anything?"

"No."

"You should, you know."

"I know. I know."

Flo bought Jules a treadmill, which she set up in her bedroom. She made him use it for twenty minutes each afternoon as a way to deal with his weight. When the canceled check came to Miss Maple, Jules was inordinately pleased to see how much money she had spent on him out of her allowance.

"Jules, honey, I don't understand what laundered money means," said Flo, sitting in a chair watching him.

Jules, hands on the rail, walked in place. His twenty minutes on the treadmill had become a talking time for them, and they both enjoyed it. "Look, let me explain," said Jules. He liked to discuss things with Flo. "Say I have a painting worth a million dollars. Arnie Zwillman buys that picture from me for that much money, but he pays for it in cash out of his briefcase. Then, with the art market the way it is, the value of the painting appreciates. That means it goes up in value, and he can then sell it on the open market, or at auction."

"Oh, I get it," said Flo. "So the dirty money becomes clean."

"Right," said Jules. "Only he wasn't talking about art."

"Honey, you can't get involved with that. You know that, don't you?" said Flo.

"I know."

"Then tell Arnie Zwillman to go fuck himself."

Jules nodded. He wished it were that simple. He turned the switch of his treadmill off. For a few moments he remained on the machine without speaking. Then he walked away from her toward the bathroom. At the bathroom door, he said quietly, "There's more to this than you know."

"What?"

"There're things about me that he knows that no one else knows."

"Not even Pauline?"

"Not even Pauline."

She stared at his back. "Like what?" she asked.

He turned around to look at her. She had never seen his face look so haunted. He opened his mouth to speak. Then he looked at his watch. "I'd better go. It's late. I have to meet Sims Lord for dinner."

"I want to hear," Flo persisted.

Jules was a keeper of secrets; he was not a person who confided in other people. Even Sims Lord, his trusted adviser, did not know everything there was to know about Jules. Sims only knew everything there was to know about Jules's business dealings. When Jules met with him later that evening, he planned to tell him about his extraordinary conversation with Arnie Zwillman, about the money-laundering proposition, but he would not be able to tell Sims the things that Arnie Zwillman knew about his life, about the girl who had gone off the balcony of the Roosevelt Hotel in Chicago in 1953. Or about Kippie. Sometimes he worried about his heart. It beat too fast when he thought about the things that were buried inside of him. He knew he should make an appointment to see Dr. Petrie, but he was always too busy, and he kept postponing it.

"Tell me," insisted Flo.

When, finally, he started to talk, he spoke slowly in a low voice, almost as if he were talking to himself, and Flo had to lean forward to hear him. She knew that if she interrupted him to ask him to speak louder, he would change his mind and not go on with his story. "When I was a young man, something horrible happened to me in Chicago, for which I bear the responsibility," he said.

IN NORTHEAST HARBOR, Maine, it always amused Neville McAdoo when he heard himself described as Pauline Mendelson's father. It amused him even more when he heard himself described as Jules

Mendelson's father-in-law. The previous summer he had celebrated his seventy-fifth birthday with a small dancing party under a green-and-white-striped marquee, given by his three daughters and their husbands. All his grandchildren came, even Kippie, who was known in the family as the California cousin. The men all wore blazers and white flannels, and the ladies, dressier than the men, were in silk prints or summer chiffons with a minimum amount of jewelry. No black tie for them. Among themselves, they chuckled at the pretensions and swank of Newport and Southampton social life, much preferring the simplicity of their own. "They have no denial of anything in those places," said Neville McAdoo. "They have no Northeast discipline." Northeast parties were never reported in the New York social column of Dolly De Longpre, who had been the recognized chronicler of society for three decades.

At that party Jules Mendelson had won the admiration of all the McAdoos when he made himself agreeable for several hours to Aunt Maud, who was known in the family as poor Aunt Maud. It was the late husband of poor Aunt Maud, Uncle Harry, who had been found dead in bed in a seedy West Side hotel in New York, dressed in women's clothing, and Aunt Maud had been a trial to everyone ever since. Kippie, who had been expelled from both St. Paul's and St. George's before going to finish up his preparatory years at Le Rosay in Switzerland, had a sort of mysterious glamour in the family. "So good-looking," the older ladies said about him. Or, "Such charm." His contemporaries had different opinions. It was at the party that Kippie had strangled a cat, as a prank, at the young people's table, to the horror and fascination of his eastern cousins. "I'll never speak to you again, Kippie Petworth," said his Philadelphia cousin, Louise Ordano, who was nearly in tears. "Lucky for you it wasn't one of Poppy's Abyssinians, that's all I can say." Cosimo and Cosima were their grandfather's Abyssinian cats, on whom he doted.

It was in keeping with Kippie's usual good luck that there had been very little commotion over the strangled cat, as it was an unknown cat that had wandered into the party tent, and it was not missed. Kippie, along with Bozzie Manchester, his New York cousin, had buried the unfortunate cat in the woods beyond his grandfather's property, and no more had been said about it.

"It's so lovely here, Poppy," said Pauline. "I always forget. I always mean to come back more often."

"The Van Degans want you for lunch," said Neville McAdoo.

"Oh, no, thanks, Poppy. I'll stay here with you," said Pauline. She dipped her napkin into a water glass and wiped away a stain on her father's white linen jacket where he had dripped carrot soup, without interrupting the flow of her conversation. "Lean closer to the table, Poppy, so you won't spill," she said. "And let me bring your napkin up higher. There. Now finish your soup. That nice girl from town made it especially for you. She said it was your favorite. What a treasure she is."

"Colleen," said old Mr. McAdoo. "Her name is Colleen. She's not a maid, you know, or a cook either. She comes in and takes care of me on vacations and weekends, when she's not at the university." Everything about Northeast Harbor fascinated her father. He took as much interest in the lives of the locals as he did in the summer people. "She's going to hotel school and wants to be the manager of the Asticou Inn one day."

"Marvelous," said Pauline. "The young today, they're so filled with ambition and purpose."

"How's Kippie?" asked her father.

"Well, sadly, Kippie doesn't fit into that pattern of ambition and purpose, but his charm continues unabated, I suppose. He's still in that rehab in France, for drugs."

Neville McAdoo patted his daughter's hand. Always slim, he had played tennis every day until a few years before his stroke. To shade his face from the sun he was wearing a white tennis hat that had been laundered so often it was soft and floppy. They were sitting on the veranda of his large cedar-shingle house, turned gray by fifty Maine winters, looking out on Somes Sound. It had been a blessing in disguise when the original McAdoo house in Bar Harbor, next to Northeast Harbor, had burned to the ground in the great fire of 1947. The once proud McAdoo fortune had diminished by that time, and the family could not have afforded to keep the place going for many more summers. With the insurance money, Neville McAdoo's father built a more practical house in Northeast Harbor, with only ten bedrooms rather than thirty, and it was there that Pauline and her sisters had spent all the summers of their lives until they were married.

"What's the matter, Pauline?" he asked.

"You always knew when something was the matter, didn't you, Poppy?" she said.

"You don't just appear out of the blue in Northeast in the spring before the season starts without something very important on your mind," he replied.

Pauline untied and then tied again the sleeves of a cashmere sweater that hung over her shoulders. She rose from her wicker chair and walked to the edge of the veranda and sat on the railing, facing her father. "I'm thinking of leaving Jules," she said.

JULES NEVER discussed the whereabouts of his wife with his mistress, but his mistress religiously followed his wife's comings and goings in the society pages and gossip columns. Cyril Rathbone, in particular, continued to have an inordinate interest in the activities of Pauline Mendelson, although he had, fortunately, seemed not to have connected Jules Mendelson and Arnie Zwillman in his account of Casper Stieglitz's party. He simply named the Mendelsons as "surprise guests at a mixed-bag evening."

"Where's Northeast Harbor?" asked Flo.

"Maine," replied Jules cautiously. "Why?"

"Is it like Malibu?"

"Good heavens, no."

"Like Newport?"

"Are you referring to Newport, California, or Newport, Rhode Island?"

"I didn't know there were two."

"There are. It is not at all like Newport, California, and it is more understated than Newport, Rhode Island."

"Understated. Does that mean classier?"

"To some, I suppose."

"Like the quiet rich? That kind of thing?"

"I suppose. Why this great interest in Northeast Harbor?"

"I hear that Pauline is visiting her father there."

Jules was silent for a moment. "And where did you hear that?" he asked.

"I didn't exactly hear it. I read it."

"Where?"

"In Cyril Rathbone's column."

"I should have guessed that. You seem to rely on that swine for so much of your information."

"I'd die happy to have my name in Cyril Rathbone's column."

"Oh, please."

"I really would, Jules. I like to read about all those people and places he writes about. It's like another world to me. One day I'd like to go to all those places, like Newport and Southampton and Northeast Harbor," said Flo.

"I wouldn't mind another glass of wine," said Jules.

"With Pauline out of town, you don't have to go home tonight, do you?"

"Yes, I have to go home, but I don't have to go home right away. I was supposed to go out to dinner, but I canceled that. I thought we might have dinner here."

"How about taking me out to dinner, Jules?" asked Flo.

"Why not eat here?"

"Because I'm sick of eating here. Chinese takeout from Mr. Chow's, or pizzas sent in from Spago. That's what eating at home is for me. I know how to wait tables, but I don't know how to cook food. I want to go out." She stood up to show her impatience.

"It's not practical," said Jules, dismissing the notion with a shake of his head.

"And why not?" persisted Flo. She placed the forefinger of her left hand on the small finger of her right hand and moved it from finger to finger as she reiterated the immediate facts of Jules's life. "Pauline's out of town in Northeast Harbor, Maine, visiting her old father. You don't have to go to one of Rose Cliveden's dinners because she's laid up in bed with a broken leg and a bottle of vodka, and besides you never go to those fancy dinners when Pauline is away. And the guy from the museum in Hartford who was coming to look at your paintings and try to get you to leave them to the Wadsworth Atheneum had to postpone because his mother-in-law committed suicide. And Sims Lord is at the bankers' convention in Chicago giving a speech in your place because you didn't want to go to Chicago. And the guy from the Louvre Museum in Paris who mended the crack in the Degas ballerina that you accidentally knocked off its pedestal because some guy got you mad at lunch after Hector Paradiso's funeral is not due in with the statue until tomorrow night. So you're free, and you're going to take me out to dinner."

Jules laughed. "Good God. How do you know all those things?" he asked.

"Because I'm a good listener, Jules. You lie here on my bed with the telephone on your stomach and make all those calls, and I just listen and remember."

He patted her hand. "Look, Flo, dear. It's not a good idea to go out to dinner," said Jules patiently. "Especially right now."

"I'm not asking you to take me to the Bistro Garden, or Chasen's. We don't have to go to a fancy place, where you're going to run into a lot of people you know."

Jules shook his head. He did not want to go out in public with Flo, but he could not bring himself to say that.

"There's even the goddamn Valley. You'll certainly never see anyone in the *Valley* who crosses over with your kind of life. Let's just have dinner together, like two normal people having an affair. Please, Jules. *Please.* I'm always all dressed up with no place to go. You don't know how lonely I get."

"Okay," he said quietly. He reached over and put his hand on her thigh and started to move it back and forth.

"Oh, no, none of that," she said, slapping his hand. "Don't get horny again. I know that trick. We'll start, and then you won't take me out to dinner. *After* dinner, I'll take care of your dick." She hopped out of bed and ran toward her closet. "A new Chanel suit came today. Black. Gold buttons. And a *very* short skirt, up to here."

"Where can we go where we aren't likely to see anyone?" asked Jules.

TWENTY-TWO YEARS earlier her father had advised Pauline not to marry Jules Mendelson. Neville McAdoo, who admired physical fitness and athletic prowess, had minded that Jules was overweight and never exercised almost as much as he minded that Jules was not eligible for any of the clubs that members of the McAdoo family had belonged to for generations. Clubs played a great part in their lives. But even Neville McAdoo could not ignore Jules's importance in the world of finance, and over the years he had come to like and respect his son-in-law.

And Jules, although he never would have admitted such a thing, was impressed with the lineage of his wife's family. He wondered in the beginning how a family that had received so much publicity through the brilliant marriages of the three sisters could have so little money. In the era of vast fortunes in which they were living, the McAdoo millions, which numbered less than five, were considered insignificant, at least in the circles in which Jules moved. It was Jules, the rich outsider, who had paid to put Poppy's old house in order again after his stroke, winterizing it, reroofing it, and adding on to the already ample veranda so that a ramp could more easily facilitate the wheelchair that had become a part of Poppy's life. Inside, the library, which Poppy always called the book room, had been made over into his bedroom, and the lavatory off the library had been enlarged to a full bathroom, with railings on the wall of his shower and tub. His greatest fear was falling and breaking a hip.

The telling of her tale was painful and difficult for Pauline. Normally so articulate and descriptive in her accounts of her life, she spoke now in a halting and disjointed fashion, looking away from her father so that he could not see the shame and pain that showed in her face. Jules was having an affair, she began. She had found out about it in the most shaming manner. "So hurtful, Poppy. No, no, I won't tell you how I found out. He has a mistress. He is keeping this woman. He is besotted with her."

"Did he tell you he was besotted with her?"

"Several times I have awakened in the middle of the night, and he is lying there next to me, wide awake, staring at the ceiling."

If Pauline had expected her father to react with ungentlemanly glee, she was mistaken. And he would not indulge in any I-told-you-so type of conversation, for he loved his daughter and could see that she was deeply unhappy.

"Have you ever seen her?" her father asked, when Pauline had finished.

"Some anonymous person sent me a photograph of her from a Paris newspaper. He took her to Paris. Did I tell you that?"

"Is she younger than you?"

"Not quite young enough to be my daughter, but almost. And pretty. Slightly common, but pretty."

"Is she in your set out there?"

"Heavens, no."

"Are you likely to encounter her?"

"I shouldn't think so."

"Are your friends like Rose Cliveden and Camilla Ebury likely to encounter her?"

One of the Abyssinian cats strolled out onto the veranda. When it came to Neville McAdoo's chair, it raised its paw to scratch at his leg. "Oh, yes, here she is," he said, delighted. He leaned over and picked up the cat. "Or here *he* is, rather. I'm never quite sure which is which. Are you Cosima or Cosimo?" He raised the cat up and stared between its legs. "Cosima, of course. I knew you were Cosima all the time." He settled back with the cat in his arms. "Are you being gossiped about?" he asked, as if the cat had not interrupted.

"If we are, I am unaware of it," answered Pauline. "At least I have not noticed any change in attitude on the part of my friends."

"Does Jules want to leave you to marry her?"

"No. I don't think so. I feel just the opposite. I feel he doesn't want to leave me, or want me to leave him. He wants both."

"Perhaps it's that relentless social life you lead out there," said Poppy. "Jules was never much for social life when you met him. Maybe this woman is just a respite from all those parties."

Pauline felt stung. "The wives of brilliant men should be socially ambitious," she said defensively. "I have played an enormous part in Jules's success, and Jules is aware of that too, but our success together is built around Jules, make no mistake about that. He is an extraordinary man. That is a thing I have never doubted, from the moment I first met him that night in Palm Beach at Laurance Van Degan's dance."

"You sound like you love him still."

"I do," she said. "Remember, I had someone to compare him to, the socially perfect and totally ineffectual Johnny Petworth."

"Oh, Johnny," said Mr. McAdoo, shaking his head sadly. "I saw him at the Butterfield the last time I was in New York, in a perfect snit over a bid in a bridge game that Win Stebbins had called wrong."

"That's what I mean by totally ineffectual," said Pauline. "I knew that marriage was a mistake during the honeymoon, but if I hadn't met Jules, I might have remarried someone just like Johnny Petworth."

"Then stick it out, Pauline. Whatever he's having will pass. He's not the first man to have an affair, you know, and it's highly unlikely that you will be embarrassed by such a person, in the way you might have been if she was one of your own set."

Her father slowly raised his hand and pointed a bony finger out to Somes Sound.

"What is it, Poppy?" asked Pauline.

"Billy Twombley's new sailboat," answered her father.

"Yes, yes, isn't it lovely?" said Pauline. Her father, she knew, was finished with the subject of Jules Mendelson.

FLO AND JULES drove to the San Fernando Valley to a steak house on Ventura Boulevard in Universal City. Listening as she did to everything that was said, Flo already knew that people in the group that the Mendelsons and their friends moved in considered the San Fernando Valley to be as remote as a different state.

"Do you have a reservation?" asked the maître d'.

"I don't," said Jules.

"I'm afraid there will be a wait of about twenty minutes," said the maître d', perusing his reservation list. "You may wait in the bar."

"I don't want to wait for twenty minutes," said Jules quietly.

"Look, there's a table over there in the corner," said Flo.

"I was about to seat a couple who have been waiting in the bar for that table," said the maître d', haughtily. He picked up two large menus to take to that couple when he fetched them.

Jules reached into his pocket and took out his money, which he carried in a loose wad, unencumbered by a clip or wallet. He peeled off a bill and handed it to the maître d'.

"Oh, no, sir. I'm afraid we don't accept tips for seating patrons out of turn." He looked down at the bill in his hand, and his expression changed. "Let me look to see if something has opened up in the John Wayne room."

"I don't want to sit in the John Wayne room," said Jules. "I want to sit at that table over there in that corner."

"Follow me," said the maître d'.

"How much did you tip him?" whispered Flo over her shoulder, as she followed the man to their table.

"Fifty," replied Jules.

"Wow," said Flo.

Seated, Jules ordered a martini and Flo ordered a Diet Coke. Out in public, Jules felt strange with Flo. In her house they could talk together for hours, but in the restaurant, even though it was highly unlikely that he would encounter anyone he knew, he found it difficult to keep up the conversation. He picked up the menu, which had a leather cover and a tassel, and glanced down it. "Let's see what they have," he said.

"Actually, Jules, I don't eat steak," said Flo.

"Why didn't you say that when I picked this place?"

"I was afraid you'd change your mind."

He looked down at the menu again. "They have lobster tails. Frozen, I'm sure. Does that appeal to you?"

"Oh, sure. I can't believe we're actually doing this, Jules."

She looked around her at the other tables. An expression of recognition came over her face.

"Do you see someone you know?" asked Jules.

"Trent Muldoon. The television actor who owns my house, that you keep telling me you're going to buy for me but never do."

"Don't say hello, for God's sake."

"I don't even know him to say hello to."

There was a moment of silence. "What did you do with yourself all day?" he asked finally.

"Read. I'm a great reader, you know," she answered.

"I didn't know, but I'm delighted to hear that. What sort of things do you read? Besides Cyril Rathbone, I mean."

"Biographies, mostly," she said, aware of the importance of the word.

"Biographies? Really? What sort?"

"Marilyn Monroe, mostly," she replied, quite unselfconsciously. "I think I've read everything that has ever been written on Marilyn Monroe."

Jules laughed.

"Oh, sure, go ahead, laugh. Typical, Jules," said Flo. She shook her head in dismissal of his attitude. "I happen to think that Marilyn was murdered. In fact, I know she was murdered. All the evidence points to it. She didn't die in her house, you know, like everybody thinks. She died in the ambulance, and they took her back to the house, where she was discovered dead."

Jules shook his own head in turn, but for a different reason. He was madly in love with a woman whose position in life was inappropriate for his position in life. This was not the sort of conversation he would ever have had with Pauline. Pauline understood world and economic affairs well enough to converse intelligently, and she could hold his interest when she discussed the events and personalities of the social world to which she had been born. No cockeyed Marilyn Monroe theories for her. "That whole story has always been absurd," said Jules.

"She was an inconvenient woman, you know," said Flo, ignoring him. She now nodded her head in a way to indicate to Jules that she wasn't telling half of what she knew about the case. "I used to hear things."

"Hear things where?" he asked.

"At the coffee shop. You'd be surprised at the things I used to hear there. And from Glyceria too. She knows things that Faye Converse told her. Faye was a friend of Marilyn's."

"What sort of things?"

"What do powerful people do with someone who's become inconvenient?" asked Flo.

"Tell me," said Jules.

"Don't you see?"

"No, I don't. What's to see?"

"You get rid of the person, and they got rid of Marilyn."

"Oh, for God's sake," said Jules impatiently. "You people with all those wacky theories."

"And you people who are always saying there are no conspiracies." There was a tone of harshness in her voice.

For a moment they stared at each other. "Is this a fight we're having?" asked Jules.

Flo smiled. "I'll back off," she said. "I don't want to blow my big night out on the town."


PAULINE walked through a cluttered side hallway, past croquet mallets, tennis rackets, boots, and umbrellas, and entered a sitting room that had little to do with fashion but a great deal to do with taste. From the lower shelf of a table behind a sofa loosely covered in extremely worn chintz, she pulled out some photograph albums.

"Here they are," she said, returning to the veranda. "I knew I'd seen them somewhere."

Her father smiled at her. He took out his round gold-rimmed spectacles and put them on. She pulled up a chair next to his wheelchair and set the albums on a table in front of them. Slowly he started to turn the pages, and in a few minutes they were laughing together as they were reminded of other times. When they came to the latest album, the pictures of his birthday party the year before, he said, "What's happened to Justine Altemus?"

"You haven't heard? She married Herkie Saybrook."

Neville McAdoo nodded approvingly. It was the kind of match he believed in. "That must have pleased her mother," said Poppy.

"As much as Lil is ever pleased about anything, I suppose," said Pauline.

"Good croquet player, Herkie Saybrook. His grandfather and I were at Groton together." He turned a few more pages and made a few more comments about people. "You haven't told me everything that's bothering you, have you?"

"No."

"Well?"

"I don't know why I feel this, but I think he is being blackmailed by a gangster," said Pauline.

"Because he has a mistress?" asked Poppy. "Hardly likely these days, Pauline."

"That's not why, Poppy. Once he told me, when we were first married, that there had been trouble in his life years ago. He asked me not to ask him about it. I only said at the time, 'Were there consequences?' or something like that. He said, and I remember it distinctly, 'One of the advantages of having rich parents is that they keep you out of jams.' Then, not wanting to embarrass him about it, I told him the story of Aunt Maud's husband being found dead in a seedy West Side hotel in women's clothing."

"You didn't tell him that?"

"I did."

"We all promised never to refer to it."

"I know. But Jules never gossips, and he would never do anything to embarrass me, ever, that much I know."

"Except have a mistress."

Pauline looked away. "We never referred to what happened to Jules again; but, whatever it is, I think the gangster, Mr. Zwillman he's called—Arnie Zwillman—I think he knows whatever it is that's in Jules's past. I used to think that perhaps he had gotten a girl pregnant when he was young, but now I think it is something more serious. Jules looked old to me for the first time, almost defeated, the other night after he saw Mr. Zwillman. Whatever it is, I think if it came to light, Jules's appointment to Brussels might be in jeopardy, and that appointment means everything to Jules."

Neville McAdoo closed the photograph album and removed his gold-rimmed spectacles before he spoke again. "All the more reason for you to stay with Jules, Pauline."

JULES took out his parking check and handed it to the parking boy.

"What kind of car, sir?" asked the boy.

"Bentley, dark blue," replied Jules.

Flo, who was always curious about other people, turned to look at a couple who were waiting for their car. "That's Trent Muldoon again," she said excitedly, tapping Jules on the arm to turn and look at the television star. "I think I'll go over and introduce myself while you're getting the car. I read in some column he's going to make a picture in Yugoslavia."

"No, no, don't," said Jules.

"Jules! Hello! Howareyou?"

Flo, without turning, immediately recognized the voice as the voice of a society woman. She wondered how they all learned to talk like that, with that slightly strident sound that announced their class and privilege. Later, alone, she would say to herself over and over again, "Jules! Hello! Howareyou?" until she had the voice imitated perfectly.

"Madge," she heard Jules say. She did not turn around, but she knew they were kissing on first one cheek and then the other, in the manner of society people. She would have liked to see Jules participate in that ritual, but she knew not to turn. "What*ever* are you doing all the way out here?" she heard the woman called Madge ask.

"A little business dinner with Sims Lord," she heard Jules answer. "And you? What are you doing out here?"

"We're on our way to the ranch for the weekend," answered Madge. "Ralph adores the food here, don't ask me why, all that awful red meat, so bad for you, every doctor says so. Where is Sims? I'd love to say hello. I haven't seen him for ages."

"I think he stopped in the men's room," said Jules.

"So did Ralph," said Madge. "How's Pauline's father?"

"Oh, fine," answered Jules. "A little stroke can't keep Neville McAdoo down."

"When is Pauline coming back?" asked Madge.

Jules's Bentley pulled up in front of the restaurant, and the parking boy hopped out. "Your car, sir," he called out to Jules. He went around to the passenger side and opened that door for Flo to get in.

Flo turned around and stood awkwardly in place, not sure what to do, and Madge White, whose daughter had become pregnant by Jules's stepson, Kippie Petworth, when they were both fourteen years old, sensed immediately that the pretty girl with red hair wearing a Chanel suit was there with Jules.

Jules, used to difficult moments in business, appeared unperturbed, as if he were in control during a complex moment in a negotiation. "Oh, may I introduce, uh, Miss, uh?—help me," he said to Flo, as if he hardly knew her himself. "I'm terrible with names."

"March," whispered Flo, embarrassed by Jules's attitude.

"Yes, yes, of course, Miss March, forgive me. I'm so terrible with names. This is Mrs. White. Miss March works with Sims."

"Hellohowareyou?" said Madge White, staring at the young woman.

Flo, confused, nodded but did not speak. Flo could see by the haughty look on Madge White's face that she understood the situation, and she shrank from the look.

A car horn honked at the delay caused by the Bentley's blocking the departure area. There were cars with impatient occupants backed up behind, waiting to be parked.

"Your car, sir," called out the parking boy again, but neither Jules nor Flo moved toward it.

A taxi pulled up next to the Bentley. As an arriving couple got out of the cab, Flo called out, "I'll take that cab," and ran toward it.

Jules, upset, called out after Flo, "I'll be happy to drop you off, Miss March." He wondered if Madge White noticed the concern in his voice.

Flo, in the cab, looked back at Jules. There were tears in her eyes. "No, no, I'm sure you and Mr. Lord have important things to talk over, Mr. Mendelson," she said. She turned to the driver. "Beat it. That Bentley is going to follow me, and I don't want to be followed."

"Where to, lady?" asked the driver. He was aware that the young lady was highly agitated, but he did not want to become involved in her drama.

"Please. Please. Move quickly," she pleaded. She gave her address on Azelia Way in Beverly Hills.

"Do you want to take Laurel Canyon or Coldwater Canyon?" asked the driver. He spoke with a heavy Middle Eastern accent.

Flo looked out the rear window of the cab and saw that Jules was shaking hands with Madge White and getting into his car. She knew immediately that he would go to Azelia Way to find her, and she did not want to be found by him. "No, listen, driver, I changed my mind. Take me to the Chateau Marmont on Sunset Strip," she said. "Take Laurel Canyon. You can go quicker on Laurel."

The Chateau Marmont was where Philip Quennell lived.

## Flo's Tape #15

"On the afternoon of the day that Pauline left for Northeast Harbor to visit her father, Jules was, as always, in my house at the regular time, about a quarter to four. He didn't tell me she had gone away, by the way. I only knew that when I read it in Cyril Rathbone's column. Anyway, we'd done it a couple of times, and he was lying on my bed talking on the telephone, just like he always did, conducting a little business before we did it again. For a guy his age, he could go more times than most guys half his age.

"But that day he needed his little agenda book that he always carried with him, that told him where he had to be at what time, and listed the sixty or seventy telephone numbers that immediately affected his personal and business life. By the way, he had me in there under Red, as in red hair, in case Pauline or Miss Maple or someone was looking through it, I suppose. Anyway, that day he was talking to someone important, I forget who now, maybe Myles Crocker from the State Department, and he signaled to me without stopping his conversation to get him his agenda out of his suit jacket.

"Well, I got the little book out and, naturally, being curious, I started flicking through it to see what fancy dinner parties he was going to that week. And that was when I saw that he had several appointments with Dr. Petrie. Dr. Petrie, in case you never heard of him, was one of the eminent heart specialists of Los Angeles. I happened to know that because Jules had attended a testimonial in his honor. Kind of a cold chill went through me. I wondered if he was okay, healthwise.

"Later, I said to him, 'You okay, Jules?' He said, 'What are you talking about?' I said, 'Your ticker?' He said again, 'What are you talking about?' I said, 'I saw in your agenda you had some appointments with Dr. Petrie.' When Jules got mad, his face got red and he became very silent. That's what happened then. He got mad. He said it was because I shouldn't have pried into his book, that it was bad manners.

"You see, I always thought the merry-go-round was never going to stop, but I should have begun to see the signs that day."

# 16

ON THE AFTERNOON of the evening that Jules and Flo dined together at a restaurant in the San Fernando Valley, another encounter took place on a street in Beverly Hills that also caused a disruption in a relationship. Camilla Ebury, the rich and pretty young widow who was having an affair with Philip Quennell, had begun to experience feelings for him that she had never felt for her late husband, and thoughts of marriage were beginning to form, although she knew almost nothing of her lover's life before she met him at the Mendelsons' party. She only knew that he was not a fortune hunter. On his part, Philip was enjoying an extremely pleasant relationship, but, for reasons of his own, he did not think of it in terms of permanence. He was merely a transient figure in the city where Camilla was entrenched. It was his intention, as it had always been, to return to his home in New York when he finished the screenplay for the documentary he was writing for Casper Stieglitz. By that time, he felt sure that the furor that had been caused by the book he had written about Reza Bulbenkian would have died down.

As with many women of her position, much of Camilla Ebury's time was taken up with good works and cultural activities. She worked long hours for the fashionable charities of the city, the Los Angeles Orphanage Guild, the Colleagues, and the Blue Ribbon Four Hundred, and her name was often listed on the committees of charitable events. She felt that it was the obligation of people born with money to devote a portion of their time to helping those less fortunate. She was also a splendid tennis player and a first-rate golfer and was often involved in tournaments. She had her own tennis court at her home in Bel Air, and she and Philip often played early in the morning before he went back to his room at the Chateau Marmont, where he worked on his screenplay. Several times a week she played golf at the Los Angeles Country Club on Wilshire Boulevard.

"All you people look alike at this club," Philip had said one Sunday evening, looking around the dining room.

She knew what he meant. "Well, we all know each other," she said. She had belonged to the Club all her life, as her father and her late husband had before her, and she knew the names of most of the members and most of the help. Every Sunday evening she and her daughter, Bunty, went to the Club for the buffet supper, just as she had gone with her father when she was a child, and Philip had started to accompany them.

"No show folk."

"No."

"No ethnics."

"Mr. and Mrs. Watkins, remember."

"Tokens."

"Well, that's the way it is. That's the way it always has been," she said to Philip, with a shrug. She hated that kind of conversation. "They have clubs too that we can't get into. Don't forget that."

Philip laughed. It was not the first time he had heard her give this rationale.

"Even the Mendelsons couldn't get into the Los Angeles Country Club, and God knows, Pauline McAdoo comes from about as good a family as you get back east," said Camilla.

"I bet if you checked into it, you'd find the problem was Jules, not Pauline," replied Philip.

Camilla didn't reply. "Here comes Bunty. Don't continue this conversation in front of her."

Philip did not play golf, but on this particular day Camilla asked him to join her there for lunch in the Club grill, where all the golfers had lunch, after she had played. He liked the look of her in her visored cap and trim white shorts and pastel-colored sport shirts. Rose Cliveden made her first appearance at the Club since she broke her leg at the lunch she gave there following Hector Paradiso's funeral. Rose was one for dramatic entrances, and she had herself pushed into the grill in a wheelchair by a nurse, although she was able by that time to navigate by herself on crutches.

"I'm back," she yelled as she came in, and all her friends in the room rushed over to greet her, and Bloody Marys were ordered for all. As always, wherever Rose was, a party began. From the arm pocket of her wheelchair, she pulled forth several gifts, handsomely wrapped. One was for Clint, the bartender, whom she had accused of making the Bloody Marys too strong on the day she fell over Astrid, and the other was for her dear friend Camilla Ebury, who was that day thirty-three years old.

"You didn't tell me it was your birthday," said Philip, when he and Camilla had settled back at their own table.

Camilla blushed. "I never tell anyone it's my birthday. Trust Rose to make an announcement. She keeps one of those birthday books. I never know when anyone's birthday is."

"What are you doing when we finish lunch?" asked Philip.

"I have an Orphanage Guild meeting at four," she said.

"Between now and four?"

"Take a shower. Change clothes. Why?"

"You're coming with me," said Philip.

"Where?"

"To buy you a birthday present."

"You don't have to do that."

"I know I don't have to. But I want to."

A half hour later, Philip and Camilla walked hand in hand down Rodeo Drive looking in shop windows, both feeling carefree, as if they were playing hooky. Philip saw a very pretty young woman coming toward him from the other direction. He was surprised enough to stop in his tracks. The young woman, who had seen him before he saw her, was also surprised, and unnerved, by the unexpected meeting.

"Hello," said Philip.

"Hello," replied the young woman.

Camilla, watching the exchange, dropped hold of Philip's hand.

"What an incredible surprise," said Philip.

"For me, too," said the young woman.

"Do you live here?" he asked.

"No. Do you?"

"No. I'm here working for a few months. Where do you live?"

"I'm in San Francisco still. You're in New York?"

"Yes." There was an awkward pause.

Camilla said, "Philip, I think I'll go back to the car."

"Oh, I beg your pardon," said Philip. "This is Camilla Ebury. Terry —uh, what's your last name these days?"

The young woman laughed. "Still Sigourney," she said.

"Terry Sigourney, Camilla Ebury," he said.

The two women nodded to each other.

"I read your book on that Wall Street guy," said Terry to Philip.

He nodded. There was another awkward pause.

"Did he really break your legs? I read that."

"Oh, no. Only a threat that didn't happen."

"Philip, I'm going to get a taxi across the street at the Beverly Wilshire," said Camilla impatiently.

"No, no, wait," said Philip, reaching out for her hand.

Camilla pulled her hand away from him.

"Listen, I better be on my way," said Terry. She turned to Camilla. "Does he still have that cute little tattoo, down there?"

Camilla, angry, blushed.

Terry looked at Philip. "Good-bye, Philip," she said. "If you're ever in San Francisco, I have a gallery. Bird prints. It's in the book." She walked on past them.

Camilla and Philip looked at each other for an instant.

"You behaved like a bitch," said Philip.

"*I* behaved like a bitch? What about her? What about that tattoo crack?"

"You brought it on, you know."

"I was jealous."

"Well, where to next?" asked Philip. "Tiffany's is across the street there in the Beverly Wilshire Hotel, isn't it?"

"Why do I feel that Terry was something more than a casual acquaintance?" asked Camilla.

Philip didn't answer for a moment.

"Who was she?"

"A subplot," answered Philip.

"How sub?" asked Camilla.

Philip paused. "I was once married to her," he said.

Camilla stopped. "Married to her? You never told me you'd been married."

"Because I'd almost forgotten I was."

"How could a marriage slip your mind?"

"I was only eighteen at the time. An elopement to Mexico. There was always a question as to whether it was legal or not."

"Was it annulled?"

"No, we were divorced."

"How long were you married?"

"Under a year."

"Take me home, will you? I have the meeting at four, and I want to get my own car."

"I haven't bought you a present."

"I don't want a present."

They drove back to Camilla's house in Bel Air in silence. When he pulled into the driveway, she picked up her bag so that by the time the car pulled in front of the house, she had already opened the door. As she was about to step out of the car, he reached over and put his hand on her arm.

"Why are you being like this?" he asked.

"I've been sleeping with you for how long now? Since the night Hector was killed, and I just realized I don't know one damn thing about you. Nothing."

"I never thought credentials were required for a love affair," said Philip.

She ignored him. "I don't know if you have a mother, father, brother, sister, or a child even."

"No to all of the above."

"Now I find out for the first time that you've been married."

"So have you."

"It's not that you were married that I mind. It's that you simply neglected to tell me an important bit of information about yourself."

"It was twelve years ago. I was married for seven months. What's the big deal?"

"There is no big deal."

"Look, I was different in those days than I am now. Wilder. Rebellious. My parents sent me away to boarding school when I was only eleven, because they were getting a divorce, and I spent the next seven or eight years wanting to get even with them. What better way than to elope to Mexico? I think of it as a youthful error, no more than that."

"What's your secret, Philip?"

"What secret?"

"You have a secret. I feel it. I know it."

Philip looked away from her.

"And you're not going to tell me, are you?"

Philip didn't answer.

"I don't want to see you anymore, Philip."

"That's quite childish, don't you think?"

She shook her head. "Let me tell you what a fool I've been. I was thinking that perhaps you were going to ask me to marry you. I even went to see my lawyers, just in case. My life is run by lawyers, part of an arrangement my father made. If we were even to think of marriage, I was told, they would draw up a prenuptial agreement for you to sign."

Philip, astonished, laughed. "I wouldn't have signed it."

"They wouldn't have let me marry you then."

"But I didn't want to marry you."

Camilla, startled, blushed. "You didn't?"

"No. Men should never marry women who are richer than they are. It's bound to fail. So tell your lawyers to flush their prenuptial agreement."

"You don't have to be rude."

"I'm not being rude. I'm stating a fact. What's wrong with a love affair? Just a plain and simple love affair. This has been a very pleasant time between us. Don't just toss it out. I have never been one to believe every romance should end up in marriage."

"So long, Philip," she said. "When you're ready to tell me your secret, maybe we'll meet for lunch sometime." She stepped out of his car.

Philip looked at her back. "I caused a girl to be paralyzed when I was driving too fast with too many beers in me. It changed my life forever," he said. Without looking back at her, he drove out of her driveway.

PHILIP QUENNELL had not made many friends in Los Angeles during the time he was there. He had met Camilla Ebury at the Mendelsons' party on his first night in the city. The mysterious death of her uncle on that same night had intensified their love affair, and he had spent most of his free time with her since then, mixing in her life with her friends rather than creating a Los Angeles life of his own. The rupture that had been caused in that love affair by the unexpected appearance on the street of Terry Sigourney brought to an instant halt any further socializing with the people he had met through Camilla. He had no desire to call on Casper Stieglitz for companionship, as he had developed an intense dislike for the man. Nor did he have any desire to associate with Lonny Edge, even to gain further knowledge of Lonny's friendship with the great author Basil Plant, whom Philip revered. He wanted only to finish the writing assignment he had undertaken for Casper Stieglitz, so that he could return to his life in New York.

He was at work in his room at the Chateau Marmont that night, when there was a knock at his door. It was the policy of the hotel to announce all visitors, but no such announcement had been made. When he opened the door, he was surprised to see the pretty young woman he knew only as Flo M. standing there. She was dressed, as he had always seen her dressed, in a Chanel suit, but she appeared to be in an agitated state. The cool, withdrawn, and slightly mysterious manner that he had grown used to when he saw her most mornings at the AA meetings in the log cabin on Robertson Boulevard was not present.

"Aren't you going to ask me in?" she asked.

"Oh, sure," he said.

He opened the door wider, and she walked past him into the room. He closed the door.

"So this is where you live, huh?" she said. "I was never in here before. I used to be a waitress at the Viceroy Coffee Shop up the street on Sunset, and all the writers who stayed at the Chateau always came in for breakfast, so I was always hearing about the place. Nice, isn't it?"

"Why do I think that you haven't come here at half-past ten at night to discuss the writers who live and work at the Chateau Marmont?" asked Philip.

"Did I know you were a writer? You didn't tell me that, did you? I think I must have just felt it. I mean, you look like a writer." She walked around his room, looking at everything. His word processor was set up on a desk and his printer stood next to it on a card table. She leaned down and read the amber print on the monitor. "You're writing a movie, I see," she said.

"Are you in some kind of trouble?" asked Philip.

"Hell, no. Do you always work in a dressing gown? That's nice, that blue-and-white-striped dressing gown. What was that, a gift from your girlfriend, I bet."

"If I didn't know it wasn't so, I'd think you were on speed," said Philip. "You're talking a mile a minute."

She opened the doors to his balcony and walked outside. "God, look at all that traffic on Sunset," she called in.

He followed her out to the balcony. She was leaning on the rail, looking down. She had taken a cigarette from her gold cigarette case with the name FLO printed on it in sapphires. She lit it with her gold lighter, and inhaled deeply.

"What's the matter, Flo?" he asked. He took the cigarette out of her mouth and threw it over the balcony.

"You couldn't put me up for the night, could you, Phil?"

"Tight quarters here."

"I wouldn't mind that," she said.

They looked at each other.

"Are you still spoken for?" she asked.

He smiled sadly. "As a matter of fact, I'm not. Why?"

"I'm not spoken for anymore either."

WHEN RALPH WHITE came out of the men's room in the steak house in the San Fernando Valley and got into the car the parking boy had brought around, the first thing Madge White said to him was, "Did you see Sims Lord in the men's room?"

"Sims? No. There was no one in the men's room. It was empty except for me," said Ralph. "Why?"

"I can't wait to tell you what just happened to me," said Madge.

Jules Mendelson had already left. He had driven his Bentley out of the restaurant parking lot with such speed that Madge thought he would surely have been arrested had a policeman been present to witness his driving. He turned off Ventura Boulevard onto Coldwater Canyon and raced up the mountain, blowing his horn relentlessly at any car not driving at the speed that he was driving, until they pulled over to the side and allowed him to pass. When he reached the top of Coldwater, he slowed down his pace because the Beverly Hills side of the canyon was more closely patrolled than the Valley side. Halfway down Coldwater, he turned left onto the street that led into Azelia Way.

All the time he was driving, he planned what he would say to her. He had not wanted to go out in public. What he most feared had happened. The fault was hers, not his. He would make her see that. At the same time, he could not erase from his memory the sad and hurt look in her eyes when he had pretended he could not think of her name.

He pulled into the secluded driveway of the house that he rented

for her. He jumped from his car, leaving the car door open. He rang
the bell. When there was no immediate answer, he took out his keys
and opened the front door and walked in without closing the door
behind him. The lights were on, as they had been left. The drinks
that they'd had before going out were still on the coffee table.

"Flo!" he called out. "Flo! Where are you, Flo?" He went into her
bedroom, her bathroom, out onto her patio. There was no sign of
her. He walked frantically from room to room. He could not imagine
where she could have gone. He knew she had no friends, except the
maid next door, and he knew she would never go to Faye Converse's
house to call on Faye's maid.

From behind the tall hedge that separated Flo's house from the
house of Faye Converse, the dog Astrid, hearing activity, came over
to call on Flo. She came in by the open front door, knowing she
would be received with great whoops of joy, as she always was when
Flo spotted her, and then be spoiled with doggy treats, as Flo always
spoiled her.

Hearing the sounds of each other, each thought the other was Flo.
Jules ran from the bedroom into the living room, where, instead, he
encountered Astrid. They stared at each other, in the same way they
had stared at each other in Hector Paradiso's house on the early
morning Hector's body lay on the floor between them, with five bullets in it, and Jules removed the note that the dying Hector had left,
before the police arrived. The little dog began to bark ferociously at
Jules, as if she feared that harm had come to Flo as well.

"Get out of here, you little piece of shit," said Jules to the dog,
menacingly.

Astrid held her ground, barking without stop and moving in on
Jules.

From Flo's mantelpiece, Jules picked up one of the two brass candlesticks with dragons crawling up their sides that Nellie Potts had
charged Flo several thousand dollars for, claiming that they were
antiques from the childhood palace of the last emperor of China.
Jules swung the candlestick as if it were a broom, and the little dog,
terrified, retreated.

"Get out of here," Jules yelled, advancing on her until he had
backed her out the front door, which he then slammed.

He went to Flo's bar. Her sets and sets of Steuben glasses were lined
up on glass shelves. Taking a wineglass, he opened the small refriger-

ator under the bar and took out a bottle of white wine from the Bresciani auction and poured himself a glass. When he seated himself, finally, on Flo's sofa, he picked up the telephone and dialed a number.

"Dudley, this is Mr. Mendelson," he said to the butler at Clouds. "I'm very sorry to call you so late. Has there been a call from Mrs. Mendelson? I see. Dudley, I will not be coming home this evening. I am going to stay here in my office. I'm still working, and I have a very early meeting. What? No, no, thank you. That won't be necessary. There are clean shirts there, here rather, in the office, and linens. But that's awfully kind of you. Will you leave a note for Willi to come to my office in the morning to shave me there? No, I shouldn't think Mrs. Mendelson will call this evening. It must be after one in Maine now. I'll call in the morning, Dudley. Good night."

WHEN JULES awoke on the sofa at five in the morning, his regular waking hour, he jumped up, furious that he had fallen asleep. He was sure that Flo had come home during the night and gone right into her room to sleep, not wanting to wake him. But she was not there. He went to his office, where he bathed and changed. Willi, who shaved him with a straight-edged razor, twice had to stop, for fear of cutting him, when Jules lurched in the chair. Every hour of the morning, he called her number. At lunchtime, he canceled an appointment and drove up to her house on Azelia Way. He had become frantic. He called the police department to see if there had been any accidents reported in a Valley cab. He called the emergency rooms of the hospitals to see if a Miss Flo March, or a Miss Fleurette Houlihan, had been admitted. He went to the Viceroy Coffee Shop. That night he went to Clouds and sat in his library alone, where he had dinner on a tray.

After two days, he called Sims Lord, his lawyer and friend. Sims Lord was not unfamiliar with the fact that Jules was having an affair. It was Sims who had purchased the sapphire-and-diamond ring for Jules to give to Flo, and the mink coat, and several other gifts that Jules did not want to have to purchase himself, for fear of talk. Sims, who was twice divorced, did not have the restrictions on his life that Jules had, and was happy to oblige. He was a Pasadenian by birth and an easterner by education. His clothes were of a cut and conservatism that appealed to Pauline's New England sensibilities. Handsome, he possessed what Pauline called a wintry look; his hair was prematurely white, and his eyes were very blue. He could be as personable as any man could choose to be, when he chose to be; and as cold as any man could choose to be, when he chose to be; both of these qualities endeared him to Jules. It was said of Sims Lord that he was a lawyer with one client—Jules Mendelson—which was an untrue statement in that he had many clients, but it was true in the sense that the affairs of Jules Mendelson had occupied 80 percent of his time for two decades.

What Sims did not know was the extent of the passion that Jules felt for the former waitress. He was shocked by Jules's appearance when he arrived at his office that morning.

"Flo has left me," said Jules. There were tears in his eyes. There was in his voice a pain that Sims Lord did not know Jules was capable of experiencing. The two men talked for hours. Jules told him everything about the affair.

"If she comes back, I want you to buy her the house, Sims. And the car. I want her to have everything in her own name. In case something happens to me, I don't want her left high and dry. Nor do I want to embarrass Pauline in any way. It is best to do these things in advance."

"Where do you suppose she is?" asked Sims, although they had asked the same question over and over.

"I don't know."

"Is there any family?"

"None."

"Listen, Jules. Now, don't jump on me."

"What?"

"There's no other guy, is there?"

"Good God." The idea of another man touching Flo was anathema to Jules.

"Have you ever thought about hiring a private detective?"

"Would it get out? I mean to the papers, or anything?" asked Jules. "There must be no publicity."

"No, no. I know just the right guy. Discretion himself. It'll cost you, but that's not a concern. His name is Trevor Dust."

□   □   □

WHEN PHILIP QUENNELL went to Casper Stieglitz's house to deliver the first draft of the documentary on the proliferation of drugs in the film industry, Flo stayed in his room. They had scarcely left the Chateau Marmont since Flo's arrival, except to attend the early morning AA meetings at the log cabin on Robertson Boulevard, or to go out to dinner at Musso and Frank's on Hollywood Boulevard, a restaurant that Philip liked, where Jules Mendelson was unlikely ever to go.

There was a soft and tentative knock on the door. Flo was wearing Philip's blue-and-white-striped dressing gown, sitting on one of the two leather chairs in the room, reading Cyril Rathbone's column in *Mulholland* magazine. "Come in," she called out, thinking it was the maid.

When Camilla Ebury walked in, Flo March knew without being told who she was. For two days, she and Philip Quennell had told each other their stories.

"Oh, I beg your pardon," said Camilla. "I've come into the wrong room."

To Flo's eyes, everything about Camilla Ebury was perfect. Her blond hair was parted in the middle and held back by two gold barrettes. Her pearls were real. Her green-and-white-print dress was silk. Even her perfume had a refined odor. She looked to Flo as if she were on her way to a committee meeting at the Bistro Garden for a fashionable charity. Flo was certain she would say, under the right circumstance, "Hellohowareyou," the way Madge White had said it the other night.

Camilla backed out the door to look at the room number, although she immediately recognized the blue-and-white-striped dressing gown that the girl in the leather chair was wearing as belonging to Philip. She saw it was the right room. "I'm terribly confused," she said. "I seem to have made a mistake."

"No, you haven't. I'm Flo March," said Flo.

"Hellohowareyou."

Flo smiled. "You're Camilla, aren't you?"

"Yes. How did you know?"

Flo looked at her. Unlike her own pretty face, Camilla's pretty face revealed no struggle in life. Things had been placed there for her, in profusion. She had remained unspoiled with her privilege, but she also took it for granted.

Camilla said, "I think perhaps I'd better go. This was stupid of me to come here."

"Now, I bet you think that he and I have got something going between us, don't you? Well, you couldn't be more wrong," said Flo. "Phil's a friend of mine, that's all. No more than that. I needed a place to stay for a few nights, and he gave me one."

Camilla looked at Flo, not sure whether to believe her or not.

"It is possible for a man and a woman to be friends without having something going on between them, even for a cute guy like Phil. I didn't used to think that, but I do now. Besides, I'm spoken for, which I told him the first day we met, and he told me he was spoken for too, and I guess you're the one."

"He said that, that he was spoken for?" asked Camilla. There was surprise in her voice.

"Yeah," said Flo. "He did."

"I'm such a fool," said Camilla. "Twice now I've told him I didn't want to see him anymore, and I didn't want him to go either time."

"You sound like you're in love with the guy," said Flo.

"I am."

"Want my advice?"

"Yes."

"Hang out here for a while. He'll be back soon. I was just about to get dressed and get out of here."

She got up and opened the closet door. From inside, she took out her black-and-white Chanel suit. "He's gone to a meeting at Casper Stieglitz's to turn in the first draft on the documentary."

"Oh." Camilla watched Flo, fascinated. The suit was obviously for evening, not morning, but she saw the Paris label in the jacket as Flo dressed in front of her. The clothes and the woman did not match. She was pretty, very pretty, and there was humor and even kindness in her face, but there was a sound in her voice that bespoke a different background from Camilla's, and a harder kind of life.

"Are you an actress?" asked Camilla.

"I once had an audition for a miniseries. That was my total experience as an actress," said Flo. "Needless to say, I didn't get the part. Ann-Margret got it. They said they wanted a name."

"I was just wondering, that's all," said Camilla. "It's none of my business."

"I'm hard to get a bead on, I know," said Flo. "I don't seem to fall into any of the identifiable categories." She pulled on her jacket. She stepped into her shoes. She picked up her bag with the long gold chain and put it over her shoulder. "Well, I guess I'm all set. When you see Phil, tell him thanks. Okay?"

Camilla nodded.

"I bet he looks real cute in his Jockey shorts," said Flo.

"He doesn't wear Jockey shorts. He wears boxer shorts," said Camilla.

"You see how little I know the guy?" She went out the door.


JULES was sitting on one of Flo's gray satin sofas, in earnest conversation with Trevor Dust, the private detective who had been recommended by Sims Lord. There were photographs of Flo on the tabletop, the eight-by-ten glossies that she'd had taken when she was still working at the Viceroy Coffee Shop, as well as more recent snapshots taken by her pool. There were also several of her Chanel suits spread out on the sofa, to show the detective how she was dressed the last time she had been seen.

The detective took off his prescription sunglasses and replaced them with his reading glasses. From a back pocket, he took a spiral notebook and checked his notes. "The taxi driver was an Iranian, named Hussein Akhavi. He's okay. Checks out. Akhavi remembers a lady answering to Miss March's description getting into his cab outside the restaurant that night. Said she was excitable, and maybe crying. He was in mourning for the death of the Ayatollah and didn't want to get involved with this woman's problems. He said she gave him a Beverly Hills address first, presumably this address, but he couldn't remember, and then changed her mind and asked him to take her to a hotel on Sunset Boulevard called the Chateau Marmont. She paid him with a twenty and told him to keep the change. But there is no record of anyone by either of her names, March or Houlihan, who registered at the Chateau that night, or since then."

"Good job," said Jules, nodding his head. "Now, I'll tell you what I want you to do. Get me a printout of everyone who was registered at the Chateau Marmont that night, as well as every night since."

"Beat you to it," said Trevor Dust. He opened his briefcase and took out an envelope, which he handed to Jules. "Here's the printout for that night. I had to pay the night clerk for this. I'll have to get it for you for the subsequent nights."

Just then, a taxi pulled into the driveway, and Flo got out. She saw Jules's Bentley and another car of a nondescript variety in the driveway. She used her key and walked into the living room of her house.

"Hi," she said quietly when she walked into the living room.

"Flo!" cried Jules. "Where the hell have you been?"

"Thinking," answered Flo.

"But you came back."

"I got sick of wearing this same outfit," she said.

Jules rushed to her side and tried to embrace her, but her eyes had caught sight of the other person in the room.

"Who's your friend here? And what are my pictures doing out like that? And all my clothes? What are you, a cop? Or a private detective?"

"I have been frantic, Flo," said Jules. "I hired Mr. Dust to try to locate you."

"I am not having a personal discussion in front of him," said Flo, pointing to Trevor Dust with her thumb. "Lose the dick, and then we'll talk."

"Right. That will be all. Thank you, Mr. Dust. Send your bill to my office," said Jules.

When Jules walked the detective to the door, Flo went to her bar and took out a can of Diet Coke from the refrigerator. She opened it and started to drink it out of the can, but then she remembered her new Steuben glasses and poured the contents into a water goblet.

When Jules came back into the room, she pointed to her goblet and said to him, "Nice glasses you bought me."

"Who were you with?" he asked.

"A friend."

"What friend?"

"Just a friend."

"Male or female?"

"That's for me to know and you to find out."

Mad with jealousy, Jules grabbed her arm with such force that the Steuben glass flew from her hand and smashed as it hit the stone floor by her fireplace. She screamed with pain. Instantly, he released her arm.

"Oh, my God," he said. "Oh, Flo, I'm sorry. I didn't mean that."

She pulled back from him with fear on her face. "Is that what happened to the girl in Chicago who went off the balcony of the Roosevelt Hotel in nineteen fifty-three?" she asked. "Did you make her so frightened of you that she backed off the balcony?"

"Flo, forgive me," he begged. He knelt in front of her and put his arms around her thighs and hugged her to him. "Forgive me. I love you, Flo. I love you. Please forgive me."

Flo March had never seen Jules Mendelson cry before.


"IS PAULINE still in Northeast Harbor?" asked Flo.

"Yes."

"Good. There's something I want to do."

"What?"

"I want to see Clouds."

"Oh, no, that wouldn't be wise."

"Why not?"

"You shouldn't have to ask that. It's Pauline's house."

"It's yours too. I just want to look, Jules. I just want to walk through the rooms. That's all."

"No."

"Why?"

"It could be disastrous."

"Who would know?"

"Dudley, for one. Blondell, for two. Smitty, for three."

"Who's Dudley and Blondell and Smitty?"

"The butler, the maid, and the guard. And there're people in the kitchen. The cook, Gertie, and the others—I don't always remember their names—but they're there."

Flo nodded. "Don't you sometimes have business meetings at Clouds?"

"Sometimes."

"How about if I'm a business meeting?"

"Oh, come on, Flo."

"No, listen. You go home. You say to Dudley, 'I'm expecting a Miss March for a meeting.' Then, at like eight or eight-thirty, I'll come up. I'll ring the doorbell. Dudley can let me in. He'll take me into the library where you'll be sitting, reading *Time* and *Newsweek*. He'll say, 'Miss March.' I'll shake hands like I'm meeting you for the first time, and then you can take me on a tour of the house and grounds. With all those people from all those museums going through the house looking at all your art all the time, one little person like me is not going to look suspicious. I want to see that picture with the white roses."

"I've had a postcard made of that picture," said Jules.

"Well, I'm not interested in the postcard. I want to see the original."

"It's too dangerous."

"Forty minutes later, I'll say good night, thank you very much, Mr. Mendelson, it was nice of you to make the time for me to see your beautiful collection, and I'll go back out the front door and get in my Mercedes and be off into the night."

"Why do you want to do this?"

"I'm interested in your life, Jules. Is that so strange? I see more of you than anyone else, but most of your life is closed off to me. You can't blame me for having curiosity about you."

"Okay," he said. "But no false moves. Dudley has eyes in the back of his head."


"OH, MY," said Flo, as she set foot in the hallway of Clouds, looking up, looking left, looking right. She was at a loss for words, and she was only in the hall of the magnificent house. The curved staircase seemed to float upward in front of her eyes, with six huge paintings on its green moiré walls. At its base, the great quantities of orchid plants in blue-and-white Chinese cachepots caught her attention. She's not even here, and the house is still filled with flowers, she thought to herself.

Flo's expectations of pleasure from her visit to Clouds were so high that she was bound to be disappointed. And she was. She could cope in her imagination with Pauline Mendelson's house, but the grandeur of the actuality was too much for her even to comment upon. She walked down the hallway behind Dudley, casting glances into rooms as she passed, each more perfect than the last. She had always thought of Pauline in terms of beautiful clothes and pearl necklaces and parties, the way she was presented in the newspapers and in magazines. She had not thought about tables and chairs that were not just tables and chairs, but tables and chairs of an exquisiteness that she, born without prospects to an unwed mother, could not even begin to comprehend. If ever, in the remote corners of her mind, she had entertained the idea that she might become the wife of Jules Mendelson, she knew at that moment that it would never be.

Jules waited for her in the library. She followed Dudley into the room. They went through the charade that she had planned. "Good evening, Miss March," he said, rising from an English chair and laying aside his magazine.

She looked into the eyes of the man whom she had made love to only three hours earlier, into whose ear she had whispered base things to incite his lust, whose body and desires she had grown to know intimately, and he appeared different to her in the surroundings of his home. She became shy.

"Good evening, Mr. Mendelson."

"Have you just arrived in Los Angeles?"

"Yes, today."

"Did you have a good flight?"

"Yes."

"I'll take you on a tour of the house and the pictures, if you'd like."

"Lovely."

"Would you care for a drink?"

"No, thank you."

"I'll ring, Dudley, if Miss March changes her mind. Will you put on the lights in the sculpture garden?"

"Yes, sir."

Alone, they were silent. She wished she had not come.

"This is van Gogh's *White Roses*," Jules said, finally, pointing to the picture over the fireplace.

"Such thick paint," she said, looking up at the picture. "Didn't I read somewhere that that picture is worth about forty million dollars?"

"That's what that article said, yes."

"My, oh my," she said.

There was a silence again.

"This room we're in is the library. It is where we spend most of our time when we are alone," said Jules, who also felt the awkwardness of the situation. He was used to giving tours of his house to the many museum people who visited Clouds, but he could not think of the appropriate descriptions and comments he usually made to say to Flo.

Flo looked around the room, without moving her position.

246

"Beautiful appointments," she said in a whispered voice.

Jules hated the word *appointments* when it was applied to the decorative arts, but he understood the extent of Flo's discomfort and, for once, did not correct her. Instead, he squeezed her hand and she was grateful.

"I guess I better be on my way," she said.

"On your way? You haven't seen anything yet."

"That's okay."

The lights went on in the garden outside. She turned to look through the windows toward the grounds. "You must see the sculpture garden, at least," said Jules. "It will look odd if you leave so soon."

The telephone rang. Jules made a move toward the instrument.

"I thought in swell houses like this the butler always answered the phone and said, 'The Mendelson residence,' " said Flo.

"He does, but that's my private line. It's Sims Lord, I'm sure. He was looking into something for me, about the house on Azelia Way," said Jules, looking at her to see if what he said had registered on her. He picked up the receiver. "Hello? Oh, Pauline. How are you? How is your father? What? No, no, there's no one here."

He looked up at Flo, and their eyes met. She opened the door to the terrace and walked out, as if to go to see the sculpture garden.

"What's that?" continued Jules, on the telephone. "You are? Oh, good. When? Yes, fine. I'll make arrangements for the plane to leave for Bangor in the morning. I've missed you."

When he finished the conversation with his wife, he rose and went out to the terrace, where Flo had gone. He passed the Rodin, which had once belonged to his grandfather. He passed the Henry Moore, running his hand over its smooth surface as he did so. He did not see Flo. He continued on to the Maillol, behind the orange tree. "Flo," he called out. "Flo!"

From behind him the terrace door opened and closed. He looked back and saw Dudley crossing the lawn to come toward him.

"Were you looking for Miss March, Mr. Mendelson?"

"Yes. She came wandering out here when I took a telephone call. I forgot to warn her about the dogs and didn't want her to be frightened."

"Miss March left, sir," said Dudley. "She said she had seen everything."

"Oh," said Jules.

□   □   □

LATER THAT NIGHT, when Jules was undressing, he removed from the pockets of his suit jacket his wallet and change and handkerchief and keys and placed them on the top of a bureau in his dressing room. As he hung his jacket on a valet stand, he noticed an envelope in the inside pocket, which he had forgotten he had placed there. He took it out. On the top left-hand corner of the envelope was the name of the private detective, Trevor Dust. He tore it open and found inside the computer printout of the hotel guests at the Chateau Marmont on the night that the taxi driver from the Valley Cab Company told Trevor Dust he had dropped Flo March off at that address. He scanned the list. Flo March was not registered. His eyes continued down the list. He was startled to find the name Philip Quennell. A blind, hot rage welled up within him.

AT NINE O'CLOCK the next morning, Jules Mendelson had Miss Maple place a call to the office of Marty Lesky at Colossus Pictures. For several minutes the two busy men exchanged pleasantries, and then Jules got down to the purpose of his call, which had nothing whatever to do with the Los Angeles County Museum, as Marty Lesky had anticipated.

"There's a man working at your studio called Philip Quennell," said Jules.

"What's he do at my studio?" asked Marty.

"He is a writer, they tell me, who is writing a documentary film for Casper Stieglitz."

"Oh, right. I met him the other night. He was at Casper's for dinner. Wrote the book on Reza Bulbenkian. What about him, Jules?"

"Send him home."

"Where's home?"

"I don't know where home is, but wherever it is, send him there."

"A good writer's hard to find, Jules."

"No, he's not, Marty. You told me yourself once. 'You can always get another writer,' you said."

"I said that?"

"Yes, you did. I remember it distinctly. Send Mr. Quennell home."

"I gottahava reason, Jules. This is not Andover. He was not caught smoking a joint. This is a studio I'm running here. I don't just send guys home with no reason."

"When's your meeting for the new museum wing?"

"Tuesday. Your secretary phoned in your acceptance."

"I'm not going to be able to make it, Marty."

"Oh, come on, Jules."

"About my pledge to the museum, Marty."

"You can't welsh on a pledge, Jules. Even Jules Mendelson can't do that."

"Fuck my pledge, Marty. What do I care about a wing with your name on it?"

"What was this guy's name, Jules?"

"Quennell. Philip Quennell."

## Flo's Tape #16

"Clouds. My God, what a house! I only saw it once, and I don't think I was even there for half an hour, but I saw enough. I mean, it was perfect. Every detail. Everything in its right place. Everything beautiful. When they make Hollywood movies about rich people, they never get the sets to look like Clouds looked.

"There are some of those ladies you read about in coffee table books, like Mrs. Paley, and Mrs. Guinness, and the Duchess of Windsor. They knew how to run those great houses for their husbands and for their friends. Well, I have to hand it to Mrs. Mendelson. She was right up there with those other ladies when it came to putting a house together and knowing how to run it in the grand style."

# 17

IT WAS BETTYE, Casper Stieglitz's secretary, who told Philip Quennell over the telephone, when he happened to call late in the afternoon to see what Casper's reaction had been to his first draft of the documentary film on the proliferation of drugs in the film industry, that Casper had decided to go with another writer.

"What does that mean, he has decided to go with another writer?" asked Philip.

"In other words, you're fired," said Bettye.

"I rather thought that was what you meant," said Philip. "No offense, Bettye, but I'd like to get fired by my boss, not my boss's secretary."

"I'm awfully sorry, Mr. Quennell, but Mr. Stieglitz is in an important conference," replied Bettye.

"Of course he is, that busy fellow," said Philip. "Will you ask him to call me?"

"How soon will you be vacating your junior suite at the Chateau Marmont?" asked Bettye.

"Who said I was vacating it?"

"I have informed the hotel that as of midnight tonight, the studio will no longer be picking up the charges for the room," said Bettye.

"What an active day you've had, Bettye," said Philip.

"I'm just doing my job, Mr. Quennell," replied Bettye.

It did not surprise Philip that the several telephone calls he made to Casper Stieglitz at his home were not returned. That evening he drove to Casper's house on Palm Circle, although he was sure he would be told by Willard, the butler, that Casper was not at home. When he buzzed the intercom at the gate, a red light went on on the closed circuit television. He heard Willard's voice. "Yes?"

"Willard, I'd like to talk to you for a moment," said Philip quickly, looking up into the camera.

"Mr. Stieglitz is not at home, Mr. Quennell," said Willard.

"It's you I wanted to see, Willard," said Philip. "I have learned some interesting information from Lonny Edge about Hector Paradiso's death, and I need some help from you in identifying someone."

Willard's voice became confidential. "Listen, Mr. Quennell. I'm not supposed to let you in here if you come by. I don't know why, but I was told to say that Mr. Stieglitz is not at home and not to let you in."

"I had the idea you were anxious to clarify the death of your friend Hector," said Philip.

"I am." There was uncertainty in his voice.

"I'll only stay a minute, Willard," said Philip.

"I'll open the gate. But, please, don't drive all the way up to the house. I'll meet you in back of the pool pavilion," said Willard.

When the gates opened, Philip drove up the driveway, past the tennis court. The night lights were on, and a game was in progress. He recognized the girlish laughter of Ina Rae and Darlene. Coming down the driveway from the house was Willard, wearing the long green apron he wore on silver-polishing days. He waved frantically to Philip to stop his car. "No, no. Don't go up to the house," he screamed. "I said to meet by the pool pavilion."

Philip nodded in a friendly fashion, as if he didn't understand, and continued up the driveway, leaving Willard behind. When he got to the courtyard, he saw that Willard had left the front door open. With great haste, he hopped out of his car and walked in the door, closing and locking it behind him so that Willard would be delayed getting in when he ran back.

He walked through the living room to the door that opened on the terrace and out to the projection room, where Casper spent most of his time. The curtains were drawn, and it occurred to Philip that Casper was screening a film.

Slowly he pulled back the sliding glass door. As he stepped into the rear of the semidarkened room, he saw Casper, wearing his dark glasses, rise unsteadily from his usual seat and go over to the bar. He was only half-dressed, wearing a black velour shirt but neither trousers nor undershorts. The heady scent of marijuana filled the air. It appeared to Philip that a session with the ladies on the tennis court had recently been completed. Casper looked at himself in the mirrored wall behind the shelves of bottles, as if he were admiring the remains of his good looks. Without removing his glasses, he turned his face carefully, first to one side and then the other, assuming an expression that erased the scowl line between his eyebrows. He held his mouth in such a way that the sagging beneath his chin vanished. Finally, satisfied with his looks, he lifted up his black velour shirt and began to urinate in the bar sink.

"That's class, Casper," said Philip Quennell, from behind. "And very sanitary, as well."

"Jesuschrist," said Casper, jumping. Through the mirror, he saw Philip walking up behind him. "You scared me. You made me piss all over myself and all over these glasses and bottles. What the hell are you doing here?"

"No, I won't have a drink, thank you," said Philip.

"Didn't Bettye call you?"

"Actually, I called Bettye, and she relayed your message. I had never heard of being fired by a secretary before, and I said I wanted to hear it from your own lips, but she said you were in an important conference, so I just came over on my own."

"I'm going to fire that fagola, Willard. I told him not to open the gates," said Casper. He reached for a telephone.

"You mustn't fire poor Willard, Casper. I'm afraid I played a trick on him to let me in. Good silver polishers are hard to find."

"What do you want, Quennell?"

"Oh, it's now Quennell, is it? I'll tell you what I want, Stieglitz. I want to know why you fired me."

"I just decided to go with another writer."

"Bettye's words exactly. Why is it I don't believe them?"

Casper looked at Philip and adopted a comradely approach. "You and me, Philip. We just ran out of gas. Don't take it personally. It happens all the time out here in Hollywood. Writers are an expendable breed. As Marty Lesky says, 'You can always get another writer.' Do you know how many writers I had on *Candles at Lunch*, for instance?"

"No, I don't, and I don't care."

Casper went back to where he had been sitting and pulled on his trousers.

"I want an answer, Casper."

Casper nervously picked up a handful of cashew nuts from the coffee table and began to throw them in his mouth, several at a time. "I was disappointed with your interview with the narcs. I didn't, uh, get a sense, uh, of the kind of obsession those guys have to catch the dealers in this war on drugs. Drugs, I don't have to tell you, are destroying the youth of this nation."

"Who do you think you're kidding, Casper?"

"What are you talking about?"

"You beat the rap for possession of ten pounds of cocaine by having some of your crooked lawyers and influential friends, like Arnie Zwill-man, the gangster, come down on Judge Quartz to suspend your sentence in return for making an antidrug movie, and all the time you're taking drugs. I could blow the whistle on you, Casper, and, may I tell you, it wouldn't read well in the trade papers."

"I do not take drugs," said Casper indignantly. "I admit, in my past, I did try drugs several times, but I have not taken any drugs since the day of my arrest, which was, as everyone knows, a total miscarriage of justice, as well as a mix-up." His voice had become strident.

Philip walked over to the coffee table and picked up from the floor an amber-colored bottle of cocaine that Casper had dropped there. He carried it back to the bar and emptied the white powder into the sink in the bar. "It ought to be even better with your urine mixed in with it."

"Get out of here," said Casper, frightened.

Philip stared him down. "Did Ina Rae run her fingers through your hair?" he asked. "Your rug is crooked. Kind of at a tilt."

Casper, enraged, rushed at Philip. "Get out of my house!"

Philip leaned toward Casper and snatched his dark glasses off him, grabbing them by the bridge over his nose.

"What do you think you're doing?" asked Casper. "I can't see any-thing without my glasses."

"I knew that behind those shades you'd have darty little furtive eyes," said Philip.

Casper sneezed.

Philip held up his hands and stepped backward. "Oh, please. I can't handle another mouthful of your half-chewed cashews all over my face, Casper. I've already had that experience once."

"The studio isn't paying for the Chateau Marmont after tonight."

"Yes, yes, I know. Your Bettye told me that. Look, Casper, I don't mind being thrown off your picture, but I have a feeling it wasn't your idea, and I want to know whose idea it was."

Casper looked at Philip but didn't answer.

"Who told you to fire me? Or rather, who told you to tell your secretary to fire me?"

"Nobody, I swear to God," said Casper.

"Oh, sure," replied Philip. "You made this decision all on your own."

"Yes, I did. I just don't think you captured the interview with the narcs in the right way," said Casper.

"That's the same scene you told me you liked so much the day before yesterday, Casper," said Philip. "Who told you to fire me?"

Casper shook his head.

Philip dropped Casper's glasses on the floor and stepped on them. "Oops, I broke your glasses."

Casper went down on his hands and knees to retrieve his glasses.

Philip reached out and grabbed him by the neck of his black velour shirt. "You know, Casper, when I was at Princeton, I saw your film *A Mansion in Limbo* three times, because I thought it was so great. I used to want to meet you. And now I have, and you're nothing more than a pathetic drug addict with a face-lift and a wig. What happened to you, Casper?"

"Let me up," said Casper.

"Who told you to fire me?"

"No one, I swear."

"Either you tell me, or I'm going to rip this rug right off your head and call your girlfriends in here from the tennis court to see their little sugar daddy without his hair pasted on."

Casper, frightened, looked up at Philip. "Don't. I beg of you, Phil. Ina Rae doesn't know I wear a rug."

"Who told you to fire me, Casper?"


IT WAS A SURPRISE to Arnie Zwillman when he did not hear from Jules Mendelson after their initial meeting at Casper Stieglitz's party, so he telephoned him at his office to set up a second meeting to discuss further the proposition he had suggested to Jules. Miss Maple, Jules's secretary, was unfamiliar with the name Arnie Zwillman and asked him all the questions that an unfamiliar person is asked by an overly protective secretary.

"Will Mr. Mendelson know what this call is in reference to?" asked Miss Maple.

"Yes, he will," replied Arnie.

"Mr. Mendelson is in conference at the moment. May I have your number, and I will tell him that you called, Mr., uh, what did you say your last name was?"

"Zwillman. Arnie Zwillman. Ring through."

"What?"

"I said, ring through to his conference and tell him Arnie Zwillman is on the phone. He'll take the call, believe me, Miss, uh, what did you say your last name was?"

"I didn't."

"Just ring through, Miss I-Didn't." He chuckled at his joke.

When Miss Maple informed Jules that a very rude person called Mr. Zwillman was on the line and had insisted that she ring through, Jules turned to Sims Lord and said, "It's Zwillman."

"You better take it," said Sims. "You're going to have to talk to him sooner or later. I checked. All records of the Chicago situation in nineteen fifty-three were expunged at the time. It's as if what happened didn't happen."

Jules nodded. He pushed the button on his telephone. "Hello?"

"You really ought to fill your girl in on who I am, Jules," said Arnie. "It's not very good for my ego to be put through the third degree. 'Will Mr. Mendelson know what this is in reference to?' she asked."

"What is this in reference to?" asked Jules.

"I've been waiting to hear from you, Jules," said Arnie.

"Well, now you have me."

"I'm interested in getting together as soon as possible. Nineteen ninety-two is just around the corner, Jules," said Arnie. "There's a lotta crapola to be worked. What you people in your line of work call modus operandi."

"I don't want to meet with you, Zwillman. Now, or ever."

"You're kidding?"

"No, I'm not kidding. And don't call me again, or I'm going to call the FBI."

"Oh, you big dangerous man," said Arnie.

"So long, Arnie."

"You're making one big fat mistake, Mendelson."

"I don't think so, Zwillman."

"You were pretty cool, Jules," said Sims Lord, after Jules hung up the telephone.

"It was good to know those records were destroyed, Sims. I'm going out for a cup of coffee. I want to get a little air."

AN HOUR LATER Arnie Zwillman informed the Secretary of State, through a highly placed intermediary, of the unfortunate event in the past of Jules Mendelson, the presidential designate for the head of the United States economic commission in Brussels during the year of European statehood, involving the 1953 death of a young woman who fell, or was pushed, from the balcony of the Roosevelt Hotel in Chicago during a romantic tryst.

The records of the death, which had been expunged by the mayor of the city at the request of the parents of Jules Mendelson, were in the hands of Mr. Zwillman and available to the Secretary of State, the highly placed intermediary was informed. The family of the dead girl had been handsomely recompensed for their loss at the time by the family of Mr. Mendelson.

THAT DAY at the Viceroy Coffee Shop Jules Mendelson did not read his financial newspapers, as he usually did. His mind was filled with other thoughts. The feeling of relief that he had anticipated when he told Arnie Zwillman that he would not meet with him again was less than he had expected it to be.

Perhaps it was the tone of voice Zwillman had used when he said to Jules, "You're making one big fat mistake, Mendelson." People simply did not call Jules Mendelson, Mendelson. He was in deep thought, stirring his coffee, although there was neither cream nor sugar in it to stir, when Philip Quennell walked up to his booth and slid into the seat opposite him.

"Hello, Jules," said Philip.

"Get lost, Quennell," said Jules, in a snarling tone of voice. While he feared Arnie Zwillman, he in no way feared Philip Quennell, and he was relieved to be able to shift his focus from one man to the other. He disliked Philip Quennell and had disliked him from the first night they met, when he arrived at the Mendelson party late, the only guest without a dinner jacket, and declined the magnificent wine from the Bresciani auction of which Jules was so proud. Each episode he had spent with him since had only increased that feeling.

"I hear you got me fired from my documentary," said Philip.

Jules did not try to disguise the contempt that crept into his face. "I don't waste my time getting low-level people fired," he said. "Move on, will you?"

"Oh, no?" said Philip, very calmly, making no effort to move. "Casper Stieglitz, after I threatened to pull off his rug in front of a couple of his hookers, let it out that you had called Marty Lesky to, as he put it, send me back home, or you wouldn't follow through with your pledge to the Los Angeles County Museum, which would have been very embarrassing for Marty, who has recently embraced culture."

Jules stared at Philip.

"What I want to know is, did you have me fired because of the crack in the Degas ballerina statue? Or because I refuse to buy your suicide story and think you are involved in a cover-up of Hector Paradiso's death? Or, what is probably the reason, because we happen to share a mutual friend in the person of Miss Flo March?"

Jules could not stand to hear the name of Flo March come out of the mouth of the handsome, self-assured young man who sat opposite him. He hated Philip Quennell's youth. He hated his good looks. But what he hated most was to think that Flo, in her anger at him, had made love to Philip Quennell, had probably performed on him the same sexual intimacies that he had come to crave from her more than anything in his life. Enraged, his face very red, he rose in his seat and leaned across the coffee shop table and grabbed Philip.

Philip Quennell did not flinch for an instant. "If you're as smart as you're supposed to be, Jules, you will remove your hands from my body immediately," he said. "I don't care how old you are, how rich you are, how important you are, I will knock you down on your fat ass right here in this coffee shop, in front of all these customers who are staring at you."

Jules met Philip's eye and knew he meant what he said. He released his grip on the young man.

"Everything all right, Mr. Mendelson?" asked Curly, the manager of the coffee shop, who ran over to the table.

"Get this guy out of here, Curly," said Jules.

"No, no, Curly," said Philip, waving his forefinger back and forth. "You don't have to get me out of here." There was about him a menace that was felt by both Jules and Curly. If Curly had thought of touching Philip to prod him out of the coffee shop, he desisted. "I am about to walk out of here on my own. I have just about finished with what I have to say to Mr. Jules Mendelson. But there is just one more thing, Jules."

"Come on, fella. Get movin'," said Curly.

Philip turned to Curly. "I am movin'. But first I'm finishin'." He turned back to Jules. Both men were standing, and people were watching. "Do not for an instant think that I will go gently into the night, Jules, despite your orders to send me home. I don't like you,

any more than I liked your crooked pal, Reza Bulbenkian. I don't like
people who can call up a newspaper and tell them not to print a story
that the public has a right to know, or tell the police not to solve a
crime, and allow a killer to walk free because you decided to dream
up some cockamamie suicide story. You're covering up for somebody, Jules. And I'm not going back to New York until I find out who
it is. For all I know, maybe you shot Hector Paradiso, Jules."

"Get lost," said Jules.

"I'm not going back to New York, Jules, despite your best efforts.
I've decided to stay awhile. So long, Jules. So long, Curly."

Jules sank back into his seat in the orange Naugahyde booth as he
watched Philip Quennell leave the Viceroy Coffee Shop. Within him,
he knew that Philip, for all his youth and handsomeness, was not a
romantic rival for Flo March's considerable favors. He also knew that
his unreasonable jealousy of Quennell, caused by Flo's spending two
nights in his room at the Chateau Marmont, had led him to make the
sort of tactical error he would never have made in a business transaction.

JULES usually arrived at Flo's house on Azelia Way at a quarter of
four every afternoon. As he had been in his office since six o'clock in
the morning, it was not thought unreasonable by anyone that he
should leave at exactly three-thirty, no matter what, and be unreach-
able until he called in for his messages an hour and a half later. What
no one knew was that by then he had made love to Flo March as
many as three times.

On the same day that he talked with Arnie Zwillman on the telephone and fought with Philip Quennell in the Viceroy Coffee Shop,
he walked out of his office at exactly three-thirty, as was his custom.
Miss Maple, who had been with him for years, was not unaware that
he seemed dispirited. As he walked past her desk, she waved good-bye
to him while she continued her telephone conversation.

"Mr. Mendelson is not available," Miss Maple said. "Oh, hello, Mr.
Crocker. If you leave your number, I will be speaking with him in
about an hour and a half and relay it to him. Oh, yes, Mr. Crocker.
Oh, yes, I know the area code in Washington is two-oh-two. I should
know it by now, shouldn't I, after all these calls between you and Mr.
Mendelson."

Jules was at the main door of his office on the top floor of the

Mendelson Building when he heard the name Crocker. He turned back to Miss Maple. "Is that Myles Crocker?" he asked.

"Would you hold on a moment, Mr. Crocker? My other phone is ringing," said Miss Maple. She pushed the hold button. "Yes, it is," she said to Jules. "Myles Crocker. State Department. Assistant to the Secretary of State."

"I know who he is," said Jules. He put down his briefcase on Miss Maple's desk and returned to his office.

Miss Maple was surprised at the break in his routine. She thought he had appeared older recently. He had seemed preoccupied since Pauline left for Northeast Harbor. He had seemed frantic for the several days he had been locked in with Sims Lord. He had seemed remote since he returned from the Viceroy Coffee Shop, reacting only to the information that a storm in Bangor, Maine, had delayed Mrs. Mendelson's departure for Los Angeles on the family plane by several hours.

Miss Maple said into the telephone, "Mr. Mendelson has just returned unexpectedly, Mr. Crocker, and will be picking up the telephone immediately."

"I've been asked to call you, Jules," said Myles Crocker. "The Secretary had been with the President all morning on the hostage crisis and couldn't make the call himself, but he will certainly be in touch with you when things calm down here."

"Yes," said Jules, quietly. He knew that he was about to hear distressing news.

"I'm afraid that I am the bearer of some bad news, Jules," said Myles Crocker.

"Yes?"

"The Secretary didn't want you to hear it from anyone else but him."

"Yes?"

"It is about your appointment to head the American delegation in Brussels."

"Yes?"

"Some information has come to the Secretary of a rather distressing nature."

"What sort of information?"

"A tragic event in a Chicago hotel room in nineteen fifty-three. There is no way that you would ever be ratified, if such a story became known, and it is thought best to simply withdraw the nomination."

Jules remained perfectly calm. "I have heard that vicious story myself. There is no truth to it. None whatever. When you are a man in my position, there are always going to be such stories spread about you. If there were anything to such a story, there would be records in Chicago, and no such records exist."

"The records were expunged at the time, Jules, but somehow, copies of them exist. At least *a* copy of them exists. A Mr. Arnie Zwillman, formerly of Chicago, has made that copy available by fax to the Secretary, and to the *Post*."

"Dear God."

"This is terribly embarrassing for me, Jules, to be the bearer of this news, after having been entertained so beautifully and so often by you and Pauline."

Jules did not reply.

"Are you there, Jules?"

"Yes, I'm here, Myles. Look, tell the Secretary he doesn't have to bother calling."

When he hung up the telephone, Jules Mendelson put his head down on the blotter of his desk and wept.

## Flo's Tape #17

"My mother used to say to me, 'Your father walked out on us when you were two.' I had romantic notions of what my father was like. I used to always think someday he'd come back and want to make life easier for us. I thought maybe he'd have curiosity about what I looked like.

"But when I grew older, I began to realize that my father hadn't ever married my mother. It sometimes even occurred to me that my mother wasn't even sure who my father was.

"Jules once said to me, 'Did you ever say that to your mother?' Of course not. Her life was hard enough as it was."

# 18

"YOU'RE LATE, Jules," said Flo. "I was beginning to think you weren't coming."

"Why are all those cars parked on Azelia Way?" Jules asked. "I could hardly get my car in the driveway. Somebody's Jaguar is blocking about half of it."

"I told those parking boys not to block my entrance," said Flo.

"What's going on?" The small street was usually silent, except for the several times a day the tour buses went by, and the voice of the tour guides could be heard announcing Faye Converse's house.

"Faye Converse is having a barbecue luncheon," Flo answered, breathlessly. She was beside herself with excitement at the activity in the next house. She had been watching the festivities through her binoculars, from her position of vantage in her bedroom window. "Look, Jules. Faye's parasol matches her caftan. She's got half the stars in Hollywood over there. Practically everyone you ever heard of. Oh, oh, my God. There's Dom Belcanto. Be still, my heart. And Pepper, the new wife. Glyceria said Dom sometimes sings at Faye's parties. Oh, look, Amos Swank, the talk show host. I just watched him last night, and there he is. And there's your favorite, Cyril Rathbone."

She handed Jules the binoculars, but he had no interest in looking at film stars cavorting at a lunch party that showed no signs of dwindling down at five o'clock. Screams of laughter could be heard.

"Don't you love the sounds of a party, Jules?" asked Flo, looking through the binoculars again. She reminded Jules of a courtesan in an opera box, enrapt with her first opera experience. "That hum of voices, and all that laughter? Wouldn't you love to know what they're all talking about down there? I may not fit in your world, but I could fit in with the movie crowd. I just know it."

Jules shook his head and walked out of Flo's bedroom into her living room. At the bar he took out a bottle of white wine from the refrigerator and poured himself a glass. He removed the jacket of his suit and threw it on the gray satin sofa. Then he sat down heavily and looked off into space. His mind was on the telephone call he had received from Myles Crocker. He imagined Myles reporting his reaction to the Secretary of State, and the Secretary of State reporting to the President, and he experienced the feeling of despair, a feeling unknown to him in his spectacularly successful life until that moment.

"Are you all right, Jules?" asked Flo, when she came in from her bedroom. She placed the binoculars on the bar.

"Fine, why?" he asked.

"You seem, I don't know, quiet, distant, something. Did I do something wrong? Are you mad at me? Because I was watching Faye's party through the binoculars? Is that it?"

Jules smiled at her. "No," he said.

"I suppose it is kind of cheap. I can't imagine Pauline doing anything like that," said Flo.

For once he did not turn away or turn red when she mentioned his wife's name. His eyes fixed on her, as if memorizing her face.

"Sometimes you look at me as if it's going to be for the last time," she said. "Are you sure you're all right, Jules?"

"I told you, I'm fine."

"I know how to cheer you up, baby." She began to sing. "*Gimme, gimme, gimme, what I cry for. You know you got the kind of kisses that I die for.*"

Jules smiled.

"I knew I could cheer you up."

She kissed him and touched his face in a gentle fashion until he began to respond to her. When he made love to her, he had never been more passionate. He could not get enough of her. His tongue probed her mouth. He sucked in her saliva. He inhaled her breath. Over and over again he told her he loved her.

Afterward, when he phoned Miss Maple to check on his calls, he signaled to Flo that he needed the little agenda book that he always carried in the left-hand pocket of his suit jacket. He covered the mouthpiece and said to her, "It's on the sofa in the living room."

Because of the party going on next door, Flo slipped on a dressing gown and high-heeled satin slippers. As she went into the living room, she heard Jules say on the telephone, "Call the house. Tell Dudley to have Jim meet her plane. Tell him to be there half an hour ahead of time, so there's no possibility of a mix-up. And hold on, I'll have Friedrich Hesse-Darmstadt's telephone number for you in just a moment."

Flo realized from Jules's conversation with Miss Maple that Pauline was coming home from Northeast Harbor, and that as of tomorrow Jules would be resuming the heavy social schedule that he and Pauline customarily followed. As she sometimes did, she felt jealous that Pauline claimed more of Jules's life than she did. Outside, she could hear the guests from next door starting to leave the party, some in an inebriated state. "Bye, Faye," guest after guest could be heard saying.

Flo reached into the left-hand pocket of Jules's suit jacket and found his agenda book. Once he had said to her, "My whole life is in this little book. All the numbers I need. All the engagements I keep." As she took it out, her hand felt a small velvet box next to it. She took that out also. She went back into the bedroom and handed Jules his book. Then she opened the velvet box. Inside was the pair of yellow diamond earrings that Jules had given to Pauline and that Pauline had returned to him the next morning. He had meant to have Miss Maple send them back to Boothby's, the auction house, to be reauctioned, but he had forgotten to give them to her when he returned from the Viceroy Coffee Shop that morning.

Flo thought that Jules had bought them for her. Ecstatic, she let out a squeal of excitement and then covered her mouth with her hand to shut herself up, as he was still on the telephone and hated for her to talk when he was conducting his business. As soon as he hung up, she ran to him and threw her arms around his neck and kissed him.

"They're gorgeous, Jules," she said. "I never saw anything so beautiful in my whole life."

"What?" asked Jules, confused by her outpouring.

" 'What,' he says." She fastened the earrings onto her ear lobes and pulled her hair back. "*This* is what."

Jules looked at her in a quizzical fashion. He was startled to see the earrings that he had bought for his wife, that his wife would not accept, on his mistress's ears. Flo's madly excited reaction to the beautiful jewels was what he had hoped Pauline's reaction would be when he gave them to her the week before. He did not have the heart to tell Flo that the earrings were not for her, or that he had just told Miss Maple to contact Prince Friedrich of Hesse-Darmstadt, the head of the jewelry department at Boothby's auction house in London, to inform him that he wanted to sell the earrings.

"Why are you looking at me in such a funny way?" she asked.

"I'm not looking at you in a funny way," said Jules. His voice sounded tired and weary. "I'm just feasting my eyes, that's all. They look beautiful on you."

"Do you think it's okay to wear the blue sapphire ring and the yellow diamond earrings at the same time?" she asked.

"I would think it's proper," said Jules.

Nothing put Flo in such a good mood as a beautiful gift. She turned the music up on the radio and slowly slipped out of her dressing gown. She began to dance around the room, wearing nothing but her high-heeled satin slippers. It was a look she knew Jules liked. He lay back on the bed watching her, as her erotic and exotic dance steps slowly began to arouse him again. He was mesmerized by her lovely young body, her beautiful creamy skin, her superb buttocks, her perfect breasts, and her ample red bush, which he could never become sated with, no matter how often he entered it, or kissed it, or breathed it, or rubbed his face in it. As she danced her way from the bedroom to the living room, he followed her. She reached behind her and took hold of his erection and led him to her newly upholstered gray satin sofa. Never losing the beat of the music she was dancing to, she perched on the back of the sofa and then allowed herself to fall backward, spreading her legs at the same time so that only her bush, open and ready to receive him, was visible to him. With one thrust he entered her and began to pump back and forth, without subtlety, a race to a mutual explosion that momentarily obliterated the great disappointment of his day.

The massive heart attack that followed was concurrent with his ejaculation, and Flo mistook the shudders of his body and the groans of pain from his lips for signs of passion. It was only when his spent penis slid out of her and he fell over backward onto her carpet that she realized what had happened. She pulled herself up off the sofa and ran to him. His face had turned gray. Drool was dripping from his mouth. She thought that he was dead.

The scream that came from Flo's lips was unlike any scream that she had ever screamed before. The sound traveled upward in the canyon, and people in houses higher up heard it, although they could not tell for sure from which house it was coming. The scream was also heard in the patio of Faye Converse's house next door.

All the guests from her barbecue lunch party had finally left, save one. Cyril Rathbone, the gossip columnist for *Mulholland*, who could not drag himself away from the great star, continued to engage her in poolside conversation, although Faye Converse was sick to death of him and his adoring chatter. He knew the plots of all fifty-seven of her films.

"How amazing you should remember *The Tower*, Cyril," said Faye politely, stifling a yawn at the same time. She could not think of anything she would like to discuss less than the plot of *The Tower*, one of her great flops, in which she had played Mary, Queen of Scots, against the advice of everyone. She wished she hadn't sent Glyceria out on an errand, for Glyceria always knew how to get rid of adoring guests who didn't know when the party was over.

It was then that Flo March's scream from the house beyond the tall hedge pierced the canyon air.

"What in the world is that?" asked Cyril. He jumped up from the lounge chair.

"Why don't you go check?" replied Faye, who intended to disappear as soon as Cyril had gone to investigate.

"Do you think it's a murder?" asked Cyril. He was wide-eyed with excitement.

"Oh, no, it didn't sound to me like a murder kind of scream at all," said Faye Converse.

"Who lives next door?" asked Cyril.

"I haven't the slightest idea," said Faye. "It belongs to Trent Muldoon, but he's rented it to someone."

"Perhaps I should call the police," said Cyril.

"You should go over and check first. It could be the television. I'd send Gylceria over—my maid, Glyceria—but she's out getting some disinfectant for the powder room for me."

"Is there an opening through the hedge?" asked Cyril.

"No, I don't think so. You have to go 'round, down my driveway, and then up that driveway," said Faye. Then she stood, expecting him to go. "It's been lovely having you here, Cyril. When you write up my party, don't mention that Pepper Belcanto drank too many tequila sours and got sick all over the walls of the powder room. All right? You know how Dom gets. Broken-kneecap time. Good-bye, Cyril."

"I'll come right back and tell you what happened next door," he said.

"Oh, no. That's not necessary."

Faye turned and walked into her house. Cyril had not expected to
be dismissed in such a fashion, but his curiosity was such that he
could not resist going to check on the source of the scream. He went
down Faye Converse's driveway to Azelia Way. From the street the
house next door was totally hidden from view by the overgrown
shrubbery and trees in front of it. Cyril slowly went up the driveway
of that house. Directly in front of the house was a dark blue Bentley,
which blocked the garage in which was parked a red Mercedes convertible. From inside the house he could hear the hysterical crying of
a woman. The front door was locked. He walked around the side of
the house to the swimming pool area. There was no one in sight.
Then he went up to the sliding glass doors and put his hands up to
cover the sides of his eyes and peered in. There on the floor was an
enormous man, totally naked. A beautiful young red-haired woman,
also naked, was administering mouth-to-mouth resuscitation.

Cyril slid open the door. "May I help?" he asked.

"Call an ambulance," screamed Flo, between breaths. Without lifting her face, she pointed to a telephone on the bar.

"What's the address here?" asked Cyril.

"Eight forty-four Azelia Way. Tell them it's next to Faye Converse's
house," said Flo, between breaths.

Cyril dialed 911. In the moments before the telephone was answered, Cyril Rathbone noticed the great abundance of Steuben
glasses on the bar shelves. His eyes wandered around the room, taking
everything in. He noticed the gray satin upholstery on the living room
sofas and recognized it as Nellie Potts's favorite fabric that season,
ninety-five dollars a yard. He wondered whose house he was in.

"Oh, hello? Nine-one-one? Oh, yes, thank God. There is an emergency at number Eight forty-four Azelia Way. Halfway up Coldwater
Canyon. Turn right on Cherokee. It will be your second or third left,
I'm not sure which. It's the house directly next to Faye Converse's
house. There is a man who has suffered something or other, a stroke
or a heart attack. I'm not sure if he's dead or not." He turned to Flo.
"Is he dead?" asked Cyril.

Flo, not stopping her breathing, shook her head no.

"Hurry," said Cyril into the telephone. "He's not dead."

When he hung up the telephone, he moved closer to the life-and-
death drama for a better look.

"They're sending an ambulance," he said.

The woman continued her resuscitation and nodded her head at the same time. Even in such a moment of crisis, Cyril did not fail to notice that the private parts of the besieged man rivaled Lonny Edge's in what he privately termed the equipment department. When the beautiful young woman raised her head to gasp for air, he saw for the first time the face of the man on the floor.

"Good God," he whispered, as he realized that the man was Jules Mendelson, the billionaire, the art collector, the designate of the President of the United States to head the American delegation in Brussels during the year of the statehood of Europe, and the husband of the exquisite Pauline Mendelson. Only a little more than a week earlier, at Casper Stieglitz's ghastly little party, Jules Mendelson and his wife had both snubbed him.

"Good God," he whispered again. Within a second, he knew that the naked redhead trying to save Jules Mendelson's life was the same girl whose picture he had sent to Hector Paradiso from the Paris newspaper, fleeing the fire in the Meurice Hotel, with Jules in the background. Later, he had sent another, anonymously, to Pauline herself. "Good God," he said for the third time.

Cyril Rathbone was, after all, a member of the news media, and he knew that he was the first person present, aside from the principals, at what would undoubtedly be a major story, if he acted quickly, before powerful forces moved in to alter the facts of the story, as powerful forces had moved in to alter the facts of Hector Paradiso's death.

"Look, miss, I have called the ambulance, and it's on its way. I have to be off," said Cyril.

Flo continued her breathing into Jules's mouth. She lifted her head long enough to say, "Get me my robe, will you? On my bed. That way." As she resumed her breathing, she pointed in the direction of the bedroom. "And bring in his pants," she called.

When Cyril was in the bedroom, he quickly called the editor of *Mulholland* and asked for a photographer to be sent immediately to the emergency entrance of Cedars-Sinai Hospital. "Can't talk," he hissed into the mouthpiece. "But trust me."

For years Cyril Rathbone had dreamed of an opportunity that would catapult him from the gossip column of the magazine to a cover story that would be discussed across the nation. His time was at hand.

"YOU DID THE mouth-to-mouth resuscitation, lady?" asked one of the five attendants who had arrived in the ambulance. Another attendant was applying heavy pressure on Jules's heart by pumping his hands up and down. A third was trying to feel for a pulse.

"Yes," said Flo. She did not take her eyes off Jules. "Wasn't that what I was supposed to do?"

"You did exactly right. You did a good job. How'd you learn how to do that?" he asked. "Most people don't know how to do it right." He had his pad and pencil out and was preparing to ask her some questions, while two other attendants were setting up the dolly onto which the stretcher would be placed.

"Where I used to work. We had to learn how to do it, in case of a customer getting a heart attack or something. But this was the first time I ever put it to use," said Flo, distractedly, all the while watching what the other attendants were doing with Jules, lifting him onto the stretcher and strapping him on. She had managed to get his trousers pulled onto him before the ambulance arrived, although she had not had time to pull on his undershorts first, or his shirt afterward. As she heard the ambulance pull into her driveway, with its siren blaring, she had hastily pulled on the clothes she had been wearing when she was watching Faye Converse's party out the window of her bedroom.

"This your husband?" the attendant asked.

"No."

"Name?"

"Mine or his?"

"His."

"Jules Mendelson," she said.

He started to write the name. "Like in the Jules Mendelson Family Patient Wing at Cedars-Sinai?" he asked.

"Yes."

"Holy shit," he said, looking at her. "Age?"

"Fifty-six, I think, or, maybe, seven. I'm not sure."

"You are not Mrs. Mendelson, you said?"

"I am not Mrs. Mendelson. That's correct."

"This your house?"

"Yes."

"Is there a Mrs. Mendelson?"

"Yes."

"Has Mrs. Mendelson been informed?"

"Only you have been informed," said Flo. "It only happened twenty minutes ago, thirty minutes ago at most. He just keeled over. Some guy came in here from the party next door and called the ambulance. I didn't see who it was, because I was giving mouth-to-mouth at the time. Is he going to be okay?"

"Should I inform Mrs. Mendelson?"

"She's on a plane, their private plane, coming back from Northeast Harbor, Maine, due in sometime this evening. I asked you if he was going to be okay."

"We'll get him into the cardiac arrest unit as soon as we get him to Cedars," said the attendant.

The other attendants had wheeled Jules out the front door of the house and placed the stretcher in the ambulance. "Okay, Charlie," one of them called back.

"Do you want to ride with us in the ambulance? I can finish these questions on the way to the hospital," said Charlie.

"Okay," said Flo.

Charlie helped her in.

"What kind of car's that, Charlie?" asked the driver. "The blue one."

"Bentley 'ninety," said Charlie. "Beautiful, huh? That'll set you back about a hundred and fifty grand. Do you know who this guy is?"

"Who?"

"Jules Mendelson, the billionaire. Like in the Jules Mendelson Family Patient Wing at the hospital," said Charlie. "So make time, or we'll all be outta work."

"No kidding? That's Jules Mendelson? No wonder central said there's photographers at the hospital waiting for the ambulance. This is one narrow driveway, and steep. I can hardly back this around," said the ambulance driver.

"Did he say there's photographers at the hospital?" Flo asked Charlie, in an alarmed voice.

"That's what central just told him on the car phone."

"Listen, you have to stop and let me out," said Flo. "Please. It's very important."

"What's the matter?"

"Look, Charlie. Isn't that your name? Charlie? I'm the girlfriend, not the wife. Do you understand? I better follow in my own car," said Flo.

Charlie did not say, "I figured as much," but Flo could read that look on his face with absolute precision. As always with Flo, people liked her, and Charlie, the attendant, did too. "Hold it up, Pedro," he called out to the driver. "The lady's getting out."

The ambulance came to a halt at the bottom of Flo's driveway. Charlie opened the rear door of the ambulance for Flo to get down.

"Jules, honey," she said to Jules's inert body, leaning close to his face. His mouth had been covered with an oxygen mask. "I'm going to take my own car to the hospital. I'll be there with you in a few minutes. You're in good hands, Jules. I love you, baby."

"Do you know how to get to the emergency entrance of Cedars?" Charlie asked her.

"Yeah. My mother died at Cedars," she said.

In her haste to scramble out the back of the ambulance, she tripped and fell onto the driveway, tearing her skirt and skinning her knee. "Goddammit," she cried out.

"Are you okay?" called Charlie, from the back of the ambulance.

"I'm okay," Flo yelled back, waving the ambulance on. The siren started to blare, as the ambulance turned left down Azelia Way. When she tried to stand up on the steep driveway, she heard the sound of Astrid barking. She knew from Glyceria that the dog had been locked up in Faye Converse's bathroom during the whole of the party, as she had, since Hector Paradiso's death, developed a reputation for biting people, and Faye did not want to risk having one of her guests bitten.

The dog came running around from the back of the house. When she saw Flo trying to get up off the driveway, she ran to her and began licking her face, wanting to be picked up.

"No, no, Astrid, not now. I can't deal with you now," said Flo. "Go back home, honey. Go back through your hole in the hedge. You have to go home now, Astrid. You can't stay here. Go ahead. Glyceria's waiting for you. *Go home!*"

The confused dog, used to being loved by her, could not understand why Flo did not pick her up, as she always did, or why she spoke to her in such a harsh tone of voice. Flo, limping because of her cut knee, ran back up the driveway to get into her car. Then she realized that Jules's Bentley was blocking her car in the garage, and she could not get hers out.

"Oh, God," she screamed, in frustration. She felt the tears that she had held back for nearly an hour, but she refused to let them come. She ran to Jules's car and opened the door. "Thank God," she said when she saw that he had left his keys in the ignition. She jumped into the driver's seat and turned on the ignition before she closed her door. The radio came on to the news station that Jules always played in his car. Astrid tried to jump into the car after her. "No, no, out," she screamed, pushing her out of the car. For an instant they looked at each other. "I have to get to the hospital," she called out to the dog in explanation, as if the dog could understand her. But Astrid could not understand her. Rejected by the person she loved most, she ran forward down the driveway, heading toward Azelia Way.

Flo had never driven the Bentley before, and she was unprepared for its enormous power. As she applied her foot too hard to the gas pedal, the car shot forward. Halfway down the driveway, before she could apply the brake to slow down, she felt a thud, and heard a thud, and then a scream. The small white furry body of Astrid flew up in the air in front of the grille and landed with another thud on the hood of the car in front of the windshield. Flo screamed. The dog rolled over off the hood onto the driveway. Flo slammed on the brakes, put the car in park, and opened the door.

"Oh, no," she moaned, unable to accept the reality of what she had done. "Oh, no." She picked up the smashed creature from the driveway, and the tears that she had held back for nearly an hour came bursting forth from her eyes. "Oh, Astrid, my little darling Astrid, I love you so much. Don't die, Astrid, don't die, Astrid. Please. Please." She looked down into the dog's eyes, and the dog looked up at her. Their eyes met. She felt the dog relax, make a quiet sound, and die.

She held Astrid in her arms. From within the car, she heard the radio. "We interrupt this broadcast. The financier and billionaire Jules Mendelson has been rushed to Cedars-Sinai Hospital by ambulance, following a massive heart attack in the home of a friend in Beverly Hills. Mendelson's wife, the society figure, Pauline Mendelson, is thought to be en route in the family plane from Maine. Stay tuned."

Flo placed the little terrier by the side of the driveway, and kissed her. "I'll be back," she whispered to the dog. She got into the car again. Tears were rolling down her cheeks, and she made no effort to control her sobs. She raced the car down Azelia Way to Cherokee Lane to Coldwater Canyon. Without waiting for traffic, she pushed

onto Coldwater, disregarding the cars that honked at her, and proceeded to Beverly Drive, passing cars all the way, until she came to
Sunset Boulevard. She ignored the light at Sunset, crossed over and
followed Beverly Drive again to Santa Monica Boulevard, blowing
her horn at any car that wasn't driving fast enough. She turned left
on Santa Monica Boulevard, again without stopping for the light,
turned right on Beverly Boulevard, and followed it until she came to
the Cedars-Sinai Medical Center. She slammed on the brakes, but
there were no places on the street for her to park the car. She realized
that she had brought no money with her and could not get into the
garage for hospital visitors. At the parking lot reserved for the doctors
and staff, she did not have the necessary plastic card to insert that
would raise the gate to allow her car to enter. Desperate to reach
Jules, she crashed his car through the wooden gate. A parking lot
guard blew his whistle at her. At the same time, a police car that had
been following her since she went through a stoplight at Beverly Drive
and Santa Monica Boulevard pulled into the lot. She opened the door
of the Bentley, oblivious to the havoc she had caused.

"Where's the emergency entrance?" she screamed to two nurses
who were having a cigarette behind one of the parked cars. They
pointed in the direction of emergency, and she ran toward it.

"Hold it!" called out the policeman to her.

"You hold it," she called back, and entered the hospital.


ROSE CLIVEDEN, who listened to the radio all day, heard the same
news announcement about Jules's heart attack that Flo had heard on
her car radio when Astrid was dying in her arms. Rose put down her
glass and sprang into action. For a moment she couldn't decide
whether to call Camilla Ebury, Miss Maple, or Dudley, the butler,
first. She had spoken to Pauline several times since she left for Northeast Harbor, and knew she was returning that very day, but she also
heard on the news that there were storms in Maine, and she thought
the plane might not have taken off, or been delayed. Pauline had told
Rose no more than that she was going to Northeast to visit her father,
who was ailing.

Rose called Dudley.

"Is Mrs. Mendelson's plane in yet, Dudley?"

"It's due in at eight, Mrs. Cliveden."

"Do you think she knows?"

"I'm sorry?" Dudley did not understand Rose's question. He knew everything about the Mendelsons, he thought.

"Do you think she's heard the news?"

"What news? About the storms in Maine?"

"You mean you haven't heard?" asked Rose. She was full of importance with her knowledge.

"Heard what?"

"About Mr. Mendelson?"

"What's happened?" asked Dudley.

"He's had a heart attack. They've taken him to Cedars. I just heard it on the news."

"Oh, no." There was a silence for a minute. "I can't understand why Miss Maple wouldn't have called here," he said.

"Perhaps she doesn't know yet either."

"How could she not know?"

"It didn't happen in the office, apparently. The report said he was visiting a friend."

"Who?" asked Dudley.

"I don't know. They didn't say on the news. Who's going to meet Mrs. Mendelson's plane?"

"Jim, the chauffeur, is going out to the airport at seven. Mr. Mendelson wanted him to be there a half hour ahead of time," said Dudley.

Rose began to give orders, as if she were in charge. "Have Jim pick me up first, Dudley. I think I should be there when she lands. She should hear the news from a friend, and I suppose I'm her best friend. And I'll go on to the hospital with her."

"Yes, Mrs. Cliveden," said Dudley.

When Dudley hung up, he yelled upstairs for Blondell, Pauline's maid, to come downstairs, and for Gertie, the cook, to come out from the kitchen, and for Smitty, the guard, to come in from the kennels, where he was feeding the dogs, and for Jim, the chauffeur, to come in from the garage, where he was polishing the cars.

"Mr. M. has had a heart attack," Dudley said, when the servants were gathered together in the main hallway of Clouds. There was a feeling of silent dismay among them, as if their lives were being threatened. Dudley had been with the family longest, and was known to have a close relationship with Jules Mendelson. Blondell thought he was crying. Then the telephone rang. It was Miss Maple.

Miss Maple heard the news from her sister in Long Beach, who had heard it on her car radio and pulled in to a Mobil station to call her from a pay phone. She immediately called Clouds to tell Dudley, but Dudley said that he already knew and that he had been about to call her, as he had just heard the news from Mrs. Cliveden, who had heard it on the radio. Dudley told Miss Maple that Mrs. Cliveden was going to the airport with Jim and would break the news to Mrs. Mendelson.

"Just what she's not going to need at such a time is Rose Cliveden," said Miss Maple.

"That's what I was thinking," said Dudley.

"I wonder if I should call the pilot and tell him to tell Mrs. Mendelson," said Miss Maple.

"I'd wait," said Dudley. "There's nothing she can do while she's in the air."

While Rose was waiting for Pauline's chauffeur to pick her up, she called Camilla Ebury to tell her the news.

"I can't believe it," said Camilla.

"It's true, all right. It's on the news," said Rose.

"Poor Pauline," said Camilla.

"I can't stay on the phone talking," said Rose. She was full of purpose. "Pauline's chauffeur is going to pick me up and take me out to the airport so that I can break the news to her. She adores Jules."

Camilla called Philip Quennell at the Chateau Marmont.

"Where did it happen?" asked Philip.

"Rose said the news said it happened at a friend's house," said Camilla.

Philip knew immediately, without being told, that it had happened at Flo March's house, but he did not tell that to Camilla. He had not told Camilla that the girl she had met and liked in his room at the Chateau Marmont was the mistress of Jules Mendelson.

Philip called Flo, and got the answering machine. At first he was going to hang up. Then he said, without leaving his name, "Flo, I'm at the Chateau, if you need me."

SINCE THE PLANE was late in arriving, Rose had several drinks at the bar in the lounge of the airport where the private planes landed. Jim, the chauffeur, twice stopped her from tripping over her crutches. By the time the plane finally arrived, an hour later than scheduled, she was sobbing incoherently over the news she had to break to her great and dear friend. When Pauline got off her plane and saw Rose in such a state, she knew that something dire had taken place. Her first thoughts were of Kippie. She was sure she was about to be told that Kippie was dead.

"Oh, my God," she said. "Kippie? Is it Kippie?"

"Not Kippie. *Jules*," said Rose, throwing her arms around Pauline.

Pauline turned ashen. "Jules?" she asked. She had decided to take her father's advice and go back to Jules. During her last days at Northeast Harbor and on the plane ride home, she had further decided to wipe the slate clean and begin again with Jules. What husband had not had an indiscretion, she had reasoned. She thought of the many advantages of her life: her beautiful home, her flowers, her friends, the traveling she did, the thoughtfulness of her husband for all her comforts. She thought of the time ahead, when she would be spending a year in Brussels, and of all the entertaining that would entail. And, most important, she knew, despite his affair, that Jules needed her and even still loved her. She could not believe that he was dead.

Jim, the chauffeur, seeing the anguished look on Mrs. Mendelson's face, understood immediately that Mrs. Cliveden had made her think that Mr. Mendelson was dead. "No, no, Mrs. Mendelson," he said. "Mr. Mendelson has had a heart attack. It was on the news. He's in Cedars-Sinai, and I'm going to take you there right now."

"What is his condition?" asked Pauline.

"We don't know," said Jim.

"We don't know," repeated Rose, through her sobs.

At the hospital, Pauline would not allow Rose to come in with her. "Take Mrs. Cliveden home, Jim, and then come back, will you please."

"But I want to be with you, Pauline," said Rose. "You need me."

"No, Rose. You must understand. I want to be alone with my husband. You have been so marvelous, darling. Thank you. Thank you. I can never thank you enough."

"Do you need any of your bags, Mrs. Mendelson?" asked Jim.

"Just that small one, Jim. For God's sake, get her out of here, and don't let her talk you into bringing her back."

"Yes, ma'am. And Mrs. Mendelson?"

"Yes?"

"Tell Mr. M. we're all rooting for him."

"That's right, Pauline. Tell Jules we're all rooting for him," Rose called out of the window of the limousine.

THE YOUNG red-haired woman with the ripped Chanel suit and the skinned and bleeding kneecaps raced into the emergency entrance of the Cedars-Sinai Medical Center in a highly agitated state. She made her way over to the admitting desk, followed by a policeman who was writing out a ticket while reeling off the charges of driving sixty-five miles an hour in a thirty-mile-an-hour zone, going through a red light, malicious damage to public property, and reckless endangerment. She turned to her pursuer and asked, angrily, "I didn't kill anybody, did I?"

The policeman continued to write his ticket.

"Or wound?" continued Flo.

"You could have," said the policeman.

"Then that ticket that you are writing out is *not* an emergency. And the reason I drove here so fast *is* an emergency. So I will take your ticket, if you ever finish writing it up, and I will handle it in the proper way, and appear in the necessary court, and pay the designated fine, or go to jail if I have to, all at some time in the future, as well as pay for the gate that I knocked down outside. But now I am here on another matter, involving a life-and-death situation, and I'm telling you, in as courteous a way as I know how, not to detain me one instant longer."

"You tell him, sister," shouted a woman with two small children, whose lover had been taken up to the emergency room with multiple stab wounds, and others waiting on benches in the emergency entrance cheered.

The policeman looked at the beautiful young woman who had just read him off. She remained unflinching in her return of his gaze. Finally, he smiled at her and handed her the ticket.

"Listen, I can't tear this up, miss. I still gotta give it to you," he said.

"Sure," said Flo, calming down.

"I hope whoever's sick is going to be okay," he said.

"Thanks." She took the ticket and turned to the nurse on duty at the desk.

"Jules Mendelson," she said.

The nurse, whose name, Mimosa Perez, was on a nameplate on her uniform, had watched Flo handle the policeman. "You must be Mr. Mendelson's daughter, right?"

Flo looked surprised at the question. Jules would have hated it if anyone had mistaken her for his daughter. Then she remembered from the time her mother had been brought to this same emergency entrance, when she was burned in the fire in the welfare hotel, that only immediate family members were allowed upstairs to talk with the doctors.

"Have to ask," said the nurse, apologetically. "Hospital rules."

Flo, unsure how to answer, nodded.

"Only immediate families are allowed upstairs," said the nurse. "Some of these reporters will stoop to any kind of low trick to get into the ICU when there's a VIP or a celeb admitted to the hospital. You should have seen this place when Lucille Ball died. I mean, it was crawling with reporters."

Flo could not bring herself to say that she was Jules's daughter, and she would never have claimed to be his wife. The nurse, eager to help the distraught but expensively dressed young woman, said, "I'll buzz you in, Miss Mendelson. Down that corridor. Turn right by the water fountain to the elevators. Take the elevator to the sixth floor. They'll direct you from there."

Flo looked at her nameplate. "Thanks, Mimosa," she said.

Mimosa smiled. "Your father's still in the operating room, but not in the Jules Mendelson Wing. I'll ring up and tell the nurse on duty that you're on your way."

On the bench next to the woman with two children whose lover was being operated on sat Cyril Rathbone, witnessing the arrival at the hospital of the mistress of Jules Mendelson. He was beside himself with excitement at the turn of events in his life that day. "Dressed in Chanel. Skirt torn. Pretended she was his daughter," he wrote about Flo March in his spiral notebook.

EVERY DOCTOR and nurse in the intensive care unit was aware that Jules Mendelson had given the hospital wing that bore his name. On two occasions, Dr. Petrie, who was in charge of the case, sent out an intern to give Flo a progress report, assuming that she was an immediate member of Jules Mendelson's family.

"We are cautiously optimistic," said the intern.

"That's only telling me that he's still alive," said Flo.

"That is more than we had hoped for when he was first admitted," said the doctor.

"Can I see him?"

"Not yet."

"When?"

For several hours Flo waited in the lounge area outside the intensive care unit, drinking Diet Cokes from a vending machine and watching television. She tried to read magazines and newspapers that had been left there, but she found it impossible to fix her attention on anything other than the matter at hand. She felt the beginnings of fear, both for her and for Jules.

In the five years since Jules had walked into the Viceroy Coffee Shop and changed her life, Flo had often longed for a friend to confide in, over events of far lesser magnitude than the event that was now occurring around her. But never had she longed for a friend to be with more than she did in those hours she waited in the lounge of the intensive care unit to find out whether Jules Mendelson would live or die.

Since she had become so intimately involved with the billionaire, she had ceased to see Curly and Belle, her friends from the Viceroy, on his advice. "Mixing with people like that, it never works," he had said to her. Only Glyceria, the maid from next door, and Philip Quennell, whom she had met at an AA meeting at the log cabin on Robertson Boulevard, had offered her the kind of friendship she craved. But she had been afraid to confide too much in Glyceria, because she knew Jules disapproved of her friendship with Faye Converse's maid. She had told everything to Philip Quennell during the two days she had stayed with him at the Chateau Marmont, when she meant to break off her relationship with Jules for good, but she was aware that Jules despised the handsome young man who had been kind to her, and she knew she could not call on him for solace.

Her attention became diverted from her thoughts by a news bulletin from anchorman Bernard Slatkin on the NBC Evening News.

"Jules Mendelson, the Beverly Hills billionaire, banker, art collector and patron, and presidential designate to head the American delegation in Brussels during the statehood of Europe, suffered a massive heart attack at a private home in Beverly Hills this afternoon.

He was found unconscious and in full cardiac arrest on the floor of the house. Medical aides who rushed to the house administered cardiopulmonary resuscitation to revive him before taking him to the Cedars-Sinai Medical Center in Los Angeles. A hospital spokesperson declined comment on Mendelson's condition."

Flo continued to stare at the television set after Bernie Slatkin had gone on to another story. She was aware that "the private home in Beverly Hills" that he spoke about was her house on Azelia Way. A chill ran through her as she realized that if Jules died, she was only a step away from being in the news herself.

"You may go in now, but you can only stay ten minutes," said the intern. "Miss?"

"What?" asked Flo.

"I said you can go in now, but you can only stay for ten minutes."

"Is he conscious?"

"In and out. You must not excite him or tire him."

"Thank you."

ARNIE ZWILLMAN looked up from his gin game in the card room of his Holmby Hills mansion, which had once belonged to Charles Boyer, and listened to Bernard Slatkin, the anchorman on the NBC Evening News.

"I said to Jules only recently when we were dining together at the home of Casper Stieglitz, I said, 'Jules, you gotta lose some of that lard, or you're going to have a heart attack.' I swear to God, I said that. Hold on there, Dom, baby. It's my deal, not your deal."

"I'M MRS. MENDELSON," said Pauline to Mimosa Perez at the admissions desk of the emergency entrance.

"Oh, yes, Mrs. Mendelson," said Mimosa, transfixed by the elegance and serenity of the woman standing before her.

Cyril Rathbone knew better than to speak to Pauline Mendelson, or even allow himself to be seen by her. He leaned back on the bench where he was sitting and raised the *Los Angeles Tribunal* to cover his face as he listened to Mimosa Perez give instructions to Pauline on how to get to the intensive care unit. Cyril followed fashion each season and could identify with precision one Paris collection from another. He wrote in his spiral notebook that Pauline Mendelson was wearing a dark green traveling suit, with tattersall blouse, by Givenchy, when she arrived at Cedars-Sinai Medical Center by chauffeur-driven limousine, after having landed in her husband's sixteen-seat 727 from Bangor, Maine, where she had been visiting her ailing father, the sportsman Neville McAdoo. He also wrote that Rose Cliveden was sent home in the same limousine by Mrs. Mendelson.

When Pauline walked into her husband's room in the intensive care unit, Flo March was still there. Jules lay unconscious on the bed. She was sitting on the edge of his bed, rubbing his hand and whispering encouragement in his ear.

"Everything's going to be okay, Jules. Just think positive. You'll be up and around in no time. It's just the strain you've been under that caused this. With Arnie Zwillman, and the statehood of Europe, and everything."

Pauline stared at the scene before her. "I would like to be alone with my husband, please," she said.

Flo jumped, as if an electric shock had gone through her. She stared at Pauline, aghast, and put her hand to her mouth. Her face was wet with tears and running mascara and smeared lipstick. Her skirt was ripped. She had washed the blood off her knees, but she knew they looked scraped and ugly. "Oh, Mrs. Mendelson," she said. Her voice was weak and barely audible. She knew that this woman would never cry in public.

Pauline went to the other side of the bed. Taking the hand of her unconscious husband, she spoke as if Flo did not exist. "Hello, Jules," she said. "It's Pauline. The nurses all say outside that you can't hear when you're in a coma, but I've never believed that. My father said he could hear everything we said to him last year when he had his stroke. Do you remember? The plane was hours late. Terrible storms in Maine. Landing problems in Los Angeles. Father sends his love. Of course, he doesn't know what's happened. Rose came to the airport to break the news to me. She was so drunk. I'll tell you about it when you're better. It will make you laugh, I know. I've talked with Dr. Petrie outside. He's terribly nice, and I'm sure he's a good doctor. They're flying in Dr. Rosewald from New York, for a consultation. I insisted on that. In a few days, if all goes well, they're going to move you to the Mendelson Wing. What's the point of giving a wing if you can't use it. Right? You'll be more comfortable there. You're going to be all right, Jules. Dr. Petrie has great hope."

Flo was overwhelmed by the assurance of Pauline Mendelson. She had never seen a woman with such beautiful posture, with such a long neck, with such an aristocratic face, or heard a woman speak with such a deep contralto voice. Like a fired maid, Flo edged her way toward the door, listening to every word that Pauline said.

As she put her hand on the knob, the door opened, and a nurse came in.

"There can only be one person in here at a time," said the nurse, in an angry voice.

"I am just leaving," said Flo.

She turned to look back at Jules once more, and Pauline turned to look toward the door. The eyes of the two women met, but Pauline's eyes moved from Flo's eyes to her earlobes and became fixated on them. The large yellow diamond earrings that Jules had given to her on the night of Casper Stieglitz's party, and that she had returned to him the following morning when they had breakfasted together in the sunrise room of Clouds, were now on Flo March's ears. Pauline's coolness and reserve evaporated. Her face flushed with anger.

"You," said Pauline. "Now I remember you. I thought you looked familiar. You're the one who backed into my car. Why didn't I realize it was you? What a fool you must have thought me that day. I think I even complimented you on your suit."

"No, I didn't think you were a fool, Mrs. Mendelson," answered Flo.

"Did it strike you funny later? Did you laugh about it with my husband?"

"Never. Never. I swear to you," said Flo.

Staring at Flo, Pauline remembered the moment on her terrace after Hector Paradiso's funeral when she had asked Jules who the red-haired woman in the Chanel suit was he had been talking to outside the Church of the Good Shepherd, and he had pretended not to know her. Even then, she realized, she was being deceived.

"Get out of this room," she said, in a low and even voice.

"I said I was going," said Flo, frightened.

But Pauline had not said enough to assuage her anger. "You tramp," she added.

"I am not a tramp," said Flo. Tears came to her eyes. The word *tramp* hurt her deeply. Once she had heard a man call her mother a tramp.

"Call it what you will," said Pauline, turning back to Jules.

Flo's anger matched Pauline's. "You can afford to be so high and mighty, Mrs. Mendelson. For your whole life, you've had everything handed to you on a silver platter. You've never had to earn your living."

"Is being kept for sex what you call earning a living?" asked Pauline.

"Yes," snapped Flo, meeting her gaze. She did not say that she took care of needs that Pauline did not, or could not, or was disinclined to take care of, but Pauline understood her meaning and her gaze without having to hear the words.

Pauline looked away. "I won't ask for details," she said.

"No, better not," replied Flo. "I might tell you."

"I asked you to leave this room before this nurse asked you to leave. So please go," said Pauline.

From the bed Jules let out a moan.

The nurse, who had been watching, said, "Yes, miss, you must let your mother be here with your father. Only one person at a time."

"Her mother!" cried Pauline, in an outraged voice. "I am not this tramp's mother. Is that how she has passed herself off?"

"Don't you call me a tramp again," said Flo. She walked out of the room.

The duty nurse could not believe the scene she had just witnessed. Within minutes she told the desk nurse outside, and the desk nurse told one of the interns, who told another of the interns. Before an hour had passed, the news had trickled down to the emergency entrance on the first floor, where Cyril Rathbone wrote in his spiral notebook, "Contretemps between wife and mistress in intensive care unit, as Jules Mendelson lay unconscious between them. 'Don't you call me a tramp,' cried Flo March."

## Flo's Tape #18

*"Cyril Rathbone says it's because of me that Jules didn't get to be the head of the American delegation to Brussels. That's not true, you know. Jules lost that appointment before the world ever heard of me. Not long before, but before. I happen to know why he lost it. I happen to be one of the few people who do know. Not even Pauline knew. Jules never told her. But he told me. Arnie Zwillman knew too. You know, the gangster? Arnie Zwillman was responsible for Jules not getting the appointment. Arnie Zwillman blew the whistle on Jules because Jules wouldn't play ball with Zwillman. Believe me, I know it. Jules knew it too. He told me that afternoon before he had his heart attack."*

# 19

CYRIL RATHBONE once had higher literary aspirations than to be the gossip columnist for *Mulholland*. At his English university, he had affected the mannerisms, flamboyant dress, and speech patterns of a latter-day Oscar Wilde, and his undergraduate plays, which were *hommages* to the great playwright, had attracted a certain youthful notoriety. However, his subsequent postgraduate forays into the West End theater in London did not live up to his early expectations. He had then arrived in Hollywood, a dozen years ago, as a promising screenwriter. He let it be known that he was the illegitimate son of a British aristocrat, an earl, who was, of course, dead. He let it be known that he had come to seek his fortune because his father's legitimate heir, the present earl, could not bear the sight of him and made his life in England impossible. His story had a romantic quality that gave him an instant social entrée. Witty and urbane, stylishly dressed in the English manner, and wickedly entertaining in his storytelling, he was snapped up by the wives of producers and studio heads as a new and amusing extra man.

People said about the hostess Pearl Silver that she must watch the airport, because she always knew before anyone else when someone new arrived in town. Pearl, who entertained at lunch and dinner several days a week, was always on the lookout for interesting new-comers, and she became the first of the movie crowd to ask Cyril Rathbone. Then Sylvia Lesky, who entertained less frequently than Pearl but in a grander manner, and was considerably harder to please, found Cyril an amusing addition at her parties. "He is a breath of spring," she said about Cyril at the time. "We need new blood from time to time. We see much too much of the same people."

Sylvia doted on Cyril for an entire season and was even instrumental in having her husband, Marty Lesky, the head of Colossus Pictures, the same studio that her father had once been the head of, sign him up as a staff writer. But none of Cyril's three screenplays, for which he had been paid handsomely by Marty Lesky, was ever produced. "Too fairyish," said Marty at the time. Cyril's option was then dropped. Afterward, he was no longer invited to the Leskys' house, where only the very successful were invited. Pearl Silver continued to have him, although more for lunch than for dinner, because he was, like Hector Paradiso, who became his friend, one of the few men who could always be counted on for lunch. Over the years, as success eluded him, Cyril changed groups several times. Then a writing stint for the society page of the *Tribunal* led to his column in the weekly magazine *Mulholland,* and the success that followed was sweet to him, although it was less than the success that he had always imagined would be his.

Some people did not believe his romantic story of being the illegitimate son of an earl. Pauline Mendelson was one of those people. To her observant eye, his excellent manners appeared to be manners learned by imitation, rather than manners acquired as a child from a parent or a nanny. He popped to his feet too fast when a lady entered the room, or held out a chair with too much flourish when a lady sat down to dine. And his accent, which was perfect to most ears, sounded altogether too florid to her well-tutored ears. Pauline was a student of English life. When she was young, her sisters thought she might marry Lord St. Vincent and live in Kilmartin Abbey in Wiltshire, but that had not come to pass. Neville McAdoo didn't possess the kind of fortune Lord St. Vincent needed to keep up his abbey, so he married one of the Van Degan heiresses instead, and Pauline married Johnny Petworth. It was Pauline who asked the present Earl Rathbone about his father's illegitimate son in Los Angeles. "An impostor, a total impostor," said the earl. "My father knew nothing of him."

Pauline was not the kind of woman who would repeat such a story, and did not. To her it was of no importance that Cyril had created such a background for himself. It was only after he became a celebrated social scribe and wanted, in that capacity, to be invited to the Mendelsons' parties at Clouds that she spoke up, when Hector Paradiso intervened in his friend's behalf.

"Do have him, Pauline," said Hector.

"Jules despises social publicity," said Pauline. "It's not good for his position in the administration."

"But Cyril is different," insisted Hector. "You know, of course, that he is the illegitimate son of the last Earl Rathbone. He's a gentleman."

"No, he's not," said Pauline.

"Not what? A gentleman?"

"That's for anyone to decide. He is not the illegitimate son of the last Earl Rathbone. It is an entirely bogus story."

"How do you know such a thing?" asked Hector.

"I asked."

"Asked who?"

"The present earl, the one who supposedly drove him out of England. He didn't drive him out of England. He never heard of Cyril Rathbone. You must never mention this, Hector."

"On my honor."

One of Hector Paradiso's lesser deficiencies was that he was utterly unable to keep a secret. When he passed on to Cyril Rathbone what Pauline Mendelson had told him, Cyril laughed in an altogether charming way. "But of course that's what Peregrin would say," said Cyril, referring to the present earl's denial of him. And he dropped the matter. But Cyril Rathbone remembered slights. He was in no hurry. He knew the time would come when he would get even.

FLO MARCH'S encounter with Pauline Mendelson at Jules Mendelson's bedside in the intensive care unit of the Cedars-Sinai Medical Center left her shattered and shamed. When she returned to her home, the first thing she saw in the glare of the Bentley's headlights, as she drove up her steep driveway, was the body of little Astrid, in the place where she had left her five hours earlier, in her haste to follow the ambulance to the hospital. It had never occurred to Flo, who secretly cherished the dream of meeting her next-door neighbor, Faye Converse, and being invited to her parties, that her introduction to the great star would finally come when she rang her doorbell to tell her that she had killed her dog.

Faye Converse, who was exhausted from her barbecue lunch party, rested after Cyril Rathbone finally left her house to investigate the screams coming from next door. She knew nothing of Jules Mendelson's heart attack, which had taken place there. She had removed her makeup and hairpieces, put on a caftan and a turban, and settled down with a goat cheese pizza, fetched by Glyceria from Spago, to watch *The Tower*, her greatest flop, on the All-Movie channel.

"You know, Jack Warner used to say to me, 'You don't have the right kind of looks for costume epics, Faye. Leave those to Olivia de Havilland.' But I insisted. I said, 'No, Jack. I want to play Mary, Queen of Scots, in *The Tower*. It's a part I was born to play.' The son of a bitch turned out to be right, of course. God, I hated Jack Warner."

"Yes, ma'am," said Glyceria.

"You know I sued him, don't you?"

"No, ma'am."

Then the doorbell rang.

"He said I was box-office poison."

The doorbell rang again.

"Whoever it is, I'm not home," said Faye to Glyceria.

"Yes, ma'am," said Glyceria.

"Imagine someone ringing the doorbell at this hour," said Faye.

"Yes, ma'am," said Glyceria.

"I really should have guards so this sort of thing can't happen," said Faye. "Dom and Pepper Belcanto have guards now."

"Yes, ma'am," said Glyceria.

"And the Marty Leskys keep a police car parked in their driveway."

The doorbell rang again.

"Aren't you going to answer it?" asked Faye.

"I didn't know if you was finished talking, ma'am," said Glyceria.

When Glyceria opened the front door, she was astonished to see Flo March, her friend from next door, standing there.

"Oh, thank God, Glyceria. I thought nobody was at home. I rang and rang," said Flo.

"What are you doing here, Flo?" asked Glyceria. She looked behind her into the house to see if Miss Converse was watching.

"I have to see Miss Converse," said Flo. "It's very important."

"She won't see nobody tonight," said Glyceria. She looked behind her again. "She's watching herself on TV, and she don't like to be disturbed."

"It's very important, Glyceria," repeated Flo.

"You won't tell her I go over to your house and drink coffee, will you?"

"Of course not. Please, Glycie."

Glyceria looked at her friend. She thought she looked tired and drawn. Her usual ebullience, which Glyceria called bounce, was missing.

"You okay, Flo?" she asked.

"Please tell her I'm here, Glyceria."

"But she just told me she didn't want to be disturbed."

Flo cupped her mouth with her two hands. "Miss Converse," she called out in as loud a voice as she could muster, after the exhaustion she felt from the last five hours. "Miss Converse, please."

"I'm going to be in big trouble," said Glyceria.

Faye Converse entered the hall of her house. "What's going on here, Glyceria?" she asked.

"Miss Converse, this is Miss March from the house next door. She says she has to see you. She says it's real important," said Glyceria.

"I'm sorry to disturb you, Miss Converse," said Flo. "It's about Astrid."

"Oh, Astrid," said Faye Converse, throwing up her hands in the air. "That wretched little dog has run away again. She's been nothing but a problem from the beginning. She bit off Kippie Petworth's finger, and she tripped my great friend, Rose Cliveden, who broke her leg. And she runs away all the time. Have you found her?"

"I killed her," said Flo.

"You what?" asked Faye.

"I ran over her in my car. I didn't mean to. I was going down my driveway. Someone had a heart attack in my house and the ambulance came to take him to the hospital. And I was following in my car. And the little dog jumped in front of my wheels, and I ran over her," said Flo. She started to cry.

The telephone rang in the library.

"Whoever it is, I'm not home," said Faye to Glyceria.

"I loved that little dog," continued Flo. "You don't know how much I loved that little dog, Miss Converse. I wouldn't have hurt little Astrid for anything in the world. I'm sorry. I'm really sorry."

Glyceria looked from one woman to the other and then left to answer the telephone.

Faye Converse listened to the young woman. She noticed how pretty she was, even though her mascara had run and her lipstick was smeared. She noticed that her suit was a Chanel, even though it was ripped and had threads hanging off it. She noticed that her knees were scraped. She noticed that she wore large yellow diamond earrings, like the ones in the Boothby catalog that Prince Friedrich of Hesse-Darmstadt had sent her. "You poor darling," she said. She walked over to Flo and put her arms around her. "This is very nice of you to come and tell me yourself that you ran over my dog. That could not have been a pleasant chore for you. I can be frightful at times, which I'm sure you've heard."

"You're not mad?" asked Flo.

"Sad but not mad," said Faye. "She was a strange little dog. Did you ever hear of someone called Hector Paradiso?"

"I knew Hector," said Flo.

"Everyone seems to have known Hector. She was Hector's dog," said Faye.

"I know," said Flo. "Some people say she's the only one who knew who killed Hector."

"I thought Hector committed suicide," said Faye.

"Two schools of thought on that," said Flo.

Faye looked at Flo. "Is your house on that side or this side?"

"That side."

"Was that you who was screaming earlier?"

"Yes, I screamed. My friend had a heart attack."

"What a terrible day you've had. I hope your friend will be all right."

"Thank you."

"There's a call for you, Miss Converse," said Glyceria.

"Who is it?"

"Mr. Cyril Rathbone."

"Oh, God. The son of a bitch is probably calling to tell me *The Tower* is on the All-Movie channel."

"He says it's important."

"Would you excuse me?"

"I better get back to my own house."

"No, no. Stay a minute. You've been so kind. Come in and have a drink."

"Oh, no, thanks. I don't drink."

"Or some pizza. You must be exhausted. We have goat cheese pizza from Spago. Have you ever had pizza from Spago?"

"Yes."

"You'll stay?"

"All right. May I use your ladies' room?"

"Yes, in there. I hope it doesn't still stink. Pepper Belcanto threw up all over the walls this afternoon, and poor Glyceria had to clean it up."

The bathroom smelled of hyacinth air spray from Floris. Flo washed her face and combed her hair. She came out of the bathroom at the same time that Faye, aghast, hung up her telephone. Cyril Rathbone had just told her that Jules Mendelson had had a major heart attack in the house next door, which belonged to his mistress, whose name was Flo March, and that there had been a showdown between Flo March and Pauline Mendelson in the intensive care unit of Cedars-Sinai only a short time before. Faye did not tell Cyril that the very same Flo March had killed her dog, Astrid, and that she had just invited her to stay and share her goat cheese pizza from Spago.

JULES remained in the intensive care unit for three nights and two days before he was moved to the finest room in the Mendelson Wing of the hospital. There were nurses around the clock. Dr. Rosewald had flown out from New York for conferences with Dr. Petrie. Dr. Jeretsky had come down from San Francisco. Dr. de Milhau had come in from Houston on the Mendelson plane. The prognosis was not promising. On several occasions Flo March, wearing a nurse's uniform, had managed to get into the room and talk to the patient.

THE WEATHER was vile. It rained all day long. Persistent downpours, sometimes torrential, were interspersed with thick mists that obliterated the city below. Pauline nodded yes when Dudley asked her if she would like a fire in the library. Even the pink and lavender roses she had cut in her garden and carefully arranged in the blue-and-white Chinese cachepots the day before could not dispel the gloom of the day. She played Mahler on the compact disc, the Ninth, her favorite, and tried to read the seventy pages of the Princess de Guermantes's evening reception in *Remembrance of Things Past*, which was always her favorite passage, but she could not concentrate.

Pauline moved over to her desk and picked up a piece of her blue notepaper. She wrote to her father. "Jules very unwell. Doctors mystified. He has suffered a serious heart attack. He's brave but naturally extremely low. I'll keep you informed. It was lovely seeing you, Poppy. Thank you for still being the best father in the whole world. Love, Pauline."

Dudley came into the room to tell her that Sims Lord had arrived at the house.

"Oh, finally," said Pauline. Seeing Sims Lord was the point of her day. "Show him in."

When Sims walked in, Pauline was struck, as she always was, by how handsome he was.

"Hello, Pauline," he said.

"Are you soaked through?" she asked.

"A bit wet, yes," he said.

"You are good to come all the way up here to the top of the mountain on such a terrible day. Come over here and sit by the fire. What will you have? Can Dudley make you a drink, or bring you a cup of coffee, or tea?"

"No, thank you, Pauline. I was in Westwood at the Regency Club when you called, and I've just had lunch."

"Thank you, Dudley," said Pauline.

Pauline sat on a corner of the sofa opposite the chair on which Sims was seated.

"The fire feels so good," said Sims. "Look how your ring picks up the flames."

Pauline looked down at her engagement ring. "This ring and you came into my life the same week," she said. "Do you remember?"

Sims laughed. He had been retained as Jules's lawyer after Marcus Stromm had been fired, the same week that Jules gave Pauline the historic de Lamballe diamond, and the same week that he had married her in Paris, with Sims as their best man. In the years since, his successful career had been both enhanced and obscured by his proximity to the dominant presence of Jules Mendelson. "I certainly do."

"I've grown to hate this ring," she said.

"Hate it?"

"For years I've enjoyed watching people react to it. It is quite blinding. Now it seems fake to me. Like my marriage."

"Oh, Pauline," said Sims.

"It's true. Don't pretend it's not, Sims. I understand your loyalty to Jules, but I know you must be aware of all that has been going on with Miss Flo March, as she seems to be called."

Pauline stood up. She took the ring off her finger. "I don't intend to wear this anymore," she said. For an instant Sims thought she was going to throw it into the fire, but she placed it in a silver box beneath the painting of van Gogh's *White Roses*.

"Someone could pick that up there," said Sims.

"I'll put it in the safe later," she said, dismissing it. "But, of course, I didn't ask you to come up here on this hurricane-like day to talk about the de Lamballe diamond, Sims. I know all about the affair. I have met this woman."

"You have?"

"She was in his room in intensive care when I arrived. She had passed herself off as his daughter. She was whispering in his ear when I walked into the room. That woman is interested in one thing and one thing only, and that is Jules's money. Imagine, with a man as ill as Jules is, possibly dying, that she should be in there grubbing for money. It's disgusting, but not surprising. I understand that she has been there on two occasions since I asked her to leave. I understand she dressed herself as a nurse and was able to get herself into his room."

Sims did not tell Pauline that Jules had told him that he must see that Flo March was taken care of, that the house on Azelia Way must be bought and put in her name, with no further haggling about price, and that a trust should be set up for her that need not be in the will, so as not to embarrass Pauline.

Pauline continued. "There is something that I want you to handle for me, Sims. I want to bring Jules home from the hospital, and I want you to tough it out with the doctors to agree. They never will with me. We all know how tough you can be. Jules always said about you that he was glad you were on his side."

"Do you think that's wise, Pauline? Jules is a very sick man. He is not out of the woods yet, not by a long shot," said Sims.

"I'll have round-the-clock nurses, male nurses, who can lift him and get him to the bathroom and wash him, and I'll have the doctors call here twice a day. I want him home."

"This will all be very expensive," said Sims.

"Oh, for God's sake, Sims. This picture alone," she said, pointing to the *White Roses*, "is worth forty million dollars, at least. Let's not waste any time on what something is going to cost."

"When do you want to do this?"

"As soon as possible."


LUCIA BORSODI, the editor of *Mulholland*, never removed her harlequin-shaped dark glasses, even in darkness. She was credited by everyone in the magazine business for saving, "absolutely saving," the floundering magazine and turning it into the enormous success that it had become. "She not only has an extraordinary story sense," a cover piece in the arts-and-leisure section of the *Sunday Tribunal* said about her, "but she has an uncanny sense of timing as well." It was Lucia, as his editor, who told Cyril Rathbone, to his consternation, that he must hold back on his story about Jules Mendelson.

"It's too early, Cyril. Don't jump the gun," said Lucia.

"But, Lucia," exclaimed Cyril, almost in tears.

"No, no, Cyril, trust me. It's the gossip columnist in you that is rushing this story, but it's a much bigger story than that, as you yourself have pointed out. You simply want revenge on Pauline Mendelson because she has always snubbed you."

Cyril blushed. If there was any doubt about his motive, the reddening of his face belied it.

"Don't you understand," Lucia said gently to the man she had just embarrassed. She understood writers and knew how to handle them. "What you have here is a story unfolding. This is not a complete story yet. You have the inside track. You were there. You saw the heart attack. You saw the girl breathing life into her lover's mouth. You have the photographs taken at the hospital. You interviewed the policeman who gave Flo March the ticket. You saw Pauline Mendelson arrive. You heard from the admitting nurse that the two ladies had hot words over Jules Mendelson's dying body."

"All that," said Cyril, like a miser gloating over his gold. "It will be the story of my career."

"But you have nothing from any of the principals. You must interview Flo March. If you get an interview with Flo March, I will give you the cover," said Lucia.

"The cover," gasped Cyril. It was beyond his wildest dreams.

"In the meantime, start planting things in your column, little hints. That will build up your audience for the story when we're ready to go with it."

SQUIB from Cyril Rathbone's column in *Mulholland*:

The cafés are buzzing. . . . Who was the gorgeous redhead who rode in the ambulance with billionaire Jules Mendelson after he suffered his massive heart attack at a secluded house off Coldwater Canyon last Friday?

MADGE WHITE, who was loyalty itself when it came to her friends, did tell Rose Cliveden, in strictest confidence, that she had actually met the girl—"so common, you wouldn't believe it"—at a steak house on Ventura Boulevard.

"No!" gasped Rose. Although Pauline Mendelson was Rose Cliveden's very best friend in all the world, as Rose frequently told anyone who would listen, Rose was not averse to hearing just the slightest little bit of gossip that just might put a chink in the armor of Pauline's perfection.

"Jules pretended he couldn't remember her name, and he told me the most awful lie about Sims Lord being in the men's room, and that the girl was actually with Sims, but, you see, my Ralph really *was* in the men's room and he would have known whether Sims Lord was in the men's room or not, and he wasn't."

Rose didn't want to hear about Ralph White in the men's room of a steak house in the Valley. "It's too sad," said Rose. "Poor Pauline. Do you think I should say something to her?"

"Heavens no, Rose. You mustn't."

"But she's my very best friend in all the world," said Rose.

"She'd die. She'd simply die, if you brought it up," said Madge.

"I suppose you're right," said Rose.

"We must keep this to ourselves, Rose. Not a word to anyone."

"Oh, darling, my lips are sealed."

When Rose hung up on Madge, she called Camilla Ebury and told her, in the strictest confidence—"No one knows but us, darling, so not a word to anyone"—that Jules had his heart attack at the home of a common prostitute. "And guess what?"

"What?"

"Madge actually saw her."

That night Camilla Ebury dined with Philip Quennell at Morton's Restaurant. Because of Camilla's great friendship with the Mendelsons, Philip had not told her that Jules Mendelson had been instrumental in having him fired off his documentary film. Camilla seemed unusually quiet throughout the meal, as if her mind was on something else.

"Is anything the matter?" asked Philip.

"No." She looked around her at the restaurant. "I never know who any of these celebrities are they make such a fuss over. Do you know any of them?"

"That's Barbra Streisand you're staring at. You certainly have to know her," said Philip. It always annoyed him that the social Angelenos he met through Camilla took such pride in distancing themselves from the film people.

"Why do you suppose she does her hair in that awful frizzy way? It's so unbecoming," said Camilla. "She should go to Pooky."

"You're changing the subject. I asked you if anything was the matter. And there is. I can tell. When you're silent like this, there is always something troubling you."

"Rose told me something today that is so upsetting I can't stop thinking about it."

"What's that?"

"I promised I wouldn't tell."

"All right."

"But I want to tell."

"Then tell."

"It's about Jules and Pauline."

Philip looked at her. "What about them?"

"Do you know where he had the heart attack?" asked Camilla.

"No," replied Philip, although he was pretty sure he did know.

"At the home of a prostitute."

Philip, understanding, nodded slowly. "She's not a prostitute," he said. "She's a mistress. It's a very different thing."

"Jules has a mistress?" asked Camilla.

"Yes. For quite a few years."

Camilla stared at Philip in disbelief. "How could you possibly know such a thing?"

"Because I know her."

"You constantly amaze me, Philip."

"You know her too."

"I do?"

"You met her. Flo March."

"You mean that pretty red-haired girl wearing an evening Chanel suit in the morning, who was sitting in your room at the Chateau Marmont?"

"Yes."

"She said she bet you looked cute in Jockey shorts."

Philip smiled.

"At least she didn't mention your tattoo, down there."

Philip laughed.

"Do you know something, Philip?"

"What?"

"I kind of liked her."

SQUIB from Cyril Rathbone's column in *Mulholland:*

The cafés are buzzing. . . . Who was the gorgeous redhead comforting billionaire Jules Mendelson in the intensive care unit when his wife, the elegant best-dressed Pauline, walked in?

"Hello?"

"Miss March?"

"Yes?"

"This is Cyril Rathbone."

"Oh, my God."

"I hope I haven't caught you in the middle of a suicide attempt."

"What's that supposed to mean?"

Cyril chuckled. "Just a little joke, Miss March."

"You've got some sense of humor, Mr. Rathbone."

"Well, you sounded so, what shall I say, so desperate. Is that the right word? Desperate?"

"What can I do for you?"

"I'd like to see you, Miss March."

"Oh, no."

"I would like to do an interview with you."

"Oh, no."

"Why?"

"No."

"You are being credited with saving his life, Miss March."

"I am?"

"The mouth-to-mouth resuscitation you did on Mr. Mendelson that you learned when you were a waitress at the Viceroy Coffee Shop."

"How did you know that?"

"I was in your house."

"You were? When?"

"I was the one who called the ambulance for you."

"That was you? The guy in my house was Cyril Rathbone, the columnist? That was you?"

"Exactly."

"Listen, Mr. Rathbone."

"I'm listening."

"I always thought I'd die happy if I could be written up in your column, just once even, but now I don't want to be written up in it anymore, even though you don't use my name."

"I think we should meet."

"No."

"Why?"

"I'm afraid I have to hang up now, Mr. Rathbone."


SQUIB from Cyril Rathbone's column:

The cafés are buzzing. . . . Is the reason billionaire Jules Mendelson is being secretly moved from the VIP section of the Jules Mendelson Wing at Cedars-Sinai Medical Center to his hilltop estate, Clouds, on Friday afternoon that a certain gorgeous redhead has managed to get into his room by disguising herself as a nurse?


OUTSIDE THE HOSPITAL and then again outside the gates of Clouds, Pauline stayed by Jules's side the whole time, holding his arm and maintaining a pleasant countenance as the photographers took their picture what seemed like a hundred times, or two hundred times, strobe flash after strobe flash.

Inside the gates, the Bentley, moving slowly, appeared at the turn in the drive and then came forward into the courtyard. The chauffeur, Jim, jumped from the car and opened the rear door. First Pauline got out. Then Jim reached in and pulled Jules out of the car. Dudley, the butler, ran forward from the house pushing an empty wheelchair. For a moment Jules stood leaning on a cane, until the wheelchair reached him. The staff who watched him out of the various windows of the house were not prepared for the drastic change in his appearance. He looked shrunken. He had become an old man, although he was not yet sixty.

Inside the house, finally, with the door closed behind them, Pauline maintained the same composure in front of Dudley. "I would like some tea, Dudley," she said, anxious to be rid of him before he said anything sympathetic, which she felt he was going to do. "And a drink. I'm sure Mr. Mendelson would like a drink, wouldn't you, Jules?"

"Yes, yes, fine, a scotch, Dudley, and a little Pellegrino water," said Jules. His complexion was pale, and he had lost a great deal of weight. When he spoke, his voice was barely above a whisper.

"But make it quite light for Mr. Mendelson, Dudley," said Pauline. "I forgot to ask Dr. Petrie if it was all right."

"In the library?" asked Dudley.

"Fine, yes, fine," they both said together.

Alone, still in their splendid front hall, their staircase floating upward, their six Monet paintings of water lilies lining its wall, their blue-and-white Chinese cachepots filled with orchid plants from their greenhouse amassed at its base, Jules and Pauline Mendelson looked at each other.

"I have to rest here for a while, Pauline," he said. "I can't make those stairs."

"Of course. Sit here. Olaf will be arriving any minute, and he can carry you up the stairs," she said.

"Imagine me being carried," Jules said, shaking his head. "I don't want you to watch me when he does lift me."

"But you didn't want to leave the hospital on a stretcher, Jules."

He nodded. "I wanted to walk out of that hospital under my own steam, no matter what. All my life I've avoided the press, and I wasn't about to allow those sons of bitches to photograph me being carried out on a stretcher. It would make me look sicker than I really am."

Their eyes met for a moment. Each knew he was far more ill than described in the optimistic propaganda about his condition that was being carefully circulated in business circles by Sims Lord and other associates. Jules sank onto the caned seat of a gilded chair, one of a set of six, which he had never sat on before in the twenty-two years that he had lived in the house.

"Did Dr. Petrie give you the pills?" he asked.

"Yes," answered Pauline.

"May I have one?"

"He said one every four hours, Jules. It's only slightly more than an hour since the last."

"I'm weary from the drive. I want one now."

She opened her bag and took out an amber plastic container. He took the pill she handed him and swallowed it.

"Is this what our life is going to be like, Jules?" asked Pauline. "Photographers lying in wait for us outside the gates of our own house? Reporters screaming rude questions at us? There is a limit, Jules, to the obligations of the marriage vows, and I think I can honestly say that I have reached that limit."

He weakly nodded his head in recognition of the truth of what Pauline had just said. Pauline again noted how old Jules looked.

"I am not the first woman whose husband has had a mistress," she continued. "I might not like it, but I could have learned to deal with it, if it was a thing that never encroached on my life; but this way— no, never. This common little strumpet has made a mockery of my marriage."

"Don't think of her as a bad girl, Pauline. She's not a bad girl. I may be a bad man, but she's not a bad girl. If you only knew her, you'd agree."

"Knowing Miss March is a life experience that I intend to deprive myself of, Jules," said Pauline. "I don't know which I dread more, having everyone I know, and tens of thousands of people I don't know, gossip about me. Or pity me. To the best of my knowledge, I have never been gossiped about in my life, and, in certainty, I have never been pitied."

Jules, drained, could only stare at Pauline. "Don't leave me, Pauline," he said.

"No, of course, I won't leave you, not now, not with you so weak and sick." She started to say more, but stopped herself. Instead she walked over to the foot of the stairs and broke a yellowed leaf off an orchid plant.

Jules nodded his head, understanding.

"How terrible, Jules, to end such a distinguished life in a cheap sex scandal. That is what people will remember about us," said Pauline.

Jules nodded again. He knew what she said was true, but he could think of no reply. "I've never sat in one of these gold chairs before," he said.

"They were a wedding present from Laurance and Janet Van Degan. Absolutely authentic, of the period. Whatshername at the Getty Museum verified them, Gillian somebody, but you didn't like them. You said you hated gold furniture. Too spindly, you said. So I put them here in the hall where they wouldn't be sat upon too often."

Jules nodded. "Thank you, Laurance and Janet Van Degan," he whispered. From the courtyard came the sound of cars and voices.

He rose slowly from his seat and looked out of the window. "What are all those cars coming into the courtyard?" he asked.

"Cars?" asked Pauline.

"Three, four, six of them, eight of them, with a lot of ladies in flowered hats getting out. What is this?"

"Oh, my God," said Pauline. "I forgot."

"What?"

"It's the Los Angeles Garden Club. I agreed weeks ago, months ago, to give them a tour of the gardens and the greenhouse. They heard about the yellow phalaenopsis that Jarvis and I have developed, and I promised."

"I'll tell Dudley to tell them you're not well and can't come out. They can come another day," said Jules.

"You can't do that, Jules," said Pauline.

"Then let Jarvis take them on the tour."

"No, Jules, no. They've paid fifty dollars each for the tour. Let's face it, it's me they want to see as much as the yellow phalaenopsis, not poor Jarvis, who did all the work."

"I was only thinking of you."

"I know."

They looked at each other.

"We're acting as though we're still very married, aren't we?" said Pauline. She touched his shoulder.

Dudley entered the hall, making a coughing sound to announce his entrance. "There are people arriving who say they are expected."

"Dudley, I completely forgot that this is the day that the garden club was coming to see my yellow phalaenopsis, and the ladies are outside in the courtyard. I'll go out and take them around. Tell Gertie in the kitchen to make tea for I don't know how many, and some cucumber sandwiches, and to use those lemon cookies she made yesterday. We'll have tea in the library. They'll love the *White Roses*, the perfect group for that."

"Yes."

"But first, help Mr. Mendelson up the stairs, and then ask Blondell to turn down his bed. Mr. Mendelson will be in the room where Mrs. Cliveden usually stays. And, Dudley, there will be a nurse arriving soon. Miss Toomey, she is called, Mae Toomey. Have the red room next to where Mr. Mendelson will be staying made up for her, and, Dudley, tell Gertie that Miss Toomey's meals will be served on trays in the upstairs sitting room, and make sure there's a television set in her room, and magazines, any of the ones that I've finished reading."

She walked over to the Chippendale mirror over the gilded console table and pinched color into her cheeks, reapplied her lipstick, and combed her hair. "There will be two male orderlies arriving tomorrow to lift Mr. Mendelson, and take him to the doctor when he's feeling better, and whatever else. They can sleep in the pool house. Have beds brought down from the third floor and put there. This dress is all right, isn't it?" Without waiting for an answer, she opened the front door and walked out into the courtyard.

"Hello, Blanche. Hello, Mavis. Welcome to Clouds."

## Flo's Tape #19

"I've heard myself called trash and tramp, and other words in that same category, and they hurt. So I want to make something absolutely clear. Except for once, only once—I mean only with one guy, not one time—was I ever unfaithful to Jules, and that was during the time I broke up with him, briefly broke up with him, after he pretended he didn't know what my name was when we ran into that snobby Madge White at the steak house in the Valley. I guess there's no protocol for a situation like that, where a guy is having dinner with his girlfriend and runs into his wife's best friend. Like, should he introduce her, or not? That's one for Dear Abby or Dr. Joyce Brothers.

"Anyway, there was this guy who took me in for a few days, after I ran away from Jules that night. He's called, uh—No, I'm not going to give his name, because he's back with the girl he had just broken up with, and I made it sound to her like nothing had gone on between us. But it did. I'd be lying to you if I said it was just a grudge fuck against Jules. This guy was really a cute guy. I originally met him at an AA meeting, and that night he was lonely and I was lonely, and we told each other all our secrets, and we did it during those days he let me hide out in his place. This guy had a tattoo in the damnedest place you ever saw. I could never get over that.

"Then I met his girlfriend. I'm not going to give her name either, because I liked her, and later she did me a good turn. Right away I could see that they really belonged together. After that I went back to Jules."

# 20

"MR. MENDELSON'S office."

"Miss Maple?"

"Yes."

"This is, uh." Flo stopped, afraid to use her own name. "My name is, uh—"

"I know who you are," said Miss Maple, recognizing the voice of Flo March from the one telephone call she had had with her, when she told her she was spending too much money.

"Red Houlihan," said Flo at the same time, blurting out the name finally that Jules sometimes used as a disguise.

"Yes, yes, I know."

"I haven't received my check."

"I know."

"For two weeks."

"I know."

"Where is it?"

"There's a problem."

"What sort of problem? I was to be taken care of for life."

"I think you had better contact Sims Lord."

"There's bills here at the house. There's men working on the new closets. Nellie Potts said they're union workers and have to be paid on time."

"Look," said Miss Maple. "I think what you should do first is tell those men to stop working on your closets. And tell Nellie Potts that you're not going to have anything more done on your house. Then call Sims Lord. Do you know Sims Lord?"

"Yes. Kind of. I've never actually met him."

"I'll give you his number."

"I have his number. Jules left his book here."

"So that's where the book is. We've been looking everywhere for it. I'll send someone to pick it up."

"No, don't. I won't give it to you."

"Look, Flo. You have to understand. I only work here. I'm just doing what I have been told to do."

"Is it her? It is her, isn't it?"

305

"Who?"

"You know damn well who. Pauline."

"You must understand, I can't talk," said Miss Maple. "You have to call Sims Lord. He's the closest person to the situation."

Flo could hear kindness in Miss Maple's voice.

"Listen, Miss Maple?"

"I really have to go."

"Do you go up to the house to see him?"

"Yes."

"Tell him. Please. Tell him she's cut off my money. He wouldn't want that to happen."

IT WAS NOT that Miss Maple was unsympathetic to the plea of Flo March that kept her from relaying Flo's message to Jules Mendelson. Each afternoon she was picked up by Jim, the Mendelsons' chauffeur, and driven up to Clouds, where she stayed with Jules for only fifteen minutes, which was thought by Dr. Petrie and Miss Toomey to be all the time that he was able to concentrate before he became exhausted and had to rest. During that brief time Miss Maple kept him abreast of the business transactions of the office, the stock market closings, and the enormous numbers of calls from well-wishers in the business and banking community. Mostly Jules only nodded in agreement, or shook his head in disagreement, although sometimes he managed to smile in recognition of the name of a business associate who had called to wish him good health. When he did speak, he spoke in a voice that was barely above a whisper, and the effort tired him. Miss Maple was shocked at the physical wasting-away of the enormous and vital man she had served for so many years. She knew that he would go into a rage if he were aware that Flo March's weekly check had not been paid for two weeks, and she was aware that such a rage might terminate his life.

IN HER DAY Faye Converse had had her share of love affairs with married men. So she was sympathetic to the plight of her beautiful young neighbor, who was so distraught over the condition of her married lover, Jules Mendelson.

"Did I ever tell you about Senator Platt of Wyoming?" Faye asked Glyceria.

"No ma'am," said Glyceria.

"Jack Warner threatened me with suspension if I didn't break that one off, after Mrs. Platt claimed she was going to spill the beans to Dorothy Kilgallen. That was when *Rittenhouse Square* was about to open, and Jack was not about to jeopardize his investment. 'Break it off, Faye, or else,' he said. That was Jack all over. God, I hated Jack Warner."

"Yes, ma'am," said Glyceria.

"And then there was Harry O'Dell. I was making a picture with Cagney, and he introduced me to Harry. Harry had millions. Did I tell you about what Edith O'Dell did?"

"No, ma'am," said Glyceria.

But Faye Converse was in an extremely awkward position in that Pauline Mendelson was a close friend of hers and she was a frequent guest at Clouds. And Jules had advised her on several investments that had made her future secure. She felt it best to distance herself from her neighbor, whom she liked. She felt also that Cyril Rathbone, who seemed to be up-to-date on every aspect of the affair, might be planning to write about it in a more serious way than in his gossip column.

The last time she saw Flo, she said to her, "Whatever you do, Flo, don't talk to Cyril Rathbone. He's trouble."

Glyceria continued to make her late morning visits to the next house, however. She noticed that Flo March sometimes didn't get dressed up anymore, the way she used to. She just pulled on her terry cloth robe in the morning and stayed in it all day. She also noticed that Flo didn't drink Diet Cokes all day, the way she used to. Sometimes she opened a bottle of white wine and drank a glass or two.

"No more hammerin'," said Glyceria one day.

"The workmen stopped," said Flo.

"How come?"

"I can't pay them. I haven't gotten a check for three weeks."

"I didn't know your gentleman was Mr. Jules Mendelson," said Glyceria.

"You didn't?"

"You never told me his name," said Glyceria. "You just always said, 'Don't come by in the afternoon after three-thirty.' I didn't know the gentleman was Mr. Mendelson."

She said "Mr. Mendelson" in such a way that Flo looked at her.

"Do you know Jules Mendelson?" she asked.

"Yes, ma'am."

"How?"

"My brother is his barber."

"Willi? Willi, who's shaved Jules every morning for twenty-five years, is your brother?"

"Yes, ma'am. Do you know Willi?"

"No, but I hear of him."

"Mr. Mendelson gave Willi the money to start his own shop on Sunset Boulevard," said Glyceria.

Flo stared at her friend.

"Tell me something, Glyceria."

"Yes, ma'am?"

"Does Willi still go up to Clouds every morning to shave him?"

"Yes, ma'am."

"Even now, when he's so sick?"

"Yes, ma'am."

WHEN MARTY LESKY, the head of Colossus Pictures, walked into Willi's Barber Shop on Sunset Boulevard without an appointment, as was his habit, it was not thought remarkable that Joel Zircon, the agent, who did have an appointment, but was considered to be no more than up-and-coming in the business, was asked to remove himself from Willi's chair and give his place to Marty. Joel Zircon was only too happy to inconvenience himself in order to accommodate Marty Lesky. The brief exchange of conversation between them was considered, from Joel's point of view, to be advantageous to his career.

"We met at Casper Stieglitz's dinner, Mr. Lesky," he said.

"Right, right," said Marty, who didn't remember and didn't want to get into a conversation with an agent on the make.

"At the party where Pauline and Jules Mendelson were," continued Joel.

"Right, right," said Marty.

"And Arnie Zwillman, and Amos Swank," said Joel, wanting to prolong his moments with the studio head as long as possible.

"Right. You ready for me, Willi?" Marty called out, and disappeared into the private room where Willi dyed the hair of his famous clients.

While Joel was waiting for Willi to finish dyeing Marty's hair, he used the time to schmooze, as he put it, with Lupe, the receptionist, and then to read the trade papers. His attention was momentarily taken up by an announcement that Hortense Madden, the literary critic of *Mulholland*, "may have discovered the lost manuscript of Basil Plant's *Candles at Lunch*, his famous unfinished novel." But Joel Zircon's attention span was brief, and he wearied of the story before he finished reading it.

The brass-studded leather entrance door of the shop opened, and a young woman entered. She hesitated inside the door, as if she felt out of place. Then she approached the appointment desk.

"May I speak to Willi, please?" She spoke quietly.

"Do you have an appointment?"

"No."

"He doesn't do women's hair."

"I didn't come to see him about my hair."

"Your name, please?"

"My name will mean nothing to him."

"He's in with a customer."

"Would you ask him if he could step outside for a minute?"

"He's in with Marty Lesky, the head of Colossus Pictures," said Lupe importantly. "I can't ask him to come outside."

"I'll wait." Flo March took a seat opposite Joel Zircon.

Lupe watched her from her appointment desk and noticed from the style that her hair had been done by Pooky, that her suit was couture, and that her bag and shoes were very expensive. She got up from her desk and went to the back of the shop.

"Flo?" said Joel Zircon. "Is that you?"

Flo looked at Joel Zircon and smiled. "Hello."

"It's Joel Zircon. Remember me? From the Viceroy Coffee Shop? You used to wait on me every morning."

"Two over easy, toasted bagel, lox, and coffee," said Flo.

Joel laughed. "You remembered."

"You can take the girl out of the coffee shop, et cetera, et cetera."

"You look like a million dollars, Flo. Ten million dollars," said Joel. "I bet you don't know where I saw you last."

"No."

"At Hector Paradiso's funeral."

"For goodness' sake."

"You cried, right? And this guy sitting behind me at Good Shepherd, Philip Quennell, who was writing a picture for Casper Stieglitz, before he got fired, he handed you his handkerchief, right?"

"Did you say that Philip Quennell got fired?" asked Flo.

"You didn't hear? What a story!"

"What happened?"

"Did you ever hear of this billionaire called Jules Mendelson? Lives in some big estate up on top of a mountain here?"

Flo swallowed. Before Joel told her what he was going to tell her, she knew what he was going to say.

"This guy Mendelson hates Philip Quennell. Why, I don't know. But he calls Marty Lesky and says get rid of Quennell." When he said the name Marty Lesky, he lowered his voice, and pointed toward the room where Marty was having his hair dyed to indicate that the studio head was on the premises. "Or—get this—or I won't honor my five-million-dollar pledge for your new wing at the Los Angeles County Museum, which is a very big deal to Marty. So Marty calls Casper and says lose him. Casper told me."

Flo stared at Joel Zircon and said nothing. Slowly she rose, as if to leave.

"But I haven't gotten to the punch line," continued Joel. "That very same day, Jules Mendelson has a massive heart attack at the home of some broad he's schtuppin' up off Coldwater, and now he's just hanging on by a twat hair. Is that poetic justice, or what do you want to call it?"

Flo began to walk toward the door. As she opened it to leave, a voice from behind her said, "Miss? You wanted to see me?"

Flo turned and faced Willi. She looked over at Joel Zircon and saw that he was watching.

"Is there a place I could talk to you in private for just a minute?" asked Flo.

"Come in here," said Willi. "My customer's in the dye room in back. Be with you in ten more minutes, Joel. Maybe fifteen."

"I'm a friend of your sister," said Flo.

Willi looked at Flo. "I didn't know Glycie had such ritzy friends," he said.

Flo opened the bag that hung from her shoulder on a gold chain and took out a letter.

"My name is Flo March," she said. "I am a very special friend of Jules Mendelson. I know you shave him every morning, even since the heart attack. Would you give him this letter, please? It's very important. Very. He will be very grateful to you for giving it to him, I promise you."

Willi looked down at the letter. Only the word *Jules* was written on the front of the envelope. "I take it this is confidential?" he asked.

Flo nodded.

"No one else should see it?"

"Oh, no. Only Jules. No one else," said Flo.

"Hey, Willi! How the fuck long are you gonna keep me waiting back here?" yelled Marty Lesky from the dye room.

Willi put the letter in his back pocket and patted it. He smiled at Flo, then turned around and went back to Marty Lesky.

THAT NIGHT at dinner at Morton's, Joel Zircon was able to say to Mona Berg, "I was talking to Marty Lesky today."

"You were what?" asked Mona, instantly jealous.

"I said I was talking to Marty," repeated Joel, thrilled with the effect the impressive name had made. "I bet you didn't know he dyes his hair."

"Of course I knew," said Mona.

Later that same night at Miss Garbo's, after he dropped Mona Berg off home, Joel said to Manning Einsdorf, "I saw Flo March today. Remember her? The waitress. She behaved very strangely."

THE FOLLOWING NIGHT the chimes in Flo March's house rang. She was sitting in front of her television set watching one of Faye Converse's old movies, drinking white wine from a Steuben wineglass. Expecting no one, she got up and peered through the closed curtains out to the front of her house. Although she could see the lights of a car, she could not see the car. She went to the front hall.

"Who is it?" she called through her front door.

"Olaf."

"I don't know an Olaf."

"I'm one of the orderlies for Mr. Mendelson. I have a message for you, Miss March."

Flo pulled open the door. Olaf was a very large young man dressed in a white T-shirt and white trousers.

"Come in," said Flo.

"I just got off my shift, Miss March. He got your note from Willi this morning. I don't know what it said, but he was very upset. Missus watches him like a hawk, you know, and also that Miss Toomey, the nurse in charge."

"Yes?"

"I'm the only one who's big enough to lift him to the bathroom, so I spend a lot of time alone with him. I have to take him on Friday to the doctor for a CAT scan, which they can't do at the house. He's going to stop here at lunchtime. He said to tell you that Mr. Lord is going to be here too. He said for you not to worry about anything."

Flo's eyes filled with tears. "Thanks, Olaf. When? What time?"

"Friday. Twelve. Twelve-thirty. One. I don't know. Depends on how long the scan takes."

"Should I have lunch for him?" asked Flo, eagerly.

"Something simple."

"Oh, how wonderful. I'll get all the things he likes. And you? And Sims Lord? You'll have lunch here too?"

"You don't have to have anything for me."

"Oh, no. I would like to. I will. Oh, thank you, Olaf. I've been so worried about him."

"I know all about you. He told me. We've gotten very close, and I don't think he likes that Miss Toomey too much."

"Come in. Would you like a drink? I have a bottle of wine open."

"No thanks, Miss March. I have to get back up the mountain. I have the Bentley outside. He wants me to get used to driving it, because he doesn't want Jim to drive when he comes here on Friday."

## Flo's Tape #20

"I often wondered why Jules never had children. It always seemed to me that he would have liked a junior, a little Jules, to leave all that money to. He hated to be written about in the newspapers, but he sure liked to have his name on buildings and wings of buildings, and what better monument could there be than a kid to perpetuate your name? I once asked him about it. I thought maybe it was Pauline who didn't want children, but Jules said no, it was he. Maybe it had something to do with what happened in Chicago, with that girl in the Roosevelt Hotel. Maybe he thought it was in the genes.

"I would have loved to have had his kid. He never knew this, but for the last year I was with him, I wasn't taking precautions."

# 21

THE WEEKS OF ILLNESS wore on, and the household revolved around the sickroom, the nurse, the orderlies, and the daily visits of the doctors. Since Jules's heart attack, Pauline had behaved in an admirable fashion that was favorably commented upon by her many friends. Despite the frequent allusions in Cyril Rathbone's column to a "redhead" who had figured in the scene of her husband's heart attack, Pauline acted as if she were totally unaware of such a story, although she was certain that everyone she knew must have been reading the same columns, or been apprised of them. She confided in no one. To anyone who called, whether it was her father, or one of her sisters, or a close friend like Camilla Ebury or Rose Cliveden, or even a museum curator who had been entertained in her home, or a high official in public office, she gave minute details of her husband's condition, as well as assurances that he was doing well. "Yes, yes, he's home from the hospital already. Isn't it marvelous? You know, Jules is as strong as an ox. The whole thing was a terrible scare for both of us. And a great warning. He has to lose weight, and now he will. I'll tell him you called. He will be so pleased. And thank you. We both so appreciate hearing from you." Callers who had heard rumors of problems in the long marriage ceased to believe them.

After Jules was brought back to Clouds to recuperate, much to the consternation of the doctors in charge of his case, Pauline began to go out to small parties in the evenings again. "No, no, of course I'll come, Rose. I'd love to come. Jules wants me to go out again. I think he loves to hear all the gossip I tell him the next day. In a few weeks he'll be up and around again himself. Long dress or short?"

When Prince Friedrich of Hesse-Darmstadt, the head of the jewelry department of Boothby's auction house, called Pauline from London to inquire about Jules, he told her that he intended to be in Los Angeles in two weeks' time, after first attending a billionaire's party in Tangier.

"I'll give a dinner for you, Friedrich," said Pauline. She was very fond of the prince.

"No, no, Pauline. I wouldn't think of letting you, not with Jules so ill," replied the prince.

"But you wouldn't believe how well he's doing," said Pauline. "I didn't mean anything large. Just ten or twelve."

"It would be marvelous, Pauline."

"Is there anyone you'd particularly like to see?"

"I long to see Faye Converse."

"Perfect. Faye just sent Jules the loveliest flowers."

FLO, LYING IN bed that afternoon, listened to the telephone ring several times. She thought of letting the machine pick up, but then it occurred to her that it might be Jules calling, and she grabbed the instrument. She worried that Pauline might have heard of their plan for Friday lunch.

"Hello?" Her voice was tentative.

"Flo?"

"Yes."

"It's Philip Quennell."

"Oh, Philip." Flo's voice relaxed.

"I haven't seen you at the morning meetings for quite some time," said Philip.

"I know."

"Are you all right?"

"Oh, yes. Things have happened, Philip. You must have heard. It's been on the news."

"I have, of course. I understand he's already gone home from the hospital."

"Yes. But it was much too early for him to be moved. He wasn't ready to go back to Clouds yet."

"Then why did they move him?"

"Can't you guess, Philip?" asked Flo.

"No, I can't," replied Philip.

"It was Pauline. She heard I went into his room dressed in a nurse's uniform, and wanted to fire the whole nursing staff. That was why she had him brought home."

"But how do you know that?"

"Mimosa Perez, one of the nurses, told me. The doctors were furious that he was taken home."

"But certainly he's being treated at home?"

"Yes."

"I assume you're not being allowed to see him."

"Correct."

"This must be a very difficult period for you, Flo."

"Yes."

There was a long silence.

"Flo?"

"Yes."

"You're not drinking, are you?"

"No!" She knew that she had answered too quickly and too emphatically. She knew that he knew too.

"I'm here, you know, if you want to talk," said Philip.

"You are sweet, Philip."

"Even in the middle of the night."

"Thanks. I won't forget your offer. And I hope that society girlfriend of yours knows what she's got," said Flo.

Philip laughed. "Would you like me to pick you up in the morning and take you to the meeting?"

"No. I'll be back real soon, Philip. Really."

"Okay."

She started to hang up, and then she stopped. "Listen, Philip?"

"Yes."

"Is it true that Jules got you fired from your documentary?"

"Did he tell you that?"

"God, no. Some jerk called Joel Zircon told me."

"Well, don't worry about it."

"I feel terrible about that. I want you to know I didn't tell him I was with you those days."

"I know you didn't, Flo."

"He had a private dick trying to locate me."

"I'm sure."

"I feel terrible about that. I feel responsible. You didn't ask me to go to your room. I just burst in on you that night."

"Jules had it in for me ever since he knocked over his Degas statue of the ballerina."


"PAULINE'S asked us for dinner on Friday night," said Camilla.

"I can't believe she asked me," replied Philip.

"Indeed she has. She's very fond of you. She asked specifically for me to bring you."

"Is it a party?"

"Small. Quite small. Only twelve or fourteen, I think. Because of Jules being ill and all."

"Is Jules up then? Is he about?"

"Heavens, no. Not yet."

"Odd time for Pauline to be giving a party then, don't you think?"

"Pauline says he's almost well again. It was just a terrible scare. She said he's on his way to a complete recovery."

"How is Pauline handling all this?"

"A model of good behavior. Everyone thinks so. Class, you know. I've always hated the word *class*, but it does say it, doesn't it? Apparently, that ghastly Cyril Rathbone has been writing such awful things in his column about the red-haired woman I met in your room. Of course, I didn't breathe a word to a soul that I had met her, and I never read Cyril Rathbone's column, but I hear about it from everyone. Mainly Rose Cliveden."

"But why is Pauline giving a party at this time?"

"For Prince Friedrich of Hesse-Darmstadt."

Philip laughed. "And who the hell is Prince Friedrich of Hesse-Darmstadt?"

"The head of the jewelry department at Boothby's auction house in London."

Philip laughed again. "Of course he is."

"Why is that funny?" she asked.

"It just is, Camilla."

"Sometimes I don't understand you, Philip," said Camilla.

"Sometimes I don't understand you, Camilla," said Philip.

ON FRIDAY MORNING, the day of Jules Mendelson's CAT scan in the Jules Mendelson Family Patient Wing of Cedars-Sinai Medical Center, as well as the day of Pauline Mendelson's small dinner party for Prince Friedrich of Hesse-Darmstadt, Flo March arose early to prepare for her lunch party for Jules and his lawyer, Sims Lord, whom she had never met. She went at seven, the time she usually went to her AA meeting at the log cabin on Robertson Boulevard, which she had not gone to for weeks, to have her hair done by Pooky and her nails done by Blanchette. Pooky said later to Blanchette that he had never seen Flo so nervous, or so unresponsive to the gossip about the fashionable clientele of the salon, which she usually enjoyed listening to. Because Pooky liked Flo so much, he did not ask her if she was the redhead everyone was talking about in the blind items in Cyril Rathbone's column.

Flo had never learned how to cook well enough even to attempt the cheese soufflés she planned to serve, but she did know how to set her table in the grandest style. Months earlier, she had cut out of a magazine a picture of a table setting that Pauline Mendelson had arranged for a lunch party at Clouds for a visiting ambassador, and using her new Steuben glasses and her new china and silverware from Tiffany and her new tablecloth and napkins from Porthault, she copied the photograph of Pauline's table exactly. Petra von Kant, the favored florist of the moment, arrived early to arrange the flowers for the centerpiece. The out-of-season tulips she had ordered from Holland were not sufficiently open to please Flo. "They're too tight, they're too tight," she wailed. "I wanted them to look as if I picked them in my own garden. You promised me they'd be open." Petra, used to tantrums from her society clients, borrowed Flo's hair dryer and blew hot air on the tulips until they were open to their fullest. Later Petra told Nellie Potts, Flo's decorator, that she had never seen a hostess who worried more about the height of the flowers in the center of her table. Petra had no way of knowing that, according to the same magazine article, it was a rule of Pauline Mendelson's that the flowers in her centerpieces never be so high as to be a deterrent to conversation, and Flo March, in her first outing as a hostess, adhered wholeheartedly to her lover's wife's philosophy. "I want people to be able to talk," she said, as if she were entertaining forty instead of four. She longed to use place cards with names written in calligraphy, but a look she caught in Petra's eye convinced her, without any words being spoken, that place cards for four would not exactly be Pauline's way of doing things.

The Bistro Garden, where she sometimes lunched with Nellie Potts and stared at the society ladies she knew were friends of Jules and Pauline, prepared her cheese soufflés with suitable instructions as to how many minutes they should be in the oven. "Thirty minutes at three-fifty," said Kurt, when she picked them up, and she repeated and then wrote down his instructions. Kurt also told her that the vinaigrette dressing should be added to the crisp endive-and-lettuce salad they had also prepared "just minutes before sitting down," and even told her how long the rolls should be heated. She wrote down everything he said, as if she were taking a course from him. She chilled the white wine from the Bresciani auction. She drove to the bakery at the Farmers Market to pick up the mocha cake, which was Jules's favorite, that she had ordered for dessert.

In the hour before Jules was scheduled to arrive at her house, she changed her clothes three times. More than anything, she wanted Jules to be proud of her that day in front of Sims Lord. She could always tell from the look in Jules's eye whether she was overdressed or perfect. She decided against wearing her yellow diamond earrings, as being too elaborate for daytime. She decided against wearing one of her Chanel suits, as being too dressy for lunch in her own house. She decided against wearing black, as being too downbeat for what she hoped would be a happy occasion for Jules. On her third try she knew she had found the right look for her that day. She wore beige slacks and a beige cashmere sweater and a gold chain belt, and only her sapphire-and-diamond ring, which she told Jules when he gave it to her that she would never take off, except when she bathed.

When she heard the Bentley come up her driveway, she rushed to the front door and opened it wide. Olaf, dressed in his white T-shirt and white trousers, was driving. Sims Lord, upright and aristocratic-looking, was seated in the backseat and stared out at her. She felt a momentary chill. If she had known the word *imperious*, she would have used it to describe him. Jules was slumped down in the backseat next to Sims Lord, his head barely showing. Flo saw him raise his hand weakly and wave to her.

Olaf greeted Flo, hopped out of the car, and went around to open the rear door. He reached in and placed one strong arm under Jules's legs and another behind his back and picked him up and carried him across the driveway to the house. Flo, instantly aware that Jules was embarrassed for her to see him being carried, turned back into her house. She was unprepared for the sight of her lover. His shirt collar looked several sizes too large for his neck. His face was drawn and gray-looking, with dark circles under his eyes. He appeared to her to be thirty or forty pounds lighter than when she had last seen him in the hospital, but she knew it was not the kind of weight loss that she should compliment him upon.

"Is there a particular chair where you want him to sit?" asked Olaf, still carrying Jules.

She had not thought about a particular chair for Jules to sit in until that moment, but she acted as if it had been one of her main concerns of the morning. "Yes, there, on the sofa, I thought," she said. "On the corner where he can lean on the arm, or even lie back if he wants to. Let me place this pillow behind him first. Is that all right, Jules?"

Jules nodded his head. After Olaf placed him in that location and arranged him so that he was comfortable, Jules looked over at Flo and smiled at her. For an instant he looked like his old self, as his broad smile eradicated the weariness of his face. Both Sims Lord and Olaf noticed it and looked over at Flo. Jules's eyes traveled around the room and rested on Flo's luncheon table. He smiled again and nodded in appreciation at the work she had done, which he knew she had done just for him.

"Oh, Jules, it's so good to see you again," said Flo. She moved over to where he was seated and knelt by him. "I've missed you so. You have no idea how much. I didn't realize myself how used I had gotten to you."

"I've missed you too," said Jules. His voice caught. He sounded as if he was going to cry, but he stopped himself.

"Sometimes it drove me mad how often you telephoned me each day, twenty times, or however much it was, but you know, I miss all those calls."

He smiled at her again. "You know Olaf?"

"Oh, yes, I know Olaf," said Flo. "He was so kind when he came here the other night. But, of course, I don't know Mr. Lord. Hello, Mr. Lord." She rose from her kneeling position and put out her hand to Sims. Although he was handsome and appeared to be friendly, he seemed chilly to her. She noticed his ice-blue eyes and his prematurely white hair. She noticed his splendidly cut gray suit and his blue English shirt with his initials on the breast pocket.

"Please call me Sims, Flo," said Sims Lord, shaking her hand. The picture that Sims had in his mind of Flo March was different from what Flo March turned out to be. He had imagined her to be pretty, but common. He had imagined her to be interested only in Jules's money. He was unprepared for her to be beautiful, and beautifully dressed. He was unprepared for her to be living in such an elegant manner. Mostly, he was unprepared to find the relationship between Jules and Flo was so affectionate.

"Quite honestly, I didn't know if you were going to be friendly toward me or not," said Flo.

"Friendly," said Jules, answering for Sims. There was no question that orders had been given in advance. When Jules spoke, his voice was barely above a whisper, but he was still in charge.

"That makes me very happy," said Flo. She smiled at Sims. "I have some marvelous white wine in the fridge. From the Bresciani auction."

Both Jules and Sims laughed.

"Jules? Will you have some?" asked Flo.

Jules looked at Olaf, as if asking for permission, and then nodded yes.

"Sims?"

"Fine."

"I have everything, if you'd like something different."

"No, white wine is fine. Especially that white wine."

"Olaf?"

"I won't, Flo. But thank you."

She went to the bar and uncorked the wine and poured it into three glasses.

Jules looked at Flo, surprised. "Are you having some wine?" he asked. "I thought you didn't drink anything except Diet Coke."

"Oh, just this once," said Flo. "This is the most wonderful celebration, after all. Welcome home, Jules." She raised her glass in a toast, and the others followed suit. "I just want to put the soufflés in the oven, and then we can talk."

"She's perfectly charming, Jules," said Sims, when Flo had left the room, but there was in the tone of voice of his compliment the slightest trace of condescension, which was not lost on Jules.

Jules, annoyed, nodded. He signaled with a wave of his hand for Sims to open his briefcase. Sims understood and did so, bringing forth the papers that he knew Jules was impatient to see.

When Flo returned to the room, there were papers and pens on the top of her beveled-glass coffee table.

"Lunch will be just a few minutes," she said.

"Something smells awfully good, Flo," said Olaf.

"My cheese soufflés," she said. "What are all those papers?"

"Read them," said Jules.

Flo took up one of the papers. It was an official-looking document, with Jules's name across the top, and the address of his office. Then, in the right-hand corner, was her name, Miss Flo March, 844 Azelia

Way, Beverly Hills, California 90210. Flo looked over at Jules and then at Sims Lord. Both men were looking at her.

"Read it," said Jules.

" 'Dear Flo,' " read Flo out loud. " 'I agree to pay you twenty thousand dollars a month for five years, commencing immediately. This money will be paid to you by the thirteenth day of each month from the proceeds of my profit from the Santucci shopping centers in Santa Ana, San Jose, and Santa Cruz. Sims Lord, my attorney and executor, has been authorized to do this. Regards, Jules Mendelson. Witness Olaf Pederson, Margaret Maple.' "

Flo looked up from the letter at Jules and burst into tears.

"That's just over a million bucks," said Jules, smiling. "You're an heiress."

"Oh, Jules," she said. She knelt in front of him again and put her head in his lap. "I knew. I always knew you'd take care of me."

Jules lay his hand on her head. "There's more," he whispered. Again he signaled to Sims Lord, and Sims passed him another paper. Flo looked up and Jules handed her the paper.

"This house is yours," he said.

"Almost yours," corrected Sims, holding up his hand in caution. "The actor who owns this house is in Yugoslavia on a film, and the papers have not been returned, but everything has been tentatively agreed upon."

"Oh, Jules. I don't know what to say." She put her arms around his neck and kissed him on the cheek. He turned to look at her.

"I think your soufflé is burning, Flo," said Olaf.

"Oh, my God!" she cried. She jumped up and ran into the kitchen. "Shit!" she yelled from the kitchen.

When she reentered the room in a few minutes, she carried one of the burned soufflés in her hand. "I just want to show you what it would have looked like," she said.

Jules, delighted with her, laughed, and Sims followed suit.

"There's still salad, and hot rolls, and your favorite mocha cake from the bakery at the Farmers Market," she said.

"Sounds good to me," said Jules.

Olaf picked up Jules and carried him to the table.

"Jules, sit here by me," said Flo, tapping the top of the chair to her right, as if she were used to giving lunch parties. "There's no place cards. Olaf, you there, next to Jules. And Sims, here, on my left. I'm so pleased to meet you finally, Sims. Jules talks of you constantly."

Sims pulled out Flo's chair, and she sat down, pleased with her performance, knowing she was doing a good job.

"Your table looks beautiful, Flo," said Jules, when he was seated. He knew how much it meant to Flo to be having guests in her house. He reached over and touched the out-of-season tulips in the centerpiece. "Pauline always said that there's no flower that dies as gracefully as a tulip." The strange remark met with silence, and then Jules said, "I can't think what made me remember that bit of esoteric information at this time."

At first, after Jules's compliments on Flo's table and flowers, conversation lagged. The weakness of Jules's condition did not allow him to dominate the small party in the way that he usually dominated the conversation at any table where he was seated, with his extraordinary knowledge of international affairs and his very high-level inside information from the business and art worlds. Olaf, who was unused to social life, keenly felt that he was merely an employee asked to sit at the table because of the unusual circumstances, and thought it inappropriate to enter the conversation. And Sims Lord was a reluctant guest, whose chilliness of manner might have made the lunch party a failure, but for the force of Flo's personality as a hostess. To entertain Jules's friends in an elegant manner that he could be proud of was a thing that she deeply desired, and she was not about to allow her first chance at it to be unsuccessful, despite her burned soufflés. In a very short time, her self-deprecating account of the events of her morning preparing for her first party had her three guests roaring with laughter. Sims Lord, who greatly liked the ladies, especially ladies who were married to other people in the social groups in which he moved, wondered to himself why none of the ones with whom he engaged in amorous escapades were as entertaining as Jules's mistress.

Jules, exhausted, could only nod with pleasure at her stories. When Flo rose from her seat to clear the table, she said, "Wait until you see this cake." When she was in the kitchen, Olaf was the first to notice that Jules had slumped over in his seat. "You all right, boss?" he asked.

Jules's head had fallen forward. He shook it slowly. Both Olaf and Sims jumped to their feet.

"Jules, what's the matter?" cried Flo, when she came back into the room, holding the cake, and saw the two men kneeling in front of Jules.

"It's all this excitement of coming here," said Sims to Olaf in a low voice, although Flo could hear. "I think we better get him back up the mountain."

Olaf, ignoring Sims, was on his feet. He picked up Jules and carried him over to the sofa, where he laid him down and began massaging his chest. Both Sims and Flo stood by and watched. In a few minutes color began to come back into Jules's face.

"Olaf, I really think we should get him home," said Sims again. Sims had become edgy and nervous. "We can't let him collapse in this house again. She'll have a fit." The "she" he referred to needed no identification.

Jules, hearing, nodded. "It would be bad for Flo," he said to Olaf. Olaf picked him up again and carried him toward the door. As Jules passed by Flo in Olaf's arms, she took hold of his hand and went with them to the car. She opened the rear door of the Bentley, and Olaf put him in the backseat.

"Good-bye, Jules," said Flo, holding on to his hand.

Jules looked at Flo. His mouth had started to hang open. He looked exhausted. He touched her hand and lifted it to his mouth to kiss, not taking his eyes off her.

"Flo, we have to go," said Sims.

"Yes, yes, I know. Good-bye, Jules," she said again. "Please call me later, somebody. I want to know how he is."

Olaf, seated behind the wheel, nodded to Flo and pointed to himself to indicate that he would call. He turned on the ignition.

"Please, Flo, we have to go," repeated Sims. There was a note of impatience in his voice now.

Flo pulled back from the car and closed the door. She and Jules continued to look at each other as Olaf backed the car around until it faced downhill. Then she ran down the steep driveway next to the car until it reached Azelia Way. The car passed her. She watched it until it disappeared onto Coldwater Canyon. She knew that she would never see Jules Mendelson again.


"NO ONE CAN give a party quite like Pauline," said Prince Friedrich of Hesse-Darmstadt, in a voice brimming with enthusiasm. The prince was in a position to know, because he was entertained by all the great hostesses everywhere, all of whom fussed shamelessly over him because of his splendid title. Rose Cliveden, who secretly longed for a monarchy, even dropped a deep curtsy to him, although no member of the prince's family had been near a throne for seventy-two years, and the principality that had borne his name had ceased to exist in the last century. It mattered not a whit to any of the ladies who fussed over him that he hadn't a cent to his name and needed his job as the head of the jewelry department at Boothby's auction house in London, if for no other reason than to pay the cleaning and laundry bills on his three dinner jackets and nine pleated evening shirts, which were the mainstay of his life. In social circles, he was considered to be a great asset to any party anywhere, because he knew all the international news that people in society loved to hear, and he had the good sense to leave his wife, whose lineage was equally splendid but who was stout and boring and thought to be difficult to seat, back in London. He had promised Pauline that he wouldn't say a single word about the billionaire's party in Tangier that he had just attended until all her guests were there, as everyone wanted to hear.

"But where is your de Lamballe diamond?" he asked Pauline, even before he inquired about the state of Jules's health, as he bent over to kiss her hand on arriving in her house and saw that it was missing from her finger. She was wearing diamonds at her neck and diamonds on her wrists, but she had put away forever her magnificent engagement diamond. No one cared more about jewelry than Friedrich of Hesse-Darmstadt, and there were few stones he admired as much as the de Lamballe diamond that Pauline Mendelson had worn for twenty-two years as a symbol of her brilliant marriage. He did not need to peer through a jeweler's eye to tell exactly how many carats a great stone had, and he could hold a prospective buyer enthralled as he recounted the provenance of an important piece, who had worn it, owner by owner, and what had become of each.

Pauline looked down at her bare finger. She could not bring herself to tell Friedrich what she had told Sims Lord, that the ring seemed to her to be as false as her marriage. "Oh," she said. "I must have forgotten it."

There were only fourteen guests that night, which, for a Mendelson party, was quite small, but every detail was planned to perfection, as only Pauline could plan such details, and each guest remarked on that perfection. It was a warm night, and there was to be a full moon. Pauline's flower gardens had never looked more beautiful, and Jules's sculpture garden had never been shown to better advantage. There were drinks in the pavilion by the pool, and the air was filled with the scent of orange blossoms from the orangerie. There was Rose Cliveden, drinking far too much, but amusing, everyone thought, at least before dinner. And Faye Converse. And Camilla Ebury, with her boyfriend, Philip Quennell. And Madge and Ralph White. And Freddie and Betty-Ann Galavant. And Sandy and Eve Pond. Except for Philip Quennell and Faye Converse, there were none of Pauline's usual arty crowd, just the group that Hector Paradiso used to say were "old Los Angeles."

Everyone asked for Jules. "He's so much improved. The doctors are thrilled," Pauline said over and over, or a variation on that statement, even though she had seen him when Olaf brought him home from his CAT scan at three-thirty that afternoon, in an alarming state. All the servants in the house were watching out the windows. Dudley had rushed into the courtyard with a wheelchair to assist, but Olaf had pushed it aside and simply picked up Jules, as if he were a child, and carried him in his arms into the house and up the stairway. It had occurred to Pauline then, as Jules passed her at the top of the stairs, unable even to speak to her, to cancel her party that evening, but later, after he seemed to revive somewhat in his bed, he insisted she go ahead with it.

Miss Toomey, the nurse in charge of his case, said over and over again that she could not understand why they had been gone for such a long time. "It's not as if Mr. Mendelson has to wait at the hospital," she said. "He did give the wing, after all. His name is on it. They should have given him priority." Miss Toomey had started to adopt a bit of the grandiosity of the family with whom she had come to live. Olaf, busy with his orderly duties, did not respond to Miss Toomey.

"Jules is simply furious that Dr. Petrie is keeping him upstairs tonight, but he sends you all his love," said Pauline.

"His sculpture garden is breathtaking," said Prince Friedrich. "I would love to run upstairs and peek in and tell him. I've never seen it lit up at night before."

"Perhaps later," said Pauline quickly. "Look, Dudley's calling us up to dinner." She put her arm in his, and they walked across the lawns to the terrace of the house.

"I was sorry you didn't like the yellow diamond earrings, Pauline," said the prince. "I thought they were exactly what you were looking for."

The image of the earrings on Flo March's ears in Jules's hospital room on the night of his heart attack flashed through Pauline's mind again. She suppressed the anger she still felt at the thought that Jules had given them to his mistress.

"Why do you say that?" she asked.

"Jules's secretary called to say he was returning them. He wanted them put up for auction again."

"He did?"

"You didn't know that?"

"When was that, Friedrich?" She tried to keep a conversational tone in her voice.

"On the very day of his heart attack. Miss Maple called me to say they would be returned, and that same night I heard from Yvonne Bulbenkian that Jules had had his heart attack."

"I see," said Pauline evenly. She stared in front of her as she continued to walk toward her house. Flo March, she thought, must have stolen the earrings after Jules collapsed in her house. She shuddered. In her mind, Flo March had become an evil woman.

"Have I said something to upset you, Pauline?" asked the prince.

"Oh, no, no," said Pauline.

Because of the warm night, Pauline had arranged for dinner in the atrium instead of the dining room. Jarvis, her head gardener, had filled the atrium with pot after pot of her yellow phalaenopsis. "It's too beautiful, Pauline," said one guest after another as they stood by the long table and admired the sight.

"You're next to me, Friedrich," said Pauline. "I've put Faye Converse on your other side."

"All my favorites," said the prince, clapping his hands. "You must tell us about the party in Tangier."

"A nightmare. An absolute nightmare. Tangier in August! You wouldn't believe the heat. All those people. And the *smells!* And no air-conditioning. And long lines for everything. And long faces everywhere. And the *placement* was a disaster. People like us seated next to people they never heard of and didn't want to hear of. If you could have seen the look on Lil Altemus's face when she saw the hotel where Cyrus put us. It was worth the whole trip." He made a face of haughty disdain, and everyone laughed. "And then she moved out and stayed on Reza Bulbenkian's yacht. Frightfully amusing, really. I wouldn't have missed it for the world."

Philip Quennell, seated on the other side of Faye Converse, watched Pauline. He had no interest in the party in Tangier, as he did not know any of the people they were talking about, and he had ceased to listen. Instead, he noticed how elegantly Pauline sat at the head of her table, her elbow on the table, her hand cupping her chin in the most graceful fashion, paying her utmost attention to her guest of honor as he recounted anecdote after anecdote about a society party, which seemed of great interest to them all. It occurred to Philip that Pauline was going through the motions of listening, but that her thoughts were elsewhere.

Dudley also watched Pauline, as he went about his duties. He noticed the tenseness beneath her calm exterior. When she charmingly excused herself from the table to attend to a hostess duty, she entered the kitchen and complained to Dudley because one of the maids was chewing gum while serving her guests.

"I wasn't chewing it, Dudley," said the maid when Pauline returned to the table. "It was in my mouth, yes, but I wasn't chewing. How in hell did she know?"

Miss Mae Toomey, the nurse in charge of Jules Mendelson's welfare, walked into the kitchen in a stormy fashion. "I am at a loss as to understand how there could be a party going on in this house on one floor while a man is dying upstairs," she said.

Dudley, ever loyal to the household he had served for so many years, had no wish to engage in a subversive conversation with the efficient nurse, and he had no authority over her to request her silence in front of the other servants working in the kitchen. He looked up and exchanged a glance with Blondell, who was helping Gertie, the cook, arrange green mints on silver dishes for the drawing room after dinner. With Blondell, who had been with the Mendelsons nearly as long as he had, he could engage in such a conversation, but he would not with Miss Toomey. Instead, he moved to the pantry, out of their earshot, and she followed him. Although he did not disagree with what she had said, he went about his chores without as much as a nod to indicate his own feelings.

When he had finished arranging demitasse cups and spoons on a tray, he looked at Miss Toomey and said, "Is Mr. Mendelson worse?"

"He will not live through the night," she said. "The man belongs in a hospital. I want to call Dr. Petrie and have him readmitted."

Sounds of laughter came from the atrium, at the completion of one of the prince's anecdotes, followed by the ringing of the table bell.

"She's calling me," Dudley said, excusing himself from the angry woman.

"More seconds for the fat prince, no doubt," said Miss Toomey. She followed Dudley toward the door. "Tell her I must speak to her. Tell her it is urgent."

As Dudley opened the door to return to the atrium, another great burst of laughter could be heard. During dessert, Dudley tried to interrupt Pauline to whisper that the nurse had to speak to her on the intercom, but she held up her hand for him not to speak until the prince had arrived at his punch line. Then, after more laughter and appreciative comments, she turned to Dudley to hear his message.

"Miss Toomey," he whispered in her ear.

"I'll call her after dessert," said Pauline. "Tell Gertie the grapefruit sorbet is divine. Perhaps you should pass it around again, and the blueberries also. Such a good combination. I don't know why we haven't tried that before."

Dudley persisted in his mission. He mouthed but did not speak the word, "Urgent."

Pauline lifted her damask napkin to her lips and then pushed her chair out. "There's a call I have to take," she said to the prince, but she did not leave the table without first seeing to his welfare while she was gone. "Friedrich, have you read Philip Quennell's book on Reza Bulbenkian? So marvelous. What's the first line, Philip? Jules was always so amused by that."

Philip, who did not enjoy being the center of attention, said, "I can't remember exactly. It goes something like this: 'Reza Bulbenkian made one of the great American fortunes by knowing all the right wrong people.'"

"Frightfully funny," said the prince, who then pulled the attention back to himself by starting on a long story about the social-climbing exploits of Yvonne Bulbenkian, and the fortune she was spending. With her guests in rapt attention, Pauline left the atrium and walked into the house and down the hallway to the library. She crossed to the telephone and pushed the intercom button.

"Yes, Miss Toomey. Forgive me for taking so long, but I assumed you knew I have guests. Is this something that can't wait?" asked Pauline.

"I'm sorry, Mrs. Mendelson, but I think you should come upstairs immediately," replied Miss Toomey. The adoring tone that Miss Toomey had previously had in her voice whenever she spoke to Pauline was missing. She was serious and businesslike and made no attempt to underplay the urgency she was communicating.

Pauline heard and understood the nurse's tone. "I'll be right up," she said. She hung up the telephone and walked out of the library. She was surprised to see that Dudley was standing outside the door in the hallway.

"Is everything all right, Mrs. Mendelson?" he asked. There was concern in his face.

"Yes, yes, of course. Go back to the party, Dudley," she said. "Perhaps serve coffee at the table rather than inside, don't you think? They all seem quite comfortable. It would be a shame to interrupt the mood."

Dudley realized that Pauline was afraid to go up the stairs and was postponing what she had to do.

"Should I call Dr. Petrie?" Dudley asked.

"No. Miss Toomey should be the one to do that, and I'm sure that's not necessary," said Pauline.

"I could ask the guests to leave, Mrs. Mendelson. I'm sure they'd all understand."

"Oh, no. Please don't. You're being an alarmist, Dudley. Mr. Mendelson is going to be fine. Now I must go up. Remember, coffee in the atrium."

She walked up the stairway, holding on to the red velvet banister. On the way up, she noticed that the third Monet painting of the water lilies was crooked again, and she straightened it as she passed, without stopping. At the top of the stairs she turned right and walked down the hall to Jules's room. She stood outside his door for a second, breathed in deeply, and opened the door.

At first Pauline could not see Jules. Olaf was on the far side of the bed, leaning over him, and Miss Toomey was on the near side with her back to the door. Hearing the door, they both turned to her.

"He is very bad, Mrs. Mendelson," said Miss Toomey. There was a censorious tone in her voice for the lateness of the arrival of the about-to-be widow. "I don't think he has long."

Pauline, frightened, stared at the nurse for a moment and then walked over to the bed. Jules lay with closed eyes. His head was turned to the side, and his mouth hung open. He was breathing in an erratic fashion, with gasping noises.

"I would like to be alone with my husband," she said.

"I'll call Dr. Petrie," said Miss Toomey.

"Not yet," said Pauline. "Not until you hear from me."

"Would you like me to stay, Mrs. Mendelson?" asked Olaf.

"Come back in a bit. I would like to talk to my husband in privacy. Can he hear me, Miss Toomey?"

"Ask him," said Miss Toomey.

"Jules. Can you hear me, Jules? It's Pauline."

Jules opened his eyes and looked at his wife. His hand moved feebly along the blanket cover, as if he were reaching for her. Pauline turned and looked as both Miss Toomey and Olaf left the room and closed the door behind them.

"Did you ever think you'd hear me say I'm scared, Pauline?" he asked. His grave illness had weakened the resonance of his voice.

"No, I didn't," she replied.

"You look very swell," he whispered. "How's your party going?"

"I should have canceled this damn party this afternoon when you came back from the hospital."

"If they criticize you, tell them I insisted you go ahead with it."

"Oh, Jules," she said, looking at him. "I feel so helpless. If you were a religious man, I would call for a priest, or a rabbi, or even Rufus Browning from All Saints."

"No, no. No last sacraments for me. I'm dying, Pauline."

She looked at him but did not reply.

"No tears, I see," said Jules, in a voice barely above a whisper.

"I've shed all my tears, Jules," said Pauline.

He blinked his eyes.

"For whatever it's worth to you, Pauline, flights of angels are not singing me to my rest."

"If you're thinking I want you to suffer, Jules, you're wrong. I don't," said Pauline, looking away from him. She held her elbows in front of her, as if she were cold, although the room was not cold.

"I remember that night in Palm Beach years ago, when I first saw you at the Van Degans' dance. You were everything I ever wanted. I'm sorry, Pauline. I really am."

She shook her head. "Oh, Jules, please, please, let's not go down memory lane."

"Listen, Pauline." There was an urgency to his weak voice. "She's not a bad girl."

"I'm not interested in hearing about her virtues."

"Take care of her, Pauline."

"You must be mad. How could you ask me such a thing?"

"I'm giving you good advice."

"No. I don't have to take care of her."

"It will be terrible for you if you don't, Pauline. There are things I know about in life. Money is one of them. Trust me in this."

The exertion of talking had exhausted him. His head rolled back and fell to the side. Pauline looked to the door. She wanted to leave the room, but an instinct told her not to. She knew that he was about to die. She moved to the bell on his bedside table to call for Miss Toomey. She noticed from the light on the instrument that one of the telephone lines was being used. She wondered if Miss Toomey was calling Dr. Petrie.

"Don't ring for Miss Toomey," said Jules. "I don't want another reprieve."

She picked up the receiver and listened in. She heard Olaf's voice, speaking rapidly. "I'm sorry, Flo. He can't talk to you. Missus is in there with him. It's almost at the end. I think Toomey suspects we were at your house today." Pauline slammed down the telephone.

"There's something you should know, Pauline," said Jules.

She could not bear to hear one more word about Flo March. She had never hated anyone before in her life, but she hated Flo March. When she spoke, she sounded weary. "No. There's nothing more I need to know, Jules. I know everything, about everything, and so does everyone we know."

"Kippie killed Hector," he said, in a voice so low as to be almost inaudible.

Pauline, stunned, gasped. Their eyes met. "No, no," she whispered, shaking her head in denial at what her husband had told her, although she knew that what he said was true.

"Open the safe in the library," he said. "There is a sealed manila envelope. Hector's note is inside."

"Where did you get it?"

"I took it from Hector's house before the police got there."

"What did it say?"

"He wrote down the name of his killer."

Pauline began to cry, as things fell into place in her mind. Kippie. Kippie did it. Kippie needed money that night, and she had refused him. And Kippie had gone to Hector. And the suicide story that she had never understood was a cover-up by Jules to protect her from knowing that her son had killed her best friend.

Pauline knelt by Jules's side, weeping. "Oh, Jules, I'm sorry. Oh, my God, Jules. You did this for me. Oh, Jules, I'm sorry. I'm sorry."

She took hold of his hand and leaned over to kiss it. She felt a resurgence of love for him, but the feeling became overwhelmed by a dark thought that leapt into her mind. "Jules? Does anyone else know what you just told me? Please tell me. Does anyone else know what you just told me?"

Jules's eyes had started to glaze over in preparation for death, but he was able to forestall that by-now-welcome event for the moment it took to meet Pauline's gaze. He saw the panic in her eyes, and he could not bring himself to tell her that it was at Flo March's house on Azelia Way that he had hidden Kippie for the six hours it took until all the arrangements had been made that changed Hector Paradiso's death from a murder to a suicide. He could not, out of respect for his wife, have the last words he uttered be the name of his mistress.

"Who, Jules? Please tell me," begged Pauline.

But Jules Mendelson was dead. Pauline, born Episcopalian, could be devoutly Episcopalian when she felt inclined toward religion, and at that moment she felt so inclined. Still kneeling by Jules's side, with her face in her hands, she said the prayers of her youth for her husband, the same prayers she had said for her mother when she knelt at her deathbed so many years before. Then she rose, still in the final stages of the Lord's Prayer, as the overwhelming thoughts of what she had to do pushed the prayers from her mind. "For thine is the kingdom, the power, and the glory, forever and ever," she said in a churchlike whisper, but she was thinking of the obligations of her life. She caught sight of herself in the mirror over Jules's fireplace. She wished she were not covered in jewels, which she had only worn for the benefit of Prince Friedrich of Hesse-Darmstadt, and which were too glittering by far for the circumstances at hand. But she could not remove them, as she had to return to her guests downstairs, and they would notice and tell afterward, after the story became public that Jules had died while she was giving a party for a prince who was no more than a jewelry salesman.

When she buzzed for Miss Toomey, the door opened immediately, as if she had been standing outside, and Miss Toomey entered and ran to the side of the bed.

"He's gone," said Pauline quietly.

"My God," said Miss Toomey. "Why didn't you call me?" She was distressed not to have been present at the moment of death.

"It was very peaceful," said Pauline. "One moment he was here, and the next he was gone. I wasn't even aware immediately that it had happened."

"I'll call Dr. Petrie," said Miss Toomey.

"I don't want anyone to know yet," said Pauline.

"But I must call the doctor."

"There's not much the doctor can do now," said Pauline. And then she repeated, with emphasis, "I don't want anyone to know, Miss Toomey. Do you understand?"

"Until when, Mrs. Mendelson?"

"Until I get rid of my guests downstairs. A half hour at most. I don't want them to know that my husband is dead. It is urgent that the press not find out. Urgent. Just stay here with him until I come back upstairs." She started toward the door.

"I'll call Olaf," said Miss Toomey.

Pauline stopped at the mention of Olaf's name. The tone of her voice hardened. "No, don't call Olaf. I don't want Olaf in this house another minute. I do not wish him to see my husband's body. I blame him for my husband's death. Get rid of him."

Miss Toomey, startled, looked at Pauline. "Yes, Mrs. Mendelson."

Pauline walked out of the room where her husband lay dead and up the hallway to the stairs. She stopped to look in a mirror hanging over a chest in the upstairs hall and checked her appearance in the manner she had of looking at herself in the mirror of her dressing table, her face to the left and then her face to the right. Extremely pale, she pinched her cheeks very hard to bring color to them. She opened a drawer and took out a lipstick that Blondell always placed there for her and applied it to her lips. Then she adjusted her hair with her hands.

Grasping the red velvet banister, she walked down the stairs. She could hear that her guests had moved inside from the atrium to the drawing room. She could tell from the conversational voices that Rose Cliveden was now very drunk and that Friedrich of Hesse-Darmstadt was annoyed by her constant interruptions of his anecdotes. The rest of her guests seemed not to be talking at all. Being a born hostess, she knew that she had been gone from her party for too long a time, and was needed to restore the room to harmony, but when she reached the bottom of the stairs, she turned in the direction of her library rather than her drawing room. She entered the library and closed the door behind her. For an instant it occurred to her that she should lock the door, but she thought it might look suspicious to Dudley if he came looking for her.

She went quickly over to van Gogh's *White Roses*, hanging over the fireplace mantel. Taking hold of the famous treasure by its frame, she unlatched a hook behind the picture and swung it outward to reveal a wall safe behind. She pulled up a footstool, stood on it, and leaned closely into the combination lock. With great dexterity she turned the lock to the left, then to the right, then to the left again, then around twice, ending up at zero. The door lifted back. Within was a small light which she switched on. Inside were all her velvet and leather jewelry boxes for her necklaces and bracelets and rings. She shifted through some papers and envelopes in the back of the safe and brought forth a five-inch-by-seven-inch manila envelope. It was taped shut. On it, in Jules's handwriting, was written the word *Private*.

Still standing on the footstool, she tore open the manila envelope. From inside, she pulled out a sheet of blue stationery, which she recognized as the stationery from Smythsons on Bond Street in London that she had given Hector Paradiso for Christmas the year before, with his name engraved in a darker blue across the top of each page. It was folded in half. With shaking hands, she opened the sheet of paper. There were stains of dried blood on the page. In blue ink, running downhill, in the shaky penmanship of a dying man, each letter becoming more indecipherable, were written the words "Kippie Petworth did this."

Pauline felt weak and dizzy. She covered her mouth with her hand and breathed great heaving sounds, as if she were going to be sick. Overlapping thoughts of Jules and Hector and Kippie filled her mind.

The library door opened, and Philip Quennell walked in. They looked at each other.

"Pauline, I'm sorry. I didn't realize you were in here," he said.

She was standing on the stool. Hector's stationery was in her hand. With extraordinary calmness, she said, "Yes, I was looking for my ring, Philip. I forgot to take it out of the safe tonight before the party, and, wouldn't you know, Friedrich would notice I wasn't wearing it the first thing when he came into the house." She turned back to the safe, pushed the piece of paper inside, and took out a leather ring box, which she opened. She put the de Lamballe diamond on her finger, shut the door of the safe, swung around the dial, and closed the painting of van Gogh's *White Roses* over it, latching it in the back. She stepped down off the footstool. "Now you know where the safe is," she said.

Philip, fascinated, watched her. "I came in to use the men's room," he said.

"It's there," said Pauline.

"I know," he answered. "I feel like we've played this scene before."

"We did," she replied. "The first night you ever came here." As she said the words to him, she remembered that she had been on the telephone with Kippie at the time. He had called asking for money. She had not known then that the call was the beginning of her life falling apart.

"Oh, I remember. Are you all right, Pauline?"

"Of course. Why do you ask?"

"You've been gone such a long time."

"There was a long-distance call I had to take. My father has not been well in Maine. The party's moved inside. I could hear the voices. Or rather, I could hear Rose's voice annoying poor Friedrich."

Philip did not want to get into a social conversation. "Is Jules all right, Pauline?"

"Yes. Fine. Why?"

"Would you like me to get rid of your guests?"

"Heavens, no. I must get back to the party. Poor Friedrich will think I've deserted him."

WHEN PHILIP returned to the drawing room, he looked around for Pauline. She had rejoined the group and was seated on a sofa between Camilla and Madge White. She sat silently, smiling, looking very beautiful, but content to listen while Rose Cliveden talked and talked, repeating the same story. Philip felt that Pauline had abdicated her authority, that her mind was elsewhere, that although she knew her guests were bored with Rose, she was making no attempt to salvage her failed party. When she smiled or laughed, he noticed that there was no merriment in her eyes to match the laughter on her lips. He thought she might not even know what she was laughing at.

Finally, when the hall clock struck ten-thirty, Faye Converse said, "This movie star has got to go home."

"Oh, I'm so sorry," said Pauline, jumping to her feet. "Let me ring for Dudley to get your coat. Darling, could you take Rose home? I don't think it's safe for her to drive down the mountain."

It was apparent to all that she wanted them to leave, but would not have asked them to if Faye Converse had not made the first move. She stood in the hallway, taking the furs from Dudley as he took them off hangers in the closet. "This is yours, isn't it, Madge?"

Outside, in the courtyard, Ralph White said to Madge, "Do you think Pauline was rushing us out?"

## Flo's Tape #21

"I got the sexual part of Jules, but I never had the feeling of living together with him. I never saw him shave, for instance. The kind of things that wives see. I never had his shoes in my closet. I like to see a man's shoes in my closet.

"I don't want you to think I'm conceited, or anything, but I can tell you for a fact that Jules really loved me. But, believe me, that had never been his intent. At first, it was like an infatuation. I think he thought that after we'd done it for a while, like the trip to Paris, for instance, that the spell would be broken, and he'd unload me with a nice gift, like a jewel or a fur coat, and probably a little cash, the way rich guys do when they unload their superfluous women. And it would be terminated with grace. And I'd go back to the coffee shop, and he'd go back to Pauline.

"I thought that was what was going to happen too. I expected him to unload me. But he didn't. After the first year, I knew it was the real thing."

# 22

WHEN ALL her guests had finally gone, Pauline went back to the library of her house. First she took off all her jewelry and placed it in the safe. At the same time, she removed Hector's final note from the safe and put it in her bag. Then she picked up the intercom and buzzed Jules's room.

"Yes?" answered Miss Toomey.

"Call Dr. Petrie, Miss Toomey, and inform him of my husband's death," said Pauline. She spoke in the same authoritative tone of voice she used when she was giving her instructions for the day to her maid or her butler or her cook.

"Yes, Mrs. Mendelson."

Then Pauline buzzed for Dudley.

"Yes?"

"Could you come in the library, please, Dudley?"

"Yes, Mrs. Mendelson."

When Dudley came in a few moments later, she said, "Mr. Mendelson has just died, Dudley."

"Oh, Mrs. Mendelson," said Dudley. "I am so sorry."

"Thank you, Dudley. And thank you for these past weeks since he came home from the hospital. You have practically run this house yourself, and my husband was very appreciative and so am I. Now, there is a great deal to be done, and I very much need your help."

"Yes, Mrs. Mendelson." Dudley turned away from Pauline so that she could not see his face. She understood that he was crying. It had always fascinated Pauline that the people who worked for Jules—his butler, his guard, his chauffeur, his secretary, his barber, his lawyer —had always cared deeply about him and stayed on with him year after year. She knew he had private dealings with them all, buying them houses, or businesses, or paying their hospital expenses, or helping educate their children.

"Will you tell the staff, Dudley?" asked Pauline. "Except Blondell. I'll tell Blondell. Tell Jim, and Smitty, and Gertie in the kitchen, and that little maid, whatshername, the one I became upset with tonight?"

"Carmen."

"Yes, of course, Carmen. Ask her not to be angry with me about the gum chewing. I was upset. I was worried about Mr. Mendelson the whole evening. I so regretted that I had not canceled the party this afternoon when he came home from his CAT scan."

"We all understand."

"Has Olaf left the house?"

"Yes."

"With all his things?"

"Yes. He said you fired him."

"I did. He deserved to be fired."

"May I know what he did?"

"Yes, but not now. Nurse Toomey has called Dr. Petrie. He should be here shortly. Alert Smitty outside that he will be arriving. Dr. Petrie is terrified of the dogs. They jumped all over him the last time. There will probably be an ambulance also. Or a hearse. I don't know what they use. Will you call Miss Maple and ask her to call the mortuary and alert them? We use Pierce Brothers, of course. Will you ask Miss Maple to be here in the morning as early as possible? Will you also get me my telephone book in my office? I have to call Sims Lord tonight and tell him, and I can't remember his home number."

"Yes, Mrs. Mendelson," said Dudley. He went to the desk and jotted down the things she had asked him to do. It did not surprise him that, even in grief and sorrow, Pauline Mendelson remained calm and organized.

"Oh, and Dudley?"

"Yes, Mrs. Mendelson?"

"Please tell the staff, and Miss Maple as well, that no one, and I mean *no one*, is to repeat this information outside the house. I do not want the press to know of my husband's death until after the funeral."

"When will the funeral be?"

"If possible, tomorrow. And it will be private."

Alone, after Dudley went about his chores, she looked at her clock. It was fifteen minutes past eleven. She counted on her fingers the time it would be in Paris. Fifteen minutes past eight o'clock in the morning. Hubert, she knew, was always up and about at seven to do his calisthenics before leaving for his atelier. She had always called her Paris couturier by his first name. He had made her clothes for twenty-five years, and she knew him well. "Hubert," she said, when he answered the telephone in his apartment. She pronounced his name *Hubair*. She told him what had happened.

"I'm so sorry, Pauline," he answered.

"Thank you, Hubert," she replied. She wanted to get right down to business. She did not want to receive sympathy. "Can you make up some things, black and gray, and maybe some white, it's so hot here, to wear for the next few months. I leave it all up to you. Nothing above the knee. Whatever you think is right, but I'm going to need a couple of black dresses immediately. I'll send the plane. Oh, and Hubert? I want one of those black veils. A total cover, don't you think?"

OLAF PEDERSON, fired by Miss Toomey, drove down the hill from Clouds. Miss Toomey, who did not like him because he had grown so close to Jules and she had not, did not know why she was firing him, and told him that. She would have liked him to stay to assist in what had to be done when Dr. Petrie arrived. Olaf realized that it must have been Pauline Mendelson who had picked up the telephone and heard him talking to Flo March on the extension and then slammed down the receiver. He had become very fond of Jules Mendelson in the weeks he had spent with him at Clouds, and he understood the deep complications of the man's life. Olaf Pederson was a decent man. He was sorry that he had upset Mrs. Mendelson, but he had promised Flo that afternoon that he would call and let her know how Jules was. His home was in the Silverlake district, but on the way he drove up Coldwater Canyon until he reached Azelia Way. There he told Flo March that her lover was dead.

WHEN THE AMBULANCE arrived to take away Jules's body, Pauline waited in the library with Dudley and Blondell until the attendants had zipped his corpse into the body bag. Then, alerted by Miss Toomey that the body was being removed from the house, the three went into the front hall to watch the attendants bring Jules Mendelson down his winding stairway for the last time. As they rounded the curve by the third of the six Monet paintings of water lilies, the shoulder of one of the attendants hit against the gilded frame of the famous picture and knocked it askew. "Be careful!" called out Pauline from below. It was unclear to the attendant whether her concern was for the welfare of the body or the painting of the water lilies.

□   □   □

THE REVEREND Doctor Rufus Browning of the All Saints Episcopal Church in Beverly Hills was contacted to conduct the private service. Dr. Browning assured the widow that the secrecy she desired would be scrupulously kept.

"But Jules was not Episcopalian," said Sims Lord, when he was made aware of this arrangement.

"Nor was he anything else," replied Pauline. Then she added, "It was not necessary for you to point that out to me, Sims. After all, I was married to Jules for twenty-two years, or twenty-three, whatever it was. I know perfectly well he wasn't Episcopalian, but he was always very fond of Rufus Browning, whenever Rufus came up to the house, and he was very generous to All Saints. Rufus will do something quick and quiet. I want this all over with before that horrible woman finds out. I do not wish the funeral to turn into a circus."

"You could always have him cremated," said Sims. "That way there's no coffin to contend with to attract attention."

"Cremated, yes. That's what should be done. He should be cremated," said Pauline, seizing on the idea.

"Oh, no, Mrs. Mendelson," said Miss Maple, looking up from her notes. "He hated cremation. He always said so. He wanted to be buried in Westwood. He has the plots, for both you and him, right next to Armand Hammer's mausoleum. Isn't that right, Mr. Lord? Isn't that in Mr. Mendelson's will?"

Sims Lord nodded.

"Well, he's not going to be buried in Westwood," said Pauline. "He's going to be cremated. Otherwise, that woman will have photographers taking her picture throwing herself on top of the grave. I know that type, believe me."

Miss Maple looked over at Sims Lord, but Sims did not look back at her. It was not lost on either of them that Pauline had become irrational on the subject of Flo March.

"Do you suppose people will say about me, 'She is the widow of a man who loved another woman' ?" asked Pauline.

"No, they won't say that, Pauline," replied Sims. "Jules loved you. I know that."

She didn't hear what Sims said. She continued with her own thoughts. "Or, 'Her husband died in the arms of his mistress' ?" she asked.

"He didn't die in the arms of his mistress, Pauline," said Sims Lord. "He died here in your house."

"To all intents and purposes he did. He had a heart attack in her arms. And he went to see her yesterday after his CAT scan. That duplicitous Olaf took him to her house. Did you know that, Sims?"

Sims Lord knew how to control the reddening of his face. He shook his head no in answer to Pauline's question. The day before, knowing that Jules was at the end of his life, he had gotten out of the Bentley when Olaf passed the Beverly Hills Hotel, as he did not want to be in the car when it returned to Clouds. It was important to him that Pauline not find out he had been party to the deception.

Pauline, unaware, continued. "I firmly believe that if my husband had not gone to that woman's house yesterday, he would still be alive. Dr. Petrie said that the CAT scan proved how well he was doing."

Dudley opened the door and came into the library.

"If it's a telephone call for me, Dudley, I'm not home to anyone except my father or my sisters," said Pauline. "Or, of course, the White House, but they couldn't know yet."

"It's Kippie," said Dudley.

"Kippie?" She stared at Dudley. "From France?"

"Yes."

"Does he know?"

"Yes."

"Who told him?"

"I assumed you would want him to know, Mrs. Mendelson."

"Yes, yes, of course, Dudley."

"Would you like us to leave the room, Pauline?" asked Sims.

"I would, yes," said Pauline.

"The staff would like to go to the funeral, Mrs. Mendelson," said Dudley, as he was leaving the room.

"Oh," said Pauline. She had moved to the telephone but had not picked it up. "But only you, and Blondell, and Gertie, Dudley. I want to keep this very small. As little attention as possible."

"Yes, ma'am, but Smitty and Jim have been with Mr. M. for years too," said Dudley.

"Yes, of course. Smitty and Jim too. I'm just not thinking," said Pauline. She turned to Sims Lord. "I suppose I have to ask Camilla Ebury too. I'll call her. But not Rose. I can't deal with Rose. And she'll tell someone. She tells everything."

"What about Camilla Ebury's boyfriend?" asked Sims.

"Philip Quennell? No, not Philip. He wasn't a friend of Jules. Just Camilla. Jules adored Camilla. No one else."

When she was alone, she picked up the receiver. "Hello?"

"*Mère?* It's Kippie."

There was a long pause, as Pauline stared at the telephone and did not reply.

"*Mère?* Are you there?"

"Yes, I'm here," she said, finally.

"Look, I'm awfully sorry, *Mère.* I know Jules and I never got along, and it was probably my fault, but I am sorry."

"Yes."

"I'll come for the service. I'm booked on the Concorde tomorrow."

"No. Don't," said Pauline.

"Don't?" he repeated, surprised.

"Don't come. The service will have already taken place. And he will already have been cremated."

"But to see you. I want to be there with you."

"No, don't." She spoke in a low voice.

"Mom, what's the matter? I mean, I'm clean this time. I'm not on drugs anymore. I've licked it. I won't embarrrass you. I promise."

Pauline did not reply.

"Mom, can you hear me? Is this a bad connection?"

"I know, Kippie. Jules told me. I know everything," she said.

Kippie was not sure what she meant. "About Flo March, you mean?"

"Yes, about Flo March, among other things."

"What other things?"

"About you."

"Me?"

"And Hector."

"What about Hector?"

"That it was you who did it."

There was a long silence. Pauline could hear her son breathing heavily, and then she spoke again in a hollow voice. "Why? Why? Hector Paradiso was my friend."

"But it's not true," said Kippie. He began to speak very quickly. "There was some hustler there, some blond trick he picked up in a gay bar called Miss Garbo's. Your great pal Hector was not the old sweetheart you always thought he was, *Mère.* He had a very complicated private life, and people who lead that kind of complicated private life get into that kind of trouble with those kind

344

of people they cavort with in the small hours of the night. You're
not so isolated up there at Clouds that you're not aware of things
like that."

"Oh, don't con me, Kippie. Just don't. I'm in no mood for being
conned. Jules Mendelson would not have gone through this complicated suicide story for a hustler from a gay bar, believe me. And it
will come out, sometime. You know it will."

"Mom. Don't you understand?"

"What is there to understand?"

"I couldn't have done it. I couldn't have shot Hector five times. It's
impossible."

"Oh, Kippie, please don't lie to me. Hector left a note. There was
blood on the paper, and your name."

"But, Mom, listen to me. That little dog, that mean little dog of
Hector's, what was that dog's name?"

"Astrid?"

"Yes, Astrid. Astrid bit off my trigger finger. Don't you remember?
You can't shoot somebody five times if you don't have a trigger finger,
Mère."

"Oh, Kippie, don't treat me like a fool. That was afterwards. He bit
off your finger the next day here at Clouds."

"But only you know that, Mère, and you just forgot it," said Kippie.

There was a silence, as she realized her son had just said to her the
same line her husband had once said. "Good-bye, Kippie," she said.
"Don't come home. Not now. Not ever. I'm going to hang up now. I
have a great deal to do."

"Mom, please. Please, Mom," cried Kippie.

But Pauline had hung up. She opened her bag and took out Hector's note. Then she picked up a package of matches from an ashtray
and lit one. Holding the note in the fireplace, she lit the piece of
paper and watched it burn until she had to drop the scorched end.
Then she walked over to a sofa and lay on it, facedown. She hugged
a pillow to her, as first the tears came and then the sobs, great heaving, uncontrollable sobs. When Sims Lord, Miss Maple, and Dudley
returned to the library to continue with the plans for the funeral, they
were touched that grief for Jules's death had finally penetrated the
stoic calm of Pauline Mendelson.

□   □   □

"JULES is dead," said Camilla, when she hung up the telephone.

"When?" asked Philip.

"Last night, apparently."

"How come it's not on the news?"

"Look, Philip. It's a secret. No one knows. Pauline doesn't want anyone to know until after the service."

"When's the service?"

"At four."

Philip nodded. "Do you know something, Camilla?"

"What?"

"I think he died last night when we were there at dinner."

"Don't be silly, Philip."

"Do you remember when Pauline got up from the table and was gone for so long? I think that's when he died."

"That couldn't be. She came back."

"Pauline's a cool customer."


NOTHING REMAINS a total secret, no matter how well planned the strategy is for maintaining total secrecy. In the ambulance that removed the body of Jules Mendelson to the Pierce Brothers Mortuary for its subsequent cremation was the same attendant, Faustino, who had been in the ambulance that removed Hector Paradiso's body to another mortuary ten months earlier, and who had reported the fact of that death to Joel Zircon, the Hollywood agent, who had been drinking and cruising at Miss Garbo's the same time as Hector Paradiso the evening before.

Jules Mendelson's death, like the death of all rich and famous people, fascinated Joel Zircon, and he pressed Faustino for each and every detail to pass on to Cyril Rathbone and his other friends. He especially delighted in Faustino's story of carrying the famous financier's body down the winding stairway and hitting his shoulder against a painting of water lilies and knocking it askew, much to the consternation of the widow, Pauline Mendelson, who had screamed, "Be careful!" Faustino felt sure her concern was more for the picture of the water lilies than for his bruised shoulder, or the body he was carrying.

At breakfast the next morning at the Viceroy Coffee Shop on Sunset Boulevard, Joel Zircon had Curly, the manager, in hysterics, doing an imitation of Pauline Mendelson screaming over her painting almost falling off the wall, as Faustino carried the stretcher with Jules

Mendelson down the winding stairway, on its way to the Pierce Brothers Mortuary. "She's a regular Harriet Craig, that one," said Joel
about Pauline.

Pooky, the hairdresser, wondered at the hilarity at the counter
between Joel Zircon and Curly, and the story was repeated to him.
He could only think of Flo, whose hair he had done the previous day
for her lunch party, and he wondered if she knew. Cyril Rathbone,
who never spoke to anyone until he'd had his third cup of coffee, sat
at his booth reading the Hollywood trade papers, and asked, irritably,
what the big joke was at the counter, and couldn't they hold down
the noise, *puleeze*, as some people wanted to read their papers, and
then Joel went through his story for the third time, adding embellish-
ments to his portrait of Pauline Mendelson with each retelling.

Cyril Rathbone rushed to the pay telephone near the men's room
and called Lucia Borsodi, the editor of *Mulholland*, waking her up,
and told her the latest development in the Mendelson saga. Lucia
knew a story when she heard it. "Get a photographer," she said to
Cyril. "Let's see if we can get a picture of Flo March being turned
away at the gates of Clouds."

When Pooky called to tell Flo the sad news, she had already heard
it from Olaf Pederson the night before. What she didn't know was
where they had taken Jules's body, and Pooky told her he was at
Pierce Brothers Mortuary in Westwood. Flo knew that Pauline would
never allow her to see Jules, so she decided to go to the mortuary and
ask to look at him once more. Jules had come through on all his
promises to take care of her, and she had the papers in her possession
to prove that.

"Do you think they'd let me in, Pooky?" she asked.

"Act like you belong. Act like a society lady. They'll let you in. It's
too early for them to call the house and check."

It was as she was leaving her house twenty minutes later, dressed in
a black Chanel suit, and carrying the centerpiece of tulips from Holland that Petra von Kant had arranged for her final lunch with Jules,
that the telephone rang again. It was Cyril Rathbone.

"I'm very much afraid that I am the bearer of sad news, Miss
March," he said. His florid English voice was very dour, as he prepared to tell her of the death of her lover. His pencil and paper were
propped to record her reaction.

"I already know what you're going to tell me, Mr. Rathbone," said
Flo.

"Oh?" He was distressed not to be the first to have reached her with the sad news, and he wondered how many other people knew. "Who told you?" he asked.

Flo did not reply.

"I wondered if I could stop by, to tell you personally how very sorry I am," he said. "I feel a very special interest because of having been in your house at the time of the heart attack last month."

"I'm sorry, Mr. Rathbone," said Flo. "I'm on my way out."

"To Clouds?" he asked, excitedly. "Are you going up to Clouds?"

"No, Mr. Rathbone."

"I could make you famous, Miss March."

"I don't want to be famous, Mr. Rathbone."

"Just one shot for my magazine. You at the gates of Clouds, waiting for news. Just one shot. It would flash around the world."

"Good-bye, Mr. Rathbone."

Flo hung up the telephone.

Cyril, rebuffed, wondered where she could be going at that hour of the morning, still before eight. On an off chance, he called the photographer that Lucia Borsodi had assigned to him for the day and asked him to "rush, rush, rush," to the Pierce Brothers Mortuary in Westwood. "Out Wilshire. Turn left at the AVCO Theater," he said impatiently, when the photographer said he didn't know where the Pierce Brothers Mortuary was. "They did Marilyn Monroe, Natalie Wood, Peter Lawford, the Zanucks, *everybody*," said Cyril. He could not abide people who had no understanding of the things that he considered to be important.

"Did? Did what?" asked the photographer.

"Laid out. Embalmed, idiot," said Cyril. "Get over there quick."

"You want me to photograph a dead body?"

"No. I only want a picture of a beautiful red-haired woman, about thirty, who will probably be wearing a Chanel suit, either going into or coming out of the mortuary."

THE PRIVATE and unannounced funeral service for Jules Mendelson at All Saints Episcopal Church in Beverly Hills was in great contrast to the elaborate service that had been held for Hector Paradiso at the Good Shepherd Catholic Church, only two blocks to the west on Santa Monica Boulevard, which had been attended by the social and power elite of the city. Outside on Camden Drive there were no limousines that might attract the attention of the curious. Jim, the Mendelson chauffeur, dropped off the heavily veiled Pauline Mendelson five minutes before the scheduled time, at a side entrance. She ran into the church, looking neither left nor right. There were no flower arrangements and there was no music. The service was attended only by members of the household and office staff who had been in the Mendelson employ for over ten years, as well as Miss Maple, Jules's secretary, Willi Torres, Jules's barber, and Sims Lord, Jules's lawyer and closest adviser. The only outsider present was Camilla Ebury, who was Pauline's great friend. Rose Cliveden, who could not bear to be left out of anything, felt certain that Pauline meant to invite her and had forgotten to in all the haste, so she arrived uninvited and knelt unobtrusively in the last pew of the near-empty church. She bowed her head in prayer, as the Reverend Doctor Rufus Browning read the prayers.

"I am the resurrection and the life, saith the Lord; he that believeth in me, though he were dead, yet shall he live; and whoever liveth and believeth in me shall never die."

While her head was bowed, a second uninvited figure quietly entered the church. It was Flo March, who had heard at the funeral home that there was to be a religious service at the same time that her lover's body was being cremated. Flo meant only to drop in to say a prayer and then leave before she was seen. She had never been in an Episcopal church before, and was unsure of how different the rituals were from those of the Catholic Church. She hastily genuflected in the Catholic manner that she had learned in her parochial school as a child and made the sign of the cross, touching her forehead, her breast, her left shoulder, and then her right, whispering as she did so, "In the name of the Father, the Son, and the Holy Ghost." She rose from her genuflection and entered the last pew. It shocked her that the church was so empty. She found it inappropriate that there would be fewer than a dozen people huddled together in the first few rows for the funeral service of such a famous man. It amazed her that there were no flowers on the altar, no music playing. She looked behind her up at the choir loft. It was in darkness. The organ was closed and covered. She listened as the minister read prayers from his prayerbook.

"Blessed are the dead who die in the Lord; even so saith the Spirit, for they rest from their labors."

All her life Flo had whispered her prayers, and it was her whispering that disturbed the Protestant worship of Rose Cliveden, kneeling in the last pew opposite hers. Although Rose was uninvited herself, she knew that she was at least a friend of the family and would be more welcome at such a private occasion than would the strange woman across the aisle from her, whom she took to be a reporter. Rose cleared her throat in a loud and theatrical way that was meant to attract the attention of the mourners in the front rows and to warn them that there was an impostor in their midst. No one turned. She got up from her seat and walked up the aisle.

Pauline sat alone in the front row. Her back remained ramrod straight, while the others leaned forward to pray. Her face was covered by the black veil her couturier had sent from Paris, along with the black dress she was wearing. Behind her sat Camilla and Blondell. Next to Blondell was Dudley, and then Sims Lord. Rose leaned in and said in a loud whisper to Camilla, "Tell Pauline that there's a reporter in the back of the church."

Rose's whisper carried, and was heard by Miss Maple, seated behind Camilla, who turned back to look. At just that moment, Flo raised her head from her prayer and saw that several faces in the front pews were looking back at her. Miss Maple leaned across Blondell and tapped Sims Lord on the shoulder. Sims looked up from his prayer.

"Flo March is in the rear of the church," whispered Miss Maple.

"Shit," said Sims, under his breath.

He too turned back to look at Flo. Recognizing her, he leaned forward and whispered to Pauline about the interloper, "It's that Flo March," as if he hardly knew her.

For Pauline Mendelson, the presence of Flo March at her husband's funeral was more than she could stand. The composure that had been so much a part of her demeanor during the months of Jules's illness abandoned her at the news that Flo March was in the church at the private service, planned in secret, so that exactly what was happening would not happen. Enraged, she rose from her seat and turned to look back at Flo. Seeing her, meeting her gaze, she brought her hand up to her veiled face, aghast at the woman's brazen behavior. The de Lamballe diamond on her engagement finger picked up the light from the rays of the afternoon sun that filtered through the stained-glass rose window above her.

"No, no. Sit down, Pauline. I'll get rid of her," whispered Sims, standing up.

Pauline disregarded Sims Lord's offer. She left her seat and walked past him down the aisle to the rear of the church with purposeful strides. The heels of her shoes echoed her anger throughout the apse. Only Dr. Browning's prayer continued as if nothing were amiss.

"Grant to all who mourn a sure confidence in thy fatherly care, that, casting all their grief on thee, they may know the consolation of thy love. Amen."

The attention of the household servants and the employees of the office was diverted from the prayers for the dead to the more fascinating drama that was being played in front of them.

"How dare you come in here?" asked Pauline. "This is a private service."

Flo, terrified, looked at Pauline. She could not make out her face through the black veil.

"I want you to leave this church *immediately*." Her voice had risen to a scream.

"I'm sorry. I'm really sorry, Mrs. Mendelson. I didn't know this was private," said Flo. "I really didn't. They told me at Pierce Brothers that there was a service here. I just wanted to say a prayer."

"*Get out!*" screamed Pauline.

No one who knew Pauline Mendelson had ever seen her behave in such a manner. Camilla rushed down the aisle after her and placed her hand gently on her back.

"Darling, Pauline. Come back so Rufus can finish the service," she said. The prayers from the altar continued.

"Give courage and faith to those who are bereaved, that they may have the strength to meet the days ahead in the comfort of a reasonable and holy hope, in the joyful expectation of eternal life with those they love. Amen."

"Someone get this *tramp* out of here," said Pauline.

Tears streamed down Flo's face as she shook her head in denial of the word *tramp*. "I'm sorry," whispered Flo again. She felt so humiliated she could not move.

Camilla looked at the two women staring at each other. She leaned over and took hold of Flo March. "Come on, Miss March," she said gently. She put one arm behind her back and held her hand with the other as she led her from the church.

From the altar the Reverend Doctor Rufus Browning began the Lord's Prayer. Sims Lord led Pauline back to her seat. The servants from the house and the employees from the office all looked down, as if they had not witnessed what they had just witnessed.

On the steps outside, Flo began to cry. "I feel so ashamed," she said. "I shouldn't have come."

"No, you shouldn't," said Camilla quietly, but there was no reprimand in her voice.

"I thought it was a funeral, like Hector's," said Flo.

"No," said Camilla.

"I better go," said Flo.

"Yes," said Camilla.

"Listen, Camilla, before I go, I want to tell you something. Please listen."

"Of course."

"It's important for me that you know this."

Camilla nodded, waiting to hear what Flo had to say.

"I don't blame her for hating me so much, but I want you to know something. I really loved the guy. It wasn't the bucks, I swear. I really loved him," said Flo.

Camilla looked at her helplessly, divided in her sympathies and loyalties.

"And Jules used to tell me he loved me. Really. At the end he even said I was his reason for living," said Flo.

Camilla stepped forward and hugged Flo. Then she turned and ran back into the church.


THE DEATH of the Beverly Hills billionaire and art collector Jules Mendelson was announced the day after his funeral. The *Los Angeles Tribunal*, the *Los Angeles Times*, the *New York Times*, and the *Wall Street Journal* carried the story on the front page. Bernie Slatkin, the anchorman of the NBC Nightly News, had a special segment on his newscast, with a film montage of events from the great financier's life, including shots of him in intimate conversations with Presidents of the United States and other world leaders at various economic conferences. Several of the weekly magazines, including *Time* and *Newsweek*, paid homage to his distinguished career.

□   □   □

HORTENSE MADDEN had worked for weeks on her story of the discovery of the lost manuscript of Basil Plant, the author who had died in drunken and drugged disgrace, without turning in the book that he considered to be his masterpiece, a novel about the smart set with whom he had been spending his time. The book, if it existed, could never be found after his death. Hortense credited Philip Quennell with some small part in the recovery of the long-missing manuscript, but in her story in *Mulholland,* for which she had been promised the cover by Lucia Borsodi, she herself was the heroine, who knew in an instant that the manuscript was the one Basil Plant's publishers had long since despaired of recovering. It was she, according to her story, who had sought out the mysterious young man called Lonny Edge, in whose Hollywood bungalow the manuscript had been located. There was a hint that perhaps, just perhaps, Mr. Edge had starred in a few pornographic films, and advertised his wares in prurient magazines, to heighten the interest in her story and suggest an unsavory relationship between the two, but as she was a literary critic, and a member of the intellectual establishment of the city, she did not dwell on the sensational. Lonny Edge, however, was reluctant to be interviewed, even though he was unaware that the mousy Hortense Madden and the blond Marvene McQueen, who was singing at Miss Garbo's on the night he went home with Hector Paradiso, and thereby became permanently persona non grata at that nightclub, were the same person.

Hortense Madden's rage knew no bounds when Lucia Borsodi called her into her office to tell her that her story had been bumped —"Just temporarily, Hortense, calm down"—in favor of Cyril Rathbone's story on the former coffee shop waitress, Flo March, who had become the mistress of one of America's richest men, Jules Mendelson, and lived in splendor in Beverly Hills, where she was credited by the doctors with saving his life after he had a massive heart attack in her house.

The picture on the cover of that week's issue showed Flo March carrying a centerpiece of dying tulips to the Pierce Brothers Mortuary in Westwood. Inside was the long-forgotten photograph of Flo March escaping from the fire in the Meurice Hotel in Paris, carrying her jewel box, with Jules Mendelson in the background.

On the Sunday that followed, Archbishop Cooning, whose mission was morality, preached from the pulpit of Saint Vibiana's Cathedral on the disgrace of a man who used his vast wealth to corrupt the morals of a girl young enough to be his daughter.

WHEN DUDLEY removed the biodegradable plastic cover from the new issue of *Mulholland*, Pauline, watching, noticed that he reacted to the photograph of Flo March on the cover.

"Did you ever know her, Dudley?" asked Pauline.

"No, no, I didn't," said Dudley, but his face flushed with embarrassment at the same time. He turned away to attend to a chore; some petals from a flower arrangement sent by the White House—"Darling Pauline, Our love and thoughts are with you, George and Barbara," the card read—had fallen onto a tabletop, and with one hand he swept the petals into the palm of his other hand, a task usually attended to by a maid.

"Dudley," said Pauline.

"Yes, Mrs. Mendelson." He was emptying the petals from his palm into a wastebasket.

"Turn around."

"Yes, ma'am."

"Was that woman ever in this house?" There was a long silence. "Answer me truthfully, Dudley."

"Yes, Mrs. Mendelson."

IF PAULINE MENDELSON were to live her life over again, she would not have made the decision she made that day, a decision that she knew at some deep level was a wrong decision even as she was making it. But her pride overtook her senses, and she made the decision that no amount of persuasion on the part of people who had her best interests at heart could dissuade her from making. She decided to cut off Flo March without a cent, even though she knew it had been Jules's intention to provide handsomely for her.

Her decision had nothing to do with money, for there was ample money. Only three days before, the day after Jules's funeral, there had been a discreet inquiry from Titus Fairholm in Melbourne, Australia, who had always admired van Gogh's *White Roses*, to see if the estate wished to sell it, at the proper time, for forty-five million dollars. Pauline knew it would probably fetch even more at auction at Boothby's. Money did not figure in Pauline Mendelson's decision.

She could not bring herself to provide for a woman she regarded as little more than a whore, a whore who had destroyed the final years of what had appeared to be a perfect marriage.

"That woman was here in my house," said Pauline. "When I was in Northeast Harbor visiting my father, she came here into my home. What kind of a person would do a thing like that?"

"Pauline, as your husband's adviser, I must caution you against this. He made arrangements. She has papers. They are signed by Jules. And by me. And they are witnessed by Miss Maple and Olaf Pederson, who was the orderly with Jules."

"I know perfectly well who Olaf Pederson is. Olaf Pederson was in cahoots with Flo March. They were only after Jules's money. I heard him talking on the telephone to her at almost the moment that Jules was dying. 'She's in there with him,' he said. The 'she' he was talking about was me, Jules's wife. I happen to know for a fact that she stole some yellow diamond earrings out of Jules's pocket on the day of his heart attack. Friedrich Hesse-Darmstadt told me himself that he had spoken with Jules only a short time before the heart attack, and that the earrings were being sent back to him in London."

"I don't know anything about yellow diamond earrings, Pauline, or about her and Olaf. What I do know is that the papers she has in her possession are legal. I can vouch for that," said Sims. Sims Lord had had a career both enhanced and obscured by his proximity to the dominant presence of Jules Mendelson. Now, emerging from the shadows of that dominance, he sought to use patience in dealing with the widow.

"Are these things written in the will?" asked Pauline.

"They aren't in the will, but the papers were already executed."

"When?"

"Last week."

"Only last week? And when did Miss March receive those papers?"

"On Friday."

"Friday? The very day Jules died, you mean? The day of the CAT scan, when Olaf, old loyal Olaf, dropped him off at her house on the way home from the hospital?"

"Yes," said Sims.

"In anticipation of death then?"

"It could be so construed, I suppose."

"I'll take her to court. This constitutes undue influence on a sick man. Remember, there are witnesses who saw her sneak into his room in intensive care at Cedars-Sinai, dressed in a stolen nurse's uniform, and passing herself off as his daughter. Remember all this, Sims."

To Sims Lord, the elegant and refined Pauline Mendelson had become a different woman since Jules's death, maddened by hatred of Flo March, but he was struck by her power. "Pauline, next to you, I was probably the person closest to Jules. This was what he wanted," said Sims patiently.

Pauline's voice rose. She had become quick to anger of late. "Whose side are you on, Sims?" she asked. "We'd better get that straightened out right here and now."

"Of course, I am on your side, Pauline," said Sims, in a placating tone. "That is a thing you never have to question. But there could be consequences, very unpleasant consequences, to what you are suggesting."

"How much does it come to, what she wants?" asked Pauline.

"Over a million. Under two, I suppose. I suggest you pay her, and be done with it," said Sims.

"Pay her over a million dollars! Are you mad?"

"That's what that ring cost that's on your finger. It's a sixth of what that Sisley picture costs behind your head," said Sims, holding out his hands in exasperation to indicate the absurdity of her concern for a million dollars. "What the hell difference does it make? Pay her."

"Never!" Pauline spat out the word. "If she is so broke, tell her to sell the yellow diamond earrings she stole out of my husband's suit pocket on the day he had his heart attack in her house."

Sims shook his head. "I'm terribly afraid you're going to be sorry, Pauline."

Pauline wondered, looking out her library windows at the lawn and sculpture garden, and beyond at the pool and pavilion, if she and Jules had ever been happy, or if Clouds was no more than a magnificent set for the performance of a marriage.

## Flo's Tape #22

"I ordered my new sofas, and I picked out the gray satin fabric for ninety-five bucks a yard. Jules used to say it was an outrageous amount to spend, but I didn't care. He had the money. If Pauline had said she spent ninety-five bucks a yard, or even a hundred and ninety-five bucks a yard, he wouldn't have thought anything of it.

"Let me tell you about these sofas, because they're important to the story, especially since Kippie Petworth dripped blood all over one of them. Nellie Potts, my high-class decorator, said they were copied from a design of Coco Chanel from her apartment in the Ritz Hotel in Paris. I liked the sound of that. I waited and waited for them, in anticipation. They took forever to make. And then finally they came. And I arranged them where they should be, and there was great excitement, and for a few days I could think of nothing else but my new gray satin sofas, and I'd sit on different places on the sofas, until I found just the right place for me to use as my regular place to sit down. And then I got used to them. And it was back to plain life again, waiting for Jules to come at a quarter to four each afternoon. Or playing with Astrid. Or drinking ice tea with Glyceria, the maid from next door. The sofas, they were nice, but they weren't it. Do you know what I mean? IT. They weren't it. They were just sofas. And I was just a mistress again."

# 23

FLO MARCH. Flo March. Flo March. Since her picture appeared on
the cover of *Mulholland*, Flo March had become notorious. People
discussed her everywhere. The discredited mistress of a disgraced
billionaire, the magazine called her. "Have you heard? She crashed
Jules's funeral, and there was such a scene you wouldn't believe it,
darling, between Pauline and this ghastly woman." Her name became
as well known at fashionable dinner parties as it was at the Viceroy
Coffee Shop, where she used to work, and where all the customers
wanted to hear about her. Curly and Belle, who defended her, became important for having known her. At the bar at Miss Garbo's,
Manning Einsdorf and Joel Zircon had stories to tell about her.
Women who had sat next to her under the hairdryer at Pooky's Salon
and not noticed her, or not spoken to her, now claimed to have been
acquainted with her. Even those closest to Pauline Mendelson could
not resist, among themselves, supplying each other with every bit of
information about the woman in whose house Jules Mendelson had
suffered the heart attack that eventually killed him. "She went
to communion at Hector Paradiso's funeral. Pushed her way right
past the casket." Or, "Of course you've seen her. She has her hair
done at Pooky's. Very pretty, in a cheap sort of way, all tarted up in
Chanel." Or, "Madge White actually met her, at a steak house in
the Valley, having dinner with Jules." Or, "She ran over Faye Converse's dog. Killed it. That sweet little Astrid, that used to belong
to Hector."

During the two-week period that her picture was on the cover of
*Mulholland* magazine, Flo March, shamed by the controversy she
was causing, shrank from contact with everyone she had ever known.
She stopped answering her telephone and did not check her message
machine. Friends came to her house and rang her bell, but she did
not answer her door. Pooky left message after message on her machine that he would be happy to come to her house before he opened
his shop in the morning to take care of her hair, but she did not reply
to his messages. Even Glyceria, Faye Converse's maid, was not able
to get into the house on Azelia Way, although she came by each
day and brought things to eat, which she left by the sliding door

that opened onto the swimming pool. On some days Flo never rose
from her bed. She had started to drink wine all day long and take
Valium.

It became Sims Lord's duty to inform Flo that the financial arrangements made in her favor by Jules on the day of his death were going
to be contested by the estate. He came to her house to tell her personally, at the behest of Pauline Mendelson, after she did not return
several of his telephone calls.

"What exactly does that mean?" asked Flo, stunned by his announcement.

"There won't be anything for you, Flo. Other than what Jules had
already given you."

"But why?" asked Flo.

"The estate feels that undue pressure was placed on Jules at a time
when he was too ill to realize what he was signing," replied Sims.

"Pressure by whom?" asked Flo.

Sims did not answer.

"By me? Is that what you mean?" asked Flo again.

"I am merely the messenger here, Flo," said Sims.

"No, Sims. You are not the messenger at all. You are a participant
in this matter. Your name is on those documents as a witness."

"I am acting for the estate, of which I am an executor," he said.

"The estate is who exactly, Sims? Pauline? Is it Pauline who feels
that undue pressure was placed on Jules? You know that's not true,
don't you?"

Flo was sitting on her gray satin sofa. A feeling of panic overtook
her. She rose from her seat so that it would not be apparent to him
that her hands were shaking. She walked by him on her way to the
bar, where she reached up for a glass and then poured herself some
white wine from an open bottle she removed from the refrigerator.
He liked the way she was dressed, in pants and a sweater. He liked the
whiff of Fracas perfume that preceded and trailed her. He liked the
way her beautiful red hair was tied back in a ribbon. He liked that she
was wearing no makeup. He realized that he was very attracted to
her.

As she passed Sims on her way back to the sofa, he took hold of her
arm and stopped her. "You didn't offer me a glass of wine," he said,
smiling at her. She understood his smile. She had seen that same
smile on the faces of older men who desired her since she was fifteen

years old. She pointed to the bar with her head and with her thumb at the same time. "Help yourself," she said.

He pulled her to him and began to kiss her. She stood there as he kissed her, but did not respond. He began to breathe heavily and pushed himself against her. She pulled back from his embrace.

"No, Sims. That's not what I'm all about," she said, waving her hand in front of her.

He continued to hold her. "Listen to me, Flo. I could take care of you. You could stay on in this house. I'd set you up."

She pulled away from him. "You've come here to tell me I'm being deprived of my rightful inheritance, and you want to knock off a quick piece of ass at the same time? Is that it?" she asked. "How did I make the mistake in my mind that you were supposed to have class?"

"Come on, Flo. You've really got me going. Feel how hard I am," said Sims. He took the glass of wine out of her hand and placed her hand on his fly.

"I'm pretty sure that your great friend Jules didn't lead you to believe that I'm that easy, Sims," she said, shaking her head.

Sims had unzipped his fly. He reached in and pulled out his penis and held it out to her, as if the sight of it, erect and strong, would send her into fits of passion and lust.

Her glance, filled with contempt, ignored his offering. "Do I really look that cheap, Sims, that you think it's all right to just pull out your dick in front of me? I don't think you'd do that with Pauline, up there in the library at Clouds. Put it away. Or jerk it off. White pubic hair never turned me on."

She sat down on the sofa and picked up a magazine, which she leafed through, while Sims Lord, red with rage, reinserted his diminished penis into his trousers and zipped himself up. Arranged, he moved toward the front door, thin-lipped now and distant. He opened her door and left without a farewell.

ONE DAY Philip Quennell came to her house and rang and rang her bell, but she did not answer. He could see that her car was in the garage and knew that she was inside. As he was about to leave, he tried the door and, to his surprise, found that it was open. He walked in.

"Flo?" he called, when he was in the hall.

Although it was bright daylight outside, the curtains were drawn, and the living room was in near darkness. When his eyes adjusted to the light, he saw that Flo was sitting in the corner of one of the large sofas. In front of her on the glass coffee table were a bottle of white wine and a water goblet from her set of Steuben glasses.

"Not safe to leave your door open these days," said Philip, taking in the scene. "There's all kinds of nuts out there."

"What difference does it make?" asked Flo, looking up at him.

"What are you doing?" he asked.

"I'm on what's known in the program as a little slip," she replied.

Philip picked up the bottle.

"Frightfully good, you know, from the Bresciani auction," she said, in an exact imitation of Jules Mendelson's voice.

"This is not going to help," said Philip.

Flo shrugged. "He hated my cheap wine that I used to buy at Hughes Market, so he sent over a few cases of his best for when he came to call. He hated my cheap glasses too, so he had me order a dozen of every conceivable size glass from Steuben in New York. He also hated my cheap sheets, so he ordered sets and sets from Porthault when he was in Paris. The only thing he liked cheap was me."

"You're not cheap, Flo," said Philip.

"Thanks, Phil Q. That's sweet of you to say, but you don't know some of the things I did with him."

"I don't want to know either."

"You're sounding priggish, Phil Q."

Philip took the bottle of wine into the lavatory off the living room and poured the remains of the bottle down the toilet.

"You sound like an elephant pissing," she called out to him.

Philip laughed. He returned to the living room and put the empty bottle in the wastebasket.

Flo watched him. "Lots more where that comes from," she said.

"Do you want me to take you to a meeting?" he asked.

"Hell, no. I'm not about to stand up in some hall and reveal all my troubles to the world. I can deal with this myself," said Flo.

"This is dealing? Lying in a darkened room with a bottle of wine?"

"Don't blow my low, Phil." She lit a cigarette and let it dangle from her lips. He sat down in the darkened room and watched her.

"Do you want me to turn on the lights?" he asked.

"No," she said. She inhaled and exhaled her cigarette without touching it with her fingers. She started to cry. "I'm scared, Phil. I'm just so damn scared."

She got up from her sofa and walked over to the bar in a weaving fashion. She reached into her refrigerator and took out another bottle of wine. She put a corkscrew into the cork, but her hand slipped, and the corkscrew cut her finger. "Do this for me, will you?" she said, holding out the bottle and the corkscrew to him.

"No," he answered.

"There's something you don't understand, Philip," she said. "I've gotten used to living like this. I didn't have a pot to pee in or a window to throw it out of until I met Jules. I was with the guy for five years. It was more than the clothes and the jewels and the car and the house. He protected me. He paid my taxes. He paid my medical insurance. He covered my overdrafts. He was good to me. I couldn't go back. I couldn't. They're going to take everything away from me."

"Who is?"

"Pauline and Sims."

"But what did you think was going to happen?"

"I thought the merry-go-round was never going to end. That's what I thought. I thought Jules Mendelson was immortal. That's what I thought. Oh, for God's sake, open this fucking bottle for me, Philip. I need a drink."

"Look, I can't deal with you when you're drunk," said Philip. "I have no patience with people who are drunk. I feel no sympathy for them. I have come here to help you, but you are too drunk to understand what I am telling you. If you should pull yourself together, call me. Otherwise, I won't bother you again."

He walked toward the front door.

"How's Camilla?" called out Flo.

"Fine."

"Tell her Flo says thanks."

Philip stopped and turned back to Flo. "Thanks for what?"

"She'll know."

"I want to know."

"She was nice to me at Jules's funeral."

"She never told me that."

"The girl's got class, Philip."

❑   ❑   ❑

WHEN SHE ran out of things she needed, like frozen dinners and sanitary napkins, she started to shop at all-night grocery and drug stores. She would leave her house at two o'clock in the morning, when she knew she would run into no one she knew or who would know her. She wrapped her hair in a scarf and wore wraparound dark glasses and drove to the Hughes Market at the intersection of Beverly Boulevard and Doheny Drive. It was when she was pushing her cart through the aisles, past the magazine rack holding the magazine on which her picture was on the cover, that she came upon Lonny Edge, whom she had not seen since her days as a waitress at the Viceroy Coffee Shop. He was dressed in black, as always, leaning against a counter, reading the article about her in *Mulholland*. To avoid him, she quickly reversed her course, but in turning, her cart accidentally bumped Lonny, and he looked up from the magazine. He recognized her immediately, even though she thought she was unrecognizable.

"Flo! What a coincidence! I was just reading about you," said Lonny.

"Hold it down, will you, Lonny?" said Flo, looking around to make sure no one heard him, even though it was after two in the morning and there was hardly a soul in the market.

"You're a full-fledged celeb," said Lonny.

"That's not the kind of celeb I ever wanted to be, Lonny," said Flo.

"You're out late," said Lonny.

"So are you."

"You know my kind of life, Flo. Normal hours were never part of my trade."

"Are you still making those dirty videos?"

Lonny smiled and shrugged. "They keep telling me I've got star quality."

Flo laughed. "I remember hearing about your star quality."

"Good to see you laugh, Flo. Want a cup of coffee? Or a drink, or something?"

"No, I have to get back," said Flo.

"Sure."

"Good seeing you, Lonny."

"Listen, Flo. I didn't know Jules Mendelson was your, you know, whatever, boyfriend? Until I heard about this piece in *Mulholland*."

"No reason why you should have known," said Flo. "Not many people did." She turned to go.

"Did you ever meet his son?" Lonny asked her retreating figure.

"His son?" asked Flo, stopping. "Jules Mendelson didn't have a son. I think you've got the wrong guy, Lonny."

"*Step*son, I mean," said Lonny.

"I don't think he had a stepson, either," replied Flo. "I mean, it's the sort of thing I would have known. I was with the guy for five years."

"Spoiled kid. Snotty kid. Named Bippie, or Kippie, or some name like that?"

Flo, hearing the name Kippie, stopped again and looked at Lonny.

"A lot of people thought I was the one who killed Hector Paradiso that night, including that dickhead Manning Einsdorf, because I left Miss Garbo's with Hector. I went home with him, sure. I balled him, sure. I even hit him around a little, because that was what he wanted. But I wasn't the last one to see him that night. The Mendelson stepkid came there before I left, looking for money, a lot of money, and Hector wanted me out of there quick."

Flo stared at Lonny. "Kippie Petworth? Was that his name?"

"Yeah, Kippie Petworth. Snobby little prick."

Thoughts began racing through her head. She remembered the boy called Kippie. Jules had arrived at her house before the sun was up, and woken her. "There is a young man here with me," Jules had said. "Let him sleep on your sofa for a couple of hours. I'll be back to get him."

"But who is he, Jules?" Flo had asked.

"He's the son of some friends of mine."

"Is he in some sort of trouble?" asked Flo.

"Nothing serious. Some kid stuff."

Flo pushed her shopping cart back to where Lonny was standing. "Are you trying to tell me that Kippie Petworth killed Hector Paradiso?" asked Flo, looking about her at the same time and speaking in a low voice, although there were no other customers in the aisle of the market at the time.

"Somebody did. And it wasn't me. And it certainly wasn't suicide, like your friend Jules Mendelson wanted everyone to believe," said Lonny. "You can't shoot yourself five times. Any asshole knows that."

Flo nodded. "I often wondered about that myself. Listen, I have to be off, Lonny. How do I get hold of you if I have to?"

Lonny took out a ballpoint pen from his jacket and wrote a telephone number on the cover of *Mulholland* magazine and then tore the corner off and gave it to Flo. Then he repositioned the magazine back into the rack, putting another issue in front of it so that the torn corner wouldn't show.

On the way back to Azelia Way, Flo thought back on the early morning that Jules had brought the young man called Kippie to her house. Until minutes before, when she met Lonny Edge at the all-night market, she had not thought of him again.

"I can't remember your name," the young man had said the next noon after he had awakened and she came into the living room. She had wanted to go to an AA meeting early that morning, but she wouldn't leave her house with the young stranger in it.

"Flo. Flo March," she had answered.

"Right. Flo March," the young man repeated.

"And I'm not sure I got yours. Kippie? Was that it?"

"Kippie. Right."

"Kippie what?"

"Petworth."

Flo laughed. "That's what I call a pretty fancy name. It's not a name you hear much in the Silverlake district."

"No, no. It's strictly Blue Book," he said and laughed.

When he laughed, it was the first time she had noticed that one of his front teeth was missing.

"I'm afraid I dripped some blood on your sofa," he said.

"Oh, my God," she said, rushing over to pick up one of the cushions of her gray satin sofa. It was covered with blood. "This is a brand-new sofa. It was only delivered yesterday. Do you have any idea how much this fabric cost? It cost ninety-five dollars a yard."

"Just have to have it recovered, I guess," he said. "Jules will pay for it."

"But I've only had it one day," she repeated. "It's brand-new."

"In the meantime, you just turn it over like this, with the blood side down, and nobody will notice the difference." He turned over the cushion and patted the clean unspotted side. "See? Only you and your decorator can tell the difference."

"Yeah," she answered, shaking her head. She was crestfallen that her beautiful new sofa was marred. She was annoyed with Jules that he had brought this careless stranger to her house, especially as he seemed unconcerned with the damage he had done, as if he were used to having things taken care of for him.

"Look, it's pointless to spend time worrying about something so unimportant as the cushion of a sofa," Kippie said, when he realized that she was truly upset over the stains he had made.

She had to admit he had charm and style, the kind of charm and style that is not acquired but innate. She tried to think of a word to describe him. "Adorable" was the word that came to mind. She wondered what he was doing in her house. She wondered why Jules had delivered him to her at six o'clock in the morning and said, "Keep him here until I come back for him. Don't ask any questions."

"Mind if I smoke a joint?" Kippie had asked, taking a joint from his pocket. He reached for a package of matches without waiting for an answer.

"Yes, I do mind," she had answered. "I don't want you to smoke a joint in my house."

He looked at her, surprise on his face. "Isn't that funny? I wouldn't have taken you for a lady who would object," he said.

"There was a time when I wouldn't have, but I do now," Flo said.

"Because I rooked your new sofa?"

"No, because I don't want any dope smoked in my house."

He shrugged and put the joint back in his pocket. "Have you got any orange juice then?"

"I'll squeeze some."

"And coffee?"

"I'll put some on. But don't talk to me like I'm the maid. This is my house you're in, and I'm apparently doing you some kind of favor by letting you stay here," said Flo.

"Did I sound like that? I'm sorry." He covered his mouth with his hand and smiled at her. She could see that he was used to getting his own way, especially with women.

She poured him coffee at the kitchen table, where he seized the *Los Angeles Tribunal* that she had read earlier and left on the table. He seemed inordinately interested in the morning paper. He turned the pages very quickly, scanning each one as if he were looking for something specific. Finally, he pushed the paper away and drank his coffee.

"What are you to Jules Mendelson?" Flo asked.

Kippie Petworth looked at Flo March, but he didn't answer her question. He realized that Jules had told her nothing.

"I asked you a question," said Flo.

"What are *you* to Jules Mendelson?" he asked in return.

Each stared at the other. Neither replied to the other's question.

Kippie Petworth had a pretty good idea who Flo March was, but Flo March had no idea who Kippie Petworth was.

Later Jules picked him up, and they left together without exchanging a word between them. Jules never brought up his name. Neither did she. Then, in the excitement of the death of Hector Paradiso, which consumed everyone's conversation for days afterward, she forgot about the young man called Kippie Petworth who had spent six hours in her house, and she never, for even an instant, formed a connection in her mind between him and the death of Hector.

When she had called Nellie Potts to tell her that she needed more of the gray satin fabric to recover one of her cushions on the new sofa, Nellie told her that the fabric company was temporarily out of stock, but she would let her know when it became available again.

THE NEXT MORNING Flo checked her date book. The day that Jules had brought Kippie to her house at six o'clock in the morning was, indeed, the same day that Hector Paradiso was found dead. She remembered also that Jules had been annoyed with her for attending Hector's funeral. She realized that if she had not gone to the all-night market and run into Lonny Edge, whom she had tried to avoid, she might never have realized that it was Pauline Mendelson's son by a previous marriage who was hidden in her house while Jules made the arrangement to cover up the murder he had committed. She remembered the young man's charm and style, the kind of charm and style he could only have inherited from his mother. The knowledge was comforting to her.

"There's something I want you to do for me, Sims," said Flo, when she called Sims Lord later in the day.

"What's that?" asked Sims. The tone of his voice was chilly.

"I want to meet with Pauline Mendelson," she said.

"Oh, come on, Flo. Be practical. Pauline Mendelson will never meet with you," said Sims.

"Perhaps you should tell her that I have some information that might be of great interest to her," said Flo.

"Forget about Pauline. That's a hopeless cause. She thinks you ruined her life. She'll never let up on you."

"Tell the great lady she's going to be very very sorry if she doesn't come and see me, Sims." When he did not reply, she added, "Tell her it has to do with Kippie."

"What about Kippie?" he asked. In the years he had been the lawyer and confidant of Jules Mendelson, he had been involved in getting Kippie Petworth out of a great many scrapes.

"I'm not talking to you anymore, Sims. She's the one I want to talk to."

"NEVER. Never, never, never," said Pauline. "There is no way I would meet with her. With people like that, it's blackmail. It's all about money."

"She said—" said Sims.

"I don't care what she said," said Pauline.

"She said it had to do with Kippie," continued Sims.

There was a silence. "With Kippie?" she replied. Pauline Mendelson was not the type of woman who perspired, but she felt moisture in her armpits when she heard her son's name, as having come from the lips of Flo March. She remembered the last thing she had said to Jules before he died. "Does anyone else know, Jules?" she had asked, but he had died without answering her. She remembered Kippie's telephone call after Jules had died. "I know everything," she had said to him. "About Flo March?" Kippie had answered.

That afternoon the Reverend Doctor Rufus Browning, of the All Saints Episcopal Church in Beverly Hills, came to have tea with Pauline in the library at Clouds. She could not bring herself to tell anyone what she knew about her son, not even her father, whom she trusted implicitly, or either of her sisters, or Camilla Ebury, and certainly not Rose Cliveden. Rufus Browning was a great admirer of Pauline Mendelson's, and relished his role as her spiritual adviser. On those occasions during the year when she attended his Sunday services, she always called him Dr. Browning when they spoke on the steps of the church after the service, but in her library, on those occasions when he came for tea, she always called him Rufus. It was not lost on either Blondell or Dudley that Mrs. Mendelson had been crying during the hour and a half that she remained behind closed doors in the library with Dr. Browning. Afterward, she telephoned Sims Lord at his office.

"I'll see her," said Pauline. "But not in my house. I do not want her here. And I will most certainly not go to her house."

"We can meet in Jules's office," said Sims.

□   □   □

"I WILL GO to court, Mrs. Mendelson," said Flo. "I have these papers that Jules signed. You will notice on these photocopies that they
were witnessed by Olaf Pederson and Margaret Maple, and Sims
Lord's name is right here in the letter."

"Those papers were delivered within hours of my husband's death
and will not stand up in court. I have been assured of that by some of
the finest legal minds in the country," replied Pauline. The words she
said were the words Sims Lord had coached her to say, but even she
could hear that the force and power she had acquired since Jules's
death were missing from her tone. "My husband was coerced by you
into signing those papers. You insinuated your way into the hospital,
first pretending to be his daughter, and then dressing yourself up as a
nurse. There are ample witnesses at the hospital who will testify to
that. I hold you responsible for my husband's death."

Flo nodded, calmly. The two women whom Jules had loved stared
at each other. Flo realized that she had the upper hand. "Jules's
health had been failing for more than a year, Mrs. Mendelson," said
Flo. "And you know that to be true as well as I do. So don't blame me
for his death. In case you're interested, which I'm sure you're not,
the ambulance attendants will tell you I saved his life. And if you're
looking for someone to blame, blame Arnie Zwillman for telling
Myles Crocker about the girl who went off the balcony in Chicago in
nineteen fifty-three, and blame Myles Crocker for telling Jules that
the Brussels appointment was off, about two hours before his heart
attack."

Pauline remained silent, devastated that Flo knew more about her
husband than she did.

Flo rose, as if she were about to leave. "I know a great deal about
Jules, Mrs. Mendelson," she said to Pauline.

"Ignore her, Pauline," said Sims. His tone of voice was icy. "This is
a woman who was paid handsomely for sexual favors and is looking
for a free ride for life."

"I'm not talking to you, Sims," said Flo. She made no effort to hide
the contempt in her voice. "I'm on to you. I've been on to you ever
since you pulled out your dick after Jules died, and thought I was the
kind of girl who'd drop to my knees."

Sims turned to Pauline. "You must understand the kind of person
this is, Pauline. She would stoop to anything."

Pauline was not unaware of a controlled reddening of Sims Lord's
face. She nodded.

"I don't believe that Miss March knows anything," continued Sims.

"Miss March knows who killed Hector Paradiso, for one thing," said Flo. She ignored Sims Lord and directed what she was about to say to Pauline. "Miss March knows because Mr. Mendelson brought the killer to her house to hide out for six hours on the early morning of the murder, while he went about the business of covering up the murder and making it appear to be a suicide."

Pauline turned pale but remained silent.

"No one would ever believe such a thing," said Sims.

"They would if they tested the blood samples on one of the cushions of my gray satin sofa, caused by dripping blood from a missing front tooth," said Flo. Her eyes never left Pauline's as she spoke. Pauline dropped her eyes and looked away.

"I'm not asking for much, Mrs. Mendelson. I'm just asking for what Jules wanted me to have. The house on Azelia Way and an income from one of his investments to continue to live in the style in which he wanted me to live. That's all. Not one cent more. With your kind of bucks, that's not much. Think it over. And should you ever wish to talk privately with me, without Sims hovering, Miss Maple will give you my number."

She opened the door of Jules's conference room and walked out.

Sims and Pauline sat in silence for a few moments.

"Pay her off, Sims. Give her what she wants. God knows, I can afford it," said Pauline.

"It never ends, once you start, you know," said Sims, finally.

"Pay her," repeated Pauline.

"It is a mistake, Pauline," said Sims.

"What do you mean?" asked Pauline. She was shaken by her encounter with Flo.

"You agree to this now, next year she'll come back for more. It's a form of blackmail. I've seen cases like this before. What was that she was talking about? The missing tooth? The blood on the cushion? I didn't understand that."

Pauline shook her head. "I don't know," she said.

"I've concluded that not only is she a liar, but she's delusional, money-hungry, and a danger to you and the memory of Jules," said Sims.

"Are you saying we shouldn't pay her?" asked Pauline.

"Isn't that what you wanted?" asked Sims in turn.

"But I thought you were in favor of honoring the agreements Jules made," said Pauline.

"Not anymore," replied Sims, flatly.

Pauline, troubled, nodded. She was afraid to pursue the subject for fear of having Kippie's name come up. She gathered her bag and rose. At the door of Jules's office, she turned back to Sims.

"What will happen to her, do you suppose?" she asked.

"She'll fall into oblivion, never to be heard from again, no doubt."

*Flo's Tape #23*

"Jules always separated his married life from his life with me. He didn't like to talk about Pauline with me, and I respected that in him, but I picked up a lot about her over the five years I was Jules's mistress, in bits and pieces, and put them all together. You talk about a privileged life. She had a privileged life, all her life. When she was sixteen, for instance, she was at this fancy girls' school in Virginia, I can't remember the name, where all the girls rode horses, and she was such a good rider and jumper that she entered the horse show at Madison Square Garden in New York and got a blue ribbon or whatever they give for the first prize. Stuff like that. She seemed to do everything just right. The only mistake she ever made was marrying that first husband of hers, because she was destined for bigger things than him.

"Listen, I have to be practical. She was the perfect wife for Jules. It's too bad we couldn't have worked out some kind of arrangement between the three of us, like they do in those European marriages. I would have settled for that in a minute. Everyone always said what a wonderful woman she was. I guess she was, until she heard about me. I suppose if I were in her shoes, I would have hated me too."

# 24

IN A SHORT TIME, the news of the financial plight of Flo March reached the ears of Cyril Rathbone. Other people's plights—divorce, job loss, cancer, AIDS, bankruptcy, arrests, suicide, adultery, and perversion—were Cyril Rathbone's fortune, and while he listened to these tales of woe, as reported to him by informants, he always said such concerned things as, "Oh, dear, how sad, how frightfully sad," but his mind was working at the same time on the manner in which he would report the news in his column. As he once said to his great friend Hector Paradiso, "What is the point of a secret if it is kept a secret?" Such sadnesses were the mainstay of his column, far more than his reportage of parties and openings and social doings. They were the very reason people tore to his page of the magazine first.

In the case of Flo March, however, his plans were more grandiose, going far beyond mere mentions in his column, because the names in her plight, Pauline and Jules Mendelson and the glittering group of greats and near-greats with whom they moved, were so celebrated. The girl, poor silly creature, was sitting on a gold mine and couldn't be made to realize it. Although Flo had not been a waitress for five years, Cyril never could resist referring to her as "the former waitress Flo March," as if that explained her inability to understand the power of her position. A book deal and a miniseries flashed through his mind. He even visualized her appearing on "After Midnight," the late-night Amos Swank show, all done up in one of her Chanel suits, telling about the mean Pauline Mendelson, who was doing her out of her rightful inheritance. Such an appearance, he knew, would guarantee that her book, if she could be induced to participate in one, would soar to the top of the best-seller lists across the country. The possibilities for promotion were staggering.

It was the great star Faye Converse, who cared about Flo, her neighbor, but didn't want to get involved in her situation—"After all, I hardly know her, poor thing, I only met her on that night she killed my dog"—who told Cyril that Flo rarely rose from her bed, and that unopened bills were piling up in great stacks on the floor of the front hall. "I don't think she can afford to stay on in that house much longer."

"But how do you know such things?" asked Cyril, disguising his delight over the report with a somber tone.

"Glyceria, my maid Glyceria, is devoted to her," said Faye about her neighbor. Faye Converse, who always told interviewers she didn't like gossip, lowered her voice to a whisper and looked about her, although she was alone at the time, in her own house, and whispered into the telephone, "I think she drinks." Then she looked about her again and said, "She is positively catatonic, poor thing."

Later that day, Cyril called Flo March and left a message on her answering machine saying that it was a matter of utmost importance that she call him. He felt sure that he would hear from Flo. But she did not return his call.

Instead, in a stroke of luck that he took to be a sign from above, as he called it, he ran into her. Cyril Rathbone put a great deal of stock in signs from above. "It was meant to be," he often said, in psychic tones. Or, "There are no accidents." Early the very next morning Flo walked into the Viceroy Coffee Shop, where he happened to be having breakfast. She stood timidly inside the door, unsure where to sit. She was, she thought, incognito, wearing large dark glasses, with her red hair completely covered by a scarf, but Cyril picked her out right away, encompassed as she was in an air of melancholy.

"Is Curly here?" she asked the cashier.

"Curly? I don't know no Curly," said the cashier.

"Belle? Where's Belle's station?" asked Flo.

"Belle don't work here no more," said the cashier.

Flo had not been to the Viceroy since she walked out of it five years before, when Jules Mendelson took her to Paris, and their love affair started. He had not wanted her to go back there, and she hadn't, although for a while she kept in touch with Curly and Belle. She stood, undecided whether to stay or leave, and then moved to a stool at the counter and ordered a cup of coffee. The waitress who took her order was new since she had worked there and did not know her. Cyril noticed that her hand shook when she raised the cup of coffee to her lips. She put it down and took out a cigarette from her gold case with the name FLO written on it in sapphires, and her hand shook again when she attempted to light the cigarette with her matching gold lighter. He knew the time had come.

Without a word to Joel Zircon, with whom he was having breakfast, Cyril picked up his cup of coffee and crossed from the booth around

374

the counter to where she was sitting. "Good morning, Miss March," he said. "What an early hour for you to be up and about. I always imagined you were one of those ladies of leisure who sleeps late and has breakfast in bed on a tray with Porthault place mats."

She looked up at Cyril Rathbone but did not reply.

He seated himself on the stool next to her. "I heard you ask for Curly," he said.

"Yes, I did," she answered.

"Dead, poor fellow."

"Dead?" She gasped and covered her mouth with her hand.

"Oh, yes. AIDS. Terribly sad. He took pills toward the end. What's that new sleeping pill everyone's taking? Halcion, isn't it? That's what he took. A marvelous decision of Curly's, don't you think?" asked Cyril.

"No, no. I don't think that at all," answered Flo.

"It's very important to know when not to exceed one's span. Curly understood that. All his friends were with him when he did it. I understand it was a glorious experience."

Flo looked at Cyril Rathbone and shook her head in disagreement. "I hadn't heard any of that. I'd kind of lost touch. I didn't even know he was sick. Poor Curly. What about Belle?"

"She went over to Nibblers Coffee Shop on Wilshire Boulevard," said Cyril. "She didn't want to stay here after Curly died. They were great friends."

"I know."

"This is West Hollywood, after all, Miss March. People come. People go. Nothing lasts."

"I suppose." She signaled to the waitress. "Check, please."

The waitress handed her the check for the coffee.

"Stay, stay. Have another cup of coffee," he said.

"Thank you, but I can't. I have things to do," she said.

"No, you don't," he replied. When she looked sharply at him, he smiled at her. She didn't have anything to do. "Please pour Miss March another cup of coffee, will you, Maureen?" He picked up the check that the waitress had left on the counter. "I know you're broke," he said.

"Not that broke," replied Flo, taking the check back from him with an abrupt gesture.

"It occurred to me that perhaps you had come here at this very early hour to try to get your old job back."

"Wrong," she replied. She opened her bag and took out a dollar tip to leave the waitress, as if that proved she was not broke.

"Pretty ring," he said, pointing to the sapphire-and-diamond ring that Jules had given her. "That should keep the wolf from the door for quite a few months."

"Oh, no. I'll never sell this ring," said Flo, looking at her ring. "No matter what. When I die, this ring is still going to be on my finger."

"A lovely young woman like you shouldn't talk about dying, Miss March. You have an extraordinary life ahead of you, if you play your cards right," said Cyril. Their eyes met. He lifted her hand and gazed at the ring. "A gift from Jules Mendelson, I assume?" he asked.

Flo did not reply. She inhaled deeply on her cigarette and stubbed it out in an ashtray.

"Very bad for you, smoking," he said.

She stood up, preparing to leave.

"Your plight has been made known to me," he said, wanting to detain her.

"My plight?"

"Your financial problems."

"Oh, I see. By whom?"

"Oh, heavens, Miss March," said Cyril. He spoke in his acquired upper-class English voice that he knew intimidated some people. "A good journalist never reveals his sources. Anyway, it doesn't matter. What matters is that it seems so appropriate that we should meet like this, by accident, here at the Viceroy Coffee Shop, where your great romance began. Of course, as we both know, there are no accidents. It was meant to be, that you should walk in here like this. Don't you agree?"

Flo, confused, stared at Cyril Rathbone, not knowing whether to stay and listen or get up and leave. "I guess so," she replied to his question, not sure whether she agreed or not.

"You are holding so many trump cards, it is a shame for you to fall apart the way you are apparently doing. I have a plan to suggest to you."

"What sort of plan?"

"Sit down, Flo. I assume I may call you Flo? It seems so formal to call you Miss March." He stood up and indicated with a flourish of his hand for her to reseat herself. After a moment, she sat down. "Why don't you take off your dark glasses so I can see your eyes?"

"My eyes are puffy," she said.

He nodded his head in a concerned fashion. "I heard you were drinking," he said.

She was frightened of him. She made no reply.

"All that fine wine from the Bresciani auction," he said. "Rare stuff, I've heard."

"I've run out of all that fine wine from the Bresciani auction," she replied.

"My, you have been drinking. Those gallon bottles of Soave from the Hughes Market must have a bitter taste after the delights of Jules Mendelson's cellar."

"What is it you want from me, Mr. Rathbone?"

"So formal, Flo. It's Cyril, please."

"What is it you want?"

"What you need first is a good lawyer," he said. "And not a Waspy frigid-type like Sims Lord. He's no friend of yours, as you may have discovered by now. He is, in fact, the leader of the opposition. Am I correct?"

Flo, riveted, nodded.

"Next, you need a good agent. And then you need a good writer. I, of course, am your writer. Your Boswell, if you will, your poet laureate. My friend Joel Zircon, over there in the booth by the window, with his head buried in the Hollywood trade papers, scarfing down the bagel and lox and slurping his coffee, can be your agent. You must remember Joel? From your waitress days? He certainly remembers you. Ghastly table manners, to be sure. Eats like a pig. But terribly clever in his chosen career. Mona Berg, the queen of Hollywood agents, increasingly relies on him. He is a young man on the way up. Joel probably even knows exactly the right lawyer for you."

"But what do I need a lawyer, an agent, and a writer for?" Flo asked.

"For your book, and your miniseries, which I am going to write in your name," said Cyril.

"What book?"

"*Jules's Mistress*. You see, I already have your title, Flo. All those bills that are piling up in your front hall, stacks of them, I hear. Now you'll be able to pay them."

Flo stared at Cyril.


ROSE CLIVEDEN had become habitually intemperate. Among themselves, her friends complained and murmured that something simply had to be done, but no one had the nerve to speak up, as Rose could not bear criticism. Instead, certain of her friends stopped inviting her. Madge White, for one, said Rose spilled red wine all over her Aubusson carpet that had been left to her by her grandmother, and ruined it, absolutely ruined it, and she would never, ever, have Rose in her house again. And Millicent Pond, Sandy Pond's mother, the matriarch of the newspaper family, complained bitterly that Rose constantly interrupted one of the former Presidents at a dinner at her house when he was trying to explain the present administration's policy in Nicaragua, and she wasn't going to have Rose back, even though she'd known her all her life. And Faye Converse, who was tolerant of everyone, was furious with Rose because she dropped and smashed two Baccarat glasses on the marble floor of her lanai, and Faye's maid, Glyceria, who vacuumed barefoot, cut her toe badly on a piece of broken glass and threatened to quit if Rose came to the house again.

When she dropped a cigarette in her bed and caused a fire in her bedroom, as well as minor burns to her arms and legs, after having drunk ten vodkas at a charity ball, Pauline and Camilla and even Madge, who relented, decided that the time had come for them to intervene in Rose's life and send her to a clinic in Palm Springs to deal with her addiction to alcohol. Rose claimed that she had no such problem. When the moment came to intervene, all of them became silent and were afraid to say to Rose what they had said about her behind her back.

"I've been dying to do that room over, anyway," said Rose to her friends, not daring to admit how frightening the experience had been for her. "I was so sick of those damn purple violets in the wallpaper and the curtains. No more chintz for me. I've had it with chintz."

"I think we're getting off the subject here, Rose," said Pauline. "I called the people at Betty Ford. They're booked ahead for months, but they will make an exception and take you immediately."

Rose was horrified at the suggestion. "All those movie stars, with their drugs, telling those terrible stories. I read about them in the *Enquirer*. That's not for me, thank you very much. Making your own bed. Mopping your own floor. Sharing a room with God-knows-who, from God-knows-where. Puleeze!"

"Either you go there, Rose, or we, who are the only friends you have left, are going to abandon you, too. Your life is out of control," said Pauline.

"No, no, I'll just stop. It's as simple as that. I mean, I stop every Lent."

Pauline, exasperated, turned to Camilla. Camilla smiled but said nothing. "Fine then. Stop. But leave me alone until you do. Don't call me. I don't want to hear from you, Rose," said Pauline. They were at the Los Angeles Country Club. She got up from the table and left, pleading an appointment with Sims Lord.

Rose was shocked by the harshness of Pauline's tone. Her great friend had never spoken to her in such a manner before.

"She's not herself. She hasn't been herself for weeks," said Camilla, in defense of her friend.

"Pauline's become bitter," Rose said, as a way of avoiding the issue about herself. "All that business about that whore Jules was involved with."

"She's not a whore," said Camilla. The picture of the husband-grabbing hussy that Pauline's friends perpetuated when discussing Flo was in conflict with Camilla's remembrance of the pretty young woman she had met in Philip's room at the Chateau Marmont and had later hugged at Jules's funeral.

"Pauline's changed," continued Rose. "Don't you feel it? She's gotten terribly tough."

"You're only changing the subject again, Rose," Camilla said shyly. "Pauline is right. She's the only one of us who had the guts to say what she said. Madge wouldn't. Even Archbishop Cooning wouldn't. You simply have to do something, Rose. You'll be dead if you don't. None of us can remember when you haven't had an arm in a sling, or been on crutches, or a walker, or a cane, all from falls when you were loaded. This time you could have burned to death. Thank God your fire-alarm system was working."

Rose, unexpectedly, started to cry.

"You should talk to Philip," suggested Camilla.

"Philip? Your Philip? That good-looking young man? I'm always happy to talk to Philip. But why?"

"Are you going to be home at six?"

"I think so. Why?"

"I'm going to send Philip over. Just talk to him, Rose. Listen to what he has to say. And don't interrupt him, the way you always interrupt everybody, like the former President. I hear the President's wife was furious with you. Please. Do it for me."

IN THE BEGINNING the arrangement between Flo and Cyril was felicitous. Joel Zircon approached several publishers and related back to Flo and Cyril that there was immense interest in *Jules's Mistress*.

"What they want is an opening chapter and an outline for the rest of the book," Joel reported. "After that, we make the deal."

"What kind of money are they talking?" asked Cyril.

"In the six figures, at least," said Joel.

That was also what Flo wanted to know but couldn't bring herself to ask. Her pool man had left her a note that morning, saying that he wouldn't be able to come anymore, as he hadn't been paid for his services. She feared that other services she had long taken for granted were going to be cut off. Whenever she thought of her financial situation, a feeling of desolation and hopelessness came over her. She had begun to realize that her only salvation was with Cyril Rathbone.

"I could always go back to modeling," she said to Cyril one day, as if she had other alternatives in her life to the one that he was offering her.

"You were never *in* modeling, Flo," answered Cyril. "This is a time for you to be practical about your future. Jules is not here anymore to take care of you. You have to think of taking care of yourself."

They met late each afternoon after Cyril finished his column for *Mulholland*. He came to her house for two hours with his tape recorder, before he went home to dress for whatever dinner or screening he was going to attend that evening. He asked her questions. At first she was guarded in her answers, always protective of Jules. She was critical about herself. "I was stupid about money. Jules was very generous with me. I spent, spent, spent," she said. "If I had saved something each week, when that enormous check came, I wouldn't be in the jam I'm in now."

"Allow me to play devil's advocate for a moment, Flo," said Cyril.

Flo wasn't exactly sure what devil's advocate meant, but she nodded in agreement for Cyril to play it.

"Did it ever occur to you that that was the way Jules liked it?" he asked.

"What do you mean?"

"As long as you didn't have any real money, you wouldn't ever leave him. After all, Jules's money was limitless. Your weekly spending sprees were nothing to him. So your curtains cost forty thousand dollars. So your new closet cost forty thousand more. So this gray satin fabric cost ninety-five dollars a yard. So what? That was peanuts for Jules. So were all your Chanel suits. Did he ever buy you a valuable picture that you could sell? No. He didn't give you any equity, Flo. Think about it."

"But he wanted to take care of me," insisted Flo.

"But he didn't, did he?"

"Yes, yes, I have these papers. Look."

"Delivered on the day of his death, Flo. Wise up. Jules was a very brilliant man. He had to know that Pauline could do what she's doing and every court in the land would agree with her. He had five years to do what he waited until the last day of his life to do."

Flo's eyes filled with tears. She could not bear to think that Jules deprived her in order to hang onto her. "I blame everything on Sims Lord," she said.

"Sims Lord is just a very high-priced hired hand, Flo. He's only doing what first Jules told him to do and now what Pauline is telling him to do," said Cyril.

"He wanted to set me up and I turned him down," replied Flo.

"Set you up how?"

"As his lady friend."

Cyril remained perfectly still. He had learned never to exclaim with pleasure when someone he was interviewing began to reveal something that the person had no intention of revealing. He merely nodded, as if what she was saying was of no more interest to him than anything else she was saying.

"Right here, on this same sofa," said Flo. She patted the cushion next to her, the same cushion with Kippie Petworth's blood on the reverse side, about which she had not told Cyril yet. "About a month after Jules died. He came here to tell me the estate wasn't going to honor the agreements Jules made for me."

"And he came on to you at the same time, did you say?"

"Oh, yes."

"Held your hand, or something?"

"Held my hand, Cyril? He put my hand on his dick. And he was supposed to be Jules's best friend. And Jules was only dead a month."

"And what did you do?"

"Took it away, of course."

"And what did he do?"

"Took it out."

"Took what out?"

"His dick."

"No!"

"Yes! Like I was supposed to go into raptures over it."

Cyril was beside himself.

"Let me tell you something about Jules," said Flo. "He was a gentleman with me. I knew he had the hots for me from the day we met in the coffee shop, but he never laid a hand on me until he took me to Paris. That was the first time."

"Yes, yes, you've already told me that. Let's get back to Sims Lord for a moment."

IN TIME, as orchestrated by Cyril Rathbone and Joel Zircon, the word was about that Flo March, the one-time waitress who had become the mistress of Jules Mendelson, was writing her memoirs, to be entitled *Jules's Mistress*. By design, Cyril's name was never mentioned as her collaborator. It was reported that Flo was dictating her remembrances into microcassettes, and that already there were forty hours recorded.

"Flo March is prepared to tell all," wrote Army Archerd in *Daily Variety*. "Her story promises to be hot, hot, hot," wrote George Christy in the *Hollywood Reporter*. Cyril Rathbone, echoing both of the above in his column in *Mulholland*, could not resist adding, "Arnie Zwillman, are you listening?"

"But why did you say that about Arnie Zwillman?" cried Flo, after she read Cyril's column.

"It's called creating a market," answered Cyril, in a patient tone of voice. He spoke to Flo as if he were a great teacher and she a backward pupil.

"But Arnie Zwillman is a very dangerous man," said Flo. There was an element of fear in her voice. "I know for a fact what he did to Jules. He destroyed his chances of going to Brussels, just like that, overnight. You can't fool around with a man like Arnie Zwillman."

"Believe me, you have nothing to worry about, Flo," said Cyril.

"I wouldn't be too sure about that, Cyril."

"Joel Zircon says his phones are ringing off the hook. Publishers can't wait to get their hands on the outline."

"What's taking you so long to write the first chapter and the outline? I've done forty hours of tapes. How much do you need?"

"Patience, Flo. Patience," said Cyril.


THAT NIGHT, late, a car drove up the driveway of Flo's house on Azelia Way. She was alone, as she was always alone those nights, and could hear the sound of the tires on the gravel of her driveway. She couldn't imagine who would be coming to call at such an hour. She could hear the sound of the engine running. Waiting, she expected her doorbell to ring, but it didn't. Her curtains were drawn, and she opened them just enough to peek outside. A car, which she at first thought was Jules's Bentley, was sitting there, idling, with the headlights on and the engine running. Then she realized it was a different color than Jules's car, a color that looked like gold. She saw also from the grille that it was not a Bentley but a Rolls-Royce. In the front seat sat two men who were looking at her house. A feeling of panic gripped her. She quickly closed the curtains. On tiptoe, she went to the front door and double-bolted it. She went through her whole house, closing curtains and making sure doors and windows were locked. After twenty-five minutes, she heard the car turn around in her driveway and pull out.

She waited for fifteen minutes more and then peered out of the curtains again. The car was gone. Everything appeared normal. She went to the front door and listened. There was no sound. Very quietly she unbolted the lock and, with the chain still on, opened the door a crack to look outside. Everything was quiet. As she closed the door again, she saw a white box that had been left on her doormat. She opened the door just wide enough to grab the package and then slammed the door again and bolted it.

In her living room, she opened the box. There was a card in an envelope, which she opened. "It's loaded," the card read. "Put it in your mouth and fire it." The note, typed, was unsigned. She removed the pale pink tissue paper. There, nestled, was a small gun. For a long time she stared at it. Then she picked it up. She could not believe that it was loaded, but she did not know enough about guns to know how to open it to check. Using both hands, she pointed the gun at the sliding glass window that opened onto her terrace and swimming pool. After several moments of indecision, she pulled the trigger, and the gun fired. The noise was deafening. The plate-glass window splintered in all directions.

She could not move from her place on the sofa. Her body was soaked with perspiration. Her breathing was heavy. She felt a different sort of fear than the fear she had felt from having no money. For reasons which she could not explain to herself at that moment, she thought of Marilyn Monroe. "They got rid of Marilyn," she remembered saying to Jules at the steak house in the Valley.

The next morning, still shaken from her experience of the night before, Flo went back to the AA meeting in the log cabin on Robertson Boulevard. She had not been there for several months, but she knew that she had to begin to put her life in order again. She wore her huge dark glasses and her hair was wrapped in a scarf. She sat away from the other people, drank a cup of coffee, smoked a cigarette, and looked around for Philip Quennell, but she did not see him. At first she was disappointed that he was not there, because she had parted from him so badly the last time he went to her house to try to help her, but then she was relieved. If he had been there, she might not have been able to do what she decided to do.

She had never raised her hand to share at a meeting before, but that morning she felt the need to speak. She raised her hand in such a tentative fashion that the speaker did not notice her at first and called on several other people. Then, when she decided that she would not raise her hand again, the speaker called on her. "The lady with the dark glasses and head scarf," he said, pointing at her.

Flo knew that she could not use her own name, even her first name, because she had become notorious. "My name is, uh, Fleurette," she said. She had always hated her real name. Even before she learned about the ways of elegant life from Jules Mendelson, she thought her real name sounded cheap, and she spoke it in a muffled voice, as she did the next words, "I am an alcoholic and chemically dependent." She looked about her, still wearing her impenetrable dark glasses, frightened. The room was silent. "I had almost a year in the program, and then I had a slip. This is my first day back."

There was applause from the group, who were celebrated for their tolerance of the transgressions of their members. Encouraged by their friendliness, Flo began to talk. She said that she had been a kept woman. "I am a mistress. Or, rather, I was a mistress. I hate that word, but it's what I am. I have been kept by a very rich man for five years. When I first met Mr. So and So, I didn't have a pot to pee in, or a window to throw it out of."

She said that she knew his business secrets and the deals she had heard when he made telephone calls from her bed during the afternoons after they made love. She discussed his heart attack and his death. She said that she had lived the life of a princess for five years but that now she was broke and about to lose the house that she thought had been put in her name. She said she knew about a covered-up murder and who the murderer was. She could not stop talking.

In a corner of the room, also disguised with dark glasses and a head scarf, was Rose Cliveden. Her hands were still bandaged from the burns she had suffered when her bed caught on fire. She had refused to go to the clinic in Palm Springs, as suggested by her friends, but, after meeting with Philip Quennell, she had agreed to go to AA meetings for two or three weeks. On this particular morning, he had promised to meet her there at the log cabin, as he guaranteed that she was unlikely to see anyone she knew, as she might at one of the more fashionable meetings in Beverly Hills, but, to her annoyance, he had not appeared. She could not relate to any of the stories told by any of the people who had shared their experiences. "I have nothing in common with any of these people," she thought to herself, as she gathered her bag and prepared to leave.

It was then, while she was slowly walking out of the frightful little room, as she later described it, that the woman called Fleurette began to speak. Rose was already at the door, tiptoeing out, when it suddenly dawned on her, when she heard the words *gangster* and *President of the United States*, that Fleurette, with the dark glasses and the good-looking suit, was none other than the infamous and notorious Flo March, who had brought such unhappiness to the life of Pauline Mendelson. Riveted, she stared at her.

"My God," thought Rose. "That's the same woman I saw outside the church talking to Jules at Hector Paradiso's funeral last year. And the one from Jules's funeral." As if she were in a theater at a play, where the second act suddenly began to show more promise than the first act had, she tiptoed back to the seat that she had abandoned and sat, rapt, throughout Flo March's sharing.

PHILIP QUENNELL, who regularly attended the early-morning meetings at the log cabin on Robertson Boulevard, arrived very late that morning. An unexpected telephone call from Lonny Edge, complaining bitterly about a description of himself that had appeared in Hortense Madden's account in *Mulholland* of his possession of the manuscript of Basil Plant's supposedly unfinished novel, had caused the owners of the bungalow where he lived on Cahuenga Boulevard to serve notice that he must vacate the premises by the first of the month.

"On what grounds?" Philip asked.

"They said the article insinuated that I was using my apartment for purposes of prostitution. I mean, I only turn a couple of tricks a week in my apartment. Most of my work I do elsewhere, in my clients' homes. But I don't exactly want to go to court over it, if you know what I mean," said Lonny.

"Listen, Lonny. I have to be somewhere. I can't talk now. I'll call you back later," said Philip.

"You giving me the runaround, Philip? You're the one who got me into all this about that fucking manuscript that was just sitting on my table peaceably for three years, until you came along and began stirring things up."

"No, I'm not giving you the runaround, Lonny. I just promised somebody I'd be somewhere. I'll call you later."

Philip arrived at the meeting as it was breaking up.

"I'm so sorry, Rose," he said, when he saw her. Knowing how spoiled she was, he expected her either to have left or to be in a foul mood with him for suggesting that she meet him on Robertson Boulevard at seven o'clock in the morning and then not showing up. "I had a sort of emergency telephone call that I had to attend to. How did the meeting go? At least you stayed to the end."

"Darling, it was fascinating, absolutely fascinating!" said Rose. He had never seen her so animated, except when she was drunk. "You have no idea what you missed. You won't *believe* who spoke."

"Who?" asked Philip, confused by her enthusiasm.

"Flo March!" she said.

Philip, surprised, looked at her.

"She's the one who was Jules Mendelson's mistress," said Rose, in explanation. "My dear, the things she said! I'm *sick* you weren't here."

"Rose, would you like to go out for a cup of coffee with me," said Philip. "We have to talk."

"Oh, no, I can't, darling. I have things to do," she said. "But I'll be back tomorrow. Every morning. It's fascinating. Better than the movies. Why didn't you tell me it's so fascinating?"

"Listen, Rose. You do know, don't you, that what you hear in these rooms must never leave these rooms," said Philip.

"What does that mean?" asked Rose.

"It means that you mustn't discuss what you've heard here, or tell the names of any of the people you might have seen here. That's why it's called Anonymous."

"Oh, darling, my lips are sealed," said Rose. She could not take her eyes off Flo and squinted to better take her in. "Pretty little thing, isn't she? You'd never know she was only a waitress, would you? See you tomorrow, darling. Love to Camilla. Big hug." She blew Philip a kiss and ran off.

Flo was surrounded by people. Unused to such friendliness, she smiled nervously as she accepted their thanks for her sharing with them. Several people offered to give her their telephone numbers. When she looked up, she was glad to see Philip standing there.

"Oh, Philip," she said, breaking away.

"Hello, Flo," he said.

"Are you still mad at me?"

"Of course, I'm not mad at you."

"You were the last time I saw you. I was afraid you'd given up on me."

"Never," he said, smiling at her. "I'm delighted you came back."

"I looked for you earlier, but I didn't see you."

"I just got here. I was very late."

"Philip, I raised my hand," she said, proudly. "I actually spoke up at a meeting for the first time."

"I heard. I'm sorry I missed you. How do you feel?"

"Wonderful. Everyone was so nice."

"What made you come back today? What made you speak up for the first time?"

"Something happened," she said. She looked up at him. Although he could not see her eyes through her dark glasses, he felt that something was wrong.

"Would you want to go out for a cup of coffee and talk?"

"Sure," she said. "But I'd rather you came up to my house for a cup of coffee. I want to show you something."

INSIDE HER HOUSE, she showed him the note, the gun, and the splintered plate glass window.

"Good God," he said. "Did you get a look at the car?"

"I think it was a Rolls-Royce. I peeked out those curtains at it. It was eerie. Two men sat in the front seat with the motor running and the lights on and just stared at the house. I think the car was gold, or some shade of yellow," she said.

"I'll tell you who has a gold Rolls-Royce," said Philip.

"Who?"

"Arnie Zwillman. I saw it one night at Casper Stieglitz's house, when Jules and Pauline were there."

Flo shivered. "Arnie Zwillman?"

"Do you know him?"

"He tried to get Jules to launder money," she said. "When Jules turned him down, he called the State Department and told them something about Jules that had happened years ago in Chicago that I can't tell you about, and the State Department told Jules, just an hour before his heart attack here, that he wasn't going to get the job as head of the American commission to Brussels."

"Were you planning to put all that in your book?" asked Philip.

Flo, embarrassed, nodded. "That's the kind of stuff my collaborator is interested in."

"You're playing with fire, Flo. You must know that. Arnie Zwillman is not a swell guy."

"I'm broke, Philip. I need bucks. My pool man quit. The telephone company is dunning me. That third-rate actor who owns this house wants me out. I don't have any choice."

"And Pauline won't help?"

"You must be kidding."

"Let me ask you a question, Flo. If you had the money that Jules wanted to leave you, would you still be writing this book?"

"Of course not," said Flo.

"That's what I wanted to hear you say," said Philip. "You wouldn't mind if I interfered a little bit in my own private way, would you?"

"How?"

"I can't tell you that yet. Trust me."

As Philip was leaving, Flo followed him to the door. "You wouldn't want to move in here with me, would you, Philip? No strings attached. Not like it was between us at the Chateau Marmont. You in that room. Me in here."

"Somehow I don't think that would go over very well with Camilla," said Philip, smiling.

Flo laughed. "No, I suppose not."

"It's nice to see you laugh, Flo."

"Before I used to be afraid because there was no money anymore. Now I'm just afraid."

AT THE SAME TIME that Philip was with Flo, Rose Cliveden called Pauline Mendelson, whom she hadn't spoken to since her outburst over lunch at the Los Angeles Country Club. "My dear, I have the most riveting thing to tell you," she said. "You won't believe who spoke at an AA meeting this morning."

LATE THAT NIGHT, Flo couldn't sleep. She got up and drove to the Hughes Market on Beverly Boulevard. As she pushed her shopping cart through the aisles, she stopped to stare at the gallon bottles of Soave wine, but she kept moving and bought twelve cans of Diet Coke instead. Ahead of her, standing at the magazine counter, was Lonny Edge. When he looked up from the magazine he was reading and saw her, he grinned his wide grin, the grin that buyers of his pornographic videos found so beguiling.

"Hi, Flo," he said.

"Hi," she answered.

"We have to stop meeting like this," Lonny said.

Flo smiled.

Lonny waved the magazine in her direction. "Last time I saw you here, you were on the cover of *Mulholland*, and now I'm *in* the magazine. Have you read this about me?"

"No."

"I'll treat you to a copy. They're trying to kick me out of my building because of this article."

"Really? What's the article about?"

"This manuscript I have that turns out to be the lost manuscript of Basil Plant. That famous writer who cooled a couple of years ago?"

"I always heard you had his manuscript, way back in the Viceroy Coffee Shop days. Curly told me that. Why would they kick you out of your apartment because of that?"

"The dame who wrote it makes it sound as if I turn tricks there, and the manager of the building has been dying to get rid of me for a long time, and he's using this magazine for an excuse. Like I'm giving his dump of a building a bad name."

"Do you?"

"Do I what?"

"Turn tricks in your apartment?"

"Hell, no, I don't. Just a couple of my regulars. Otherwise, I go out. Anyway, I want to get out of that kind of business. I'm over thirty now. Time to get serious about my life."

"Well, we've all got our problems, Lonny," said Flo, moving her shopping cart past him.

"I don't know where the hell I'm going to move to. I've lived in that bungalow ever since I came to this town."

Flo stopped and looked back at him. An idea came into her head, which she then rejected. "Good luck in finding a place," she said.

## Flo's Tape #24

"After Jules died, when Cyril Rathbone's article in Mulholland magazine came out about me, with my picture on the cover—oh God!—
Archbishop Cooning started to give these sermons every Sunday from
the pulpit of Saint Vibiana's. Oh, my, the things that he said about
him! Poor Jules. He said Jules corrupted my morals. When I was a kid
back in parochial school, we used to hear about Archbishop Cooning,
only he was just Bishop Cooning then. He was always carrying on
about virginity and stuff like that, saving yourself for marriage, ha ha
ha. We were all scared of him, but the nuns thought he was great,
especially Sister Andretta.

"Which brings me to Cyril. I always knew he was vile. Jules hated
him. And Pauline did too. And yet, I put my fate in his hands. That
was a mistake, one of my many mistakes. Any vestige of sympathy I
might have received from Pauline over Jules's estate, I lost when I said
that Cyril Rathbone was going to write my book. I mean, just from
that article he wrote about me in Mulholland, I should have known.
When facts failed, he just embellished his accounts with whatever
came into his head.

"I didn't tell him everything. Some of it I held back. The part about
Kippie Petworth, for instance. For about five minutes I had the upper
hand in the situation, with the information about Kippie that I had
learned from Lonny, that he was the one who killed Hector Paradiso.
But when I met with Pauline, I saw the look of terror in her eyes when
I approached the subject of Kippie. I mean, terror. And I backed down.
I didn't press my advantage. Like I felt sorry for Pauline Mendelson,
this rich lady who'd had every whim of her whole life attended to.

"I'd like to have had that out with Jules, about Kippie. That he hid
the kid out in my house, and I was there squeezing orange juice for
him. I don't think Jules should have done that to me. But people like
that, Jules and Pauline and their whole crowd, they really didn't think
the rules applied to them."

# 25

THE DEATH OF Jules Mendelson was a great sorrow to Dudley. He felt that never again would he be able to serve so great or so kind an employer. He had been generously provided for in Jules's will, and had also received a handwritten letter from Jules, delivered after his death by Sims Lord, asking him to stay on with Mrs. Mendelson at Clouds, for which there would be a substantial added remuneration for each year he remained in her employ. The muffled scandal of Jules Mendelson's love affair was a thing that Dudley chose to overlook, as if it had not happened. When pejorative remarks about the great man's behavior came to his ears, and a great many had, he faced his informer with a look of such hauteur that it silenced further discourse on the subject and caused the informer to retreat in shame. It was, he felt, up to him to see that there was no lessening of the established standards of the house.

When Philip Quennell, a half hour after leaving Flo March's house, rang the buzzer at the gates of Clouds and asked over the closed circuit television system if Mrs. Mendelson was at home, Dudley was quite put out. Although he knew that Mrs. Mendelson was fond of the young man who had become the boyfriend of Camilla Ebury, he felt that it was an impertinence for him to arrive at the gates of such a house as Clouds and ask to see her, without having called first to make an appointment. Dudley was not unaware that Jules Mendelson had despised Philip Quennell, and he joined his late employer in blaming Philip for causing the crack in the statue of the Degas ballerina.

"Is Mrs. Mendelson expecting you?" asked Dudley over the closed circuit system.

"She is not, no," replied Philip, looking up into the television camera.

"I really don't think it is convenient for her to see you, Mr. Quennell," said Dudley, taking upon himself the task of speaking for the lady of the house. Although he was in no way impolite, he allowed a mild note of annoyance to creep into the tone of his voice. "Perhaps you should telephone Mrs. Mendelson later today and try to make an appointment to see her."

Philip was not to be dissuaded so easily. "I realize I have come without calling first, Dudley, but could you please ask Mrs. Mendelson if she could see me for a few moments," said Philip, in an insistent voice.

Dudley, annoyed now, made no reply. He turned off the system and called Pauline on the intercom to tell her that Philip Quennell had arrived at the house without an appointment and wished to see her.

"Heavens," said Pauline over the intercom.

Although Dudley could not see Pauline, he imagined that there was a look of surprise on her face. "I've asked him to call you later to make an appointment," said Dudley.

"No, no, I'll see him, Dudley," said Pauline. "It's just that I have things to do. I have to meet with Jarvis in the greenhouse first, and then I'll be up. Have Mr. Quennell wait in the library."

Dudley, without saying anything welcoming to Philip, pushed the button that opened the gates, and Philip proceeded up the long driveway to the house. When his car pulled into the courtyard, Dudley opened the front door.

"Mrs. Mendelson has asked that you wait in the library, Mr. Quennell," said Dudley. He walked in that direction with Philip following him. "Mrs. Mendelson is with Jarvis in the greenhouse and will be up shortly."

He opened the door of the library and Philip went inside. As always, when he entered that room, Philip walked over to the fireplace and looked up at the painting of van Gogh's *White Roses*.

"Is there anything you'd like? Tea? Coffee? Drink?" asked Dudley, as he turned away and put into alignment a row of magazines on the fireplace bench.

"No, thank you. I'm fine," replied Philip, as if he were unaware of the butler's lack of civility.

After ten minutes, Pauline walked into the room through one of the French doors that opened onto the terrace. She was carrying a basket of roses that she had just cut in her garden. "Hello, Philip," she said.

Philip hopped to his feet. "Pauline, I know this is inexcusable, to drop in on you without calling first. I think I have upset your butler."

"Oh, don't worry about it," she said. "I hope you won't mind if I put these flowers in a vase while we talk." Without waiting for an answer, she took a blue-and-white Chinese vase and carried it into the lavatory, where she filled it with water. "I'm having a guest for lunch. I'm afraid I can't ask you to join us."

"Oh, I wouldn't dream of staying. It's extremely kind of you to see me. I'll only be a few minutes." He was beginning to feel nervous about his mission.

Pauline came out of the lavatory and took a pair of clippers from her basket and began to strip the roses and cut off the ends at an angle. "You haven't fought with Camilla again, have you? That's what I imagined," she said.

Philip smiled. "No."

Then she started to arrange the flowers in the vase, with the expertise of a person who had spent a lifetime arranging flowers in rare Chinese vases.

"It's not unlike your painting," said Philip, pointing to her arrangement.

"Mr. van Gogh's picture always influences me, but certainly you didn't come here to talk about flower arrangements," she said.

"No." He shook his head. "I came here to talk about Flo March."

Pauline's body stiffened at the mention of the woman's name. She put down her clippers for a moment, breathed heavily, and then picked them up again and went on with her arranging.

"Have you become her spokesperson?" she asked. The expression on her face had changed, as had the tone of her voice. "If so, please contact my lawyer, Sims Lord. I have no wish to hear any message from her."

"No, Pauline. I am not her spokesperson. Nor am I bringing you a message from her. Nor am I speaking in her defense. There is something I think you should know. Please listen to me."

"Does Camilla know you've come here, Philip?"

"No, she doesn't."

"What do you think she'd say if she knew?"

"She'd say that it was none of my business."

"She'd be right."

"She would be right, I know, just as you are right to be annoyed with me because I am interfering, but I anticipate a catastrophe if you don't listen to some reason, and it is worth your disapproval."

Pauline continued with her work. "I've always liked you, Philip. You must know that. I've been a good friend to you. But I think you have overstepped the bounds, and I would like you to leave my house and not come back."

Philip nodded. He walked toward the door of the library. As he opened it to leave, he turned back. "There are things she knows, Pauline."

"Please go," she said.

He continued to talk as if she had not spoken. "She is a desperate woman, and desperate women do desperate things. She is being manipulated by an unscrupulous man who despises you."

"And who is that?"

"Cyril Rathbone."

"Oh, puleeze," she said, laughing dismissively. "A ridiculous man. An impostor. He holds a grudge against me because I would never invite him to my house."

"You must understand that that makes him dangerous. He is writing a book in Flo March's name, called *Jules's Mistress*. Did you know that?"

Pauline's silence told that she had not known. "A whore's trick," she said, finally.

"Cyril Rathbone has taped her for forty hours," said Philip. "She has told him things that could be embarrassing to you."

Pauline wanted Philip to go, but she wanted him to stay also. "What sort of things?" she asked. In order not to show the interest she had in what he was saying, she continued to arrange the roses in the Chinese vase.

"I don't know. I haven't heard the tapes. I must ask you something, Pauline. And you don't have to answer me. In fact, don't answer me, because it is none of my business. But I'm still going to ask you. Does she know something about you? Or Hector? Or something about your son that no one else knows?"

"Is that what she said?"

"Alluded to, but didn't say."

Ashen-faced, Pauline turned away from Philip. "The woman is a liar. She would say anything."

"You're wrong, Pauline," said Philip. "That is just not so. She would prefer not to write this book. I can tell you that for a fact. She has told me that within the hour, but she is desperate. Put yourself in her place."

"Once you start paying off a blackmailer, it never ends. Anyone will tell you that," said Pauline.

"It's only what Jules promised her. It's less than what that ring on your finger is worth."

Without looking at her finger, she lifted up her left hand and pulled the ring back and forth with her right. Since Jules's death, Pauline had begun to wear his ring again, the huge de Lamballe diamond. When people commented on it, as they invariably did, she had taken to looking at it and smiling and then telling the story of how Jules had given it to her in Paris on the week she married him. The story was told with affection for the husband she had been married to for twenty-two years. People remarked later that there was no trace of bitterness in her toward Jules for the humiliation he had caused her. "It's so typical of Pauline. She's a lady through and through. After all, she is a McAdoo," her friends said.

"Good-bye, Philip," said Pauline.

"Good-bye, Pauline."

He knew that he had failed in his mission and lost the friendship of Pauline at the same time. Dismissed, he walked down the hallway toward the front hall. At the instant he arrived there, Dudley entered the hall from another of the six doors that opened onto it and went straight to open the front door. But he had not opened it for Philip's exit from the house, as Philip thought, but for the arrival of another guest who was standing there.

"Mrs. Mendelson is expecting me," said the man. He spoke with an English accent.

"Indeed, Lord St. Vincent," said Dudley.

Philip Quennell and Lord St. Vincent looked at each other as they passed. Dudley did not introduce them.


"I CAN'T UNDERSTAND it," said Flo. "People are interested, very interested in my book. There is great excitement. And then, suddenly, those very same people are no longer interested. We're never going to sell my book."

"You are entirely too quick to be defeated. You don't seem to understand how strong a position you are in, Flo," replied Cyril.

She shook her head. "I'm not in a strong position. There are forces working that have nothing to do with us."

"You dramatize."

"They're no longer interested because the person to whom they have to present the idea has already been gotten to by someone," said Flo.

"Oh, come on. Who has such power?"

"Friends of Pauline."

"What sort of friends?"

"One of the former Presidents who has dinner in her house."

"I don't believe that."

"Oh, yes."

THE INITIAL enthusiasm in publishing circles that Joel Zircon reported for Flo March's book, *Jules's Mistress*, seemed to abate overnight. Publishing companies that as recently as a week earlier had claimed they were ready to make a deal, once the first chapter and the outline were turned in—which they assured Joel was only a formality—were now difficult to get on the telephone.

"It's been a long fucking time since someone didn't return *my* telephone calls," complained Joel Zircon to Mona Berg, when they were having lunch. Joel had been given a promotion in the Berg Agency. "I can't understand it."

Mona, ever practical, had an instant solution. "Go the miniseries route," she suggested.

"Meaning?"

"You take your first chapter, and your outline, and you go to the networks, and say, 'I have here the first chapter and the outline of *Jules's Mistress*, Miss Flo March's book, which all the publishing companies are snapping at my heels for, but I have decided to skip that step and come straight to you while the story is still hot, hot, hot.' "

"Yeah?"

"Then you start teasing them a little. Drop the big names. Jules Mendelson. Pauline Mendelson. All those Washington people. And bank presidents. And cabinet ministers. You'll have them eating right out of your hand."

"*Former* cabinet ministers."

"All right, all right. *Former* cabinet ministers. Don't get picky with me when I'm doing your creative work for you."

"Sorry. Go on."

"Use words like billionaire, and high society, and mansion when you describe it. They always like that."

"Great idea, Mona. You're the best in the business."

"I know," said Mona.

□   □   □

"SOMETHING'S GONE OFF," said Joel.

"Meaning?"

"They're not going to do the miniseries."

"I thought you said they were going to buy it."

"They changed their mind."

"Why?"

"They said mistress stories are not commercial."

Flo pulled the covers up over her and turned toward the wall. "Somebody got to them," she said.

"What do you mean?"

"Just what I said. Somebody got to them."

"Oh, come on."

"You don't know these people the way I do."

JOEL tried the other two networks. There was enthusiasm at the lower echelons, followed by rejection when the idea was presented at the highest levels of programming.

"I must be losing my touch," said Joel to Cyril. "I thought if anything was sure-fire, this was it. I mean, it has all the elements."

"I have an idea," said Cyril.

"What's that?"

"Get Flo an appearance on the Amos Swank show. Have her tell her story to late-night America. Beautiful young girl with a story to tell can't get it published because the powerful of the country are conspiring against her."

"I'd stay up late to look at that."

"So would most of the country."

"Is Flo up to that?"

"What do you mean?"

"She don't look so steady to me."

"What do you mean?"

"She's falling apart again."

"Don't worry about Flo. I'll get her in shape."

THERE WAS GREAT excitement when the date was set for Flo to appear on "After Midnight," the Amos Swank show. She began to pull herself together again. She went each morning to the log cabin to attend the AA meetings. On the advice of Philip Quennell, she did not raise her hand and discuss her life anymore at the meetings.

"People know who you are now. They talk about you. They're not supposed to, but some of them do," said Philip. He did not tell her he suspected that Rose Cliveden had repeated everything she had said to either Pauline or Sims Lord. He only said, "Don't go out for coffee with Rose C."

"Why not?"

"She's a talker."

"But she was so nice to me."

She went to a gym and began to work out. She went back to Pooky to get her hair done, and to Blanchette to get her nails done. She brought Pooky back to her house with her to help her decide what she should wear on the night of her appearance. She had not been able to afford new clothes since Jules died, but Pooky assured her that the Chanels in her wardrobe were classics and timeless. He took the one they picked out for her to wear on the Amos Swank show to a dressmaker friend of his in the San Fernando Valley and had it short-ened to the latest length. "Wear the sapphire-and-diamond ring," he said. "That's all. Don't wear the canary diamond earrings."

"You're a pal, Pooky," she said.

Cyril took on the job of coaching her. He brought her video tapes of Amos Swank interviewing other celebrities to study. "Sit like this," he would say. Or, "Don't use that expression." Or, "If you talk about Lonny Edge, make sure you say porn star."

"I'm not going to talk about Lonny Edge, Cyril."

Flo was frightened.

A CALL TO Mona Berg from Freddie Galavant, who had once been an ambassador and was a close friend of people in high places, warned her that if her agency represented the book or miniseries of the whore Flo March, the IRS would never give her a moment's peace again. Mona called Joel Zircon into her office and said, "Drop it."

"But I almost have a deal."

"Drop it," repeated Mona.

Joel dropped it.

□   □   □

BECAUSE DOM BELCANTO, the ballad singer, was the main guest on the Amos Swank show that night, Arnie Zwillman gave up his nightly card game to stay home with Adrienne Basquette and watch his great friend. "I never miss one of Dom's appearances," he said to Adrienne. It was not until the opening credits, when all the guests were billboarded, that he realized that Flo March, "the girl who wrote the book that everyone is afraid to publish," as Amos Swank himself described her, was to be the final guest on the show, after Dom Belcanto, who was plugging his new album, *My Cigarette Burns Me*.

"That fucking broad's a loose cannon," said Arnie to Adrienne.

PAULINE MENDELSON, who led a busy life, almost never watched television, except for the news, and certainly never watched the Amos Swank show. "I never know who any of those people are," she used to say to Jules, about the roster of guests on the show, who were mostly the leads in television series she had never seen, or comics from Las Vegas, where she had never been. But she was to be the chairperson of a benefit for the Blind Children's Home of Los Angeles, which she agreed to do before Jules's death, and Dom Belcanto, who did "marvelous things" for charity, as his publicist was quick to point out, had agreed to sing at the dinner at the Century Plaza. So that night she watched, as she had to meet Dom the next day to discuss the benefit.

FLO HAD MET that afternoon with the researcher from the Amos Swank show, who had been most sympathetic with her story and assured her that her segment, although it was to be the last one of the show, could be the most popular, except for Dom Belcanto's.

"You mean that I won't get to talk with Amos Swank until we go on the air?" asked Flo. "Even get to meet him?"

"That's right," said Laurette. "Amos feels it's better for the spontaneity of the show when you meet on the air for the first time."

"How will he know what to ask me if we don't talk first?"

"That's what I'm here for," said Laurette. "I've read Cyril Rathbone's piece in *Mulholland*, and I've read your first chapter, and the outline. Dynamite. Really dynamite. We talk through your story, you and I, and then I go and talk it through with Amos, and decide what parts are the most interesting, and then I write the questions, and they're put on the teleprompter," said Laurette.

"That's how they do it? Really?"

"And there'll be a large audience tonight because of Dom Belcanto. The whole country will be watching, believe me. What a draw that guy is," she said.

"I don't want to talk about Mr. Mendelson's stepson," said Flo.

"No, no, no, not to worry," said the researcher.


"DO ME A FAVOR, Cyril. Wait outside somewhere. You make me nervous," said Flo. She was in the chair in the makeup room.

"I just wanted to stress about the letter that Jules wrote you leaving you the million dollars," said Cyril. "Did you give them the Xerox of it, so they can show it on the monitor?"

"Please, Cyril. I went through everything with Laurette this afternoon. She has the letter."

The makeup artist, Jess, placed Kleenex all around the collar of her Chanel blouse so that the pancake wouldn't come off and cause a stain. The makeup artist admired her hair. "I never saw such beautiful hair," he said.

"Thank you," said Flo. "Everyone's so nice here. I can't get over it."

"We've been together a long time here on the show. It's really like a family," said Jess.

"Do you think I should kiss Amos on both cheeks when I make my entrance?" Flo asked.

"How well do you know Amos?"

"I've never met him," said Flo.

"No, I wouldn't kiss him then."

"That's what I thought. I saw Roseanne kiss him when she went on, so I thought I'd ask," said Flo.

Flo was very nervous as the time approached, but she was also very excited. She had always wanted to be in show business. She loved being in the makeup room, having Jess work on her. She loved sitting in the green room talking with the other guests who were going to be on the show. She wished she had pursued her career in show business. She used to want to be no more than the second lead in a situation comedy, but she felt now that she could do more important roles. It occurred to her that maybe this appearance could lead to some acting jobs. She thought about getting new pictures taken. And an agent. She would need an agent. Maybe Joel Zircon would handle her as an actress as well as an author.

"Miss March?"

"Yes?" She looked up to see a page in a dark blue uniform. "Is it time to go on the set? I'm so nervous."

"Would you come with me, Miss March?" said the page.

"Thank you."

"Mr. Marcuzzi would like to see you in his office," said the page.

"Who?"

"Mr. Marcuzzi. The executive producer."

"Oh, my," said Flo.

"He's in the West Building. On the fifteenth floor."

"Is there enough time before I go on?"

"There must be. He runs the show."

She followed the page through the corridors leading from the studios in the East Building to the executive offices in the West Building. The page stepped aside as she got into the elevator and then pushed the button for the fifteenth floor.

When the elevator doors opened, Flo got out. Cyril Rathbone was standing there. He stared at her.

"Cyril, are you supposed to see Mr. Marcuzzi too?" asked Flo.

"They canceled the segment," said Cyril.

"What?" she gasped.

"You heard me."

"I don't believe it. Laurette spent two hours at my house this afternoon. We went over everything. They just did my makeup."

"And then they canceled you," said Cyril.

"But Mr. Marcuzzi wants to see me."

"He wants to see you to tell you you're not going on, that's why he wants to see you. Do you know what he said? He said, 'Amos don't like guests who write books. He don't read books. He likes big stars, like Dom Belcanto, or girls with big tits, like Roseanne, or animal acts.' You don't need to hear it twice," said Cyril. The annoyance in his voice was with her for her failure rather than the failure of the Amos Swank show.

Flo felt faint. Beneath her theatrical makeup, she had become ashen-faced. She felt that if she couldn't sit down, she was going to fall down. Opposite the elevator bank were three windows with deep sills. She walked over to one of the windows and leaned against the sill. "Somebody made a call again," she said. She spoke more to herself than to him. She stared out the window. Her face revealed an awareness of the hopelessness of her situation. She was deep in thought at what had just befallen her, but there was no aid from Cyril for her distress. To Cyril, she had become an unimportant person, and therefore her thoughts were unimportant thoughts.

She looked down, out the open window. Fifteen floors below, the traffic on Ventura Boulevard raced by. She leaned slightly out the window and stared down. Thoughts of her mother filled her head, moving from welfare hotel to welfare hotel with all her worldly possessions in torn shopping bags.

In that instant Cyril saw the possibilities of the thought that was forming in Flo's mind. He resisted his initial impulse to reach out and grab her. "I was there. I tried to stop her," he would say to the police. "I screamed, 'Don't, Flo! Don't!' But she eluded me."

"Jump," said Cyril behind her, in a low voice. "Go ahead, Flo. Do it."

Flo slowly turned her head to him, and their eyes met. He looked eager and excited, and was breathing heavily. "It's all over for you," he said, talking rapidly, in a low but urgent voice. "You have nothing to live for. Jules is gone. In the long run, he forgot about you. You're broke. You're never going to have any money again. No one wants to see you. No one wants to know you. Do it. Jump, Flo. It'll be all over the papers. It will be a sensation. People will remember you for years, Flo. Death can be a beautiful experience. Go on, Flo. Go on."

Flo stared at him, transfixed. He nodded at her. She looked back at the street below and knelt on the windowsill with one leg, still looking down. She then raised her other leg to the sill. Perched now, she stared down. The traffic on Ventura Boulevard raced below her, the headlights and taillights mesmerizing her. She leaned out farther on the ledge.

"Go on," whispered Cyril, from behind her. "Do it." He repeated and repeated the words as if he were arriving at an orgasm, and she, his submissive accomplice, obliged in the act as she moved farther and farther out on the ledge. She raised her arms.

At that moment the elevator stopped on their floor, announced by a bell and the opening of the door. "Going down," called out a passenger from inside.

The spell was broken. Flo leapt backward onto the floor. Pale, almost fainting, she stared up at Cyril Rathbone and slowly pulled herself away from him, with fear in her eyes, like a dog that had been whipped by its master. Tears streamed down her cheeks. She tried to raise herself from the floor, but her legs were too weak to rise.

"Going down," called out the voice from the elevator again, and the door started to close.

"*Hold it!*" screamed Flo. She half rose to her feet and ran into the elevator. Cyril followed her. Inside, a janitor with a trolley of cleaning utensils nodded to them. Flo held on to the railing of the elevator for balance. Cyril began to speak to Flo, but she turned away from him. With shaking hands, she wiped the tears from her face and, in an automatic gesture, unscrewed her lip gloss and ran the stick over her lips without looking into a mirror. The elevator descended in silence.

"I'll get the car," said Cyril when they got out.

Flo shook her head. "Never mind. I'll get a taxi," she replied.

"No, no, darling Flo. Don't be silly." His voice had returned to its florid tonality, as if what had just happened between them had not happened.

"Yes." She leaned against the wall, exhausted.

"Would you like me to get you a glass of water?" he asked, nervously.

"Why did you do that to me?" She barked out the sentence at him, as if it were one word.

"It was a joke, Flo. I was kidding. You know I didn't mean it."

She stared at him. "That's some joke, Cyril. That's really funny. Amos Swank could have gotten a lot of mileage out of that bit of comic business." She walked away from him.

"Flo," he called after her.

She stopped and turned toward him. "Stay away from me, Cyril," she said. She pointed her finger at him for emphasis, and repeated, "Stay away."

THE IRANIAN taxi driver from Valley Cab kept looking at her in his rearview mirror. She looked familiar to him. He thought she might be a television star from one of the series at the studio where he had picked her up, but he couldn't remember which one. She gave him her address on Azelia Way off Coldwater Canyon, in Beverly Hills. The address had a familiar ring to him. He looked at her in the mirror

again, but she was deep in thought. He watched her as she opened
her bag and took out her wallet. She kept looking at the meter and
then looking down at the money in her hands, probably counting to
see if she had enough.

"Driver," she said, "when you get to Sunset and Coldwater, you
can let me out. I'll walk the rest of the way."

"You can't walk, Miss. It's pitch dark, and it's almost two miles up
Coldwater to the Azelia Way turnoff."

"Listen, driver. I don't have enough money with me to go any
farther. I didn't realize that when I got into the cab. I'm very sorry. I
was supposed to get a ride home with the person who brought me to
the studio, but something came up and I had to take a cab, and I
didn't realize I didn't have enough money with me."

The driver snapped his fingers. "The Chateau Marmont, on Sunset
Boulevard. That's it, right?"

"What?"

"Didn't I drive you once from a steak house in the Valley to the
Chateau Marmont? You were crying and upset about something?"

Flo smiled. "And you're the same driver? You seem to catch me on
my peak nights."

"You tipped me ten bucks that night. I never forgot that. Most
people, it's fifteen percent of the fare, if that, no more. You didn't
even think about it. You paid, and then you handed me ten bucks. I
thought, this lady has class. I'm not letting you out on the street, lady.
I'm taking you all the way home." He turned off the meter. "This
ride's on me."

"That's very nice of you," said Flo.

"Some private detective came after me a few days later. Did you
know that? Wanted to know where I took you. I had it all on my call
sheet. This address on Azelia Way, where you first told me to take
you, and then that was crossed off, and the Chateau Marmont was
written in."

Flo looked at the driver's permit in the cab and saw his name.
"Hussein? Is that right?"

"Hussein. That's my name."

"I want you to know I really appreciate this, Hussein. Not too many
classy guys around these days."

When the cab turned right off Coldwater Canyon to Azelia Way, a
car came down toward them. As it passed, Flo looked out the window

and saw that it was a gold Rolls-Royce. Two men were seated in the front seat. They did not look in her direction. A chill went through her. As the cab proceeded up the hill toward her driveway, Flo looked out the back window toward the Rolls.

"You wouldn't do me a favor, would you, Hussein?" she asked, as the cab pulled into her driveway.

"What's that?"

"Would you just wait here until I get in my house?"

"I'll go to the door with you," he said. He got out and opened her door, as if he were a chauffeur rather than a cabdriver.

At the front door, as Flo took out her keys to unlock the door, she saw that the door was pulled to, but open.

"Maybe you forgot to close your door when you went out," said Hussein.

"Maybe," said Flo. She pushed it open.

"Want me to go first?" asked Hussein.

"Would you mind?"

Inside the house, Flo looked around her. Everything seemed to be in order. She looked in her kitchen, in her unused maid's room, and finally in her bedroom. She opened one of the drawers of the wardrobe in her dressing room and felt behind some boxes for the Louis Vuitton jewel case that she was photographed carrying out of the Meurice Hotel in Paris during the fire. When she opened it, she was relieved to see that her yellow diamond earrings, which she considered to be her last gift from Jules Mendelson, were still there.

"Everything okay?" asked Hussein.

"Seems to be," said Flo.

"Are you going to call the police?" he asked.

"No, nothing seems to be missing. I want to thank you a lot. I really appreciate this. If you give me your address, I'll send you the money after I go to the bank tomorrow."

"This was on me," said Hussein. "Good luck to you. You seem to have a lot of difficulties in your life for such a young lady."

Flo smiled. "Good luck to you, Hussein."

When she was alone, she put the chain lock and dead bolt on the front door. She walked through her house and pulled down the shades and blinds and closed all the curtains. She turned on every light. In her bedroom, she began to undress, taking off the Chanel suit that Pooky had thought was the right one for her to wear on the

Amos Swank show. She sat down at her dressing table and rubbed cold cream on her face to remove the television makeup that Jess had been putting on her when the page asked her to go up to Mr. Marcuzzi's office. As the thought of what she had almost done on the fifteenth floor of the West Building in the Valley Studios went through her mind, she felt faint again. She went into the bar and looked for a long time at the gallon bottle of Soave from the Hughes Market. She pulled out the cork and then emptied the wine in the sink, turning her head away so that she would not be attracted by the heady aroma. Then she reached into the refrigerator and took out a can of Diet Coke. She opened the tab on the top and started to drink it from the can. Looking at herself in the mirrored wall of the bar, she remembered how Jules had hated her to drink from the can and poured the liquid into one of her Steuben glasses. "I'm still trying to do things your way, Jules," she said into the mirror. "And it's getting me absolutely nowhere."

As she turned to walk back into the living room, her stockinged foot stepped on a hard object. Looking down, she noticed Cyril's tape recorder on the floor of the bar. She leaned down and picked it up. It had been smashed with a hammer. The microcassette that had been in it was gone.

SHE COULD not sleep. She brought the pillows from her bed into the living room and lay on her gray satin sofa, with a package of cigarettes and a few magazines. Every time she heard a car go up Azelia Way, she stopped to listen until she was sure it had passed her driveway.

She picked up *Mulholland.* There was Hortense Madden's article about the missing manuscript of the late writer Basil Plant, which had been located, possibly, at the bungalow on Cahuenga Boulevard of Lonny Edge, the pornography star.

She looked at her watch. It was two o'clock in the morning. She knew it wasn't too late to call. She wondered if he would even be home yet. She dialed the number.

*"It's Lonny. I can't come to the phone now. Leave your name and number, even if you think I already have it, and the time you called, and I will get back to you as soon as possible. Wait for the beep."*

She did not wish to leave her name on his machine. Just as she started to hang up, she heard Lonny's voice. "Hello? Hello?"

"Lonny?" she said.

"Ina Rae?" asked Lonny.

"No, it's Flo."

"Flo?" She could tell that he did not recognize her.

"From the Viceroy. From the newsstand at the Hughes Market."

"Flo, my God. How are you? I was expecting someone else."

"I gather. Ina Rae. Who's Ina Rae?"

"Oh, don't ask."

There was a silence.

"Are you all right, Flo?" asked Lonny.

"Sure."

"What's up? It's two o'clock in the morning."

"Are you still looking for a place to live?"

"Yeah. I sure am. They're kicking me out of here. I was gonna move in with this friend of mine, Ina Rae, but it's not gonna work out. Why?"

"How much are you prepared to pay?"

"Six, seven hundred a month. Why?"

"You can't get much for six or seven hundred a month these days, Lonny. Can you swing a thousand?"

"Maybe. Why? Do you know a place?"

"I have a maid's room in my house you could move into, as a temporary measure," she said.

"Really? You mean at your house in Beverly Hills?" There was excitement in his voice. "That would be great."

"Now, listen. No monkey business between us. No turning tricks in my house. No dirty videos. Strictly a roommate proposition. And two months' rent paid in advance."

"Why would you want a guy with a reputation like mine living in your house for, Flo? Are you that broke?"

"Yes. I'm that broke, Lonny. They're about to turn off my telephone."

"Why do I think there's more to this two A.M. call than that you're broke," said Lonny.

"Because I'm scared, Lonny. I'm scared to be alone here."

## Flo's Tape #25

"I was like a feather in the breeze. Except for Phil, this friend of mine from AA, I didn't know who to believe. I really had nowhere to turn. I suppose that's how I ended up with Lonny for a housemate. Lonny Edge, imagine. The thing is about Lonny, he's actually a nice guy, but he's in a line of work that most people don't have much truck with, at least publicly. My God, the stories he used to tell me about some of those famous people he visited in Bel Air and Holmby Hills, the kind of people you'd read about in the papers as being oh-so-proper. Lonny told me everything about Kippie and what happened that night at Hector's. It was all about money again. Kippie needed money, and his mother wouldn't give it to him, and neither would Jules, apparently. So he went to Hector's and surprised him with Lonny. I mean, what are those people hanging on to all that money for? Is it worth it, to cause all the trouble they cause, just to hang on to all the money?

"Probably the only smart thing I ever did was to go to the Wells Fargo Bank the morning after Cyril tried to talk me into jumping out the window of the Valley Studios and get the tapes and bring them back here to the house."

# 26

CYRIL RATHBONE, awakening, remembered with regret what he had said and done the night before. He knew only too well that the impulse that had driven him to seize the moment of Flo March's despair and urge her to jump out of the window on the fifteenth floor of the administration building of the Valley Studios—which seemed logical to him at the time, promising him personal headlines as well as a spectacular finish for his book—had severed forever her association with him. He was not able to erase from his mind the combined look of fear and hatred on her face when she had told him to stay away from her. Even so, he tried to reach her by telephone and then by a Federal Express letter, explaining his act, in a revised version of the facts and thoughts that had flashed through his mind at the time; but there were no replies, and he knew there never would be. He was history, as far as Flo March was concerned.

The thirty-nine hours of microcassette tapes that she had recorded were in a safety deposit box at the Wells Fargo Bank in Beverly Hills, for which they both had keys. When he went to the bank several days after the evening of her dismissal from the Amos Swank show, he found that the safety deposit box was empty. Without Flo, his dreams of expanding his career from social columnist to book writer were dashed.


IN HIS COLUMN, Cyril Rathbone began writing of the widowed Pauline as Pauline, Mrs. Mendelson, the sort of style used for dowager peeresses of the realm. Pauline had started to go out again in the city, appearing at small dinners of close friends and at cultural events, but at all times she avoided the cameras of the social and fashion press, which had followed her for so many years. "Pauline, Mrs. Mendelson, arrived for the opening of the ballet after the curtain had gone up. These days she guards her privacy," wrote Cyril in one column.

Although it appeared to be an accidental meeting, it was no accident that Cyril Rathbone should happen to pass Pauline Mendelson on Bedford Drive at the precise moment she left Pooky's salon, after having had her hair done and nails manicured, beauty chores that were usually performed at her home. That morning at breakfast at the Viceroy Coffee Shop, Pooky had told Blanchette, the manicurist, that Mrs. Mendelson would be coming into the shop at eleven and, no matter what, she must not be kept waiting, even if it meant canceling the previous appointment, as she had to leave the salon by eleven-fifty in order to be back at Clouds for a lunch she was giving for a visiting ambassador. Pauline Mendelson was the kind of customer for whom such adjustments were made. Cyril, in the booth behind the hair stylist, could not help but perk up his ears.

At eleven forty-five Pauline's chauffeur, Jim, parked the Bentley directly in front of the entrance of Pooky's salon and stood holding the car door open for her. Exactly at eleven-fifty the doorman opened the red lacquer door of the hairdressing salon, and Pauline emerged, in the rushed manner of a celebrity. Her hair was covered with a scarf, and she walked with rapid strides across the sidewalk, looking neither left nor right, hugging her bag to her, as both the doorman and the chauffeur tipped their hats. Cyril, carrying a briefcase in one hand, affected a rapid walk himself, looking neither left nor right, as if he were on his way from one important meeting to another and time was of the essence. Midway in the sidewalk they collided, and both almost lost their balance. Pauline's bag fell to the ground. Cyril's briefcase fell to the ground.

"Good God," he said, with a trace of annoyance in his florid English voice, as if the fault were not his own. He picked up his briefcase.

Jim, the chauffeur, rushed forward and grabbed Pauline's arm to keep her from falling, and then reached down to pick up her bag. "Are you all right, Mrs. M.?" he asked.

"Yes, Jim, fine. The thing is, I wasn't looking where I was going." She turned to apologize to the man. "I'm terribly sorry," she said. "I'm afraid it was my fault."

"No, no, please," said Cyril. "Forgive me. My mind was a hundred miles away. Did I hurt you? Oh, my word, Pauline. I didn't realize it was you."

Startled, she nodded in a distant manner when she realized that the man she had collided with was Cyril Rathbone.

"This is too extraordinary," he said. His voice took on its psychic tone of wonderment. "I have been thinking of you. But then, as I'm sure you know, there are no accidents, even though we seem to have had a minor collision." He smiled, as if he had made a joke.

Pauline did not wait for him to continue. She proceeded over to her car and entered the backseat. As Jim was about to close the door, Cyril stepped over, held it open, and leaned into the car. No such proximity to her would come his way again, and he knew it. "It is urgent that I speak with you, Pauline. Urgent."

"I'm afraid that I am terribly late," she said, retreating into the far corner of the Bentley.

He wanted to say, "Yes, I know, the ambassador is coming for lunch," but he didn't. Instead he said, "You will be very grateful to me for what I have to tell you. It is of the utmost importance to you."

She looked at him, without replying.

"It concerns Miss March. I have heard her tapes," he said.

Pauline shook her head, not wanting to listen. Jim, the chauffeur, moved around the driver's side of the car and opened the front door. Pauline did not want Jim to hear what Cyril Rathbone was about to say.

"I'm in a frightful hurry," she said, holding up her hand at the same time to forestall any further conversation.

"So am I," he replied. "I'm late for an appointment." He patted his briefcase, as if it contained state secrets. "But you must hear me out."

"We'll go straight home, Jim," she said to her chauffeur.

"Please, Pauline," insisted Cyril.

She spoke without looking at him. "Call Miss Maple, my husband's secretary. Ask her to set up an appointment."

FOR NEARLY three decades Arnie Zwillman, about whom there was much media speculation, had managed to elude the photographers, journalists, and investigative reporters of the *New York Times*, the *Wall Street Journal*, the *Los Angeles Times*, and the *Los Angeles Tribunal*. As story after story appeared over the years on mob activities in trucking, in Las Vegas, in the record business, in the motion picture industry, in drugs, in prostitution, in pornography, in everything, his name came up time and time again, but always as a mysterious figure, an éminence grise, rarely seen, never photographed, inaccessible in the extreme, except for occasional forays to the Friars Club for cards, which were his passion. His social life was limited to his current wife, whom, with the diminishment of desire, he changed with regularity every seven years, and to the company of such celebrated cronies as Dom Belcanto, the ballad singer, and Amos Swank, the late-night talk show host, and their current wives.

It was to Amos Swank that Arnie Zwillman had made the call the night before, after his program was on the air, during the first commercial, to request that his last guest of the evening, Flo March, be dropped from the lineup.

"Dump the cunt," he said.

"Roseanne? Dump Roseanne?" replied Amos, horrified by the thought.

"Not Roseanne. Flo March."

"That puts me in a real bind, Arnie," said Amos. "We're on the air. I can't get a replacement."

"Tell Dom I said to sing a few more numbers," answered Arnie. "The public's tuning in to see him, not the March broad."

Later, when Arnie listened to the only tape that had been found in Flo March's house, his face was a study in displeasure. The encounter that had taken place between Jules Mendelson and him in the den of Casper Stieglitz's house, while the rest of the party was watching a movie, was recounted in detail, as told to Flo by Jules himself. The words "laundering money" appeared frequently, as well as the methods for doing so during Jules's tenure in Brussels, as suggested by Arnie to Jules.

It was Arnie's firm belief that only the unexpected interruption of Pauline Mendelson, who had been offended by a lesbian reference made by the drugged Casper Stieglitz, had prevented the deal from being solidified, there and then.

"Christ, this March dame should have been a secretary. She must have taken down everything Jules told her in shorthand while she was taking down his pants to blow him," said Arnie. His remark caused loud laughter in the room, but Arnie Zwillman was in no mood for laughter. He raised his hand and the laughter curdled. "Where's the rest of the tapes? There's supposed to be forty hours. This is only an hour. I want to hear the rest of the Kippie stuff."

"That's all we could find," said Jo Jo, his aide.

"They're probably in some safety deposit box. Get that fruitcake, Cyril Rathbone. Scare the shit out of him," said Arnie.

"IT'S MR. RATHBONE. I am expected," said Cyril, sounding more English than ever, as he peered up into the camera of the closed circuit television at the gates of Clouds. Dudley, looking back at him in the monitor in the butler's pantry, was not kindly disposed toward the writer from *Mulholland* magazine, after what he considered to be the shameful and traitorous article he had written about Jules Mendelson and the woman called Flo March, an article that he knew had caused mirthful glances and suppressed laughter in the butlers' pantries of the other important houses of the city. Dudley went so far as to express disapproval to the lady of the house when she had told him that Cyril Rathbone was expected, but Pauline Mendelson had merely shrugged and not replied, as if it were an occasion over which she had no control.

As Cyril drove up the long driveway of the Mendelson estate, turning right to enter the magical part that could not be viewed through the gates at the entrance, his heart beat faster. It had always been a disappointment to his editor, Lucia Borsodi, that he did not have access to the great house. It had not mattered to her that no other social columnist in the city had access either, or that the late Jules Mendelson loathed social publicity. Lucia Borsodi told him over and over that in New York, Dolly De Longpre, the famed doyenne of the breed, had access to all the best houses of both the old and new society, and even, when she visited Los Angeles, as she did once a year, was invited to dine at the Mendelsons', which was an annual rebuff to Cyril. But, finally, he had arrived at the private and exclusive estate that for years had been his dream to enter.

As he drove his car into the courtyard, he gazed ahead with joy. The vast house before him was everything he had imagined it was going to be. The front door opened before he reached it, and he walked into the hallway, without even looking at Dudley, drawn to the sight of the sweeping stairway and the six Monet paintings ascending upward, as if it were a magnet.

"Oh, marvelous, marvelous," he said, looking up, looking left, looking right, at the treasures everywhere, forming sentences in his mind of the descriptions he would write. Catching sight of himself in a Chippendale mirror over a console table, he was pleased with his smart appearance, in his well-cut seersucker suit, blue shirt, and pink tie.

Dudley, who refrained from offering a greeting, led him down the corridor into the cool shadows of the library. Outside it was very hot, but blue-and-white-striped awnings kept the sun from the beautiful room. Immediately responding to the luxury, Cyril felt comfortable. To the right, over the mantel, was van Gogh's *White Roses*. He wanted to stop and look, but the butler opened the doors to the terrace and went outside. "Mrs. Mendelson is cutting roses in the garden," he said. He raised a hand and pointed toward a large sculpture of a sleeping woman. "Beyond the Henry Moore, to the left, is the rose garden." He then turned and reentered the house.

Cyril felt disappointment. He loathed the sun. His fair skin was of the variety that burned and blistered. He would have much preferred to have his meeting with Pauline in the cool library, sitting on fine chairs beneath fine paintings, holding cool drinks in fine glasses. He would have liked a tour, room by room, antique by antique, painting by painting, as he had so often heard from Hector Paradiso honored guests were sometimes treated to, if they expressed interest in the treasures of the house.

The outdoor locale had been Pauline's idea. Whatever the disagreeable man had to say to her, she wished it to be out of the earshot of Dudley and the other servants. As Cyril walked across the acre of lawn, he wished he had brought his straw hat to protect his sensitive skin from the strong rays of the sun. At the same time, he noticed and memorized the extraordinary pieces of sculpture that Jules Mendelson had collected. "Beyond the Henry Moore," the butler had said. He wanted to remember that.

Pauline's back was to him when he saw her. She was leaning over to clip an enormous pink rose, which she then held to her nose for an instant. She wore gardening gloves and a large straw hat. On the lawn beside her was a basket in which were several dozen roses of different hues of red and pink. He watched her as she waved away a wasp that buzzed too closely to her. Even unobserved, he noticed that she retained her elegance, and the picture of her was pleasing to his eye.

"Pauline," he called out, excitedly, as if he were a guest at a garden party approaching his hostess, rather than the almost author of a salacious book about Pauline's late husband and her late husband's mistress. Although he knew she must have heard him, as the distance between them was not excessive, she did not turn around immediately, and he called out again, "Pauline."

Pauline had not turned around because she could not bear it when the feline old Etonian, who never actually went to Eton, called her by her first name. She felt the intimacy to be an impertinence, but she did not correct him. Instead, she called him Mr. Rathbone.

"Hello, Mr. Rathbone," she said, bestowing on him the overly gracious smile that people like her reserved for underlings who had overstepped the bounds. He recognized her look and refrained from requesting her to call him Cyril. Nor did he attempt to kiss her on the cheek, as he had at Casper Stieglitz's party when she pulled back from him and said she had a cold. There were garden chairs by the pavilion, and she indicated with a gesture that they would sit there.

"This is all very beautiful, Pauline," he said, looking around at the house and grounds.

"Thank you," she replied.

"The Maillol sculpture is to die for," he said.

She nodded at the mention of the sculpture that had been her husband's favorite, but she made no attempt to apprise him of the fact that it had been her husband's favorite, nor did she attempt to engage in hostess talk, as it had been he who insisted he had urgent information to impart to her. To indicate to him that the moments between them were to be brief, she neither removed her gardening gloves nor settled back in her chair.

Although such signals as she gave him caused him to be nervous in her presence, he adopted a languid posture when he seated himself, as if he were used to such afternoon tête-à-têtes in the rose garden at Clouds.

"Such a hot day," he said. With his hand, he shielded his eyes from the sun and wished there were an umbrella to pull up for shade.

"Yes," she agreed.

"I long to see your famous yellow phalaenopsis orchid plant," he said.

"Mr. Rathbone, please," she replied, closing her eyes and waving her hand. "No garden club tours today. You spoke on the street of a matter of urgency. Let us deal with that matter and forget about my yellow phalaenopsis."

Even then, holding all the aces as he did, he would have tossed them aside to become her acolyte, the way Hector Paradiso had been, but he realized she was not to be won over by his compliments or charm. Rebuffed, he smiled in defeat. "As I often write in my column, Pauline, there is no one tougher than a tough society lady," he said.

"True," she agreed.

"You've never liked me, have you, Pauline?" he asked.

"With very good reason, Mr. Rathbone. But, again, let us get to this matter of urgency." She pulled back her glove and consulted her watch, with no attempt to disguise the gesture.

He ignored her request. "In a moment. There's something I would like to straighten out first. Was it because you didn't like me that I was not asked to deliver the eulogy at Hector's funeral last year?"

"Oh, for God's sake," she replied impatiently.

"You know, don't you, that it should have been I who gave the eulogy." He tapped his forefinger on his chest to indicate himself. "After all, I was his best friend."

Pauline did not respond, but she had the ability to speak without uttering a word, merely raising her eyebrows, and make her meaning very plain.

"After you, I mean," Cyril said quickly, correcting himself. "That ambasssador who gave the eulogy hardly knew him. I always felt it was you who prevented me from giving the eulogy."

"Was there not a morals charge pending against you at the time, involving a beating, or something?" asked Pauline.

Cyril, surprised, blushed deeply and said nothing.

Pauline continued. "I seem to remember that my husband was informed of that fact. Archbishop Cooning was already of two minds as to whether or not he should officiate at the funeral Mass, despite the fact that Rose Cliveden had contributed a hundred thousand dollars to the refurbishing of the archbishop's residence in Hancock Park. Under those circumstances, your candidacy as eulogist was considered by the planners of the funeral, of which I was not one, to be, uh, unseemly. I think that was the word that was used at the time. Unseemly."

Cyril's silence continued.

"There is a bee on your shoulder," he said, finally.

"It's not a bee. It's a wasp," she said, brushing it off her shoulder with her gloved hand.

"Pesky creatures," said Cyril, waving his hand frantically to discourage the wasp from coming in his direction. He did not like to say, for fear of appearing unmasculine, that he was terrified of wasps. "Should we not go inside?" he asked.

"It's gone," she said, unconcerned. "Tell me, Mr. Rathbone. As we seem to be playing the truth game, were you the one who sent me, anonymously, the photograph of my husband and Miss March fleeing the fire in the Meurice Hotel from the Paris newspaper?"

"Yes, I thought you should know," he said.

"Oh, I see. You did it out of kindness, you mean?" she asked. "Your reputation for duplicity clings to you, Mr. Rathbone." Reserve, propriety, and good manners were born within her, but she made no attempt to disguise the disdain in her voice.

"I felt you should know," he repeated.

"Of course, you did," she said, with no lessening of the edge in her tone.

"Hector saw the picture. I sent it to him, but he didn't have the nerve to show it to you," said Cyril.

"Hector was a gentleman. One of the many differences between you and that fine man," she replied.

Smarting now from her contempt, he no longer tried to be winning. "There is a book being written about you and your husband, as I am sure you have heard," he said.

"It would be hard not to hear about it, as you have covered it extensively in your column," she replied.

"I have heard the tapes that Miss March has recorded," he said. "There are forty hours recorded thus far."

Pauline folded her gloved hands.

He began to pour out to her the story of her husband's long affair with the former waitress, sparing nothing, feeling no constraint. He knew now he could never make her his friend, so there was no longer any point in constraint. He leaned forward toward her and hissed out her husband's history, truths and untruths intermingled, wanting only to wound.

"When Jules left all the parties early, right after dinner, leaving Hector to bring you home, because he had to be up so early in the morning to take his calls from his offices in Europe, he really got up so early because he wanted to see Flo, because he needed to knock off a quick piece on the way to work, to hold him over until his regular visit in the afternoon. His sexual appetite was insatiable. He reappeared on her doorstep every afternoon at a quarter to four, without fail, no matter what the business crisis, first things first. In the several hours he spent with her each afternoon, before returning home to you for his glass of wine in your sunset room, to discuss the events of the day, before you dressed for dinner to attend whatever the party of the evening was, he came three and sometimes four times, each time varying the position. He could not get enough of the woman. It's all on the tapes, Pauline."

Pauline sank back in the wrought iron chair.

"There is more," said Cyril.

She looked at him. "How much more?"

"Much more."

"Are you going to make me pull this out of you, sentence by sentence, Mr. Rathbone? Or are you going to tell me? After all, that was what you came here for, was it not?"

"It is simply that it is indelicate," he said. The insincerity in his voice was so apparent that he heard it himself.

"Then be indelicate. I'm sure it will not be your first indelicacy."

"You see, I have the forty hours of microcassettes. Actually, I mean that I have thirty-nine of the forty hours. There was one cassette left in my tape recorder which is still in Miss March's house. She seemed very private about it. Something about our mutual friend Hector's death. Even to me, she would not reveal the entire contents."

Beneath the wide brim of her straw hat, Pauline closed her eyes. She was determined not to allow Cyril Rathbone to witness a tear escaping.

"For a price, I would be able to turn everything over to you," he said.

"So that's what this matter of urgency is about," she said. "I should have known. Blackmail."

"Your son, your bad-boy son, Kippie, isn't that his name? It has something to do with your son," said Cyril.

Pauline raised her eyebrows in an arch of displeasure meant to disguise the fear that she felt, but she did not trust herself to speak, as that fear might have become apparent. Another wasp buzzed near her. She looked down at her shoulder and, with her gloved hand, flicked it off her in a nervous fashion that had nothing to do with the wasp but everything to do with the words that were coming out of the mouth of Cyril Rathbone.

He leaned forward toward her again, aware that finally he had succeeded in reaching her vulnerable point. A smile twisted his lips as he continued elaborating on the details. "Apparently—this is all according to Flo March, of course—your son, while on temporary leave from his drug rehabilitation center in France, was arrested in the Los Angeles airport for carrying drugs. He needed ten thousand dollars immediately. You refused him, apparently. As did the gangster Arnie Zwillman, with whom your son enjoys a peculiar sort of friendship. And so he went late that night to visit your best friend, Hector, catching poor Hector, apparently, in the middle of a sexual act of a deviant nature with a well-known video star of the pornographic variety named Lonny Edge, whom Hector picked up in a gay bar in West Hollywood called Miss Garbo's on the way home from a very swanky party in your house that you declined to let me cover for my column. Incidentally, of no moment here, Mr. Lonny Edge has subsequently become the housemate of Flo March, to help cover the destitute woman's living expenses, since you saw fit to cancel the bequests made to her by your husband. At any rate, your son, Kippie, was so hard-pressed for the ten thousand dollars that you would not give him that he offered himself sexually to your friend, Hector, although that sort of thing was not remotely his inclination. When Hector refused, there was a bit of a scuffle, apparently, and Hector produced a gun, and—"

The wasp that Pauline had flicked off her shoulder flew into Cyril Rathbone's mouth and stung his tongue. In an agony of pain, he could not even scream as his tongue swelled with the poison of the sting. His eyes rolled in his head, imploring Pauline for help.

Pauline stared at the spectacle of the writhing man in front of her. Sweat broke out on his face and body. His shirt became soaked, and the sweat seeped through to his seersucker suit. He tried to stand and then fell to his knees in front of her. She picked up the basket that held the roses she had been cutting.

Pauline drew out her clippers and started to work on her roses. "You must always clear away any foliage that will be beneath the water level in the vase," she said, bringing her gloved hand down the stem and pulling off the leaves. "And then, when you cut off the bottom of the stem, make sure always that you do it at an angle, like this, do you see? Now, these roses from my garden have particularly thick stems, which makes it difficult for the water to penetrate, so I always suggest, when I talk to the newcomers at the garden club, to peel away half the stem, like this."

Cyril Rathbone twisted and turned. With his mouth wide open, she saw that his tongue was hugely inflated and vividly red. Saliva dripped out of his mouth and rolled down his chin. He began to choke, holding his hands to his throat, and terrible noises emanated from his mouth.

"I hope it hurts terribly, Cyril," she said calmly.

Finally, she had called him by his first name, but he was by then beyond caring. Cyril Rathbone fell over, dead.


PAULINE walked across the lawn and into the house through the French doors in the library, carrying her basket of roses. As she did so, Dudley passed in the hallway beyond.

"Dudley," called out Pauline.

"Yes, Mrs. Mendelson?" he said, entering the room.

"That man from *Mulholland* magazine?"

"Mr. Rathbone?" he replied.

"He seemed to be in some sort of distress. A coughing fit, choking or something. Perhaps Smitty or Jim should go down and check on him."

"Yes, Mrs. Mendelson. I'll buzz Smitty in the kennels."

Pauline deposited her roses on the table and continued on to the hallway and up the stairs. Midway up, she turned. "And, Dudley," she called.

"Yes, Mrs. Mendelson."

"I think you should call an ambulance." She continued up the stairs. "And the police."

*Flo's Tape #26*

"It often surprised me that Jules didn't have a bodyguard, or body-guards. So many of the film stars went around surrounded by them, as did many of the millionaires in the city who were nowhere near as rich as Jules. Of course, there were guards at Clouds and attack dogs, and they kept a fake police car in the driveway to scare off the curious, but he never went out in public with guards. He thought they attracted too much attention. And he said if anybody was going to get him, they'd get him anyway. He didn't think it looked right for a presidential designate, which he was, to go around with guards just because he was rich.

"One time when I was in the Bentley with him, driving back to my old neighborhood in Silverlake to pick up some mail, he opened the glove compartment and took out a gun that he held in his lap while we drove. I hated that. But he said there were people out there, mad people, who were out to get people like him."

# 27

BY THE TIME Pauline had bathed and changed, both the ambulance and the police had arrived and parked their vehicles in the courtyard. She sent word down to Dudley by Blondell not to allow the attendants to carry Cyril Rathbone's body through her house to get to the ambulance, but to carry it around by the side of the house behind the kennels. From her bedroom, where the windows were open, she could hear one of the attendants say, in a Hispanic accent, as he was lifting the remains of Cyril Rathbone into the ambulance, "They're dropping like flies in this house. This is my second time here. Last time I accidentally hit the picture on the stairs, and you should have heard the lady squawk."

Pauline waited until the ambulance had departed before she came downstairs to meet with Captain Nelson and Officer Whitbeck of the Beverly Hills Police Department.

In the library where they were waiting, the two policemen wandered around the magnificent room, silently looking at objects on tables and the pictures on the walls. Officer Whitbeck occasionally cleared his throat to get the attention of Captain Nelson, and then pointed to a treasure he thought the captain might have missed in his perusal of the room.

"Do you think it's okay to sit?" asked Officer Whitbeck, eyeing the green leather English chair that had been Jules Mendelson's favorite, wanting to lounge in it.

Captain Nelson shook his head. "We better stand," he said.

The library door opened and Pauline entered the room. Wafts of expensive perfume preceded and trailed her. "I hope you've been offered a drink, or something, Captain," she said, going toward him and shaking his hand. "I'm Pauline Mendelson." They had heard and read about the beautiful and very rich widow.

"No, thank you, Mrs. Mendelson," said Captain Nelson. "This is Officer Whitbeck."

Pauline smiled at Officer Whitbeck. "Please, for heaven's sake. Don't stand. Take a seat. Sit there, Officer Whitbeck. That was my husband's favorite chair. You must forgive me for keeping you waiting. I stayed upstairs until the ambulance attendants had removed

Mr. Rathbone's body. It brought back such sad memories. My husband recently died."

"Yes, yes, of course," said Captain Nelson, unable to take his eyes off her.

The sheer social power of her overwhelmed the room. Although neither policeman knew anything about fashion or style, each was aware that Pauline Mendelson was wonderfully dressed, in printed silk and quiet gold jewelry, as if she were on her way to a tea. She sat perfectly and with a gesture turned the meeting over to them, as if she were in their power; but they knew, as she did, that they were in hers.

"I'm so sorry, ma'am," said Officer Whitbeck. "But we have to ask you a few questions."

"Of course," she said.

"About your guest, Mr. Rathbone," continued Officer Whitbeck.

"But I barely knew Mr. Rathbone, Officer Whitbeck. He wasn't a guest, in the sense that he had been invited here by me. It was such a strange thing. He is a writer of some sort for *Mulholland* magazine. He had taken a great interest in a yellow phalaenopsis that my head gardener and I have developed, and asked that he be allowed to visit my greenhouse."

"A yellow what?" asked Officer Whitbeck, who was taking notes. "Can you spell that?"

"It's a breed of orchid," said Pauline. "Usually white, but Jarvis, my gardener, and I were able to develop a yellow variety, which I'm proud to say has caused quite a stir in horticultural circles. My garden is my passion. The Los Angeles Garden Club has been here to see it, and it's been photographed for several of the gardening magazines. Mr. Rathbone wanted to see my phalaenopsis, for something he was writing, I suppose. I was cutting roses in my garden when he arrived. There they are there." She pointed to the basket of red and pink roses that she had left on the library table. "I must put them in water before they die. Do you mind? It's terrible for them to just lie there in this heat. We can talk at the same time."

"No, no. Go right ahead, Mrs. Mendelson," said Captain Nelson.

"The next thing I knew he had started to cough and choke, and I asked Dudley, my butler, to send the men down to see if he was all right," called out Pauline from the lavatory, as she ran water for the flowers.

"Do you know his age, Mrs. Mendelson?"

"You'll have to call his magazine. I really didn't know him. Was it

424

a heart attack?" she asked, as she came back into the room with the roses in a vase. "I'll arrange these later."

"He was stung in his mouth by a wasp," said Captain Nelson.

"Good heavens," she said.

WHEN THEY were gone, she picked up the telephone and dialed. "This is Mrs. Jules Mendelson. I would like to speak to Mr. Pond. . . . I see. . . . Well, ask him anyway. I'm sure if you buzz in, he'll take my call. . . . Sandy, darling, it's Pauline," she said when the publisher came on the telephone. "Such a strange thing has happened. I need your help. This awful man who keeps writing these terrible things about Jules and that woman. What? . . . Yes, yes. That's his name. . . . Rathbone . . . I'll tell you what-about-him. He just died in my house."

MUCH WAS MADE in the press of the bizarre death of Cyril Rathbone, the controversial columnist for *Mulholland* magazine, who had "choked to death after having been stung on the tongue by a wasp in the sculpture garden of the mountaintop estate of Mrs. Jules Mendelson." The only other mention of Pauline Mendelson's name in the account in the *Los Angeles Tribunal*, however, was to say that she had not been home at the time. Exactly what Cyril Rathbone was doing sitting alone in Pauline Mendelson's sculpture garden, where his body was discovered by the butler, was a mystery that caused much speculation, as it was a known fact in social circles that the lady of the house despised him and had never invited him to her home.

No one contributed more to the speculation than Hortense Madden, the literary critic of *Mulholland*, who had also, for quite different reasons, despised Cyril. She reveled in each grotesque detail of his demise, as reported to her by the ambulance attendant, Faustino, whom she managed to track down, as well as by the undertaker, who had both embalmed Cyril and laid him out in the closed coffin. Their descriptions of the size and the color of Cyril's tongue fascinated her, and she made them repeat certain particulars, which she wrote in a notebook, like a reporter at the scene of a crime. She even begged to have the coffin opened for a final look at Cyril, but the undertaker refused her request, on professional grounds, as she was not a member of his family.

425

"My dear, the tongue was swollen to four times its size, ready to burst, apparently. Bright red, turning black," Hortense breathlessly reported to Lucia Borsodi. "Imagine what he must have been saying to Pauline at the time to have God pick that moment and that manner to take him."

God was not someone who regularly appeared in Hortense's conversation or thoughts, and Lucia, for propriety's sake, drew a halt to the conversation. "But Pauline Mendelson wasn't even there, Hortense," she said. "He went there to see her yellow phalaenopsis."

"I don't believe that story for a single moment," said Hortense with a dismissive gesture. "You mark my words, Pauline hotfooted it out of there as fast as she could, as soon as Cyril choked out his last breath."

"Well, I must write a eulogy," said Lucia. "I haven't a clue what to say."

"Say that in whatever corner of hell Cyril is residing, he is most certainly bragging to the other devils that he managed to die in Pauline, Mrs. Mendelson's, sculpture garden," said Hortense.


ON THE ADVICE OF Sandy Pond, Pauline left Clouds as soon as she had finished speaking with him. "Reporters will be calling. It's just as well not to be there," he said. "You've had enough publicity since Jules's death."

Fortunately, Jules's Bentley was parked in the courtyard, with the keys in the ignition, and she hopped into it and drove down the mountain to Camilla Ebury's house, without a word to Jim, her chauffeur, who was in the kitchen with Gertie, the cook, getting the grocery order, which had to be picked up at Jurgensen's Market.

When Camilla looked up from her serve and saw her unexpected guest coming toward the court, she halted her second serve and waved to Pauline. Camilla said something to Philip, and he turned to look at Pauline. Both knew that Pauline was not the sort of person to drop in on people, even on a friend as close as Camilla Ebury was, and Camilla suspected that there was something wrong.

"Keep playing, keep playing," said Pauline. "I don't want to interrupt your game."

"Is everything all right?" asked Camilla.

"Of course. I was just passing, and I thought I hadn't seen you for a bit and that I'd stop in for a glass of iced tea. But I don't want to stop your game. Hello, Philip."

"Hello, Pauline," he replied, in a polite but guarded fashion, remembering the unpleasant conclusion to their previous encounter.

Pauline smiled at Philip in a friendly way. "I've never seen you in shorts, Philip. What marvelous legs you have. No wonder Camilla is so mad about you."

"Pauline!" said Camilla, blushing and laughing.

Philip was surprised by Pauline, as her friendliness belied their last leave-taking, when it had seemed that they would never see each other again.

"I'll ring for some iced tea," said Camilla.

"No, no. Finish your set," said Pauline. "I'll watch."

Camilla could never picture Pauline spending a leisurely sort of afternoon, or even a leisurely hour, lying back on a chaise watching a tennis game. She was always so frenetically busy, in her garden, or with her correspondence, or her charities, or her guest lists, or her seating charts, or her flower arranging. But she sat back on Camilla's chaise in a totally relaxed fashion and watched the completion of the set with total concentration, even occasionally making the appropriate remark on a good serve, or lob, or backhand.

When the set was completed, they returned to the house and talked for over an hour on matters of no consequence, in the sort of conversation that Pauline was usually contemptuous of as a waste of valuable time.

"Am I in the way?" asked Philip, thinking there was a point to the visit that his presence was delaying. "Would you two ladies like to talk alone?"

"No, no," cried Pauline. "Tell me, what is it you're writing now? I hope you're not still involved with Casper Stieglitz. Will you ever forget that night? Wasn't it a nightmare?"

"Philip's moving back to New York," said Camilla.

"When?"

"Next week."

"Next week? Philip, why?"

"I've finished here. I came for a few months, and I've stayed almost a year. It's time."

Pauline looked at Camilla, who appeared downcast at Philip's decision.

"And here I am interrupting one of your last days together," said Pauline, getting up to leave.

As they stood in the driveway and watched the Bentley pull out onto Copa de Oro Road, Camilla remarked to Philip, whose arm was around her waist, that she hadn't seen Pauline in such good humor since before Jules's death.

When Philip read in the *Tribunal* the next morning that Mrs. Mendelson had not been at home at the time of Cyril Rathbone's death, he understood.

"THERE GOES MY Thursday-afternoon income," said Lonny Edge, tossing the *Tribunal* aside.

Flo March was too young even to think of reading the obituary pages of the newspaper, unless the death announced was of sufficient news value to rate headlines, like Rock Hudson's, or Lucille Ball's, and she did not know that Cyril Rathbone had died until her new housemate happened to mention it, over their morning coffee.

"Cyril Rathbone is dead?" asked Flo, shocked. "How?"

"Got stung on his tongue by a wasp."

Flo thought for a moment. "Not inappropriate," she said.

"What does that mean?"

"The guy had a tongue like a viper. Where did this happen?"

"At Pauline Mendelson's house."

"At Pauline Mendelson's? You have to be kidding!"

"That's what the paper says," said Lonny.

"Let me see that," said Flo. She took the paper and read the account. "I wonder what he was doing at Pauline's."

Lonny shook his head.

"He hated Pauline. And Pauline didn't like him. Jules used to tell me that. I bet I know what he was doing up there at Clouds," said Flo.

"He was a regular of mine. Every Thursday afternoon at four. Rain or shine. Always brought doughnuts."

"You get fat eating doughnuts, Lonny. You were beginning to get a gut," said Flo.

"Hey, I didn't think you ever noticed me, Flo."

"Don't get any ideas."

Lonny laughed. "He was kind of a snazzy dresser. He always wore seersucker suits and a pink tie. Not my kind of taste. Kinda English. I'll miss the guy."

"I won't."

"No?"

"He wanted me to jump out a fifteenth-story window."

Lonny stared at her. "You got any more cigarettes? I'm out."

JO JO had reported back to Arnie Zwillman that he had not been able to locate Cyril Rathbone, either at his office at *Mulholland* magazine or at his condominium in the Wilshire district.

"Not like you to let me down, Jo Jo," said Arnie, from the telephone in his steam room.

When Arnie read about Cyril's death in the *Tribunal* the next morning, he understood and called Jo Jo immediately. "This means that the dame is the only one who has the tapes, so they're either in her safety deposit box or her house."

"That's what I was thinkin'," said Jo Jo.

"I wonder what the fruitcake was doing up at Pauline's house," said Arnie.

THE FUNERAL SERVICE, which was held in the tiny chapel of a mortuary near the Paramount Studio, was sparsely attended, as might be expected for the funeral service of a man who was unloved. According to Hortense Madden's count, there were only fifty seats in the chapel, and not all of those were occupied. Most of those present were employees of the magazine, whom Lucia Borsodi had given orders to attend, even including the man who ran the photocopying machine. In the back, by a spray of pink gladiolus that would have offended Cyril's eye, sat Lonny Edge, the pornography star. Hortense Madden, who had a fertile imagination, was quick to figure out the connection.

Neither of the two ladies in whose lives Cyril had become intertwined at a literary level in the months before his death, Pauline Mendelson and Flo March, was present, although Pauline, to avoid criticism, as Cyril had died in her garden, sent flowers. The flowers she sent were not from her own garden or greenhouse, which was her usual habit, or from the fashionable florist Petra von Kant. Instead she dispatched her maid, Blondell, to send them, and Blondell, with no instructions from the mountaintop as to choice, chose the pink gladiolus, which Lucia Borsodi relegated to the back of the chapel.

"YOU WERE my husband's friend, Sims," said Pauline.

"Yes."

"You knew him better than anyone."

"Perhaps."

"There are tapes that Miss March has recorded. Did you know that?"

"No."

"Forty hours, so far. Apparently, there are revelations on those tapes, if I am to believe what that frightful Cyril Rathbone told me, that could prove embarrassing. Business revelations. Personal revelations."

"Did you believe him? Half of what he writes is bullshit. Everyone says so."

"I did believe him, yes."

"Did he say more?"

"That was when the wasp flew into his mouth and stung his tongue."

There was a brief silence. Sims asked, "Are you crying?"

"A bit. Yes. Something has to be done, Sims. These tapes, if they do exist, must be stolen."

"Easier said than done. I wouldn't know how to go about such a thing."

"I have an idea," said Pauline. "Did you ever hear of someone called Arnie Zwillman?"

"The guy who burned down the Vegas Seraglio for the insurance money?"

"Yes. Ghastly man. I met him once. He has that sort of extra-clean look that gangsters sometimes have. I think they bathe more often than other people."

"What about Arnie Zwillman? He tried to shake down Jules. He was responsible for Jules not getting the appointment to Brussels."

"He's on the tapes too, apparently. All that business about Brussels and the laundered money."

"I'm missing a beat here, Pauline."

"It seems to me that Mr. Arnie Zwillman would know a thing or two about breaking into Miss March's house and stealing the tapes," said Pauline. "I mean, isn't that the sort of thing those people do?"

## Flo's Tape #27

"*Last night, when I couldn't sleep, I watched* Laura *on television. There was this character called Waldo Lydecker played by an old movie star, probably long dead now, named Clifton Webb. I kept thinking to myself, 'Who does this guy remind me of?' and then I realized it was Cyril Rathbone, and not just because the two of them were gossip columnists. They even dressed alike, and they talked alike.*

"*I heard from the lady at the Wells Fargo Bank in Beverly Hills that Cyril had a fit when he found that I had taken the tapes out of the safety deposit vault. We both had keys. I bet the reason he was up at Clouds to see Pauline had something to do with these tapes. Knowing Cyril like I came to, he was probably trying to blackmail her with what was on the tapes.*

"*I'm surprised he didn't come up here and try to get them away from me.*"

# 28

AT FIRST, after Jules's death, when the money stopped coming, Flo March's economies had been relatively painless. She stopped renewing her magazine subscriptions when they came due and purchased cheaper brands of bottled water. Then she gave up her daily excursions to the boutiques on Rodeo Drive and began marketing at Hughes in West Hollywood instead of at Jurgenson's in Beverly Hills. The man who regularly cleaned her swimming pool stayed on as long as he could without getting paid, because he liked Flo and realized she was in trouble, but he eventually left. In his absence, the water in the pool developed a scumlike surface, and the drain became clogged by leaves. Then Flo let her gardener go, when Lonny Edge suggested that he could do just as good a job as "the little Jap" was doing, but Lonny soon tired of the chore and forgot to turn on the sprinklers, and kept postponing mowing the lawn or tending the garden, so the grass became long and brown, and the garden was choked by weeds, sights that would not please any landlord's eye, and they were certainly displeasing to the eye of Trent Muldoon, the television star, when he returned to look at his home on Azelia Way after a long absence.

He pushed the front doorbell and could hear pretty chimes ring inside the house. The chimes were but one of the many improvements his tenant had put into the house. There was no answer, but he could see that there were two cars in the garage. After several minutes, he rang again. This time the door was opened by a sleepy Lonny Edge, dressed only in a towel wrapped around his middle, who had been awakened from his late-morning siesta by the pool by the sound of the chimes.

"Yeah?" he asked.

"I would like to see Miss March," said Trent.

"She's asleep. She don't get up till noon."

"Would you tell her Trent Muldoon is here."

"Trent Muldoon," said Lonny, breaking into a wide smile as the television star's face came into focus. For a moment he could not remember the name of Trent Muldoon's canceled series, which he used to watch, but he was still delighted to be in his presence. "I thought I recognized you."

"Would you wake her up, please?"

"Sure thing. Come in, Trent. Wait here in the living room. You can sit right there on her gray satin sofa. I'll get Flo."

It was then, when he was alone in the room, that Trent Muldoon saw how the plate glass window had been shattered by the gunshot that Flo had fired in the room. She had not replaced the glass in the window, because the cheapest estimate had been eighteen hundred dollars, which she could not afford. She had taken her canary diamond earrings to a dealer in antique jewels in Beverly Hills. The extent of her financial plight was so well known that the manager of the shop took advantage of her immediate need for money and offered her a sum of less than half of their worth. At the last moment, she could not bear to part with them, as they had been Jules's last gift to her, so she sold the jeweler only one of the earrings for the value of the canary diamond. It had been Flo's intention to replace the smashed window, but she used the money to pay off her most pressing bills, and then there was nothing left.

Trent Muldoon was standing by the window, running his fingers over the shattered plate glass, when Flo walked into the room, followed by Lonny. She was barefoot, wearing only a terry cloth robe and dark glasses, and her hair was uncombed.

In her years of being tutored by Jules Mendelson, she had developed an eye for style and an understanding of manners and good taste. Even with her head and heart pounding, even without looking in the mirror of her bar for verification, she knew exactly how she appeared to Trent Muldoon at that instant, as he looked up at her from the shattered window. She knew that she presented a picture without style or taste, and that Lonny Edge, the porn star, standing behind her with only a towel wrapped around his middle, detracted even further from her diminished image. She put her hands to her head in a vain attempt to bring some kind of order to her hair.

"I can explain that," she said, about the window, before he had a chance to speak. "This box was delivered to me, in the middle of the night. Like a corsage box. And I opened it, and there was a lot of wrapping paper inside, you know, like pink tissue paper, and at the bottom of the box was this gun, and there was a note, and the note said, 'Put it in your mouth and fire it,' I swear to God. In my whole life, I'd never held a gun in my hand, and I didn't know what to do with it, so I aimed it out there to the door and fired it, just to see if it was loaded; and as you can see, it was, and the door got shattered.

Now, it's being fixed. I can assure you of that. There is a new plate glass window on order."

She looked at him. She knew how she sounded. She looked at Lonny. She knew how he looked. She wished she had never asked Lonny to come to share her house with her.

"I'm very sorry about this, Miss March, but I'm afraid that I have to instruct my business manager to go ahead with eviction proceedings," said Trent. "It's been four months since you paid the rent, and my house has been not only neglected, but destroyed."

"Hey, please, Trent. Or, Mr. Muldoon, I mean. Give me a break, will you. Don't make me move. I love this house," she said, trying not to cry. "If I'd known you were coming, I'd have had it looking all spick-and-span, the way it's always been. I've been going through some bad times. I'm getting straightened out. You'll get your rent, and the plate glass window will be fixed. I swear to God."

Trent moved across the living room without answering and walked out of the house.

"Hey, Trent." She ran after him, calling out, "Listen, please. Look at all the money I put into this house. You have to see the closet space. It was designed by Nellie Potts. She's the best decorator in Beverly Hills. It cost thousands. And the wet bar. I put in the wet bar and the mirrored walls."

She stood at her front door and continued to talk to him as he got into his Ferrari and closed the door and started the motor and backed out of her driveway, which was not going to be her driveway much longer. "How can you kick me out of here, Trent, when I've increased the value of your house? Please. Just give me three months. I need three months to get my book finished. Please. Please. I spent a fortune on your lousy house."

Trent Muldoon was not hard-hearted. He knew what it was to go through a bad spell, and he felt sorry for Flo March. But an instinct told him that she was not going to have a comeback, as he was, if the picture he'd just completed in Yugoslavia turned out to be the hit the Italian producer told him it was going to be. He knew panic and desperation when he saw it, and Flo March was panicky and desperate.

WHEN THE eviction notice was served, Flo became too paralyzed with fear of what was ahead of her to be able to find a place to move.

She had thirty days to vacate the premises, but it was only at the end of three weeks that she began to look for a new place.

"Don't mention my name, Lonny, when we look. Nobody wants to touch me with a ten-foot pole," said Flo.

She disliked every apartment or condo she saw, when she compared it to what she had on Azelia Way. "If I have to live in a dump, at least I'd like to live in a dump in a better neighborhood," she said about each one she saw.

Each day she cursed herself for spending so much money when she had money. Driving with Lonny Edge in his car to look at places that she could not afford and would not have liked to live in if she had been able to afford them, she repeated over and over again the litany of her expenses. "The curtains alone cost me forty thousand dollars, and the closet with all the built-ins, that was another forty. Right there, there's eighty thousand. Do you want to know what I spent on mirrors?"

"Hey, hey, hey. You're sounding like a broken record, Flo. You've told me all this a hundred times. I'm sick of hearing it," said Lonny.

"I know. I know. Listen, Lonny," said Flo.

"Yeah?"

"Can you get me some Valium? My nerves are jangled. I need to calm down."

"I thought you couldn't have any pills in AA."

Flo ignored what he said. "Could you get me some, Lonny? After the move, I'll calm down again."

"Sure."

They had started to argue. They were mismatched and tired of each other. She didn't want to be seen with him in public and was afraid that he would leave her. She had stopped going to the AA meetings in the early mornings again. She could not bear to see Philip Quennell. She did not want him to know what dire circumstances she was in, or that Lonny Edge was living in her house. She had heard through an AA acquaintance she ran into at the Hughes Market that he was moving back to New York. She tried to call him at the Chateau Marmont to say good-bye, but he had checked out. The forwarding number was at Camilla Ebury's house.

"HELLO?"

"Is that you, Camilla?"

"Yes."

"This is Flo March."

"Oh. Hello."

Flo spoke very quickly, as if she was afraid of being cut off. "Listen, Camilla. I know you're Pauline's friend, and I don't want to put you in a spot talking to me, so just let me talk quick, and you don't have to say anything. First, thanks for being so nice to me at Jules's funeral. You didn't have to do that, and I was very touched, and, second, I need to talk to Philip. I heard from someone he's moving back to New York, and I have to speak to him before he goes. I think my phone's tapped, so he better not call me here. Ask him if he'll be at the meeting on Thursday. We can talk there. Okay?"

"Of course. I'll tell him," said Camilla.

"You know I'm not after him, don't you, Camilla?"

"I know that."

"It's just a business thing I want to discuss."

"I'll tell him. And Flo?"

"Yes?"

"Good luck to you."

LONNY EDGE was very vain about his body and took great pains to keep in shape. Each afternoon since he had moved into Azelia Way, he drove down Coldwater Canyon to Beverly Park and ran around the track for three miles. Several days in a row, he noticed a gold Rolls-Royce parked in the alley near the completion of the run. Lonny always stared at expensive cars and had curiosity about the people in them. After the second day, he noticed that the two men in the front seat were looking at him. After the third day, he responded when they nodded to him. On the fourth day he did not think it amiss when they asked him if he needed a ride. He didn't need a ride, but he got in the backseat of the Rolls anyway. He was used to being picked up, and he missed the adventures of the streets in the expensive neighborhood where he now lived.

The adventure was of a different sort than he expected. But it involved wealth, more money than he had ever imagined would be his. He had only to unlock a door.

"What do you mean, unlock a door?"

"Just that. Leave the door unlocked. Very simple."

"And then, you do what?"

"Pay a visit. That's all. There's some tapes in that house I want."

"Tapes? You mean, my videos? You don't have to break in for that. You can buy them at the all-night bookshop on the corner of Santa Monica and Havenhurst for thirty-nine ninety-five."

"No. Not your videos, Lonny. Audiotapes. Forty hours of audiotapes. Microcassettes. Those little ones."

"I don't know anything about that," said Lonny.

"They're there. They used to be in a safety deposit box at the Wells Fargo Bank in Beverly Hills, but they're in that house now."

"And Flo?" asked Lonny.

"What about Miss March?" asked Arnie.

"Nothing would happen to Flo, would it?"

"Heavens, no. I have no interest in her whatever. It's just the tapes I want."

They dropped Lonny back at Beverly Park.

Later, back at the old Charles Boyer house, Arnie Zwillman telephoned Sims Lord. "I saw him. I took him for a ride."

"And?"

"Lonny Edge has an IQ that hovers around room temperature."

In the background, Jo Jo, listening, laughed, but Arnie raised a disapproving hand, and the laughter curdled.


IT WAS LONNY who came up with the housing solution. He reported to Flo that he had run into his old landlord from his bungalow on Cahuenga Boulevard. The new tenant had caused a small fire, and the landlord said that Lonny would be welcome back.

"But I thought the landlord and you parted on very bad terms," said Flo.

"We did."

"I thought he accused you of turning tricks in your bungalow," she said.

"He did."

"Why would he welcome you back then?"

"I told him I'd given up all that. I told him I'd turned over a new leaf."

Flo nodded. It seemed to her that there was a beat missing in his story.

"Also, if they go ahead with publishing Basil Plant's book, I'll be in the news for having discovered this long-lost masterpiece, and he liked that," said Lonny.

"But I thought you said it was just a tiny little place with hardly enough room for you," said Flo.

"It is."

"Then why would you want me to move in with you?"

"You did me a favor when I needed a place. I'm just returning the favor."

She missed Jules more and more. She missed having him make decisions for her.

"Listen, it could be just a stopgap for you, Flo," said Lonny. "You could put your furniture in storage, rather than rush into some place you don't like. Then, when you find something, you can move on. It might be just the thing for you, to drop out for a while, and you certainly won't run into anyone you know from Beverly Hills over in my old neighborhood."

"Okay," she said. She had no other choices.

FOR ONE WHOLE DAY Flo and Glyceria stood on a ladder and unhooked all her curtains.

"They'll never fit anyplace else," said Glyceria.

"I don't care. I don't want Trent Muldoon to have them," she answered.

"What are you going to do with them?" asked Glyceria.

"Do you want them, Glycie?" asked Flo.

"Hell, no. I've only got three little tiny windows in my place," said Glyceria.

"Then I'll put them in storage. I think I'll break the mirrors in the bar before I leave," said Flo.

"No, don't break them. He could cause you trouble. I'll take them off the walls for you," said Glyceria.

ON THE LAST NIGHT she spent in her house, the front hall was lined with cartons and packing cases going into storage, and with shopping bags filled with things she was taking with her to the bungalow on Cahuenga Boulevard. Her gray satin sofas and her other upholstered furniture were tagged for the warehouse, as were her Chinese brass candlesticks with the dragons climbing up the sides. Glyceria helped her wrap her Steuben glasses in newspaper, and her Tiffany plates and silverware in the boxes and bags they arrived in. The moving vans were coming the next morning at ten. She had only to pack her clothes. All her Louis Vuitton bags were out and open, but she had not yet taken her Chanel suits off their satin hangers, or emptied the many drawers and shelves in her dressing room cupboards of her blouses and sweaters and nightgowns and underwear and stockings.

Hidden away behind the lingerie that she had ordered from Paris, from the same shop on the Rue de Rivoli where Pauline Mendelson had her lingerie made, was the small brown bag with the thirty-nine hours of microcassette tapes that she had removed from the safety deposit box at the Wells Fargo Bank in Beverly Hills on the morning after Cyril Rathbone had tried to talk her into jumping out the fifteenth-story window of the Valley Studios.

"Here's your key to my place," said Lonny. She was relieved that Lonny Edge had, as he put it, "things to do" that evening, and absented himself from Azelia Way. She thought that perhaps he had returned to the nocturnal habits he had said were a part of his past. Men called him at the house, and he had spent several evenings and afternoons away, without explanation, since the decision was made to move into his old bungalow on Cahuenga Boulevard. She noticed that he had a great deal more cash on hand than he usually had, and he exhibited a show of generosity toward her that she was unused to from him. He stopped bickering with her over inconsequential financial matters. When she asked him to go to the Hughes Market to get her things, he went without complaining and paid for even her personal items, like sanitary napkins and nail polish, without insisting on being reimbursed. Sometimes he brought home pizzas and made her eat.

"I don't think you should stay here tonight, with the house all upside down like this," said Lonny. "Too depressing. Go over to my place. I'll be there after midnight. I'll bring you back here in the morning before the movers come."

"Okay, Lonny. Give me that address once again on Cahuenga."

"Seventy-two-oh-four and a quarter. Up Highland Avenue to Odin. Turn right under the bridge to get to Cahuenga," said Lonny patiently. It was the third time he had told her the address.

"Right. Right. I'll remember. I just want to stay here for a while by myself. You know. Memories. There were good times in this house, believe it or not."

"Sure, Flo," said Lonny. He leaned over and kissed her on the cheek.

She wanted to be alone on her last night on Azelia Way. Over and over again, she walked through the rooms of the small and elegant house where so much had happened to her. It was not a house with happy memories, but she loved it because it had been hers, or almost hers, and in her mind she relived the joys and sadnesses she had experienced there. She wondered to herself if she would ever again live in the manner that she had lived there. Finally, late, she lay down on her gray satin sofa. She picked up the cushion with Kippie Petworth's blood, now faded to a dark stain, on the reverse side and placed it behind her head. She meant just to lie there for a bit and rest, to think of her life with Jules Mendelson, as well as the life that was ahead of her. Her sole asset was her tapes. She felt sure that she could get someone to help her put them into book form. The someone she wanted to help her was Philip Quennell. She knew that he would understand both the shortcomings and the greatness of Jules Mendelson. She knew that he was not seeking revenge, the way Cyril Rathbone had been seeking revenge on Pauline Mendelson. The prospect of working with Philip Quennell was pleasing to her. She dwelt on the pleasing thought. She had not meant to fall asleep when there was so much work still to be done, but she did.

SHE WAS AWAKENED by a sound. She knew there was someone in her house. At first she thought it might be Lonny, returning for her when he discovered she wasn't at the bungalow on Cahuenga Boulevard, as she had promised him she would be. But the sounds she heard were not the Lonny sounds she had become accustomed to during the month they had been living together on Azelia Way, the sounds of slammed refrigerator doors, belches, and the television set turned on far too loud. She lay where she was on the gray satin sofa without moving, as if she were still asleep. From behind her she heard a breathing sound and realized that the person in her house was in the same room, by the fireplace. Very slowly she sat up on her sofa and turned her head to see the figure of a man rifling through the packing boxes on the floor. The definition of his face was obliterated by a woman's stocking pulled over it.

"Lonny, is that you?" she asked, even though she knew it wasn't Lonny. Her voice was tinny and high-pitched. She could feel the frightened beating of her heart pounding against her chest. Her fingers stiffened. Her lips, her nose, even the follicles of her hair began to tingle with fear. "What are you doing in my house? Why are you ripping those cartons and bags apart? Who are you? What are you looking for?"

The man did not reply. Very quietly, he stood up. She saw in his hand one of the brass candlesticks from China with the dragon crawling up the side, and a red tag on it to identify it as one of the pieces to go into the moving van for storage the next morning.

"That's Chinese," said Flo. She was breathing very heavily. "That's an antique. One of the dynasties, Jules told me. Ming, maybe. I could never get it straight. What are you doing with it? Why are you coming toward me like that? Please. Don't. Is it the tapes? Is that what you want? Those damn tapes. Is that it? Take the tapes. They're in the other room. Oh, no."

She watched the brass candlestick descend to bash in the side of her head. "Oh, dear God," she said. She raised her hands to cover her face. "No, not my face. Please don't hit me in the face, please, mister. Not my face, please." The sapphire in the diamond-and-sapphire ring that Jules had given her, which she told Cyril Rathbone would be on her finger when she died, smashed from the force of the next blow. Her lipsticked lips moved again, but her attacker knew that she was only saying a prayer. "Oh, dear God, help me, help me" were her last audible words. The sounds that came from her mouth through the next eight blows were prayers, "HailMaryfullofgracethelordiswiththee," indecipherable to her attacker, asking God to forgive her sins, asking her mother for help, asking Jules to let her die before she was hit again, because she knew, before the first blow landed, that there was no rescue for her.

## Flo's Tape #28

*"I know I should be thinking about this damn book, but all that I can think of these days is what's going to happen to me. It's a terrible feeling to think that the best things that have happened to me have already happened, and everything else is going to be downhill from here. But no matter how hard I try to visualize what my life will be like from here on, I can't seem to come up with a picture. What the hell does that mean?"*

# 29

"PHILIP. Once you said to me that you had caused a girl to be paralyzed and that it had changed your life forever," said Camilla.

Philip Quennell's romance with Camilla Ebury had lasted the better part of a year. During that time she had given thoughts to marriage, but he consistently made it clear that he resisted permanence in love. In his past there was a nameless girl whose life he had thwarted, for whom he felt a responsibility that precluded such thoughts, and Camilla learned to accept what she had for as long as it lasted. They had loved and fought and parted and made up and loved again, and the arrangement, finally understood by each of them, brought pleasure to both.

On their last night together before Philip returned to New York, they dined alone in Camilla's house and then made love with the same ferocity and frequency as they had on their first night, following their meeting at Jules and Pauline Mendelson's party on the evening of his arrival in the city.

Philip got up from the bed. Camilla watched him as he opened the door of her closet and took out his blue-and-white-striped dressing gown and put it on. He walked over to her dressing table and pulled the chair from its place so that the back of it was facing the bed. Then he straddled it and looked at her as he started to speak.

"Her name was Sophie Bushnell. Her name *is* Sophie Bushnell, I should say. She is alive, but alive in a wheelchair because of me."

"I want to hear, Philip," said Camilla.

With his finger he traced the design on the back of the chair as he talked, looking at it. "We were in her car, but I was driving, too fast, over a causeway that separated the part of town where she lived from the part of town where I lived. We had been drinking. I hit an abutment. She broke her neck."

He raised his eyes and looked at Camilla.

"Is there more?"

"Yes."

"What?"

"I was trouserless at the time." He rose from his seat and walked into her bathroom.

"Is that why you're so afraid to commit?" she asked when he came out.

"Pretty good reason, don't you think?"


"I'LL MISS YOU," she said later, laying her head against his chest.

"Me too," he answered. He placed both his arms around her.

"You've turned me into a wanton woman."

"It's what you were born to be."

"It won't really be over, will it?"

"You know it won't."

"There'll be other times."

"Of course."

"You'll come out?"

"Sure."

Philip could not bear leave-takings. It was arranged between them that there would be no morning farewells. When he kissed her good night, he told her he would be gone before she awoke in the morning. Philip was always up before six to attend his AA meeting at the log cabin on Robertson Boulevard, and Camilla, more often than not, slept late; so the morning of his leaving was no different from their usual routine, except that she did get up and make him a cup of coffee while he was shaving and showering. Their last kiss was just a peck, as if he were off to the office for the day or, with his packed bags, off on a business trip, although he would not have honked his horn twice at the end of the driveway if he were just off for the day or for a business trip.

He planned to see Flo March at the meeting and take her out for a cup of coffee afterward, before he left for the airport.

"You don't have to worry about me," Flo had said to him at the meeting the day before, when they made their coffee date.

"I do worry. You're the most fragile tough girl I ever knew," he answered.

"Is that good?" she asked.

"I don't know." He had an urge to kiss her.

"How's Camilla?" she asked, understanding his urge.

He laughed.

"You don't think my life is complicated enough?" she asked. "I'll give you a nice AA hug, though."

444

They both laughed.

"Listen, there's something I want to talk to you about before you go," she said. "Of a business nature."

Driving toward West Hollywood, he imagined that what she wanted to talk about had to do with the book that she had been writing with Cyril Rathbone before his death. His plan was to advise her to leave Los Angeles and start anew someplace else, where her name was less well known.

He saved a seat for her by putting his car keys on the chair next to his, but Flo March did not appear at the meeting. When the room became crowded, and there were not enough seats for all, he picked up the keys and relinquished the chair. Every time a latecomer entered the room, he looked anxiously toward the door. A feeling of unrest came over him. He tried to focus his attention on the talk being given by a former surgeon who told of operating on a patient while he was drunk, but he could not concentrate on the man's pain. Halfway through the talk, he rose and went outside. There was a public telephone on the corner of the street. He dialed Flo's number. The ring had a peculiar tone, and then the recorded voice of an operator came on and said that the number he was dialing was no longer in service. He wondered if the telephone company had disconnected her phone for nonpayment of her bill, or if she had ordered it to be disconnected because she was moving. His feelings of unease about Flo returned.

When he got into his car, he found that it was blocked by the cars in front of him and behind him, both of which had parked too closely, and he could not get out. He knew he would have to wait for the end of the meeting for the occupants to come and move their vehicles. Just then a yellow cab turned the corner to drop off a latecomer in front of the log cabin. Philip recognized that it was Rose Cliveden, hiding behind dark glasses and a head scarf that were meant to disguise her, although no one at the meeting would have known who she was, even if she announced her name and bank balance.

He ducked down into his car, not wanting to be waylaid by Rose. In her sobriety, she talked as much as she had talked when she was drinking. Turning, she saw him and waved as she approached his car.

"I need your advice, Philip," she said. "I'm scheduled to speak tomorrow on my three-month anniversary, and I have the most awful confession to make."

"Rose, I'm in rather a hurry this morning," answered Philip.

"You see, I never heard the word grandiosity until I came into the program, and I'm afraid I've been very guilty of it," she said, as if Philip had not spoken. "For years, almost thirty, I've always told people I had an affair with Jack Kennedy, in the Lincoln Bedroom in the White House. I think I even discussed it with you on the first night we met. Do you remember? You said to me, 'What kind of a fuck was Jack Kennedy?' And I told you he was a marvelous lover until he came, and then he couldn't stand to be touched, because of all that Irish Catholic guilt. Do you remember all that?"

"Yes, Rose, I remember, but—"

"Well, I just made it all up."

"Rose, please, I must go," he said, but there was no getting rid of Rose Cliveden when Rose was discussing herself.

"It wasn't true. I never went to bed with Jack Kennedy. But I told it so many times I began to believe it. I thought it made me a more interesting woman. How do you think that would sound when I speak on my anniversary tomorrow? Is that the sort of thing they like to hear?"

Philip looked outside the car as the taxi that Rose had gotten out of began backing up in order to turn around. He began to talk very quickly. "That's not really the point, Rose, whether they would like to hear it or not. You see, it's not an entertainment when you speak. You only have to say that you made up stories to enhance your importance during the years you were drinking," said Philip. "But I really must go, Rose. I have to be somewhere."

"Do you think I should write Jackie and apologize for telling that awful story?"

"No. Good-bye, Rose. I'm going to try and grab your taxi. I can't get my car out of here."

As Rose disappeared inside the log cabin, he opened the door of his car and ran after the cab, waving his arms to attract the attention of the driver.

"Please," he said, when he got to the cab. "Can you take me to Azelia Way? It's halfway up Coldwater Canyon."

"Can't, fella. I'm a Beverly Hills cab in West Hollywood. I'm not supposed to pick up customers off the streets out of my own district, or I could get a fine. Sorry."

"This is important," said Philip. He didn't understand why he felt a sense of urgency. He took a twenty-dollar bill from his pocket and handed it to the driver. "Nobody's looking. Nobody's going to report you. It's only twenty minutes past seven. The streets are still empty."

"Does the fare come out of the twenty?"

"No. The twenty's on top of the fare."

"Hop in."

When they turned off Coldwater Canyon onto Azelia Way, the taxi driver said, "Oh, Azelia Way. That's where Faye Converse lives."

"The house I'm going to is the first house past Faye Converse's house," said Philip.

"I know her maid," said the driver.

"Uh-huh," said Philip.

"Glyceria."

"What?"

"Her maid's name is Glyceria. I drive her to the bus station every night. Faye pays."

"It's right here," said Philip. "Turn here."

"Oh, no, fella. That driveway's too steep. I'll never be able to turn around up there. You can get out here."

Philip paid the driver. He hopped out of the cab and ran up the hill. The grass had turned brown and had not been cut. The shrubbery along the path to the front door looked ragged, in need of clipping. When he got to the door, he rang the bell. There was no answer. Then he rang again. He tried the front door, and it was unlocked. When he opened it, he called out, "Flo?" He waited a moment. Then he called again. "Flo? Are you here, Flo? It's Philip. Can I come in?"

There was no answer. He peered inside. There were cartons and packing cases and shopping bags along the walls of the hallway, in preparation for moving, but they had been torn apart, and the contents were scattered. He wondered if there had been a robbery, or if vandals had gotten into the house. As he walked in, he saw that the living room was in shambles. He walked down the hallway to the bedroom. The bed had not been slept in, and there were half-packed bags on it. The door to the elaborate dressing room that Flo had had built was open. All the drawers were pulled out, and blouses and sweaters and stockings and belts and lingerie were hanging out of them, as if the place had been ransacked.

"Flo?" he called out again.

Slowly he walked out of her bedroom back into the living room.

The back of the gray satin sofa was facing toward him. There was a pair of her shoes on the floor, one halfway under the sofa, the other by a chair. A brass candlestick with a dragon crawling up the side had been dropped on the floor, its bloody base staining the white carpet. He leaned down and picked it up. There were pieces of red hair mixed in with the blood. He rose and walked very slowly over to the sofa and, with dread, looked down at the body of Flo March. Her red hair was matted with blood. Her hands covered her face, as if to protect it, and the sapphire in her ring was smashed, as was the finger on which it was worn. There were contusions on her forearm.

All the blood drained from Philip's face as he looked down at his beautiful friend. "Oh, Flo," he breathed out. On the bar was a telephone. When he picked it up, there was no dial tone, and he remembered that it had been disconnected. He ran out of the house. In order to get to Faye Converse's house next door, he had to run down the long steep driveway to Azelia Way and then run up the driveway next door. He rang and rang the bell, but there was no answer. He called out her name, "Miss Converse!" and then called out the name of Glyceria, the maid, but the house was closed up. Faye Converse had gone to New York to promote her new perfume, and Glyceria had not arrived yet for work.

He ran down to Azelia Way and then up to Flo's house again, hoping that the keys to her car would be in it, but they were not. Again he ran down the driveway and then down Azelia Way to Coldwater Canyon. He was sweating from all the running. The heavy morning traffic down the canyon had started. He tried to hail a ride, but the cars passed him by without stopping. He began to run frantically. A passing motorist dialed the Beverly Hills police on his cellular telephone.

"There's a crazy guy running up and down Coldwater Canyon," he said.

BLONDELL, Pauline Mendelson's maid, who had been with Pauline for over twenty years, tapped on the door of her bedroom and entered without waiting for a reply. She was carrying a small tray with a cup of tea, which she placed on a table by Pauline's bed. She went over to the curtains and pulled them back to let in the morning light.

"For heaven's sake. What are you doing, Blondell? What time is it?"

"Early. Are you awake?" asked Blondell.

"Just slightly," said Pauline. "Come back in an hour. I'm going to try to sleep some more."

"I thought you would want to know—"

"I've had a terribly sleepless night again."

"—that that woman who was in the church at Mr. Mendelson's funeral—"

"Oh, puleeze. I don't want to be awakened to hear anything about her," said Pauline.

"She's dead, Mrs. Mendelson."

"What?" Pauline sat up in bed.

"Murdered," replied Blondell.

"What?" Pauline said again.

"It's on the news."

"How?"

"Beaten in the face and head with a brass candlestick."

"Good God. Do they know who did it?"

"They've arrested a man who was running wildly away from the house down Coldwater Canyon."

"Do they know who it is?"

"They didn't give his name."

IN THE OLD Charles Boyer house, Arnie Zwillman was doing laps on his treadmill when he watched the same newscast that Blondell had seen. He was not bewildered by the reports of the death of Flo March, that troublesome creature—or fucking cunt, as he was more likely to call her—but he was utterly bewildered by the reports of an uniden- tified man running wildly away from the scene of the crime. It both- ered him enough to turn off the treadmill and go to the telephone in his workout room.

"What the fuck is going on?" he asked when the person whom he dialed answered.

"They arrested the wrong guy," was the answer he received.

PHILIP QUENNELL, in custody in the Beverly Hills police station, remained totally calm as he was fingerprinted and booked. His atti- tude and demeanor were a source of immense annoyance to the policeman, Officer Whitbeck, who had picked him up on Coldwater Canyon and arrested him fleeing from the scene of the crime.

"You're in deep shit, fella," he said more than once.

"No, I'm not," replied Philip. He knew that in time it would be ascertained that Flo March had been dead for several hours by the time he arrived at her house. He knew that Camilla Ebury would give evidence that he had spent the night at her house. At least fifty people would remember that they had seen him at the early morning AA meeting on Robertson Boulevard. Rose Cliveden would swear that she had talked to him on Robertson Boulevard at seven-twenty. His car would be discovered parked on Robertson Boulevard, and the taxi driver of the Beverly Hills cab would be located and have on his log the hour that he had driven Philip to the house on Azelia Way.

"I think it's highly unlikely that I would have suggested taking Officer Whitbeck back to the house on Azelia Way if it had been I who crashed in her head," Philip said to the captain.

"Get yourself a lawyer and tell him your story," said Captain Nelson.

ON THE TELEVISION NEWS, a detective from homicide determined the cause of Flo March's death as multiple skull fractures and inter-cerebral hemmorhage due to blunt force trauma. He said it was not simply a blow that had killed Miss March, but blows, many blows. He estimated nine. Pauline Mendelson watched on the television set in her library. The detective described the blows as gaping blunt lacerations of the scalp. More than one of the blows, possibly as many as four, would have been sufficient to kill, although it was believed that the fatal blow was one to the left side of the head, over the ear. The face of the young woman was, by contrast, relatively unmarked. Robbery was immediately ruled out as a motive, as a yellow diamond earring, thought to be of considerable value, remained in one ear lobe, and a sapphire ring, smashed by the murder weapon, remained on the victim's ring finger. There were multiple lacerations on both hands, as well as fractures of the fingers of both hands.

"THEY HAVE ARRESTED Philip Quennell," said Sims Lord, later.

"Philip Quennell! No, that couldn't be true," said Pauline, in disbelief.

"It's true. They found him running down Coldwater Canyon away from the house."

"That doesn't mean he killed her."

"People do not speak well of him."

"What sort of people?"

"Casper Stieglitz, the producer, for one. Marty Lesky, the head of Colossus Pictures, for another. And Jules, you must know, despised him."

"That doesn't mean he killed her," repeated Pauline. "I don't believe it." She rose and walked around the library. "Oh, my God. How could this happen? Do you know something, Sims? If I had paid Flo March the lousy million dollars she wanted, none of this would have happened." She went to the telephone.

"Who are you calling?"

"Camilla Ebury."

IN THE WEEKS OF his residence there, Lonny Edge had never felt comfortable in Beverly Hills. Even in the privacy of the secluded house on Azelia Way, people in such lowly capacities as the man who cleaned the swimming pool had looked askance at him when he paraded nude by the pool, and Trent Muldoon, the television star, had given him the same kind of disapproving look when he answered the door with only a towel wrapped around his middle. Lonny Edge was not used to indifference when he showed his disrobed body. He felt slighted when he did not observe desire in the eye of his beholder.

"They're a big bunch of snobs in Beverly Hills," he complained during that time to his friends at the Viceroy Coffee Shop. "Even the cops in Beverly Hills have attitude."

When the cops from Beverly Hills knocked on the door and identified themselves at 7204¼ Cahuenga Boulevard, accompanied by their fellow officers from the station house on La Brea, Lonny Edge was nervous at first, thinking that his immoral past had caught up with him.

"Just a moment," he yelled out, tearing down from the wall the poster from his best-known video, *Hard, Harder, Hardest*, in which his jeans were revealingly dropped to his pubic hair.

"Yes?" he said, when he opened the door.

"May we come in?" asked Captain Nelson.

"Yeah. What's the matter?"

"We wanted to ask you some questions."

"About what?"

"Flo March."

His relief knew no bounds. "Oh, Flo. Sure, I know Flo. She's my roommate. Not exactly roommate, per se. Housemate is a better word for it. Why?"

"When did you see her last?"

"Last night I saw her. Why? I've been living there in her house on Azelia Way. But we were moving out today. I better get over there. The movers were coming by ten. She was supposed to be here last night. I don't know why she didn't come, and the phone is out of order, or disconnected, or something, I don't know what. I didn't want her to stay alone there last night, because she was depressed and all. What's this all about? You know who Flo March is, don't you?" He said her name as if it were the name of a movie star that they should recognize. "She's been in all the papers. She was the mistress of Jules Mendelson. You know, the billionaire? With all the art? A close personal friend of a lot of the Presidents. Lived up on top of the mountain, at the estate called Clouds? You know of Pauline Mendelson? The socialite?"

The police officers stared at Lonny. Finally, Captain Nelson spoke. "Would you come with us, please, Mr. Edge?"

"Where?"

"To the Beverly Hills police station."

"Hey, what the fuck is this, man?"

"Just routine questioning," said Officer Whitbeck.

"You can't routine question here? What are my neighbors going to say, me going out of here with a whole posse of cops?"

As the two policemen approached him, Lonny made a dash for the front door. One of the two leapt after Lonny in a pantherlike motion and made a lunge for him, grasping him around the chest from behind.

"What's going on here?" screamed Lonny, fighting off the assault.

When he was subdued, the officers jerked his hands behind his back and clamped handcuffs on his wrists. Another knelt on the floor and clamped shackles on his feet.

"How come you killed your girlfriend, Lonny?" asked Officer Whitbeck.

"Flo? Flo's dead? Oh, no. Oh, Flo. Oh, no. You're not going to pin this on me. No way. I know too much about all these people. Pauline Mendelson's son killed Hector Paradiso. Kippie Petworth, that's his name," he screamed. With one officer on each side of him, they pulled him out the door and across the courtyard to the stairs that went down to Cahuenga Boulevard. "I saw him. I was there. Kippie Petworth, Pauline Mendelson's son, shot Hector five times, and Jules Mendelson covered it up and told the world it was a suicide. That's why they killed Flo March. She knew. She knew too much."

"The guy's nuts," said Officer Whitbeck to Captain Nelson.

WHEN GLYCERIA, Flo's friend, who had helped her pack to move, showed up for work at Faye Converse's house, she was immediately made aware of the dire happenings in the house next door. By that time Flo's body had been removed to the morgue, and the news of her death was in every newspaper and newscast. Two men in two separate jails had been booked for the murder. The driveway in front of Flo's house was filled with reporters, some of whom peeked in the windows.

Avoiding them, Glyceria made her way to the back of the house, to the swimming pool area where she used to sit with Flo in the early days of their friendship, when little Astrid brought them together. It surprised her that the sliding glass door with the smashed window was ajar. She wondered why there was not a police guard on duty, or why a house where a murder had taken place was not sealed.

FOR A six-hour period, two men in two separate jails were booked for the same murder. When finally Philip Quennell was released from the Beverly Hills jail, with abject apologies for having been wrongfully booked, he emerged into a glare of television lights and strobe cameras. His money and credit cards and watch and cuff links were still in the sealed manila envelope that the arresting officer had handed back to him as he was discharged. His tie had been lost. He felt soiled and looked weary as the reporters crowded around him.

"Flo March was my friend," he said. "I am heartbroken that her life has ended in this terrible way."

"Are you bitter that you were falsely arrested?"

"No."

"Are you going to sue?"

"No."

"What was it like to discover her body?" asked a reporter.

Philip sheltered his eyes from the bright lights of the television camera. As he looked past the crowd of media people surrounding him, he saw Camilla sitting quietly on a bench watching him.

"Excuse me," said Philip as he pushed through the reporters and made his way to where Camilla was. "Am I glad to see you."

"Oh, Philip. Are you all right?"

"Let's get out of here," he said.

"They towed your car, but I was able to get your bags."

On the steps outside, he said, "I'm really glad you were there. I can't tell you how much it means to me. I want to hug you and kiss you, but I don't want to have them take our picture at the same time. Do you know what I feel like?"

"Crying?"

"That's right. How'd you know that?"

"Because I love you. Come on. My car's in the lot," said Camilla.

He took hold of her hand and they headed for the parking lot. "There's something I must ask you," he said.

"What?"

"When you heard I had been arrested."

"Yes?"

"Did you think it was true? That I killed her?"

"No. Not for an instant."

## Flo's Tape #29

"Lonny's expecting me over at his little bungalow on Cahuenga, but I really want to spend my last night here in this house. God, how I love this house. What memories, including the lousy ones, but that's what makes a house a home. I wanted to think about Jules in private, because after tomorrow, when the moving men come, everything's going to be different for me. Sure, he had a lot of faults, but he was good to me. If I had it all to do over again, knowing what I know now, would I still have gone with Jules? I think about that a lot, and I've finally come to an answer. Yeah, I would."

# 30

NOT A SINGLE SOUL, except for Philip Quennell, who made the arrangements, knew that Camilla Ebury paid for the cost of Flo March's cremation and burial in the Westwood cemetery.

INA RAE attended every day of Lonny Edge's three-week trial. She was distressed that he was so pale and thin and listless, but she reported to Darlene that he was as handsome as ever and always seemed pleased to see her in the courtroom. Throughout the trial, Archbishop Cooning, who was militant on morality, preached from the pulpit of Saint Vibiana's on the tragic life of Flo March. The archbishop did not blame her alleged killer, Lonny Edge. The archbishop laid the blame directly on the late billionaire who had corrupted the young woman and led her into a life of luxury and entrapment. Poor Jules, his friends said in private. It was a good thing he was dead, so he didn't have to hear what the archbishop had to say. He always hated to have his name in the newspapers.

It was as if Lonny Edge's life mattered less because he had been involved in what was considered an unacceptable style of existence. He now resides in San Quentin, and will remain there, in all probability, for the rest of his life, which is not expected to be a long time. There have been rumors that he has a fatal disease. It has been reported that he looks more than twice his age and weighs but a fraction of what he weighed when he appeared in his pornographic videos, and that lesions cover his once-handsome face.

Nothing has gone right for Lonny. The lawyers for the publisher of Basil Plant's lost manuscript of *Candles at Lunch* argued successfully in court that the manuscript had been stolen before Basil Plant's death, and that Lonny was due no payment whatever. This was particularly distressing to Marv Pink, the lawyer who agreed to represent him on the condition that 50 percent of the proceeds from the sale of the manuscript be turned over to him. The book will finally be published in the spring. There is great interest in it from both the book clubs and the movies.

□   □   □

PHILIP QUENNELL has visited Lonny in San Quentin several times. Philip is one of many who do not believe that Lonny killed Flo March, but that he merely left the door to her house open that night in order to allow unnamed people to enter and search for her tapes, believing that she would be in his apartment on Cahuenga Boulevard at the time.

"Lonny's fingerprints were not on the murder weapon," he said over and over to no avail. It was not a point that was stressed in the courtroom. He could never understand why so little was made of the fact that the drawers and packing cases in Flo's house had been ransacked. Lonny Edge had lived in the house, and wouldn't have needed to ransack anything. One of the many things Philip could not figure out was why one of the cushions of Flo March's gray satin sofa was missing. The tapes, if they existed, and Philip Quennell believes they did exist, have never been found.

KIPPIE PETWORTH has not come to the bad end that Arnie Zwillman and the headmasters at several fashionable schools predicted he would. At least, as yet. He has become the young lover of Mrs. Reza Bulbenkian, who dotes on him completely and keeps him in very smart style in an apartment on Beekman Place in New York. Yvonne pays a publicist to keep her name in the papers, praising her parties and her clothes, and to keep Kippie's name out. Her husband, Reza, of course, is totally unaware of the arrangement.

Kippie's mother, Pauline Mendelson, became Lady St. Vincent, and lives at Kilmartin Abbey in Wiltshire. There is no contact between mother and son. She brought with her very few reminders of her past life, other than the vast Mendelson fortune, which was now hers, and two artworks that she did not sell. She tried to hang van Gogh's *White Roses* in several locations of her new home, but it seemed inappropriate among the Canalettos in the drawing room, and out of place among the Raphael drawings that lined the walls of the library. The insurance company disallowed it to be hung in any of the hallways, for security reasons, or in any of the rooms that the public was allowed to wander through on visiting days. Finally, Lord St. Vincent suggested to Pauline that she hang it on the wall of her morning room, where she attended to her correspondence, menus, and invitations each day, but she found the picture too overpowering for the small room, as her attention was constantly drawn to it for the memories it evoked of the twenty-two years it had hung over the fireplace in the library at Clouds. She did not wish to sell it, because of the attention it would cause on the international art market, and donating it to one of the many museums that had craved its possession would also have attracted the kind of media coverage that would resurrect the history of her previous marriage and the brutal death of Flo March. Finally, she had it wrapped in blankets and tied with twine. It has been placed in one of the storage rooms of the abbey, along with the great silver pieces that have not been brought out since the wedding of Lord St. Vincent's daughter nine years ago.

The last time Philip Quennell saw Pauline St. Vincent, she was seated in the backseat of a Daimler in Beauchamp Place in London, staring straight ahead. He was sure that she saw him, but she gave no sign.

Clouds was sold to a Japanese who had lately become involved in the motion picture industry, having purchased Marty Lesky's Colossus Pictures. Mr. Ishiguro's plans for the beautiful house were more grandiose by far than anything the Mendelsons had ever dreamed. An indoor ice skating rink and a bowling alley were but two of the planned additions. In time Mr. Ishiguro came to feel that it would be less expensive to tear down the house and build again on the same site. The house has now been leveled, although the kennels and the greenhouses remain. Construction on the new house is expected to be completed in three years.